of Liberty

SE

Michael Phillips

The Secret of the Rose

DAWN OF LIBERTY

Tyndale House Publishers, Inc.
Wheaton, Illinois

Published in association with the literary agency of Alive Communications, Inc., P.O. Box 49068, Colorado Springs, CO 80949.

Library of Congress Cataloging-in-Publication Data

Phillips, Michael R., date.
    Dawn of liberty / Michael Phillips.
      p. cm. — (The secret of the rose ; 4)
    ISBN 0-8423-5959-1 (HC : alk. paper).
    ISBN 0-8423-5958-3 (SC : alk. paper).
    1. Evangelistic work—Europe, Eastern—Fiction. 2. Conspiracies—Russia—Fiction. I. Title. II. Series: Phillips, Michael R., date. Secret of the rose ; 4.
PS3566.H492D39   1995
813'.54—dc20   95-14556

Printed in the United States of America

03   02   01   00   99   98   97   96   95
9   8   7   6   5   4   3   2   1

To
a new and rising generation of
Christian writers, thinkers, and pray-ers
who will carry the legacy of men like
Baron von Dortmann
and
George MacDonald
into the twenty-first century,
and will eternally impact the way
Christians think about their faith.

Contents

• • •

Part IV: New Times . . . and Old

Part V: Evangelism and Intrigue

Part VI: Disunity, Twentieth-Century Style

Part VII: From Out of the Past

Part VIII: Past Meets Future

Part IX: A Different Vantage Point

Part X: Which Direction Destiny?

Part XI: *Das Christliche Netzwerk*

Part XII: Climax of the Quest

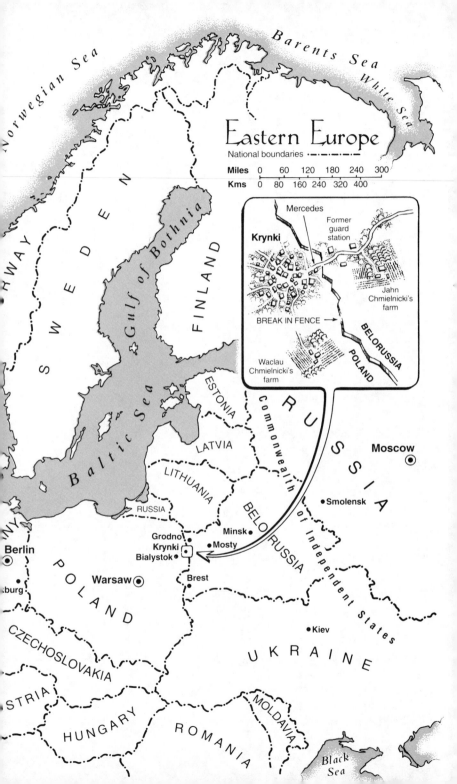

Eastern Europe

National boundaries ·—·—·—·—

| Miles | 0 | 60 | 120 | 180 | 240 | 300 |
| Kms | 0 | 80 | 160 | 240 | 320 | 400 |

Norwegian Sea

Barents Sea

White Sea

NORWAY

SWEDEN

Gulf of Bothnia

FINLAND

Baltic Sea

ESTONIA

LATVIA

LITHUANIA

RUSSIA

Moscow

Smolensk

Commonwealth of Independent States

RUSSIA

Grodno
Krynki
Bialystok

Minsk

Mosty

BELORUSSIA

Berlin

GERMANY

burg

POLAND

Warsaw

Brest

Kiev

CZECHOSLOVAKIA

UKRAINE

USTRIA

HUNGARY

ROMANIA

MOLDAVIA

Black Sea

Inset: Krynki

Krynki

Mercedes

Former guard station

Jahn Chmielnicki's farm

BREAK IN FENCE →

BELORUSSIA

POLAND

Waclau Chmielnicki's farm

Prologue

• • •

In all his purposes for the world, the Creator allows time to help accomplish them.

Whether it be in an individual heart, in the relationships of a family, or in the history of a nation, time teaches, time heals, time strengthens, time deepens roots and gives perspective. For time is an essential element of growth, and a necessary catalyst for the development of maturity and wisdom.

The best things are never arrived at in haste. God is in no hurry; his plans are never rushed.

When he fashioned time, the Creator divided it into segments. Night and day became its measured portions. Months were marked by the sequences of the moon, and the years by repeating quarterly spans of changing climate. He made all things to grow according to these patterns, passing ever and again out of dormancy into fruitfulness and back again, repeating over and over the growth cycle of life's miracle.

Just as he created such natural phases to prescribe duration for growing things, he likewise defined by parallel intervals the progression of the earthly sojourn of his people.

The pilgrimage of one Baron Heinrich von Dortmann had now graduated through the fullness of its natural seasons. His days on this earth had been ones of learning, teaching, loving, and serving, that the bonds of his temporal life might in the end break into the freedom of eternal childness for which he had humbly prepared himself.

His God was not only his Creator but even more was his friend. His was a life whose single prayer was that he might know his God-friend more intimately, and that his life, his words, and his deeds might cause others to know him likewise. His was a life that must spread out, that must plant and nurture and reproduce, and which constantly poured itself, into his wife and daughter first, and then all those around him.

He was a man who visibly evidenced the life-spreading, the life-giving, the life-creating character of the primary and foundational essence of the Trinity. For the purposes of the Creator are everywhere bound up in that highest aspect of his triune nature—Fatherhood.

The Fatherhood of God is one that must not merely create, it must continually imbue with *life,* it must generate his *Own* life.

In each tiniest corner of creation does the begetting of the Father's substance and being continue every instant, impregnating new generations of seeds and trees, flowers and grasses, animals and men, with that mysterious yet delicate potency . . . to *live!*

The flourishing fruitfulness of creating Fatherhood invisibly fills every molecule, forever passing itself on and on—every apple containing the seeds to produce ten new trees, each of which is capable of growing ten thousand new apples, which can each produce ten million more in their turn.

In all growing things does this miracle of reproduction and proliferation show us the Father's smiling face. "Look," he says, "look around you. Life is springing up everywhere—because I put *Myself* into all I touch, into every atom of the universe."

Men and women are drawn to the earth; many do not even know why. They cultivate gardens and tenderly care for its trees and flowers and shrubs. The wise among them, however, acknowledge what gives the garden its glory. Kneeling down to plunge their fingers into the moist earth, they recognize that the miracle of God's very creation is before them. When they pluck a blossom from a cherished rose, to offer in affection to a loved one, they perceive their participation in the greatest truth in all the universe—that the goodness of the Creator has been lavished abroad upon the earth for his children to behold, discover truth from, and then enjoy . . . if they will but look up, behold his face of love, and learn to call him Father.

Such a man was Baron Heinrich von Dortmann, late of the kingdoms of Prussia and Pomerania, now child in the heavenly kingdom of his Father, a man for whom the earthly ground he cultivated served as but a foreshadowy likeness of that heavenly garden to which he was now giving his efforts, and the roses he so lovingly tended while here were but faint images of flowerage of a more enduring kind.

In truth, the baron's life itself was a seed, placed in good soil and nurtured by heavenly purposed rains and sunshine, germinating, sending its roots deep and its trunk high, that in time it might bear its appointed fruit: those living blossoms, whose blooms were the radiant faces of others who had become the Father's children by the death-energized sprouting of his life-seed.

Existence continually regenerates itself. Such is the *life* placed into the very universe by its Creator that it can do no other than propagate and rejuvenate. As growing things do not reproduce only once, but pass along not merely the capacity to exist and breathe and grow but the power likewise to *renew* that life, so too did the spiritual life-legacy of Heinrich von Dortmann now spread out and flow into those whom his life had touched, extending in ever-widening concentric circles to future generations, in outflowing ripples of purposefulness in God's kingdom.

The autumn and winter seasons of his life, spent in prison and then in the mountains of Bavaria—though perhaps dormant to the onlooker—were years destined for eternal purpose, during which a multitude of prayer-seeds for family and nation were expectantly planted in the soils of heaven.

The story of the baron's life is necessarily, therefore, one in which the roots from his plant passed on life to an ever-increasing number of human-plants after him, nourishing and enabling them to flourish and bear fruit—thirty, sixty, and a hundredfold. Some of the spiritual seeds planted as a result fell in unexpected places, and the life that would burst forth from them would astonish many. Such, however, is the Father's way. He sends his sunshine and rain to fall on the just and the unjust. Nothing comes back empty. No word from his mouth returns void, but accomplishes the purpose for which he ordained it.

And so, as all life ultimately flows in that great eternal round back into the heart of its Creator, the characters of our saga advanced through the cycles of life. The baron, reunited at last with his beloved Marion, had ascended into the springtime of a happy new time that will know no winter.

Matthew and Sabina had now passed through that wonderful autumn when the bounty of harvest yields fruit from years of labor, and found themselves entering the restful, memory-filled winter years. Now had come the season to observe with glad expectancy the flowering spring and summer for a new generation, even as the country they loved prepared to emerge from its dormancy of separateness and embark upon a new national epoch of unity.

Generations pass that others may be born. The cycles of human life give no occasion to sadness, but rather rejoicing. Should winter's death not come, no eternal springtime could follow. Heinrich and Thaddeus had faded from earthly view, and soon likewise must Sabina and Matthew accompany them beyond the mists of earth's horizon.

Such passings are no end but rather signify completion, fruition, and fulfillment, necessary that new beginnings might begin. What appears to earthly eyes as life's sunset is only the back side of the dawn opening into the greater life toward which we are bound.

God our Father, do we doubt that all things ultimately work for our good and to the growth of your kingdom, both here and in the life to come? Open our eyes to apprehend your designs, that we might fall ever more harmoniously in step with them. Accomplish your eternal purposes in the men and women around us, even those in whom we see no possible light of your presence. Strengthen our faith, Lord, to believe that you indeed love all men and women and are constantly sending rain and sun into the cold chambers where they live so alone with themselves, to soften the seeds planted there by a thousand circumstances of life and by the words and deeds of your people. Awaken the long-dormant hearts of those who have resisted you. Enliven the seeds planted in the human soils throughout the earth, and cause a hundredfold fruit to grow from the plants that spring forth from them. Cause fruit to grow and seeds to be planted from our lives, as we have witnessed in that of the baron and from his legacy. Make us fruitful progenitors of your life, our Father, we pray from the depths of our hearts.

And what is the season at *Der Frühlingsgarten?* What will the breaking of winter's spell in this new German year hold in store for the posterity of the lineage of that ancient family Dortmann and its former estate?

The grounds south of the baron's beloved *Lebenshaus* were not only an earthly garden. The flowers tended by his hand contained no mere temporal tidings. Verily the secret of the rose contains as many depths as does the Father's life itself, for within its blossoms he has hidden his own messages of love for his children to discover.

The baron's Garden of Spring now encompassed his whole nation, and a dawn of many awakenings was at hand.

PART I

Cold War—
Treachery and
Bravery

1979

1
Interlude of Isolation

• • •

East Berlin

WHAT DID IT ACTUALLY FEEL LIKE, SHE WONDERED, THAT rough, thick vertical gray slab of stone and cement that so deeply represented life in this city and stood as the symbol of Europe's division?

To her it had always been. It had existed right there, less than two kilometers from her home, every day of her young life.

Familiarity notwithstanding, however, *Der Mauer* yet remained to the impressionable eyes pausing a moment to behold it a compelling yet confusing enigma. Its proximity drew her in a way she could not understand, as a slumbering evil presence, awaiting some future moment of wakefulness.

Her parents told her often of the summer days when it had been built, when soldiers, dogs, and tanks patrolled every inch of the border, when escape attempts had been a monthly, sometimes a weekly or even a daily occurrence, and when many had been killed.

She had also heard the numerous stories of her father's own involvement. Only eighteen years had passed. Yet for her, those were events of another era, another lifetime. She had grown up with the Wall and had known nothing else.

Most Berliners had managed to accustom themselves to the silent symbol of separation during the interlude since. Being whose daughter she was, however, she had also grown up with the conviction constantly reinforced that everything that could be done *must* be done to help people from this side get to the other. Her father was a leader in the underground network, and her family, and those like them, would never get used to the barrier. In what ways lay open to them, they would always, even if it cost their lives, resist the tyranny that Communism had imposed upon their countrymen. So at least said her father.

Between deserted buildings of Markgrafenstraβe she continued to stare down the two empty blocks at the somber stone barrier, whose height was strung with coiled and deadly barbed wire. Partially visible on her right stood one of the hundreds of guard towers, occupied by soldiers of her own race who now took their orders from Moscow.

An eerie feeling swept suddenly through her, as if foreshadowing a day when the sleeping gray serpent would wake, and when her destiny *would* take her closer to the Wall than she dared walk today.

For this moment, however, she could only gaze from a distance and wonder what it all meant.

With an unconscious shiver, Lisel Lamprecht jerked her head back in the direction she had been bound, and continued her way along Leipzigerstraβe with the package that had been the object of her errand. She continued occasionally to glance at the Wall down the side streets she passed, for its direction paralleled hers for another short while, before she veered left on Gertraudenstraβe.

But though she knew it not, events were approaching that would alter her outlook about everything and would eventually bring her—as something within her subconscious had just sensed—face-to-face with the Wall. When that day arrived, she *would* press her hand against the cold stone, challenging its presence. Perhaps she would even see the other side like those her father and mother now helped.

For today, however, she was but one German teenager caught up in the silent clash over ideology that overarched world events. She was of the *next* generation, those who had been taught of but did not remember the great war. Therefore she could not quite grasp the complexities and implications of the very different kind of conflict that had been being waged throughout the world ever since.

Though history is rarely neat, nor the cleavages into which events order themselves so tidy as pundits later organize them, that forty-five-year conflict in the latter half of the twentieth century known incongruously as the *Cold* War divided itself roughly into two uneven segments surrounding the assassination of President John Fitzgerald Kennedy in 1963.

This most dangerous war the world had ever seen produced but a handful of casualties, and those mostly accidental. Yet for nearly half a century the globe of humankind had stood poised on the brink of wholesale destruction the likes of which could only be imagined by the most pessimistic of doomsday prognosticators.

Prior to the Cuban missile crisis of 1961 and the shattering events on the streets of Dallas in November of 1963, much of the steadily mounting East-West tension was played out on the visible world stage, where diplomatic bravado and technological prowess were the criteria used to judge superiority. The late forties, fifties, and early sixties acted as a prelude, during which both sides postured and bluffed and threatened, developed and tested their bombs, increased their stockpiles of nuclear weapons, and then raced for the conquest of space. The Soviets pushed out their borders, and the Americans sought to eradicate Communism from their land.

Nineteen sixty-three was the year Lisel would always consider significant as that of her birth. The rest of the world would remember 1963 as the year when everything changed.

The two men who had squared off eyeball to eyeball over Cuba, and who had come to symbolize the essence of the new age of conflict, were gone—Kennedy cut down by an assassin's bullet; Khrushchev shortly thereafter ousted from power.

As Lisel grew from infancy into childhood, the world's attention turned elsewhere, to Southeast Asia, whose faraway jungles began to witness a cold war that was suddenly heating up. It was a localized clash between democracy and communism that, if the superpowers did not keep it contained, could escalate into World War III.

It was a time of change. The world was being reshaped at many levels and in a host of diverse ways.

The Beatles forever revolutionized pop music, Vietnam permanently mutated the American perception of war, and Watergate cynically altered the political climate of Washington. But the Cold War went on, its most serious battles being waged far from the public spotlight.

Lisel matured and began to cast her young gaze abroad upon her world. She lived in an environment of tension and danger. Subtleties of the conflict between Moscow and Washington increased. No longer did presidents and premiers yell and threaten. Détente replaced ultimatum, test bans replaced nuclear detonations, and congenial words masked hidden motives.

Indeed, the sixties and seventies had transfigured everything about how people looked at their world. But silently the behind-the-curtain theater of the Cold War continued unaffected by it all.

Foot soldiers of the conflict took over from world leaders—men and women like Lisel's own parents, those whom in most parts of the world would have been considered an unremarkable citizenry. It was now these who waged an invisible war for that most basic of human rights and desires—that commodity known as liberty. Much of the Cold War turned silent and sinister, its battles fought in ones and twos, in neighborhoods and candlelit basements, from behind drawn curtains, along deserted byways, and in lonely prison cells, hidden from the public eye.

And now, during her sixteenth year, while the world anxiously watched the heated chess game playing itself out between Iran's Ayatollah Khomeini and President Jimmy Carter of the United States, this silent, unseen drama continued unaffected. The eyes of the world were riveted upon Tehran, yet it was still the Cold War between democracy and communism that remained the global dividing matrix between good and evil, between autonomy and servility—aligning nations, creating adversaries, separating families, and artificially disrupting long-established ethnic unities.

At the heart of this focal center still sat the divided nation of Germany, formerly the cause now the victim of events it could no longer control. As the superpowers played out their impersonal maneuvers on the gameboard of the world, nowhere did a rising postwar generation feel more helpless and ill-used by their gambits than in the figuratively and actually divided capital of Berlin.

It was a land where the Cold War made enemies of friends, family, and neighbors, where *Stasi* informants lurked everywhere, where KGB infiltrations had been effected at every level of life, and where treachery loomed always nearby. Desiring freedom too greatly, or helping others who did, was a lethal business. The blood that was often spilled in consequence, and the tears of those left behind, was all too real.

The global standoff continued year after year, nowhere symbolized more visibly than at the Friedrichstraβe border crossing known as Checkpoint Charlie, not far from the shop out of which Lisel had recently come.

All the while, the most recognizable symbol of this unseen drama remained the gray, malevolent, unbreakable, unscalable barricade slicing its way through the center of Berlin, separating a nation . . . dividing a world.

Yet if it was an era producing treachery, it also gave rise to bravery. For seasons of danger produce heroes as well as martyrs. Of the courage and selflessness of both, the world seldom hears. From time to time, however, individual stories become known . . . and those who hear them are changed forever after.

The energetic young East Berliner quickened her stride once the Wall was at her back, walked for another ten minutes through a drab neighborhood, then turned from the street along the uneven concrete of a broken walkway, and was soon entering her home.

2
Sisters of Danger

• • •

"DO YOU HAVE THE PACKAGE, LISEL?"

"Yes, Papa," she answered.

"No trouble?"

"None, Papa."

"Good," replied her father, taking the small parcel. He unwrapped the paper hastily and began examining the book his
daughter had apparently just bought. He did not pause long
enough on any page to read, however, for he was uninterested in
the content intended by the author. Rather he now leafed through
the volume in order to piece together a cryptic communiqué from
his shopkeeping contact.

Within five minutes he satisfied himself that he had thoroughly
deciphered the message.

"We must bring an important man into Berlin next week," he
announced to wife and daughter as he rose from the chair where he
had been sitting intently studying the book.

"How, Hermann?" asked Frau Lamprecht.

"The friend of my cousin will pass him off to us in the wood
south of the city," he replied.

"Can I go with you, Papa?" asked Lisel.

The big man did not answer immediately. "Hmm . . . perhaps it
might be time," he mused at length.

"May I visit Girdel?"

"There will be no occasion, Lisel."

"I have not seen her for a year."

"When we are about the business of the network, the safety of
those who place themselves in our hands must be our only thought."

Even as he spoke the words, Hermann's thoughts trailed back to a time long past. It had not then been his own daughter's safety he had been thinking about, but that of another.

So many memories, so many individuals—it all seemed from another lifetime. She now occupying his thoughts had been an important part of this work he was engaged in. She was one of its founders and most loyal members. She had finally used her own *Network of the Rose* to flee herself.

Hermann smiled at the thought of the successful escape to freedom through the cemetery.

Karin had tried so strenuously to convince him to accompany them. Now he wished he had confided in her the reason he had had to remain behind—that he was planning to be married soon. But at the time he thought the less any of them knew about one another the better.

He had been a different man back then. Smiles and tender thoughts had not been part of his nature. Having a wife and daughter had tempered his gruff exterior. He wished he could see Karin again, though he knew that was not her real name. He wished she could see him, now that he too was on intimate terms with the Master whom she had always served.

Hermann sighed. But he had not laid eyes on his former comrade since that day, though occasionally there were reports. He only prayed his own Lisel might become so brave a woman.

In the brief seconds while Hermann reflected on his former associations and what they had been through together, his daughter found herself likewise remembering the first day she had seen her friend Girdel.

The two girls could not have been more than four or five at the time, far too young to possess the slightest inkling of the import of the meeting that had brought their fathers and several others of like commitment together. While the men of God prayed and plotted together, Lisel and Girdel had played in the innocence of childhood.

Ever after, though the occasions of visits were not many—for the mutual work of their fathers was necessarily a clandestine one—they remained friends and grew as sisters, not realizing to what an extent theirs was a sisterhood of danger.

Neither were they aware of the parental discussions concerning how much to include growing boys and girls such as these in the secretive activities that bound them together. Like the baron, whom none had known but most in this region had heard of, the faithful men and women of the network desired that their convictions outlive their own brief mortal years. Thus they prayed to be able to inculcate in their offspring a vision of helping the larger family of God's people, and they necessarily sought opportunities to teach them such work firsthand. But for the fathers and mothers in this particular part of the world, such was a dangerous legacy to pass on to their sons and daughters, and they did so with great soul-searching and prayer.

Seeds must be planted. Some must die in order that others might bear hundredfold fruit.

Girdel, a year older, had now been active in her own father's affairs for some time. But Hermann, more cautious—brave enough yet newer to the life of intimate faith than Girdel's father—had been reluctant to allow Lisel to participate quite so fully with him. Today's thoughts of Karin, however, suddenly made him aware how quickly his daughter's womanhood was approaching and that he could not prevent its coming.

He sighed, then took Lisel's hand and led her out of the kitchen and to the worn couch, where he motioned for her to sit down beside him. She did so. They remained several moments in silence.

"Do you remember about the rose?" he asked.

"Yes, Papa. I could never forget that."

"We have not spoken of it in several years. Do you still wear the locket your mother and I gave you?"

"Of course, Papa. It is the most special thing I have. I am wearing it now."

She reached up, pulled at the thin chain at her neck, and a moment later the tiny gold-plated locket appeared between her fingers. Hermann smiled at the sight. It was not an expensive piece of jewelry but a mere trinket. It was not its value that made it precious, but rather what he had placed inside the tiny chamber, and what they symbolized.

"Do you recall what I told you that day?" he asked.

Lisel nodded.

"The mystery of life is found in seeds," began Hermann. "When they are planted with prayer . . ." He paused, obviously waiting.

". . . blossoms of love will grow," added his daughter, completing the sentence for him.

They laughed together.

"I'm happy you remember," he said.

"I will never forget the seeds you have planted in me, Papa."

They fell silent in the small room. The daughter's soft hand still rested in the large, rough palm of the father, content as a newborn fawn in a spring wood, and showing no anxiety to take flight.

"You are growing older, Lisel," said Hermann at length. "You are nearly a woman."

Lisel glanced down, trying to keep back the blush of embarrassment she could feel rising in her cheeks. "I don't know, Papa."

"It is true, my child—and a lovely woman at that."

Now came the red in earnest. Lisel said nothing. A long silence followed, but a comfortable one that neither was eager to break.

"Yes," said Hermann at length, "I think you *may* accompany me, Daughter. The work must be carried on, and one day I will be too old to continue it myself."

"Then may I visit Girdel, Papa?"

"Soon, Lisel . . . soon. Once we have the man safely in the hands of our people on the other side, I will make arrangements with our friends for a visit."

"Oh, thank you, Papa."

A moment more they sat, then stood. Lisel joined her mother in the kitchen.

Hermann's mind was suddenly full of a melancholy mixture of thoughts and emotions concerning his daughter that he could never have put into words even had he tried. He was no philosopher, but a man whose life evidenced his convictions. Yet the sensations surging through him at this moment were no less profound that he did not possess the capacity to analyze them or formulate them into specific thoughts.

He turned and sought what solitude could be had in the confines of the small space they possessed behind the house.

The tiny plot of ground where there was room for but a few green things to keep alive was a far cry from that magnificent *Frühlingsgarten* where she whom he had known as Karin Duftblatt had spent the early years of her life. He walked out in the direction of the single rose plant that grew on the premises. She had given it to him twenty years before when telling *him* of the mystery of the seeds, a truth that, once he had fully apprehended it for himself after she was gone, he had later passed along to his own daughter.

Hermann Lamprecht was a humble man and could hardly have known that the tears now filling his eyes were tears from the universal Fatherhood of the world, the same tears that had driven Heinrich von Dortmann to *his* garden to pray—with words perhaps more eloquent but in substance identical—the same prayer upon many occasions years before. Nor could he have possibly foreseen how the two prayers, separated by more than a generation, were intertwined as they entered the eternal heavenly ear, and thus whose answers were destined to interweave as well.

Hermann lifted up to the heavens the strange burden that had so suddenly seized his breast, and uttered the simplest form of that profoundest parental cry in all the universe, that entreaty born in the very Abba-heart of God, which echoes back his own divine love that is continually calling the sons and daughters of his creation back to himself: *God—take care of my child . . . protect her, watch over her, and keep her in your hands.*

They were the only words Hermann could bring to his lips. They were enough. His Father heard and would use them to consummate his purpose.

3

Evil Chase

• • •

East Germany

WITH UNCANNY PRECISION A LARGE, DARK MERCEDES roared through the black and empty night.

The narrow, half-paved back roads through the Brandenburger Wald southeast of the city scarcely widened in some spots beyond the breadth of the vehicle itself. Though more than sixteen hundred kilometers separated him from his home, he still considered Poland and the DDR his turf. He had done duty here in the latter during his younger days, assigned to the *Stasi* office of the now-influential German politician Gustav Schmundt.

He knew all the escape routes like the back of his hand and had been tracking the moves of the network for two weeks now—from eastern Poland, across the border near Eisenhüttenstadt, and finally here—to the moment of final showdown. He knew they considered their present charge an important one. No old woman wanting to see loved ones in the West, no idealistic student hoping for a so-called better life.

This time they had a big fish in tow. The biggest! He was one of the leaders who had taken over when the Jewish rabbi had fled, and who had in the years since become the Moscow leader of the underground Christian organization, known by various names in different parts of Eastern Europe, sometimes *Das Christliche Netzwerk,* sometimes merely as *The Rose.*

He should never have let him go that day they met as young men on the streets of Moscow. But now at last the moment for his revenge had come.

Andrassy Galanov stood ready to drop the net over his arch rival who had evaded the rest of the KGB for more than fifteen years. At least he thought it was the same man. He would know for certain soon . . . very soon!

For this confrontation his superior had sent him west three weeks ago with his own personal vendetta against the Christian leader hanging in the balance.

"You get him, Galanov, do you hear me?" he could still hear the furious voice shouting across the cornfield. "I want him! Don't show your face again if you return empty-handed!"

A quick glance back revealed Leonid Bolotnikov, the top agent of the empire, pistol in hand, standing over a dead peasant's body, fist lifted in rage, as the three men they'd trailed half the night disappeared into the surrounding wood.

Minutes later the revving of an automobile engine sounded through the trees.

They had been outmaneuvered. A night of pursuit lost!

Even as the escape vehicle sped away and the sound faded into the distance, in his ears echoed further angry shouts from his director. "After him! Don't let him get to Berlin, or you'll rot in Siberia!"

The kingpin of the underground network—the man they called *Der Prophet*—had eluded them, for the present.

Within an hour of the failed capture, an automobile bearing the thirty-six-year-old agent careened recklessly southwest toward Minsk. His uncle had liked to use Siberian threats too. When applied to his nephew, however, Andrassy knew they were mere empty tirades, and he hadn't paid serious attention to them. But Korskayev was dead, and now Bolotnikov was head of the entire KGB, and when *he* spoke, even an experienced and self-reliant agent like Andrassy Galanov occasionally trembled. Bolotnikov was a man with both the power and the determination to carry out his threats.

Galanov crossed into Poland early the next afternoon and reestablished contacts in Warsaw, making use of some of Korskayev's old files that night. It had taken several days to sniff out the cooled trail of *Das Netzwerk's* moves. But there was a heavy and dedicated Christian element in the region of Bialystok according to his uncle's records, and once he had picked up the unmistakable clues of their presence, everything confirmed that indeed his quarry was close to his grasp. He smelled the urgency in their movements immediately. After questioning his own operatives and a few of the Christians he'd been able to lay his hands on, he knew that only hours ahead of him they were passing *Der Prophet* from hand to hand along the very underground circuit that the fugitive himself, along with the two Germans for whom his former *Stasi* boss possessed such a fixation, had helped to establish.

Steadily across Poland Galanov drew closer.

This time no hole in the system would allow the man to escape. He would ensnare him! No foul-ups! Tonight destiny would shine its face upon him. He would deliver the hated and troublesome apostle into the hand of his chief. No one would get out—especially not the so-called *Prophet*.

Galanov would kill if he had to . . . he would not let the man into the West.

His headlamps danced about, sending luminescent beams into the thick clumps of pines bordering the way on each side. Like menacing eyes probing the blackness, with every bend and twist of the road they sought their prey with eerie divination.

Behind the wheel, foot nearly to the floor, sat the latter-day Saul who considered himself guardian of the reputation of the Committee of State Security, otherwise known as the KGB. His fascination with the Christian underground had begun during his brief stint in Berlin, and over the years, though he knew it not, it had grown to resemble his uncle's deviant hatred. Truly did he carry on into the next generation the twisted vendetta of he who had been known in these regions as Emil Korsch.

Even as the lights of his car glared into the night, his own eyes glistened with the evil fire of their dark intent. If only he could do what his KGB chief himself had failed to do! Promotion would be his. Perhaps a position in the Kremlin—maybe as Bolotnikov's top assistant or some other high post in Chairman Brezhnev's government.

It won't be long now, he thought as the automobile raced along.

No other noise sounded for miles. The night remained empty and black.

Respectable people had taken to their beds hours ago. In this region, so close to the borders of the partitioned city, nothing but trouble could come to one caught abroad after midnight.

4

Network Preparations

. . .

WHILE THE OLD ADVERSARIES OF THE ROSE SPED THEIR way, Hermann Lamprecht awoke and began preparations for the night's clandestine activity. He still harbored grave doubts about his daughter accompanying him. She had been involved around the fringes of the network and its people in minor ways for years. But this was a more important and more dangerous assignment.

But he had promised. And she was a stouthearted girl.

And he knew the time could not be delayed forever when he would have to start treating her like the full-grown woman she nearly was. He had sensed it before praying for her protection, and the feeling had grown even stronger afterward. Her younger brother was only eleven, and he too was anxious to become involved. Hermann could not shield them from the realities of life in this part of the world forever.

He dressed quickly, then roused his wife and Lisel from their few hours' sleep. While Frau Lamprecht made coffee and put a few other items of food in a bag, Lisel excitedly dressed for the adventure.

Twenty minutes later they were ready, promising the anxious but faithful wife to be home before noon.

Hermann possessed the papers justifying his being out in the middle of the night, though he did not anticipate being stopped by the authorities. He had long ago learned what routes would avoid them.

They proceeded by car through East Berlin, through Grünau and Müggelheim, past the city's eastern border at Gosen, then southwest into the wooded region, where, within thirty minutes, he turned off the road and parked the car. Here they would wait for two hours before proceeding to the designated place of meeting on foot.

Once the handoff was made, he and Lisel would make their way back to the car with their delivery, drive him via side roads to Glasow, then retrace their steps homeward.

Meanwhile, in another part of the district of Brandenburg, two darkly clad individuals hastened along. They had left Fürstenwalde by foot, walking some three kilometers to a solitary barn far removed from any human abode in the middle of one of the wheat fields of an East German collective farm.

The man in front puffed from the effort, for they strode with long and quickly paced steps. He baked bread and rolls and sweets for the village by day, and in truth carried a few kilograms more around his midsection than was good for him. By night he did the network's business and did it bravely in spite of the exertion—and the hazards.

Behind him followed a tall, strongly built man of some forty-five or fifty years, though darkness rendered certainty of age difficult. *Herr Brotbacker* had heard of *Der Prophet* and had even picked up vague rumors that hard times had befallen the Russian patriarch like the rabbi before him. A plan was said to be in place to get him out, but as to specifics no one in any of the neighboring fellowships knew anything. He had no idea that the man he now led across the grain fields to Brother Hugo's old deserted barn was none other than he who had smuggled behind the Iron Curtain the very Bible the baker so treasured, stashed in his small apartment under the bed where his wife now slept.

Neither man had spoken since leaving the lights of town.

Finding their way inside the structure of the barn, now decaying from disuse under East Germany's communal farming system, the German breadmaker assisted his silent Russian brother aboard an aging wooden wagon already hitched to a sturdy plow horse. Still without sound of human voice to disturb the sleeping night, he walked across the packed dirt floor and opened the large door, which was kept well-oiled and thus swung without so much as a creak in spite of its age.

Farmer Hugo, already waiting atop the wagon with leather reins in hand, clicked his tongue, urging his faithful equine collaborator into motion. The baker closed the door behind them.

As the clomping footfall of the horse and the groan of the wagon's wheels faded across the field, he began the walk back to town. He would be able to catch about two hours sleep before the morning ovens and loaves of rye demanded his attention. Now the mysterious traveler bounced slowly along in the hands of the farmer, who would pass him on at the next rendezvous point to someone neither *Brotbaker* nor Hugo had ever met.

Thus did the *Network of the Rose* operate. No one knew much. Words remained as few as possible. A look, a brief smile, the scantest of necessary instructions, passwords having to do with flowers and growing things, perhaps a parting nod. Hardly any of those now involved knew anything about that daring young lady who had been so instrumental in helping establish the network after the war, nor how she and her father had eventually made use of it themselves to escape to the West. Nonetheless, carrying on the work remained the vital imperative—preserving the chain, keeping strong its links, protecting God's people. The less each knew of what his brothers and sisters of the underground were about, the safer for all. The last decade had begun to witness a few changes and eased restrictions since the days of Khrushchev. But lives still could be lost. Shootings occurred at the Wall with continued regularity. Caution remained a matter of life and death.

Two and a half hours later, the lone pilgrim, a stranger in the hands of his brothers, weary now from night after night of intermittent and tedious travel, having slept but little in the back of the wagon before being passed along again several times from one silent accomplice to the next, approached a small clearing in the wood where two dirt roads intersected.

A faint flicker of light shone through the darkness, then disappeared. It was the sign by which the man who had the sojourner in tow—neither baker nor farmer this time, but in fact a converted local Communist official attached to the constabulary—knew that his leg of the clandestine itinerary had come to an end. He had never seen the face behind the brief flash of light, nor would he—for the protection of all. At this juncture came the final handoff save one, and vulnerability mounted the closer they came to the city.

"Come with me—quickly." A hand reached across through the night to clutch that of the nomadic evangelist.

Turning to retrace his steps to his own home, the official heard but a few words more and did not hesitate in his return through the trees. They were on their own now. *God be with them,* the converted Communist silently breathed.

The transient Russian now noticed that two persons had come to meet him. The second, slighter of build and shorter of stature, stood a little behind the man who had spoken. The man's daughter, seventeen and already active in the network's activities for years—without knowing that her friend Lisel was also out with her father on this fateful night and awaiting them on the other side of the forest—had, like Lisel, begged to accompany him.

"There is always the possibility of danger, Girdel," her father had replied to the request.

"Is it not you who have always taught me to fear nothing that we have placed in God's hands?"

The man had smiled and nodded. He had indeed so taught her, and how could he therefore deny her request?

"Make haste," whispered the German to the refugee. "We must get you to the safe house before dawn."

With that, the three disappeared quickly from the rendezvous site, father and daughter leading the man for whose escape already so many had risked so much.

5
Ultimate Test of Faith

.   .   .

AN HOUR AND TWENTY MINUTES LATER, FATHER, daughter, and prophet exited the cover of trees through which their path had taken them. The first gray hints of dawn made the horizon faintly visible in the east, though the protection of darkness still covered them.

They were close now.

Safety lay but twenty minutes beyond. The contact who would drive the fleeing Russian to the safe house already crouched in wait on the opposite side of the large field they had just entered.

In the distance, suddenly the sound of a car's engine came into hearing.

Indistinct at first, gradually it loudened. The leader of the trio stopped briefly, listened, then quickened his pace. The automobile bore in their direction—and fast. It might mean nothing. They had to make every second count nonetheless. If nothing else, the approaching car signaled that the end of their cloak of night came nearer every second.

The huge car rounded a curve, and suddenly headlights blazed above them in the air.

The small band broke into full flight across the barren pastureland. No hope of cover lay anywhere. At the far end, a large figure had risen from a hollow and now stood impotent to help, watching in mute agony as the most feared of all nightmares played itself out before him. Silently he prayed. Beside him stood a girl, tears rising in her stunned and innocent eyes.

The three fugitives sprinted courageously, measuring half the distance to their would-be rescuers.

But it was too late.

Their persecutor had spotted them, and the enormous Mercedes rumbled over the flat grassy expanse, bouncing high over the ruts with the wild fearlessness of an army tank, spotlighting the fleeing forms ahead of it in the naked exposure of their helplessness.

Another ten seconds—the chase took no longer.

The revving engine screamed by them, then sputtered into silence as the machine skidded in an arc in front of the tiny company. It cut them off, sending a choking cloud of gritty dust all about, momentarily dimming the headlamps. Even before the Mercedes reached its final stop, its door flew open and the driver burst out onto the turf, automatic pistol brandished in his hand, eyes aglow in the intoxication of at long last outwitting these Christians he so despised.

A silence pregnant with suppressed passions followed. Only the laboring lungs of the three renegades broke the stillness of the dusty air. They stood still as statues while their adversary scanned them from head to toe.

Slowly a cunning smile spread over his face.

"So, Rostovchev," he said at length, speaking in Russian, "it *is* you they call *Der Prophet*. I suspected as much."

"We meet again, Comrade Galanov," replied the tallest of the three. He did not return the smile, yet his tone hinted nowhere of hatred. It was the first time the East German and his daughter had heard the voice of the man they had been attempting to lead to safety.

"Under less than pleasant circumstances for you, I must say, than the Moscow street where I last saw you seventeen years ago," replied the agent, punctuating his words with a wave of his gun. The smile, still on his face, gave evidence that he enjoyed this moment of his triumph.

"Danger comes with walking as a Christian."

"Bah! And idiocy along with it!" The smile vanished.

"In the eyes of the world, I suppose, it must look that way."

"Always preaching, eh, Dmitri?" rejoined the other sarcastically. "Well, no matter," he added. "It would seem I have you checkmated at last. My chief will be pleased to see you again."

"I doubt Leonid Bolotnikov is capable of feeling pleasure," replied the one called Rostovchev. "Hatred too thoroughly consumes him, though no doubt seeing me dead would give him an evil kind of satisfaction."

"I am sure it will."

"And you as well?"

"Let's just say that I shall provide it for him."

A momentary pause followed.

"Tell me, Andrassy," said Rostovchev, "when did you take up the KGB's cause again? I understood you had gone to work for the French after returning from Germany years ago."

A huge laugh bellowed from Galanov's throat. It revealed glistening white teeth in a face that under any other circumstances would have been considered well sculpted. But the traitorous glare of his eyes undid the attraction. Even the most cursory of glances confirmed this man as one to stay away from. On his head grew a thick crop of healthy, reddish-brown hair, rumpled and unkempt from his frenzied night behind the wheel.

"The French!" he repeated, still laughing. "Morons every one! *Ja, ja,* Comrade Prophet, they think I work for them, because I turn over something insignificant every couple of months. Fools—they're the easiest of all to double-deal in this game!"

"So you're still a KGB man at heart."

"I am a Russian."

"I cannot profess to surprise."

"Bolotinikov pays better than the French too," said Galanov, chuckling again.

"You really ought to give our side a try, Andrassy."

"You're as Russian as I."

"I meant our Christian side," he said, staring deeply into the agent's eyes with a heart full of compassion.

The other hesitated a moment, returning the stare, then seemed to shake himself free from its spell. "Bah!" he snapped.

"You just might find that there's more to what we believe than—"

"None of your sermons!" snapped the KGB agent.

"It's about life, Andrassy. Nothing but death results from the tangled game you play."

"Shut up, Rostovchev!"

"I have prayed for you for years, that you would one day know the life I know."

"That's absurd!" bellowed Galanov with a laugh of incredulity. "What business is it of yours to pray for me? You are more a fool than I took you for!"

"We are under orders to make such our business."

"Orders—orders from whom?"

"From him whom we call Master."

"Enough of this moronic chatter—into the car!"

"It's you I'm concerned for, Andrassy. I only wanted to say—"

"Death *will* result, just as you say—*yours!*"

"Whether I live or die is in his hands."

"We've wasted enough time pretending as friends!" retorted Galanov with disdain. "You know how it works, Rostovchev. Now into the car, and your two spying friends with you. It'll be the firing squad for you, the gulag for them!"

"Please. These two are innocent of any crime. They are Germans. Let them go."

Again Galanov laughed. "Let them go free, so they can continue helping our enemies escape into West Berlin!"

"Christians are not your enemy," said the evangelist sadly.

"What kind of fool do you take me for? Bolotnikov would shoot me if I returned to tell him a wave of compassion had come over me and I had let the kingpin of *Das Netzwerk* go free. Now come, all three of you—into the car!"

Dmitri Rostovchev slowly began to make his way forward in the glare of the headlight. As he did, the East German who had remained silent thus far spoke hurriedly to his daughter, hoping the KGB agent would have difficulty hearing their soft voices.

"Geh, Girdel!" he said. *"Schnell—mit dem Prophet. Hermann warten dahinten im Feld. Lauf, Tochter!"*

The girl hesitated. *"Nein, Papa—du muβt auch mit,"* she replied in a pleading voice.

"Ich folge," he answered. "The light is still thin enough. In a few paces you will be out of sight. Run to our friend waiting on the other side of the field!"

Suddenly he lurched forward in front of the prophet. Before the surprised man of God knew what was happening, he found himself shoved with strong arms into the darkness, away from the two beams of the Mercedes.

"*Geh, Tochter!*" he cried. "Take him and run!"

Without further hesitation, Girdel obeyed, gripping the hand of Rostovchev and yanking him after her.

"Stop!" cried Galanov, hardly aware of what had happened until it was too late. His eyes had grown accustomed to the visibility provided by the lights of his car. All at once he realized he could see only the ridiculous German standing there. Dmitri and the girl had disappeared!

He advanced in rage, crying out for them to stop. "Don't make me shoot, Rostovchev!" he shouted. "You only make it harder on your—"

But further words did not come from his lips. With unexpected swiftness the German sprang forward with a powerful lunge and threw himself upon the KGB agent, knocking him to the ground.

Momentarily stunned by the assault, Galanov crawled to his knees, then sought his gun in the dirt. The next instant a punishing kick from the German's boot sent the pistol across the ground.

The German bolted after his daughter and the prophet.

"Stop, Rostovchev!" cried Galanov behind them, as he climbed to his feet and scanned about frantically for his gun. "You can't get across the border, not now! I'll alert the guards. Come back or I'll kill you all!"

•   •   •

Hermann was sure the three running toward him had seen him, for they were coming straight in his direction. The moment he saw the Mercedes leave the road and come screaming across the field, however, he knew they had been spotted.

"Get down, Lisel," he cried. "Get back to the hollow."

Terrified, she obeyed.

Only a moment or two longer Hermann watched.

The next instant his senses returned to him. He fell back to his belly, and now crawled quickly after his daughter. He could do nothing for the others now but pray.

Still the three ran, though separated, toward the contact they had seen earlier, but who had now disappeared from sight.

Seconds went by. Only the muffled thudding of feet broke the silence.

Suddenly explosions of gunfire rang through the morning air. More shouts from the enraged Galanov, whose footsteps now pursued the fleeing Christians.

Sharp reports from the automatic pistol continued to ring out in rapid-fire succession.

A cry.

The sound of a fall.

Running footsteps.

More shots.

All at once the gunfire stopped. Stillness descended over the field, but only briefly. Without warning, the engine of the Mercedes turned over, then revved to full throttle. The next instant it tore across the field in the direction Galanov had last seen his prey heading.

Lying motionless on his belly in the grass, the German who had imperiled his own life for his brother heard the car rumble past about thirty feet to his right. Slowly he rose to his feet.

But he did not walk far. In the gathering light of dawn he could make out a form lying ahead of him.

The Mercedes rampaged into the distance, its driver maniacally flying after what turned out to be a stray cow at the far border of the pasture. By the time he discovered his fatal error and spun the huge car around, not a single sign of life met his eyes. The man he had come west to capture already lay hiding in a culvert, safely in the hands of the waiting emissaries who had come out from Berlin.

Back in the middle of the field, hidden by grass tall enough to keep him out of sight, a German father knelt over the body of his only daughter, weeping bitter tears of anguish and grief.

But even in the season of severest earthly trial, the words of his whispered prayers of agony rose heavenward not only for his daughter, for his wife, or even for himself. They had all chosen the perilous road where faith had to be put on the line daily, knowing that in this region of the world, martyrdom was no mere ancient myth from the days of early Christendom, but a present reality. They knew the sacrifices that could be exacted from them.

"O God, O God!" he whispered from depths of his spirit known but to a holy few. *"God, my Father, forgive the man they call Galanov for his great sin against your name and your people. Put forgiveness and compassion in my heart toward—"*

His words broke off. Convulsive moans of silent lament shook his manly frame. He lay his head upon the girl's chest, still warm from the life so recently extinguished, and wept the tears of a father giving over his only child into the hands of the Father of them both.

6
Hidden Change

• • •

BESIDE HER OWN FATHER, IN SPITE OF THE THIN LIGHT OF dawn, Lisel Lamprecht realized well enough the truth of what she had just witnessed. She had recognized her friend's cry . . . and heard the fall which followed.

With eyes wide and mouth gaping open in paralyzed horror, unconsciously she tried to rise and take a step toward the grim scene. Hermann stretched out his arm and pulled her back to the ground beside him. Stunned, she did not resist.

The tears which had risen in her eyes moments earlier now broke into convulsive sobs, though they lasted but an instant—only long enough for her equally grief-stricken father to clamp his great hand over her mouth and pull her close beside him where he lay next to the Russian.

"We cannot help her now, Lisel," whispered Hermann. "Her father will take care of her and do what he is able."

Longing to join his network comrade, yet knowing to do so would only endanger them all, Hermann lay ten minutes more in the silent safety of the culvert until the Mercedes was well out of sight and hearing.

No words were spoken. But in the silence of that brief interval, vulnerable, trusting, impressionable Lisel Lamprecht—though she hardly knew it at the time—felt the innocence that had till then been hers as a child of God slowly slip away and into the past. It was the moment the young daughter of the network would always look back on as that when she could no longer make herself believe in the God to whom her mother and father were so dedicated.

If this was what resulted from so-called faith, she would later say, she wanted no part of it.

Meanwhile, she lay silently weeping for her friend, unconscious of the acrid, life-changing metamorphosis taking place within her heart.

Had her father, or he called the Prophet, realized what was occurring in the depths of the soul lying on the ground beside them in the now-expanding light of dawn, they would surely have sent more of their earnest prayers in Lisel's direction.

But their mutual Father gave tender heed to every heart's cry lifted up that morning on anguished murmuring lips from the desolate field outside Berlin. His faithfulness would be abated by neither death nor the willful heart that thinks it rejects him.

He would do that which his very nature compels him to do—he would love as only a true Father's heart is capable.

He would keep them—both Lisel and her departed friend Girdel—in the bosom of his infinite care. He would answer both their fathers' prayers . . . and all would be well.

Even had Hermann left his hiding place sooner, he would have found the area deserted. The limp, broken body of the dead girl was already being borne by her weeping father as quickly as possible back the way they had come. He would seek no help from the others that would endanger the mission.

When Hermann rose, the air was still.

His friend was on his way back to Kehrigkburg, where he would mourn with his wife and where they would bury their daughter. KGB agent Galanov was miles away, recklessly canvassing every possible route of escape westward in the direction of the village of Großbeeren, where previous experience told him the traitors must be bound.

Hermann emerged from the culvert, glanced about, determined that they were safe, then led grief-numbed daughter and the Prophet out of hiding and quickly back eastward to the wood where his car was waiting.

He would drive the Russian fugitive to the safe house in Glasow. From there, others would get him safely across the border. He and Lisel, as he had promised his wife, would be home before midday.

PART II

Outbreak of Freedom

1989

7

Earthquake at the Border

• • •

East Berlin

SHE COULD HEAR THE SHOUTS WHILE STILL BLOCKS AWAY.

The whole city seemed lit up. It was a massive crowd. Two or three thousand people must be at the border. She had never heard anything like it.

Lisel Lamprecht had known something huge was at hand the moment she'd arrived back in Berlin.

It was just after eleven-thirty. Weary from travel, for the last three hours of the long drive from Czechoslovakia she had been anticipating nothing more when she reached home than flopping into bed.

But those plans were not to be.

She walked into the apartment and found it deserted. None of the others were home. She glanced around briefly, then went out again into the city, this time by foot, drawn by some irresistible force.

Something was up. Already thought of sleep had disappeared.

It was dark, the middle of the night. Yet noises in the distance carried an ominous sound.

Everything felt different . . . excitement was in the air!

Her pace quickened, heart beating, perspiration beginning to flow. Was it elation or panic that now caused her chest to pound and her brain to race? She couldn't tell. Suddenly they seemed strangely intermingled.

Lisel hurried along. Many others were out, some running. All movement led toward the border.

What was going on at the Wall!

Was it the sound of confrontation or jubilation that became louder and more deafening the closer she got? Was this the moment they had all waited for . . . or was full-scale war about to break out? How could so many people be at the border and she not hear gunfire? Why were the *Stasi* allowing such a mass demonstration?

Had some new protest been mounted, some huge demonstration she knew nothing of?

Or was she too late? Had the arrests already been made and the noise of the crowd merely the angry sounds of protest? Perhaps the guns from the guards had already carried out their lethal work.

Perhaps death had come again to those committed to freedom. Perhaps she was too late.

She turned down the familiar street known as Markgrafen. She had stared down this same street hundreds of times, with its vacant buildings on each side, stared down the two empty blocks toward the somber, gray, silent, imposing barrier.

The sight that met her eyes on this historic night jolted her senses with such a current of electric anticipation that for a few seconds her disbelieving brain ceased to function.

What seemed ten or twenty thousand people filled the streets stretching up and down the Wall as far as she could see! She saw no guards, no *Vopos,* no *Stasi,* no uniforms of any kind!

What could it mean!

Unconsciously Lisel's feet increased their pace. Now she was running, shoving, making her way through the gathering crowd, struggling forward, hastening toward destiny.

. . .

The years during which the evil barrier had separated the German people seemed so long, as if they would never end. It had only been twenty-eight years, yet it seemed forever. Only a few months ago, East Germany's Communist leader Erich Honecker had declared that the Wall would remain for one hundred years.

Twenty-eight years—one year for each of the twenty-eight miles of Communist suppression that snaked its way like a shameful blemish through the very heart of this proud European capital, scarring the soul of its people, dividing a continent, separating a world.

Through the decade of the sixties the Wall grew formidable. Through the seventies it sat unchanging, taking on aspects of the eternal. A new generation of Germans was born who knew nothing else but that *the Wall* was there—and always would be there.

The eighties opened with no hint that this next decade would end other than it began. The arms race had slowed but not been eliminated. Global standoff continued.

Who could have foretold, however, what shifts in the seismic plates of international relations were about to jolt the earth? The historic globe-quake would be set off by the rise to prominence of two new leaders: Ronald Reagan in the West and Mikhail Gorbachev in the East. These two would symbolize the final episode in the confrontation known as the Cold War.

Even as the Russian leader attempted to bring modernization and change to his nation, unknown to the world the Soviet Union was in fact already unraveling from within. An easing of Moscow's tight grip on the rest of the Eastern Bloc seemed the only way for Gorbachev to save his own nation. This loosening, however, resulted in an ideological fracturing of the solidarity of the all-powerful Communist leadership.

Sensing perhaps by some divine intuition of timing for which he seemed uncannily capable, U.S. president Reagan, standing in 1987 at the Brandenburg Gate with his back to the ugly barricade, boldly challenged the Soviet leader for all the world to hear: "Mr. Gorbachev," he said, "open this gate. . . . Mr. Gorbachev, tear down the Wall!"

For years the fault lines had already been rippling their way through the structure of the Soviet system, invisibly weakening the internal fabric of the Iron Curtain. From almost the beginning of his tenure, the new Russian premier spoke of "new thinking" in Soviet foreign policy. Practical realities involved in this relaxing of the Brezhnev Doctrine came slowly, but soon the world realized a genuine change was at hand.

All in their own way wondered what it signified for them.

Gradually leaders and groups and opposition parties in several of the Warsaw Pact nations began to test and push, seeing in what ways they might tentatively express a hint of independence from Moscow.

Was Gorbachev's "new thinking" for real? There was but one way to find out.

The answer came during the incredible year the world would never forget: 1989. A series of occurrences headlined the year's newscasts that only a short time earlier would assuredly have led to full-scale war throughout Eastern Europe. But now they came without so much as a whimper of protest from the Kremlin, while the rest of the world stood by and watched events unfold with nervous and astonished disbelief.

Poland—where malcontent union leader Lech Walesa had been a thorn in Moscow's side for a decade—and Hungary led the way.

In January, Hungary's Parliament voted to allow independent political parties.

Such moves a decade before would have resulted in Russian tanks moving on Budapest. Yet the stout Hungarians went even further. Shortly thereafter, they slackened control of their westernmost border, eventually withdrawing their guards altogether.

Escapes grew more commonplace. Western Hungary, accessible to all Eastern Europeans, gradually became a favorite "holiday" locale.

No reprisals from Moscow.

It seemed times had indeed changed from the Brezhnev era!

In April, Poland's government legalized the long-troublesome labor union known as Solidarity.

No reprisals from Moscow.

In May, Hungary's leaders took the unthinkable initiative of sending out the country's army to dismantle the barbed wire along its shared border with Austria.

Suddenly the long-impenetrable Iron Curtain had sprung a leak!

The human trickle that had already been climbing over it now simply walked undisturbed into Austria. The Iron Curtain between Hungary and Austria was down!

Word began to spread throughout Eastern Europe like a grassfire blown by a mounting breeze. The trickle became hundreds, then thousands, then tens of thousands fleeing to freedom in the West.

Yet no reprisals were forthcoming from Moscow.

The "new thinking" was for real!

No Soviet tanks rolled out to squelch these outbreaks of independence.

In June, Poland held free elections. The former Communist state was beginning to look like a democracy! And the results were even more stunning—the once-outlawed Solidarity Party scored overwhelming victories.

In August, high-ranking Solidarity leader Tadeusz Mazowiecki, handpicked by Lech Walesa himself, became the country's first non-Communist prime minister since World War II.

Still there were no reprisals from Moscow.

Suddenly that which had been given hollow lip service by Moscow—that each of the Warsaw Pact nations possessed freedom in how it chose to function—had overnight become reality. One by one, each of the satellite nations found opportunity and means to test its own limits, then gradually broke free, tentatively and unevenly, guided now more by internal forces and pressures and timetables than by the strict Communist orthodoxy that had molded direction since the Second World War.

Czechoslovakia now followed Hungary. Thinking they could perhaps get rid of a few malcontents, a special train to the West was established to allow those who chose to emigrate. But Czechoslovakia's Communist leaders, like Communist leaders everywhere, hugely misjudged how widespread the hunger for freedom actually was.

Every train was filled to capacity. The emigrating human tide became a flood. The flood steadily mounted into a tidal wave. In October the so-called freedom train bore untold thousands from Prague to a new life in West Germany.

That same month in East Germany, Communist Erich Honecker was forced out and replaced by Egon Krenz. Hungary continued to push hardest of all, its ruling party repudiating Communism altogether. Its split with Moscow was as unbelievable as it was irreparable.

Then, two weeks later, in the boldest step to date, Hungary declared itself an independent republic.

And *still* no reprisals came from Moscow!

The revolution of 1989 was underway. The stage for cataclysm was set.

East Germans were now pouring out of that country through the Curtain's breaches in Hungary and Czechoslovakia, 225,000 already in the year. The rate had risen to 300 Germans an hour disappearing to the West.

Already in just a few short months an astonishing 1.5 percent—and that the youngest and most vigorous heart of the workforce—of East Germany's *entire* national population had vanished south, either to Prague or Hungary, there to find their way west into Austria or West Germany.

And the flow was increasing. The heart of the DDR was evaporating.

As the months of autumn progressed, the strain on East Germany over the westward flight of its people mounted daily.

A change had to come, some response from new leader Krenz, a Communist himself. Otherwise the exodus would continue and even mount higher. If it went on for another six months, as much as 10 or 20 percent of the entire population could be gone!

What would eventually result from the surging tide of freedom now so brazenly challenging the old Communist order? Chaos or crackdown seemed the only alternatives.

Sometime in the early days of November of that fateful year, the Communist leaders of East Germany decided to take a calculated risk. The thirst for freedom was obviously gaining momentum. They could not hope to stop it.

If they did nothing to stem the tide, their country would eventually disappear before their very eyes.

If, on the other hand, they brought in soldiers to seal off the rest of the DDR's border as had been done in Berlin twenty-eight years ago, a full civil war could erupt—a war they might not now win. Moscow had already demonstrated that it would offer no help—the rest of the Warsaw Pact was on its own.

What if, therefore, East German Communist leaders reasoned with themselves, *they did not try to stop the flow, but legalized it? What if they even went so far as to open the border between East and West Berlin?*

It was a daring proposal!

They would thus show the people of the world that freedom existed in East Germany. Its people could come and go as they pleased. There would be therefore no reason for them to emigrate.

The few faces in attendance at that highly confidential meeting took in the suggestion with somber nods that indicated deep reflection in altogether new directions. Communists had never dared voice such things. Yet all of a sudden it seemed there was no other way to save their crumbling edifice.

Where or when or how the decision was made will be for future historians to discover. Perhaps the full truth will never be known, lost like so many things in the deep vaults of Communist secrecy.

But however it was reached, it was a risk, and a decision, that would change history.

Lisel Lamprecht was away from Berlin on November 9 when the stunning announcement had been made.

Returning from Prague after delivering a carload of refugees to a safe house where they would be taken to the freedom train the following day, she knew nothing of that day's press conference.

East Berlin's Communist Party boss, Günter Schabowski, himself a Politburo member, had announced, almost casually, that as of midnight that very evening, East Germans would be free to pass, without special permission, across any of the DDR's borders—*including* the crossing points through the Wall in Berlin.

Rapidly word spread through both halves of the divided city.

The die had been cast. There could be no turning back now. Even had they wanted to, the DDR's leaders had thrown control of their own futures into the blowing winds of liberty.

Well before midnight, a huge crowd of West Germans had gathered at Checkpoint Charlie in the American sector of Berlin, well supplied with champagne and beer to celebrate. By eleven-thirty they were shouting and crying out to the East German border guards, *"Tor Auf . . . Tor Auf!"*

•   •   •

Lisel was now being swept along by the growing throng, at length divining the momentous truth that the hated barrier had been breached. It was 12:15 A.M., though she was utterly unconscious of time.

Surging forward through the mass of hysterical humanity, suddenly Lisel found herself standing before the Wall itself. She had looked at it from a distance for so many years, fought against the tyranny it represented. Suddenly she stood facing it without danger.

The sounds of the shouting crowd faded as she recalled that day returning from the bookshop so long ago when she had wondered what the Wall felt like.

Slowly she reached out and placed her palm flat against the rough gray concrete. It did not feel so unusual now. There was nothing to it but cold, lifeless cement. How could such an inanimate substance have symbolized so much?

For several moments she stood, unmoving, hand pressed against the stone barricade. Gradually sounds began again to intrude into her brain. *"Lisel . . . Lisel!"* Someone was shouting her name.

She looked around, then glanced up. One of her FA colleagues was sitting on top of the Wall, shouting down to her. "Lisel," he cried, "come up . . . come up!"

The next instant a rope was dangling down in front of her.

What seemed a hundred hands grabbed toward it. But this was an opportunity Lisel had waited, and worked, and fought for for years, and she would seize it herself!

Pushing her way, she grabbed hold of the rope and began scrambling upward.

Unconscious of anything but the height to be scaled, she pulled and scraped her way, until at last she saw her friend's hand reaching down toward her.

Upward she stretched, as far as her arm would extend. It had been a long struggle, not only for her, but for the Alliance, and all the people of this land . . . and the climax was at hand.

8

Outburst

• • •

THE DECADE BETWEEN 1979 AND 1989 HAD BEEN A TUMUL-
tuous one for Lisel Lamprecht.

She had left home at seventeen, a year after the incident that
fateful morning outside the city that had shocked her entire emotional system so deeply. It was a day she still could not think of
without emotion, though it roused as much silent anger in her heart
now as pain.

In that most irrational yet common of fallacious human
misreactions, the smoldering embers left alive from the trauma came
to burn most of all toward her own father. The anguish over the loss
of her friend sat deep in her soul for a year, brooding, chafing,
gradually changing from hurt to indignation, feeding upon evil
suggestions from demons of bitterness, accusation, and doubt until
one day it erupted in an unplanned and unpredictable torrent against
poor, unsuspecting Hermann.

What triggered the incident was insignificant enough. There had
been hundreds of such days before. Yet on this particular morning,
without warning the long-festering fuse ignited into full flame.

Lisel had not asked to accompany him nor shown the slightest
interest in the network's affairs since that morning both would forget
if they could, nor had Hermann been inclined to push her toward
increased involvement. The enthusiasm she had shown earlier had
vanished altogether, and both he and his wife recognized that time
was necessary for the healing of such wounds. Lisel was still young,
they said to themselves, and they must do their best to give her room
to grow without pressure.

Over the following year, however, they began to sense more than just the quietude of pain, but with it a deepening independence within the heart of their daughter.

Grieved, they were yet powerless to resist the change. All attempts to display tenderness, to talk with Lisel as they once had, fell as on ears of stone. The normally smiling and energetic girl gradually became more and more unresponsive and distant. By the time of her seventeenth birthday, Hermann and his wife found themselves wondering if she was their daughter at all.

What could have happened, they asked one another a hundred times, and with the thousand looks of silent anguish that passed between while they watched Lisel walking like a moving statue through the room, without so much as a glance of recognition toward either.

She took to leaving the house more and more on her own. The mention of new friends crept into what little conversation went on. Occasionally they saw someone waiting on the sidewalk, or a strange car parked on the street, when their eyes followed from inside after Lisel's announcement that she was "going out" for a while.

Neither approved of such new habits, nor favored these associations about which they knew nothing. Yet they feared any attempt to speak some word of parental caution might only drive Lisel further away.

An expression of hardness and resolve came to replace the happy features that had previously characterized the growing girl's smiling countenance. Even her younger brother, twelve now, felt the change and was affected by it. He was too young to know the same aches that sat like lumps of frozen tears in the hearts of his father and mother. But Lisel was his older sister, and, notwithstanding the five years separating them, they had always been friends. He missed her now and silently wondered why she no longer had time for him.

Lisel herself was well enough aware of the pain she was causing the other three of her family. But she was only seventeen and was resolute to prevent herself from caring. Thus she squelched the hundreds of opportunities presented her to heed the voice of conscience, and in so doing slowly deadened the capacity of her inner ears to hear at all.

The *Self* is perhaps more fully *alive,* and more staunchly *determined* to occupy the throne of the soul, during the years between fourteen and eighteen than in any other period during all the human span of years.

Alas that for the great majority of men and women it must come fully alive at all, and reach for the energetic measure of independence to which it feels entitled, before the realization follows that the foremost purpose of life—that very reason for which we have been given the thing called *life* at all—is nothing more nor less than to *deny* that Self the independence it seeks, indeed to *kill* its Self-life altogether that true *life* might emerge from the altar upon which we have slain it.

This is the great human dichotomy—that which inevitably rises within us as the most *natural* expression of our humanness is the very enemy to everything our deepest nature desires to become.

In truth, there is no higher life to be gained than that born from *death* of Self. In pursuing the independence Self lusts for, we only race further and further from the *life* the heart longs for.

The eternal opposite of Independence is *D*ependence. The world counts the latter a great evil, the one condition of being to be avoided as if it were the worst of all plagues. In actual fact, no life can be ours until Independence dies, and we recognize the utter *Dependence* of the entire universe.

Dependence upon the eternal Fatherhood of creation is the only air which to breathe gives life. Only sons and daughters can live under the dependent canopy of that Fatherhood. Those who have rather determined that independence is their life's objective can find no home there. They will suffocate, for the tingling air of that region will not enter their lungs.

The great business of life, indeed the *only* business of life, is to become children. Out of childhood we grow, and into a new and higher childhood we *must* grow if we would become capable of breathing the air of the high mountains of true personhood.

Between the two, however, stand the fateful, and for many fatal, years of independence. They may come at fourteen, they may arrive at six, they may delay till thirty-seven. Likewise, the duration of these backward-progressing years of growth may be two or five or sixty.

When they come matters not. How long they last matters a great deal. For however long a man or woman allows the demon Independence to rule determines the steepness of the subsequent uphill climb toward Childness, which is the only and the eternal goal of earthly existence.

Alas, therefore, for those who must allow the Self its season of reign. For in so doing they give this lethal enemy Independence an entrenched foothold from which it will then take the remainder of their mortal days to dislodge. How much better to deny the Self its would-be throne early, and thus get on with the true business of life the moment adulthood arrives.

Lisel, however, was far from such realizations. She had allowed the demon to enter through the wounds in her heart. And now it spoke its lies of independence into the ears of her Self, callousing her to the capacity to care that she was hurting those three who loved her most in all the world.

Some would say she could hardly be blamed for such a reaction. But we are *all* to blame for exalting the Self, however harsh may be the pains inflicted upon it. The first lesson of the higher Childhood into which we must grow is that each alone determines the direction and speed of his or her character development. What we become we have *chosen* to become—there is none other accountable besides ourselves.

The storm came without warning one Sunday morning.

"Where are you going, Lisel?" asked her mother, as Lisel put on her coat and walked toward the door.

"Out—with some friends."

"What friends?"

"Just . . . *friends,*" she replied, irritation showing through in her voice.

Hermann walked into the room, hearing the last of the exchange and noting his daughter's expression. "There is no reason to talk in that tone to your mother," he said, more abruptly than he had been accustomed to speaking for many months.

Lisel sighed, hand on the door-latch, but said nothing. Neither parent observed the silent thundercloud gathering upon her forehead.

Hermann was annoyed with his daughter, yet immediately repented the manner in which he had addressed her. "Why don't you come with me instead," he said, attempting with modest success to give his words a tone of brightness. "I have to drive down to Großbeeren to see Josef."

Still Lisel remained silent.

"It has been too long since you went anywhere with me," added Hermann, doing his best to keep up his cheerful expression, though his daughter was making it extremely difficult.

"On your *network* business, you mean?" she said, the disdain with which the word passed her lips more than obvious.

"Yes—you used to want to come with me."

"Things have changed."

"You no longer want to be a part of the work?" At last Hermann began to lose the calm demeanor he had been struggling to hold in place. In certain moods he hurt for his daughter, and he had shed many prayerful tears on her behalf. But she could still drive him to vexation on a moment's notice with her uncaring attitude and biting, sarcastic tongue.

"That is exactly right—*I do not,*" Lisel shot back emphatically.

Hermann opened his mouth and began to vent long months of pent-up frustration, but only managed a handful of words. "I have had about all the cynical words and haughty looks from you that I—"

Suddenly she was shrieking at him—screaming like she would never have dared to before. "You and your idiotic network!" she cried, spinning around from the door and facing her dumbfounded father.

"How dare you speak like that, Lisel," said Frau Lamprecht, now approaching and angry also in her turn. "You know as well as anyone that your father has given his life—"

"And for *what?*" she interrupted again, bitterness apparent in every word.

"We have helped many people to freedom," replied Hermann, astonished at what he was hearing.

"You *think* you're helping, but you're accomplishing nothing! The Wall is still there, despite everything you think you're doing!"

"There are many ways to be free."

"You do nothing but help one person at a time," Lisel shot back. "A person here, a person there . . . what good does it do? *It will never do any good!* Even if everyone did like you and all your praying, complacent friends, nothing would ever change. This corrupt system will go on forever! Religious talk about freedom inside means nothing!"

Her face was red as the torrent of anger that had built up over the last year at last burst its dam and spewed out of her mouth. In shock now, both Hermann and his wife stood speechless and gaping.

"The system has to be torn down so that everyone can be free," Lisel went on. "My friends understand that. No, I want nothing to do with your impotent and absurd network! Who do you think you're fooling with all your stupid religious games! You're not fooling me!"

At last was Hermann's tongue loosened. "Stop with your irreverent outbursts!" he cried. "Stop this instant, or I'll—"

"Or you'll what!" she yelled back in challenge.

A brief silence filled the tense atmosphere of the house. By now the commotion had brought Lisel's brother to the door of the room, where he listened with wide eyes and a terrified heart. Never had there been such an explosion under this roof before.

"Ha—I thought so!" spat Lisel with derision. "What are you going to do? . . . *You'll do nothing!*"

The threat from the mouth of his own daughter again revived Hermann's brain, but now was the tongue of his old Adam fully awake. "I'll silence you myself," he cried. "However much this evil rebellion has entered your heart, you are still my daughter and I—"

"Silence me—*how?*" she yelled tauntingly. "Will you take me on a mission so that I can be killed too? That will silence me all right—just like Girdel!"

The stunning words fell with such force from her lips that Hermann was numbed into instant silence. His face went white as a sheet.

"Yes—that's right! You may think I have forgotten, but I will never forget that day! *It's your fault*—yours and Girdel's father's and all the rest of you. You may as well have *all* killed her! You talk about freedom, but how free is Girdel? How many more like her have to die? Will I have to die too! Yes, you may silence me, but I'm not going to wait for that to happen! I'm going to make sure my life counts for something before everyone dies and the Wall is still there. *Your daughter,*" she repeated, *"—I stopped being your daughter on that field out there when I watched Girdel's blood spilling out on the ground. That's when I knew I wanted no more of this life here!"*

The next instant the door slammed behind her, while Hermann's poor wife sought the big man's arms and shoulders in which to bury her grief-stricken tears.

Slowly and silently their twelve-year-old son turned and wandered back toward his room, face ashen, heart smitten through as with a cruel knife of dreadful loss, and understanding nothing of what he had just heard.

None of the three had seen Lisel since that day.

9

A Prodigal Daughter

• • •

LISEL QUICKLY FOUND WHAT SHE CONVINCED HERSELF
was a home and family among the friends she had already made in the
organization known as the Freedom Alliance.

Not even returning that night for any of her things, she took up
residence with several other girls in the group. The oldest was but in
her mid-twenties, for the entire Alliance was made up of young
people. They were kind to her, in the way young people of shared
vision extend bonds to anyone of like mind instantly closer than with
the estranged families many have left behind. They helped Lisel get on
her feet, taught her to stay out of the government's way, and in time
she managed to obtain enough work to contribute to the household,
to the cause, and to her own sustenance as a self-supporting young
East German woman.

Her faith was all but dead the moment she turned her back on her
parents and walked out the door of the house where she had spent
the first seventeen years of her life.

Lisel quickly afterward discarded the remnant shards of her Christian beliefs. It did not take more than a conversation or two with
others further along the road of doubt and unbelief than herself to
convince her that Christianity was a belief system as outmoded as the
Communism their movement and cause was fighting against. Impressionable and unable to probe the deeper fallacies of their faulty logic
and shallow reasoning, Lisel accepted the conclusions of her older
peers without dispute and made their self-exalting religion of activism her new god.

It was a long time before she considered religion seriously again, and then only in the way of formulating an analytical response to it. Her companions were mostly of similar age and liked to talk, not merely about how to obtain freedom for their nation but about the higher cognitive and metaphysical issues of life, into which discussions the myth of God could not help but play a pivotal role. Nor was she alone in voicing an agnostic perspective of so-called rationalism. Many in the Freedom Alliance had likewise rejected what they viewed as the simplistic notions of Christianity. This common ground served yet further to deepen their mutual confidence that they had entered an age of enlightenment never known by their small-thinking and religiously superstitious parents.

As Lisel saw it, therefore, her rejection of the Christian faith was completely in step with views held by most young people her age, all of whom saw things in a much more reasonable and informed manner than had previous generations. Nearly all her comrades in freedom's cause shared her perspectives. To her, it was a logical progression for any modern and intellectually honest individual to go through. Though she would always grieve for Girdel, she eventually viewed her friend's death almost as the moment when her own liberation from the myths of her past had been born.

She had wrestled with the implications of that fateful day long and hard during her final year under her parents' roof. She and her brother had always been taught that God was on their side. If that was true, then *why did he let Girdel be killed?* That had been the horrible and spiritually cataclysmic question.

As long as she could remember, her parents had taught her that God was good. She had assumed it to be true without ever stopping to question it. They had said God would protect them, that he took care of those who believed in him.

For the first time in her young life, suddenly at sixteen that principle was shattered. She began wondering if everything else she had been taught and had always assumed . . . *was true at all.* The tragedy in which she had been so closely involved brought to the surface questions and doubts she had never so much as considered. And as the questions persisted, she found nothing in all she had been taught that would make them go away.

She had tried as long as she could to believe in God and work with her parents in his service. But where had it all ended but in pain and suffering? She did not want to wind up like Girdel, dead because of a naive faith.

What else could it possibly be, she concluded at length, than just that—a *naive* set of beliefs that, when put to the test, made no difference at all? And if they didn't, they couldn't be true.

If there was a God, he would *surely* have kept that bullet from finding Girdel's body. *How could there possibly be a God?* she asked herself over and over.

Then came the explosion, and just as suddenly as it had begun, she was storming out, slamming the door behind her.

That was nine years ago, when she was seventeen. She had seen neither father nor mother nor brother since.

During the years she had gradually risen in the ranks of the underground East German freedom-fighting movement known as the Freedom Alliance.

Without knowing it, she was following in her father's footsteps more than she realized, though her activities were political rather than spiritual. Nothing could prevent the intrusion of thoughts upon occasion about her upbringing. But through the years Lisel became skilled at sending such potential reflections away from those tender, sensitive areas where personhood dwells, and thus remained, as much as it is possible to be, content in her unbelief.

How long they had worked and fought and sacrificed for this moment of freedom. Now suddenly it was happening so fast, more rapidly than they'd dreamed possible . . . so fast.

The tugging on her hands and the shouts in her ears brought Lisel once more back to the present incredible moment of triumph.

10
The Wall Comes Tumbling Down

• • •

SCRAMBLING UP THE LAST BIT OF THE WAY, MANY HANDS now grabbed hold of Lisel's arms and shoulders, pulling her up toward them.

She was atop the Berlin Wall!

Tentatively she got her feet under her, then rose on the narrow and uneven top. Standing to her full height, she threw her hand into the air, fist clenched, calling out shouts of victory with thousands of voices just like hers.

All around, the night air was filled with sounds of riotous tumult.

Lisel suddenly realized she was looking down upon *West* Berlin, where a throng even larger than she had just come through spread out like a sea in the night along every street. Whistles and cheers, automobile horns and lights blended in a cacophony of happiness and celebration.

Photographers and television cameramen were pointing their instruments up at those poised on the top of the Wall. With a shout and a gesture, she waved down to them. She could not hear their cameras clicking, but the tiny explosions of light gave evidence enough that her picture was being taken by a dozen at once.

Lisel laughed in joyous abandon, now looking up and again allowing her gaze to spread slowly out over the massive throngs of well-wishers from West Berlin.

As she stood peering across the historic midnight scene, slowly the tumult began once more to fade from her hearing, as it had only two or three minutes earlier upon pressing her palm against the rough stone surface below.

In the midst of so many thousands, perhaps even half a million individuals, gradually twenty-six-year-old Lisel Lamprecht found herself engulfed by a phantasmic wave of aloneness. Her eyes and ears remained wide, and she knew her wits were still with her, for her own awareness continued at normal pace. Yet she could feel her sensory consciousness giving way to another dimension, as if a waking dream was stealing over her in the midst of the din.

Time slowed until she could no longer feel the movements of those about her. The noise entering her ears faded, until nothing was left but the silence of her own thoughts. On the ground, movement no more registered to her senses with realism. Every figure decelerated into slow motion, then ceased altogether. She stood, gazing upon the sea of humanity, now stilled and silent that she might contemplate it at her leisure.

Gradually from amid the surging tide of impersonality, in dreamlike vision, faces now rose up, like a vapor rising from the sea, and became focused just above the mass—happy, exuberant, shouting, joyous faces.

Movement returned to the scene, but only a silent animation upon the ten thousand faces of the crowd. Lisel could see eyes flashing and lips moving and heads turning in joy, yet still no sound from their voices reached her ears.

Faces . . . faces spread out for miles in front of her and behind her and along the Wall in every direction. Jubilant, smiling, celebrating faces—faces aglow in victory, the triumphant moment they had all been waiting for.

She could see them shouting, but why could she not hear their voices? They were trying to tell her something—what was it they were saying?

A inner minor chord struck into the midst of the spectral revelry. Suddenly a chill swept through Lisel's body.

Something wasn't right . . . something was wrong—very wrong with the scene she was witnessing in her mind's eye.

A change now began to come. The faces were changing now, a million of them . . . turning grotesque and vaporous . . . their features slowly vanishing back into the mist of the sea of humanity out of which they had come.

She tried to twist away, as if she sensed what was coming, to shake herself free from this waking vision turning now into a nightmare. But she could not turn, and continued to stare ahead. She opened her mouth and tried to force another celebratory shout, as if the sound of her voice would break the spell. But she could no more utter a sound than had this dream come upon her in the midst of a deep slumber.

The mistlike swirling figures continued to alter their aspect . . . growing, rising again . . . becoming larger, too large, a huge fog rising up and coalescing into a great cloud of pure white . . . all the former faces now fading into a single face . . . huge, as big as the city itself.

Large and pale was the new face that emerged out of the cloud. But it was no more a cloud, but became now like the moon, shining eerily, its features gradually coming into view, lips moving soundlessly as had all the individual faces which had drifted skyward and melted into it.

A chill of ice set Lisel trembling from head to foot. What was the great mouth of the dream-face saying?

Suddenly she knew she was reading the man's lips. She knew what they were uttering—it was a message meant only for her. *We have helped many people to freedom. There are many ways to be free, Lisel—what you see here is but one of them.*

It was the face of her father!

No! Lisel tried to cry. But she could cause no sound to come to her voice. Again she attempted to force her head away.

But her father's face continued to loom large in the eye of her memory. No expression of rejoicing was upon the moon-face she knew so well but had tried to forget. Rather, tears fell from his eyes, and an expression of grieving sadness filled his countenance. There could be no doubt he was beseeching his daughter to return to home and family.

Try as she might, Lisel was powerless to shake the image. Deep inside did she realize that this moment signified a victory for him too? Had not he, in his own way, been fighting for freedom just like she? But, as his words had said, freedom of a different kind.

The last words he had spoken to her nine years ago—those very words her brain had just seen on his lips—were true: He *had* helped many people to freedom.

But she didn't care! She would not *let* herself care.

No victory celebration could alter the fact that the barrier existing in Lisel's own heart was as solid as the material at this moment under her feet and showed no signs of weakening anytime soon. Yet in the few brief seconds of her vision, at long last some tiny, long-dormant place within Lisel's soul had at least turned in the direction of awakening to recognize the self-erected wall of separation she had built up within herself.

It should well be so, for prayers had been sent against many barriers, not only that upon which the young prodigal stood. Some walls, however, are erected with materials more difficult to topple than mere bricks and cement. And for all eternal things, especially the perfecting of sons and daughters, time is necessary for their accomplishment.

If that inner wall was to come down, the time *could* have been on this night—for *any* moment is fit occasion to will the Self into submission to the Spirit. But for Lisel Lamprecht, that moment would not be tonight.

No, Lisel repeated to herself, more determined this time. Her father's was an unwelcome presence intruding into her brain, piercing like a poisoned arrow out of the past sent to destroy the joy of the moment.

No! she said yet a third time, finally with success at generating a peep of sound. She would not think of him now! She would *not* allow him to ruin this wonderful moment!

She clapped her hands to the sides of her ears and shook her head back and forth, as if the motion would rid her of thoughts she did not now want to ponder.

Then, thinking to exorcise the demons of her past but in reality yielding to those of the present, at last Lisel summoned the sheer determination of will and forced a great cry out of her mouth.

Suddenly the vision vanished, and again she found herself gazing out upon the tumult of Berlin's humanity, returning to its hysterical appearance, accompanied by the instant return of boisterous sound and frenetic motion to the scene.

Lisel whooped and yelled for another thirty seconds, as happy now to have put the nightmare behind her as to celebrate freedom's triumph, then yielded to the invitations of those on the other side to jump down from the barrier and join them in the free West.

Moments later, Lisel was engulfed in hugs and shouts and handshakes and more hugs from a throng of people she did not know and celebrating the occasion with a long swallow of champagne from a bottle that had been thrust into her hand.

Minutes later ten thousand voices rose spontaneously as one to the emotional strains of at least one portion of Germany that had not been separated these last twenty-eight years, for the anthem and heritage it represented belonged to every man, woman, and child the world over who considered himself a German:

Deutschland, Deutschland über alles,
Über alles in der Welt,
Wenn es stets zu Schutz und Trutze
Brüderlich zusammenhält;
Von der Maas bis an die Memel,
Von der Etsch bis an den Belt:
Deutschland, Deutschland über alles,
Über alles in der Welt.

11

Knitted Prayer Strands of the Rose-Tapestry

• • •

MEANWHILE, AS THESE MOMENTOUS EVENTS ROCKED THE city of Berlin with reverberations that shook the entire globe, throughout all of Europe every man or woman who had been touched personally by the effects of the Wall—a statement that could be made about nearly every German in both the BRD and the DDR—reflected on their own private histories and considered what this portentous change might mean for them.

At last had the prophetic words of Goethe's *Faust* concerning German *Zerrissenheit** again for a new generation, like many times already in the past, been put to rest: "Two souls, alas, reside within my breast."

Now approached a new season for the outworking of Nietzsche's analysis of his own race: "The German soul is . . . more intangible . . . more contradictory, more unknown . . . than other peoples are to themselves. . . . It is characteristic of the Germans that the question 'What is a German?' never dies out among them. . . . The German soul has passages and . . . caves, hiding-places and dungeons therein. . . . The German himself does not exist: he is becoming."

Many, like those who had gathered at the Wall, celebrated with riotous abandon. Others rejoiced more quietly.

There were many kinds of tears shed the next day, tears of gladness, tears of reminiscent regret, tears of complex nostalgia.

---

*"torn condition"

A small number in the East—those who divined potentially unpleasant changes in the wind for people like themselves who had exerted power over their countrymen in the old order—grew nervous.

Those few who grasped the higher truths of Romans 13:1 and Matthew 16:19 sought their knees: What might these great events portend for God's people? They would inquire of the Father.

In the middle of the Soviet sector of the city, an aging man and his wife, who had not been inclined to seek the border the previous evening, quietly prayed together as the gathering dusk descended over their small East Berlin home.

Their thoughts were not occupied with taking flight to the suddenly opened and accessible West. They had had numerous opportunities before this, and in truth could have been living on the other side years ago had such been the lot marked out for them.

The weighty events of the past twenty-four hours signalled little immediately new for them, although it would surely alter—and joyfully!—the work with which they had been involved for the whole twenty-seven years of their married lives.

What was on their minds this day—and had been continuously since hearing the news—was the question of what impact this might foreshadow in other directions. Shakings of this magnitude among the powers of the earth were unlikely without echoing repercussions throughout the spiritual realm. What additional loosenings in the heavenly places might now result? Could this breaking of the enemy's grip on earthly principalities signify a like relaxing of his hold upon the souls of men and women?

Such at least was their hope . . . and the prayer of their hearts.

They were thinking of their son and daughter, the latter of whom they had not seen for nine painful years. One wall had been torn down. But for these two, an even more significant one yet remained. Separations in the world were being breached, and they would see the one that ran through the middle of their own home healed most of all.

With the news, therefore, they found a dedication rising up in their weary but faithful hearts to redouble their prayer efforts against it.

Their prayers had been unchanged in ten years, though they had been uttered in a thousand variations, sometimes with mere groanings and sighings when words could not be found.

On this evening, however, words came easily, for their hearts were full of renewed hope.

"Keep our dear Lisel in your care, heavenly Father," prayed the mother. *"Turn her thoughts again toward us, and let her know that we will always love her. Heal the wounds she is carrying so that she might become a child once again."*

"Protect her, Lord," Hermann now prayed as he had hundreds of times before, taking the hand of his wife. *"Uphold her with your hand of grace, that when she returns to you, she will know you have been with her all along. Take care of her . . . and bring her home."*

"And thank you, Lord Jesus," continued Frau Lamprecht, *"for your watchful care and ministration to Lisel's brother. Keep him also in your hands, and strengthen his faith to continue praying that his arms might soon wrap themselves around his sister once again."*

• • •

Two mornings after that fateful midnight in Berlin, 720 kilometers to the east, word had just come to one of the members of a small fellowship of Polish believers not far from the Russian border concerning the astounding events that had just taken place in Berlin.

As Waclau Chmielnicki set the newspaper down on the table in front of him, so many thoughts flooded his brain. It was a dream come true, the answer to so many years of prayer—freedom at last!

Or at least the beginnings of it.

Who could tell, however, what this momentous day in Berlin would signify for them in Poland? Perhaps it would mean nothing at all. This was not Germany, after all. Poland adjoined the Soviet colossus, and Moscow was not likely to allow freedom to encroach quite *this* close.

Unconsciously he cast his gaze out the window toward the east. The border sat right out there, he thought—under his very nose. He could walk out and touch the fence. He rejoiced for his German brothers, but as long as that fence separated him and his cousin, he would remain wary of the Soviet beast.

He could not help thinking back to the days when he, as a mere boy, had taken part in his father's activities in the Brotherhood. What a thrill it had been to participate in their underground prayer meetings and to see so many pilgrims and sojourners and refugees that came through their region and received help from his father and his friends.

Then had come the Jewish man, followed quickly by the arrest of their young leader. Everything had changed after that.

They had always been aware of the danger, but after that it always seemed closer. Kochow Rydz had gradually become the acknowledged leader of the group, but then several years ago he had been arrested too. By then Waclau himself was old enough to coordinate certain of the Brotherhood's activities.

Now his own father was dead, Andre Palacki and his wife were also gone, as well as Karl Laski and Michal Malik. Kochow had been released after seven years and was now back among them, though the years in prison had aged him noticeably.

Waclau shuddered at the memory of first sight of him upon his return. How much worse it must have been for Dieder, according to Kochow's descriptions. But Palacki had still not returned to the region of Bialystok. Perhaps the time was now approaching when—

His own son Leeka walked into the room, interrupting his reflections. Waclau showed him the newspaper, then attempted to explain what the great event signified.

"Papa," his son asked, "does this mean I will be able to visit Uncle Jahn?"

"I'm afraid not yet, Leeka, my boy," replied Waclau. "I fear the fence between our house and his will yet divide us for a time."

Chmielnicki rose. It was time to assemble the Brotherhood once more, he thought. They must pray for their friend and mentor Dieder Palacki, who, though free from his years of imprisonment, yet had to guard his steps. Perhaps this news from Berlin foretold the day for which they had all prayed, when he might rejoin the fellowship without fear for the rest of their safety.

He would spread the word around Krynki, then drive into Bialystok tonight to see Kochow. No doubt he would have heard about the events in Berlin and perhaps already be in contact with the others.

O Lord, Chmielnicki prayed silently, *make it possible for us to see our brother Dieder again!*

• • •

A few hours later, far to the south and east, in that region bordering the Mediterranean known as the Land of Promise, where the freedom of nationhood had come forty-one years earlier, a Jewish man and woman likewise knelt in prayer. Their petitions, however, were offered neither for themselves nor offspring nor once-imprisoned colleagues, but rather for the great German city where they had been reunited years earlier through a tunnel under a wall that suddenly was no more.

"Thank you, blessed Father," prayed the Hebrew Christian Joseph Aviz-Rabin—he in fact who had been in the thoughts of the praying Pole just hours before, and who had himself suffered in a Russian prison for eight years—*"for the freedom you have brought to Berlin."*

"And we thank you again, dear Lord," added his wife, Ursula, *"for the freedom you gave us there, and for miraculously reuniting us after being separated so long, and for the joy of that meeting. May all those whom the Communist evil has separated likewise now be joined as we were."*

"We pray for our American friends, God," now said her husband. *"Give us opportunity to see them again, and to visit Germany once more."*

"We join in prayer," said Ursula, *"for the tearing down of many walls between men's hearts. May this event cause unity and healing, and may many come to know you as a result."*

"Amen . . . ," added Joseph. *"Amen!"*

• • •

In a lonely room in Wroclaw in southwest Poland, the man responsible for the praying Jew's conversion to the Christian faith also now found himself drawn into intimate dialogue with his Father in heaven. He too had heard of the sudden opening between the two halves of the German city and realized it to be no isolated event.

What might be its meaning for him?

Changes had been coming to his native Poland throughout the whole of this year even more rapidly than in the DDR. Now Poland even boasted a democratically elected government. With these new developments in Berlin, even more Westernization was likely to come, and at an accelerated pace.

There was no going back now. Surely it was safe for him to come out of hiding and begin traveling and speaking more openly within his own country.

He sensed it was time to let his voice be heard.

"O God," said Dieder Palacki, *"show me what you want me to do, where you want me to go, what you want me to say. Make me an instrument for the strengthening of your church. Give me courage to say what must be said."*

He paused, then added, *"Let me never speak any but your words, Father. Lead me to those to whom you would have me speak, and let nothing but your messages for them leave my lips."*

•   •   •

Some four thousand miles to the west, completing the interconnections of prayer whose strands were woven together as in a great heavenly tapestry of yet invisible but soon to be revealed purpose, at the epicenter of freedom itself, in the U.S. capital of Washington, D.C., two other aging saints watched in prayerful and disbelieving wonder as the events in the land of their early years together unfolded.

Suddenly the woman who had not watched more than twenty hours of television in the whole of the last twenty years found herself glued to the small set in her husband's den. Unable to keep from weeping from the many emotions surging through her, she sat taking in every newscast and documentary she could locate, beholding the answers to years of prayer before her very eyes.

"Thank you, Lord . . . thank you!" were the only words she could breathe.

Immediately the conversation between husband and wife began to revolve around scheduling a return trip to Germany at the soonest convenient opportunity.

12
What Dangers Ahead?

• • •

Moscow

MEANWHILE, YET FURTHER TO THE EAST, KGB AGENT AN-drassy Galanov contemplated what he had just read in this morning's edition of *Pravda*. He had heard about events in Berlin two days ago, but reading of it and seeing photos brought back many memories.

Though it had been an inauspicious season in his life, Berlin did represent the place where he had achieved his start. He thought about the German *Stasi* chief, wondering what would become of his former boss now, a Communist in a country suddenly discarding the old order.

Galanov knew that Schmundt had given up the secret police some time back in favor of politics, and had since risen high. Would his be the fate of Honecker, ousted in favor of the new . . . or would he survive the shake-up now going on in the DDR?

Posing the question concerning his former associate quieted Galanov still further and brought him face-to-face with an even more sobering question: What would become of *him* in this sudden restruc-turing sweeping through Europe?

Gorbachev had already made reforms sufficient to have caused considerable squirming among the old guard in the military and the Politburo . . . not to mention the KGB. The once powerful and feared agency was not what it had once been.

No toppling of walls was going on here in the Soviet Union. Communism was not being thrown out—that could never happen, even with Gorbachev at the helm.

There was no denying, however, that all the old lines were being redrawn—more slowly and subtly, perhaps, than this sudden and unthinkable demolishing of the division between East and West that had occurred in Berlin.

Yet the astute observer could detect whiffs of similar currents in the wind . . . even here.

Galanov wasn't sure he liked the odor.

Freedom carried an aroma all its own, and a great deal depended on which side of the fence you happened to be standing on *before* its winds began to blow.

What might happen here? he wondered. *Where could all this lead?*

In Germany and Hungary and Poland, already all the old loyal Communists were being thrown out. What if those same west winds of liberty one day stretched all the way to Moscow, even to the Kremlin?

What *might* happen?

Where might the KGB find itself then?

The question set off shock waves in Galanov's brain. He had reached his present heights by preparing himself for any and all eventualities and contingencies, by always remaining one step ahead of his adversary.

That was how he had managed to climb so high in this regime, even higher than his dear departed, cunning, and sinister uncle.

He winced inwardly at the intrusion of an unwelcome memory. He had not been one step ahead of that Christian fool calling himself the Prophet. The failure of *that* attempt ten years ago still gnawed at him, and the memory of Bolotnikov's subsequent tongue-lashing stung.

But he had used the failure to good purpose and had been, if not even more ruthless, certainly more effective as an agent for the state's security, even working his way back into Bolotnikov's good graces, though the man was no longer head of the agency.

But how could he remain one step ahead of the adversary now, when the adversary was the invisible and illusive commodity called *change?* How could he order his steps if he could not see which way that enemy might suddenly turn?

Had he been the praying kind, now might be a time such as to employ that ancient rite on his own behalf. Bah! What was he thinking! Where had the notion of such an absurdity come from!

Still, it might not be a bad idea to begin planning a strategy—privately, of course—for his own survival, just in case Gorbachev's reforms got the best of the Soviet leader and began to take on a life of their own . . . in the event that one day, even in this country, Communists and party members—and even KGB agents!—began to be looked upon with less favor than in past years.

Insurance was always a good idea, a hedge against the fickle winds of new times. He did not want to find himself facing the fate of Kádár in Hungary or Honecker in the DDR, or suddenly being thrown into prison for his years of loyalty to the Soviet system.

He was safe for now. But in the meantime, he would keep his eyes open for danger . . . and for opportunity.

PART III

Reaching the Post~Cold War World

1992

13

Destination: Berlin

. . .

Washington, D.C.

READYING FOR TAKEOFF NEVER LOST ITS THRILL.

The airport stimulated one's senses in and of itself: businessmen with briefcases, broadcast messages, foreign tongues, uniformed pilots, and three-piece suits lending an air of sophistication—the place reeked with the sensation that important goings-on were in the wind.

Especially here at Washington's Dulles International Airport, where capital politics and global decisions were constantly in the wind. Anyone you bumped into might be a senator or ambassador or foreign diplomat. Any parcel or bag might contain briefs and papers bound by courier to a head of state at some distant corner of the earth.

Every overheard call at the bank of pay phones gave snatches of world-significant conversation. Just being in the midst of it elevated your perceptions, drawing you subliminally into the fancy that you too were part of it all—an intrinsic element in some daring, unspoken plot, an enterprise upon which the fate of the world hinged.

It was all make-believe, of course. Yet the very ambience of the place contradicted reason, telling you that maybe it *was* true and that *you* possessed the key, the clue all these other people were looking for.

Tad McCallum's mind drifted back to the reality of the present as he flipped through the magazines on the plane's rack. Selecting two, he turned and made his way down the aisle to his seat with his two companions for the adventure.

Sometimes, he had to admit, the travel became tedious. It was regular enough in his line of work that there were times he would rather stay home and work in the office. But he loved what he did, and much of it could not be done from behind his desk or in front of a computer screen. And usually by the time he reached the airport, the intoxication had set in again. Especially for an assignment in Europe.

Even if Germany was the place of his birth and his second home, there remained an old-world mystique that always came back the moment he walked through the airport's doors and began thinking of where he was bound. It never failed to inject him with the exhilaration of walking into the middle of adventure. Maybe he was only an unknown translator and research assistant for a news bureau that was still unknown alongside AP and UPI. Still his pulse quickened, his imagination soared.

The final level of intoxication arrived the moment you had stowed your bags securely away and had eased into your seat, glanced out the window, and sighed with satisfaction. You had eluded them all so far and had gotten safely to the plane! You could relax until time for phase two of the operation at the other end.

Faraway places, intrigue, mystery, romance. He was John Wayne, Harrison Ford, or Michael Douglas in disguise. Who could tell what might be awaiting him once they touched down in Tangier or Monaco or Istanbul, and he stepped onto the tarmac to discover—

"Find anything interesting?" a voice beside him interrupted his fanciful reverie as he eased into his seat.

"Oh . . . oh, yeah—a couple I hadn't had a chance to look through at home yet," he replied, stuffing the magazines in the seat pocket in front of him and adjusting his seat belt.

"We'll be in the air soon," said the occupant of the window seat, leaning toward both the men beside her with a happy smile of eager anticipation. The voice that had spoken contained a smooth and musical timbre, a sound of youthful vibrancy that belied the years indicated by the shade of her hair, though the light gray that fell away from her head down to nearly shoulder length yet hinted—for one, such as her husband, with loving eyes to see it—at the bright yellow strands of blonde it had gradually replaced over the years.

Sabina McCallum, though in her sixty-ninth year, still radiated the energy to which a seventeen-year-old boy—the man, in fact, now sitting beside her—had been drawn like a magnet just over half a century earlier, at the garden party of their first meeting in Berlin before the war. The wrinkles of age were visible enough; however, the creamy texture of her skin had aged as gracefully as her voice, and by any standards she was still a beautiful woman. The light from her flashing blue eyes was undimmed and, if anything, shone with even more of the sparkle of the youthfulness toward which such as she are bound—those, that is, who have made it the business of their lives to live as children of their Father.

"I've never seen you so excited before a trip, Mom," laughed the young man.

"She's hardly slept all week, Tad—you should have seen her last night!"

"That's not exactly true, Matthew," rejoined Sabina, now laughing herself. "But you both have to admit, this is like no trip we've ever taken before. I still cannot believe it. Imagine—Germany united again!"

The man beside her, Matthew McCallum, the lady's husband, also appeared remarkably fit for one who had the previous year achieved the status of septuagenarian. His hair, still thick, had retained more of its original brown than hers its yellow, though it was more than half gray throughout. That he was strong and had kept his well-proportioned physique conditioned was obvious. He jogged, swam, or bicycled at least three times a week, and he and Tad knocked a handball around at each other regularly with the happy competitive intensity only a father and son can share.

Retired from the diplomatic service now for about seven years, his schedule had been no less active than during his many years in Uncle Sam's employ. He had written five best-selling books, and monthly received more invitations to speak at churches and conferences and retreats and other functions than he could possibly accept. During the last twenty years he had become a recognized Christian spokesman, whose experience in politics and world affairs gave especial credibility and interest to his perspective. After his father-in-law's death in 1969, followed by his own father's passing a year later, he and Sabina and their six- and seven-year-old son and daughter moved back to Washington, where Matthew's diplomatic duties could more effectively be carried out. With her father gone, Sabina confessed that Germany held no more life for her and that she needed a change.

Matthew then undertook to carry out a promise made to Baron von Dortmann and began, through his own writings, to restructure, interpret, and make public the material, principles, and perspectives in the wise old German's journals. The result had been more successful than either Matthew or Sabina had anticipated, and in the time that had passed since, Matthew had become a well-known and sought-after personality and author in his own right.

Once his own history was known, with his background extending to the war and his connections with John Kennedy, along with the story of the daring escape out of East Berlin in 1962, the notoriety surrounding the name McCallum increased even more. He and Sabina found themselves the unwitting victims of the tendency of Christians to make stars of their showcase personalities, but they managed throughout it to retain their privacy and therefore made as few appearances as possible.

The circumstances surrounding the telephone call Matthew had received six months earlier, however, had been unique. After much prayer he had accepted the invitation to attend the Berlin conference.

It was to Sabina's homeland, therefore, that the two elder McCallums, along with their son—who would be attending for reasons of his own job-related responsibilities—were now bound.

14

Reevaluation

• • •

"IT WILL BE AMAZING TO SEE IT ALL NOW," SAID MATTHEW in reply to his wife's comment.

"Oh, Matthew, do you really think we will be able to visit *Lebenshaus* again?" asked Sabina, giving voice to the question that had never left her mind since moments after learning the Berlin Wall had been toppled in November of 1989.

"I've pulled every diplomatic string I know to pull," answered her husband. "Not that I still have much weight to throw around," he added with a laugh. "But there were still a few debts I had outstanding around Washington, and I called them all in. I'll talk to the Germans and Poles as soon as we land to follow up on my previous inquiries. That's one of the reasons we came a week early, remember."

"Oh, I can hardly even stand to think about it. I'm so excited, but I don't want to let myself get my hopes up."

"I can understand wanting to see *Lebenshaus*—I want to see it too, after hearing about it all my life!—and to be in Germany again now with reunification imminent. But what I don't understand, Dad," said Tad as he leaned toward both his parents, "is why you decided to come to this conference. I thought these kinds of huge Christian gatherings were just the kind of things you'd been trying to avoid since your books became widely known."

Matthew smiled thoughtfully. "That's the same question I've been asking myself ever since I accepted Darrell's invitation," he said with a chuckle. "I'm not sure I know myself."

"And you still don't know?"

"No . . . I don't suppose I do—other than that, after your mother and I prayed about it for several weeks, it was something we felt the Lord wanted us to do."

"Are you looking forward to the convention now that the decision's made and you're on your way?"

"I can't say as the thought of it has my senses riveted with enthusiasm."

"What about you, Mom?" asked Tad.

"I'm just a tourist and spectator," replied Sabina with a gay laugh. "They didn't ask *me* to participate, so I have no intention of bogging my spirits down thinking about it like your father. If I am able to lay eyes on *Lebenshaus* again, that's all I care about."

"What are you going to do?" Tad asked Matthew.

His father shrugged. "I'm not really sure yet. Darrell has asked me to be on a panel or two. He'd probably get me up in front of the whole conference if he thought he could talk me into it. But I'm feeling more and more uncomfortable about the whole thing."

"Why?"

"Because the older I get, the more I find myself feeling like a very quiet and private man down inside my heart and mind, where I live."

"You're just like Thaddeus," put in Sabina with a fond smile of remembrance, "—your father, I mean," she added, "not your son."

Matthew smiled. "The trouble is," he went on, "the older I get also, the more everyone is determined to make me a speaker and celebrity. I don't like it."

"That's the price of writing best-selling books. You *are* a personality in the Christian world, Dad," said Tad, "there's no denying it."

Matthew sighed but offered no further comment.

"Are you glad you accepted the invitation?" asked his son.

"Yes," replied Matthew. "Your mother and I have been looking for an opportunity to come back to Germany, and with you covering the conference, I suppose it seems like the right thing to do."

The sound of the captain's voice over the plane's intercom broke off their conversation. It was followed by the first movements of the huge 747 as it backed away from the gate and then began making its way across acres of pavement toward the runway. As they proceeded, the German-accented voice of the flight attendant gave out seat belt, oxygen mask, and other safety procedures and information.

Tad, Matthew, and Sabina did not resume their conversation for some time, and within ten minutes the deafening jet engines behind them were lifting the plane at a steep angle into the sky above Washington. The next minute the 747 began its bank eastward where Chesapeake Bay and then, ten or fifteen minutes later, the Atlantic would come into view.

15

New World Order:
Price Tag and Opportunity

• • •

BY THE TIME THE THREE MCCALLUMS RESUMED THEIR conversation, Lufthansa flight 431 for Frankfurt had reached its cruising altitude of 37,000 feet. They loosened their seat belts and sipped the coffee they had just been served.

As children of parents who had married late in life, both Thaddeus Heinrich and his sister, Marion Rebecca, younger by fifteen months, had enjoyed a singularly close relationship with both father and mother. As youngsters, they had been equally intimate with the two grandfathers after whom the former was named. Though the memories had grown dim, thoughts of those early years when all six had shared the mountain chalet above the Bavarian village of Oberammersfeld brought warm and happy feelings of contentment. But such were his parents, Matthew—son of former U.S. Ambassador Thaddeus McCallum—and Sabina—daughter of former German baron Heinrich von Dortmann—that these close familial bonds and contentedness did not abate with the passing of the two older men and the move to the States. As Tad and Mary grew, they discovered that their best friends in life were none other than their own mother and father. Consequently, Tad remained at home while attending the University of Maryland, where he studied journalism, history, and political science.

His father's retirement had nearly coincided with his own graduation, a year following his sister's marriage. The two men had spent the following summer together remodeling a portion of the McCallum home into a small apartment for Tad, with an office and separate entrance so that he could remain with his parents and yet live with a certain degree of independence. The arrangement had met with the hearty approval of the whole family. Sabina was especially delighted. She had expended a great many tears at losing her daughter to marriage only a year before and was not yet prepared, she said, to let her son launch out on his own quite yet.

Tad had worked for a short time for one of his father's colleagues in the State Department before taking his present position with World News Service. Equally fluent in German and English, he had been hired initially as a German translator as well as consultant for WNS's European Bureau in Washington.

At twenty-eight, Tad McCallum had now been with WNS just under five years. During that time the range of his responsibilities had widened considerably. He still functioned in the capacity of translator in a variety of German-English and English-German situations, but was also called upon as a research assistant and even occasionally to write briefs, documentaries, or news features of his own in one of the two languages.

Knowing that his parents would be attending, and because of his deep personal interest both in the future of Germany as a half-German himself and in evangelism as a Christian, he had requested his present assignment. Now he and his father and mother were on their way to the Berlin Church Leadership Conference for the Post–Cold War Era, where his chief duty involved writing a summary news feature, in both German and English, which WNS would release to the media the day following the conference.

"Listen to this," said Tad, who had been perusing the latest issue of *Time,* which he'd nabbed from the magazine bin on his way into the cabin. "This is some time to be going to Europe!"

"Did something new happen?" asked Sabina, leaning over from her window seat.

"No, just the same thing that's been going on for the last two years—change. Everything is turning upside-down. Listen to this article by Lance Henry. It's called 'Europe: The New Silent Revolution.'

"When people and nations squeeze closer, pushing
against one another, the result is inevitably either conflict

or unity. The world has seen more than enough of the former through the centuries—now suddenly the era for the latter seems to have arrived.

"With the remarkable events of the 1980s, culminating in the toppling of the Berlin Wall in 1989, the reunification of Germany in 1990, followed by the dismantling of the Warsaw Pact and Soviet Union, a new revolution in Europe has begun. It has been, and will continue to be, unlike any that has preceded it, unlike any the world has seen before. Not only has this new European revolution been nearly bloodless, it is a revolution of unity rather than disparity—a revolution whose factions say, 'We lay down hostilities and join *with* you,' rather than, 'We take up arms to fight against you.'

"Indeed, with the end of the Cold War, the first truly global revolution began. A revolution of peace is shaking the very foundations of the world. And with the new political alignments being so suddenly and quickly created, new spiritual awakenings are alive as well, offering clarity and perhaps even cosmic focus to this new age of harmony."

Tad put down the magazine and grew pensive.

"What is it?" asked Matthew.

"I just found that last sentence triggering my thoughts, which then went sailing off in a hundred directions. I've been reading and thinking about it for the last several months—wondering where Christians fit into all this talk of the new world order."

"In other words," said Matthew, "what is to be our response?"

"Right. All the old lines of demarcation are gone. The entire course of social and political direction is changing. God is shaking up everything. It's a unique time in the history of the world."

"Maybe the conference will provide some answers."

"Somehow I just don't see the answer coming from conferences and mass agendas for evangelism."

"Now it's you who's playing the skeptic."

"Maybe so," laughed Tad. "Don't get me wrong. I'm as delighted with the end of the Cold War as anyone. I'm excited about

Germany's reunification. But I'm just not sure we can place too much stock in it."

"None of these changes are going to alter the intrinsic sinfulness at the core of man's being, is that what you're getting at?" asked his father.

"Exactly. It's wonderful that we're no longer on the brink of nuclear holocaust, but the world is still going to face trouble in the days ahead. That's exactly what Henry says later in his article:

> "Revolution has indeed come to Europe—without bombs or tanks or guns, but no less revolutionary in its remaking and reorganizing impact upon peoples and nations who find themselves suddenly thrust into a new era. The Europe of the 1990s is no mere decade changed from the Europe of the 1980s, but rather one altered by centuries. Between 1980 and 2000 will yawn a gulf, not of two decades, but of a millennium.
>
> "But where is this revolution leading? What will this priceless but uncertain and tenuous commodity called 'freedom' bring? Has liberty indeed dawned, or will there be an interim period during which many will have to settle for something less? What does liberty mean for the people of Poland and Hungary and Czechoslovakia and Russia, whose recent harvests are poor and whose economies are in shambles?
>
> "What does it mean for those of former West Germany and former East Germany who want their full slice of the affluent German pie? How much will they share the German abundance?
>
> "Who will provide the aid to rebuild? Even now, major aid packages are being considered in Bonn and Washington and London. How far should the Western nations go financially?
>
> "Such are the questions asked after every war—be it a hot or cold one—and they form an intrinsic part of the revolutionary equation."

"He's put his finger on it," remarked Matthew. "I was just with some of my old friends last week who are still working in government. They're all saying the same thing, from the Oval Office on down: Where's the money going to come from to finance the new age of peace?"

"The president's been talking about the new world order, yet who's going to foot the bill?"

"Right," rejoined Matthew. "Let's face it, the United States is broke."

"One of your congressional friends with presidential ambitions will probably draft a new world order Marshall Plan," laughed Tad.

"*My* friends—I've been out of the game too long to have any friends left in Congress. *You're* the one with all the connections on Capitol Hill now!"

"Nah, WNS is still too small a player in the news business for any of the big boys to pay much attention."

"Don't kid yourself, Tad. They know who you are—and not just because you're my son. Just the fact that CNN relies so heavily on your bureau gives it a certain degree of clout. And everyone knows you're one of the rising stars in WNS."

"Aw, Dad, I'm only a translator."

"They rely on you for much more than that. You were just telling me the other day that Lockhart was asking you to get more involved in the investigative side of it."

"Bob was feeling overworked that day!"

"You told me just two days ago—when Sabina and I were packing, you remember—you said you were going to try to put together another article while we were here, something in addition to your assignment to cover the conference."

"Hmm, yeah—you're right," replied Tad.

"'A real piece of investigative journalism'—those were your exact words, I believe," added Matthew. "What exactly did you have in mind?"

"I'd been thinking of something that would probe a little deeper into what the Wall's coming down really signifies."

"There, you see—you mark my words, you're going to be more than a translator for WNS before long. It wouldn't surprise me for your exploits to surpass my own one day," added Matthew with a laugh.

"How could they, with no Iron Curtain left now for me to break people over like you did!"

"You mean *under,* don't you?" put in Sabina, leaning over with a smile, remembering the day she and her father had escaped to the freedom of the West.

"I'm sure the days of bravery and daring exploits aren't over forever," rejoined Matthew. "You'll have your own share, no doubt. You'll probably get involved in something next week for that story you're talking about that'll put you in the headlines!"

Tad laughed.

"Speaking of breaking out under the Wall," Matthew added, turning toward Sabina, "you didn't finish telling me about that letter from Ursula a few days ago. I'd forgotten to ask you more about it. Everything's still on for them to meet us next week, isn't it?"

"Joseph's still coming to the conference," answered Sabina, "but Ursula's now having her doubts."

"Why?"

"Because she and Joseph just had their third grandchild," laughed Sabina. "That's the part of the letter I *did* tell you about."

"Boy or girl?"

"Oh, Matthew, you're impossible—a girl."

"So what does that make the count for them?" asked Matthew, trying to divert the attention away from his own forgetfulness.

"Two granddaughters and a grandson. But with four children of their own, I have the feeling that is only the beginning. Their quiver will be *full* of grandchildren in another ten years."

"That is exactly how your father would have put it," said Matthew, leaning over and kissing Sabina. "You are the baron's daughter in every way."

Sabina smiled. There was no greater compliment she could be paid.

"And speaking of quivers," added Matthew, turning back now toward their son with a sly grin. "If you don't get moving before long, Tad, my boy, your mother and I are going to be joining your four grandparents on the other side with *our* quivers still empty!"

Tad laughed. "You can't rush those kinds of things, Dad. You ought to realize that. I know well enough that you were over forty when you and Mom married."

"Just barely over!"

"I'm only twenty-eight. I've got loads of time. Believe me, when the right young lady comes along—who is as right for me as Mom was for you—I'll take notice. You're the one who is always reminding me not to be in a hurry and to wait for the one God has for me, even if I wait for years, like the two of you did. Besides, I'm sure Mary and Bill will see to it that the family line continues."

"I suppose you have me there on both counts!"

"But we're not getting any younger, Tad," added Sabina with a smile that displayed contentment rather than chagrin at the fact. "Or hadn't you noticed?"

"The two of you act younger than most of the people I know who are half your age," answered Tad. "I suppose I'm so accustomed to the way you are that I don't pay much attention to your years."

Matthew and Sabina exchanged a smile of deep satisfaction and happiness. Their son was a young man to be proud of.

Gradually the conversation slowed for a time, and Tad returned to the magazine article. After several minutes he lifted his head and glanced back toward his father.

"It just keeps coming back to me that the whole thing revolves around the question we were talking about before: Who is going to pay for the changes?"

"Well, I don't think there will be a new Marshall Plan, like you mentioned. I doubt any serious proposal will be mounted along those lines. We don't have the industrial health to pull it off like we did in the forties."

"But don't you figure the rest of the world will expect it of us?"

"Possibly," Matthew shrugged.

"So where will the billions come from to reconstruct Eastern Europe? I can hardly see Japan pouring billions into the rebuilding of Russia—a natural enemy for thousands of years. And I doubt Germany will be the pot of gold everyone expects either."

"It's the healthiest of the Western nations right now."

"But don't you think that will cause more problems in the long run than it solves? You told me you saw signs of it years ago even in the fifties and sixties when you were assigned there."

"I did observe some things when I was working for Jack Kennedy, and even later during the Johnson administration. But what exactly are you referring to?"

"That the have-nots of Eastern Europe will run from capital to capital, looking for whoever possesses the fattest bank account. By their perception, after it becomes obvious how quickly the U.S. bank is going to run dry, that will be Germany. The expectation is that if you've got nothing, you have a right to what the *haves* possess. I think that will eventually result in considerable pressure being placed on the Bonn government. Or should I say the Berlin government!"

"They haven't transferred it to Berlin yet, have they?"

"No, but plans are already underway, as I understand it, to move it a little at a time. I don't think it's set for completion until 1996 or so."

"In any event, about what you were saying, I suppose that *is* one of the hallmarks of the new age," said Matthew. "Everyone has a right to a handout, a free ride."

"The minute the Wall came down, East Germany wanted in on West Germany's wealth. And in the euphoria of it all, West Germany wanted to share. But the stresses of the East's expectations are already being felt. And then the rest of the Eastern Bloc wants in on it too. Now that some time has passed, the reality is that the rebuilding process has been more costly than anticipated and has taken a great deal of money out of West German hands."

"You've done your homework on this situation, I can see that!" said Matthew.

"Working for Bob Lockhart drills that into you mighty quick. WNS isn't going to make an impact unless its people know their stuff and are on top of the major stories. That's his constant theme."

"So what else does your homework tell you?"

"That immigration is as big a problem as financing the reconstruction," answered Tad.

"Immigration's always been a problem for developed nations."

"It's growing into a crisis in Western Europe. Foreigners are streaming into the cities of West Germany. Jews from Russia, gypsies from Romania begging on the streets, Turks in huge numbers. There's a massive movement from Asia, including almost a hundred thousand Vietnamese. With the borders open, suddenly it's a flood. They're taking jobs, they're sapping the economy, taking advantage of the welfare system, with the result that inflation is on the rise and the high German standard of living cannot help but suffer in the end."

"The growing pains of the changing times, I suppose."

"Perhaps. But I think there are more serious issues in the European consciousness occurring than meet the eye—especially in Germany. That's one reason I'm excited to be going, besides visiting all the old familiar places again, and maybe even Mom's old home—to see it all firsthand. I have the feeling all this change is going to rub some rough edges raw and bring about responses no one anticipates. In fact, I can see room for the wrong kind of world leader to capitalize on the new range of forces and new fears that are bound to surface."

"What are you implying—the rise of another autocrat, a dictator?"

"Probably not. Whatever comes, it won't be like anything we've seen before. Even though the Cold War may have ended, greed and the lust for power haven't. I can envision highly fertile ground for a New Age, smiling, 'peace-loving' world leader who is yet a wolf in sheep's clothing. It's just the kind of thing the Bible foretells, and it seems to me Henry opens the door for it in his article."

"What does he say?"

Tad again picked up the *Time* and read aloud:

> "The balance of power, the very basis of power, is shifting. From military to economics, from old alliances left over from the Second World War and modified by the Cold War, suddenly everything is new. The United States seems to be in a cycle of decline. Germany and Japan represent the new global powerhouses. And the entire fabric of Eastern Europe and Russia is being remade from the inside out.
>
> "Out of this will emerge new leaders and new powers. The soil is too fertile and the climate too ripe to expect anything less. It is a cultural, social, political, and perhaps even spiritual rebirthing of Europe. Yet not even the most astute historian or politician or sociologist can predict who the offspring's parents are or what it will look like or what it will grow up to be.

"See what I mean?" said Tad. "There are many possibilities for the unknown. And when you factor in the spiritual dimension, which of course none of the world's analysts seem to be aware of, it becomes even more dynamic."

"Sounds to me like you're already halfway started on that story you were talking about on the deeper implications."

"Yeah, but I need an angle, something fresh—something personal that gives all this change a face, real flesh and blood."

Tad paused a moment.

"Hmm . . ." he intoned unconsciously.

"What is it?" asked Matthew.

"Oh, there's a picture of the Wall to the side of the article—you know, that scene the night it came down, throngs all around, people on top of it shouting and celebrating. I was just thinking how great it would be to interview someone who was there that night . . . maybe even one of these young people in the photograph."

"It would give an interesting slant to it."

"Well . . . something to think about. I'll have to see what I can do once we're in Germany."

Tad resumed the article, continuing to read portions of it aloud to his parents.

"In many respects, former East Germany, the onetime but now defunct DDR, lies at the very heart of this silent birthing revolution, bridging the gap between the wealth of the West and the crying needs of the East. In East Germany, with Berlin at its center, do all the forces for revolution converge. And it is to Germany that many look for answers to this complex range of questions, simply because it is *there,* situated at the crucial vortex of all these forces, the Mason-Dixon line of the 1990s.

"The unrest of revolution is clearly visible throughout Germany, especially as one walks the streets of Berlin, arising simply from the uncertainty of what comes next.

"German Chancellor Kolter and his coalition in the Bundestag represent the political focal point. The rest of the former Iron Curtain nations look hopefully to the German parliament for compassion and generosity at the specially reconvened session on the eighteenth of this

month to decide upon aid to the East. Meanwhile
Russian leader Boris Yeltsin must wonder where the
future direction of power lies for the Soviet
Commonwealth.

"You see what I mean—we're heading right into the heart of it,"
said Tad, putting down the magazine.

"I suppose there's no better place for them to have planned this
conference."

"Berlin sits right at the crossroads."

"Perhaps," Matthew replied, then paused thoughtfully. "I don't
know though," he added after a moment. "I'm not so sure that the
Christian groups and leaders who are pushing for this great evangelistic thrust know what's being birthed either, to use the article's term.
I don't think the methods the evangelical community has used in the
past are going to result in revival erupting everywhere. I don't think
it's going to be that easy. These are unique and momentous times,
perhaps the prelude to Jesus' return. I think evangelism is going to
have to be new too. There—that's my two cents worth."

"That's more than two cents!" Tad laughed. "I would rate that a
couple hundred dollars' worth at least."

"Well, who knows, maybe a week in Berlin at this conference will
answer all our questions."

"One thing's for certain."

"What's that?"

"If we want to feel the pulse of the future . . . what better place to
go than to its very heart?"

16

Sabotage

• • •

Outside Kiev

AS THE PLANE BEARING THE THREE MCCALLUMS FLEW away from the setting sun, several thousand miles away where night had already descended a man dressed in black and carrying only a set of heavyweight wire cutters approached an unlit portion of a chain-link fence. He had walked to the back of the factory through a dense wood, not the way he came to work every morning on the road to the front gate. But his present assignment was far different from what he was paid to do after punching in every morning and going to his assembly station at the plant.

He would be paid for tonight, of course. And handsomely!

So well that he had scarcely thought twice before accepting the offer. Even in newly democratic Ukraine, pay was still miserable, and there was never enough for anything extra. This one hour's work would get his wife a refrigerator and his two children new shoes. Marta was supposed to be handsomely compensated too, and he would do anything for her. If he was lucky, there might even be something left over for him. But his personal reward would come later, after they had . . .

Actually, the man who had hired him hadn't exactly said what would come afterward. But the strong suggestion that he could find himself *foreman* of the entire assembly section one day was enough. With the three thousand rubles they were paying him, he was willing to take his chances. He was a member of the fledgling union himself, and he wished neither it nor any of his fellow workers harm. But this was an opportunity he couldn't pass up. And the man had assured him that it would be to everyone's advantage in the end.

Pavlovich knelt in the moist grass at the end of the wood, pulled out the heavy wire cutters, and began snipping through the links of the fence. There was enough light to see by, but it was still dark enough to keep him hidden. The complex security systems in his country were not intended to keep people *out,* but rather to keep them in. The only guard on duty tonight was well inside the compound and on the other side anyway. Pavlovich knew him well enough and knew that he was probably asleep by now, with half a glass of vodka on his desk.

He was through the fence in ten minutes. He would hardly have needed to run to the back door of the factory, but he did so nevertheless. The man had given him a key. Pavlovich hadn't asked where he'd stolen it. It didn't matter.

Once inside, he did have to be careful. Sound traveled and echoed about the bare floors and machinery in the tomblike quiet—enough that even a half-drunk guard might hear.

The work would take him probably an hour. Several tiny explosive charges had to be set, some papers pilfered from two or three files, a handful of dirt mixed into the oil of one of the large hydraulic lifts, and finally one of the supporting guy-wires for the overhead crane sawn three-quarters through. This last act could not help making some noise, but he would go slowly and watch himself.

They hadn't told him the precise purpose behind the sabotage of the auto factory, but none of his nighttime activities would destroy the plant. He was told it was designed to make the management look bad. The records he'd stolen, along with other evidence they would take care of themselves, would point the finger for the damage and shutdown straight at the managers, who were none too popular right now. Pavlovich was perfectly willing to go along and do his part. Especially for three thousand rubles.

Ever since the first day they'd heard the word *perestroika,* there'd been talk about how much better it was going to be. Well, that had been six or eight years ago. Gorbachev hadn't made it any better, neither had Yeltsin, neither had their new right to vote, neither had the group of Americans who had come to the plant five months ago to help modernize it and set up the union. Now they had a union, but still nothing had changed. Conditions remained terrible and pay low, and Pavlovich had waited long enough.

He'd heard enough about change. Now it was time he did something to help it along.

He set the last of the charges, then went to work with the tiny diamond-bladed hacksaw they had given him to cut through the guy-wire. It was tedious work, but the special saw made little noise, and one by one the individual steel wires began to snap. He would have to cut through about fifty of the seventy-five or so that combined to hold up one corner of the crane. When they notified him, he would add an extra 2,300 kilograms to the load. Since loading the crane was his job, that wouldn't prove too difficult. He would make sure there was no one in danger underneath, then give the signal to the crane operator above. He would raise the hoist, and a few seconds later the wire would give way and the load come crashing to the ground.

That, along with the other things, would cause pandemonium. The plant would have to shut down temporarily. The union would call an investigation. The managers would be implicated and thrown out. The union would install its own people, Pavlovich among them, in the management positions. Repairs and modernizations would be made, pay increased, hours shortened, and the change that had been talked about for so long would finally begin.

Pavlovich knew that several of his colleagues were influential union leaders, one was even on the state committee. What he did not know was that the subversion of which he was a part was not the mere localized mischief of one automobile factory as it had been represented to him by the man who had approached him last month.

How could a man of Pavlovich's limited education and intelligence fathom the wide-sweeping breadth of a conspiracy intended to domino from several such factories into a sweeping nationwide worker revolt throughout the motherland?

17
Nefarious Transaction

• • •

Bonn

THAT SAME NIGHT, IN ANOTHER PART OF EUROPE TO THE west, a man waited on a darkened street corner. In spite of the summer warmth, he was wrapped tightly in an overcoat, a wide-brimmed hat pulled well down over his forehead. By all appearances, he did not want his face seen.

In a few minutes a large white automobile pulled alongside him. The door opened, he stepped quickly inside, and the auto pulled forward, turning into an underground parking garage below one of the many dozens of buildings once in governmental use but now with an uncertain future after reunification. The long process of removing the inhabitants to what would eventually be the new capital of Berlin was slowly underway, but would not be completed for several years.

It was late. No other cars were about.

The white vehicle wheeled inside the garage. The automatic gate closed behind them. The driver pulled to the far wall, then shut off the engine.

"You were not followed?" said the driver of the car in a deep, resonant voice without turning around.

"Nein, Herr Bundesminister."

"Are you available to perform certain services for me?" asked the driver. The commanding strength of his voice made it sound as though nothing but an affirmative response would be tolerated.

"I am at your disposal, as is my custom."

"The usual fee?"

"Information is negotiable. If there are those you wish removed, yes, the usual forty thousand D-marks per."

"You have new equipment?"

"Always."

"You sound rather cocky, Herr Claymore." The pale, deep-set eyes of the man in front squinted slightly, and he was tempted to turn around and pierce them straight into those of his lackey. But with calm determination he restrained the urge, letting only the imperceptible movement of his thick, dark eyebrows indicate his displeasure. In this business, although you had to be careful, you had to use whomever was available. And as much as he hated him, the fellow whose only known label was the nickname for Bonnie Prince Charlie's famous two-handed broadsword was the best he'd ever been able to find. He didn't know what the man looked like, and he didn't ever want to know. Things like this were best kept that way.

"I make sure of myself," replied Claymore, as full of annoyance at the self-important politician as the latter was of condescension toward him. "Nothing I do can ever be traced. What is it you want this time?"

"Information first. Perhaps other things later. I want you working solely for me for the next two weeks. I will pay you a retainer on top of the other fees. You need to be ready to move at a moment's notice. Is your Russian visa current?"

"I can travel anywhere from England to Japan without difficulty—yes, all is current."

"It may require carrying weapons across the Russian border."

"That is no problem. I have done so many times."

"The next two weeks are critical. There is no telling where I may need to send you."

"Give me instructions in the usual way. You can depend on the result."

"First of all, a man you have watched for me before, the head of the CSDU. Keep an eye on him. I must reel him in soon, and if there are new affiliations, relationships, idiosyncrasies to add to my dossier on him, I want to know. He is too straight for any dirt. But one never knows what one may turn up. I've heard a rumor or two about his past that bear investigation."

"How long?"

"Two or three days. Time is short."

"And then?"

"Then I don't know. It depends on other things. But be ready to catch a quick flight east."

The next moment the engine of the car revved to life. It pulled cautiously out of the garage, then eased into the adjoining street. The driver did not stop for several blocks. When he did, it was along a dark stretch of the avenue where the streetlight was out. He continued to stare straight ahead until he heard the back door of the car slam. Immediately he accelerated.

Neither man had seen the other's face.

18

Honoring the Past, Looking to the Future

· · ·

Over the North Atlantic

"THE SUN IS TURNING RED AND ORANGE," COMmented Sabina, glancing out the plane's window, "and we've been in the air less than two hours."

"It's only—what—6:15 or so, Washington time," replied Matthew, looking at his watch. "But the sun will be gone soon."

"It'll be a short night, flying away from the sun," added Tad.

"And just about the time you drift off to sleep," laughed Matthew, "they wake you for breakfast!"

"It's a good thing we have a week to unwind and get our systems back to normal before the conference. Are the two of you going to spend the whole time in Bavaria?" asked Tad.

"We want to see the house and visit our friends in the village," answered Matthew. "But you know how anxious your mother is to investigate the current status of *Lebenshaus*. I doubt she'll be able to wait until after the conference."

Sabina laughed.

"You're as anxious to see it as I am!" she said.

"I confess you're right. I've got some people lined up to see about it. We've got so much to see and do—I can't imagine we'll have enough time."

"We need to try to see if we can locate any of the old network people as well," added Sabina.

"And I want to see all the places you've been telling me about all these years," added Tad, "—not only *Lebenshaus,* but the cemetery, the house in East Berlin where you lived, Mom—"

"If it's still there."

"—and the prison outside Potsdam where Grandpa was held, where you first saw each other on the sidewalk in West Berlin in '61, the woods where you took Mom on that horseback ride, Dad—"

Both Sabina and Matthew laughed to be reminded of the happy days that seemed so long ago and yet only like yesterday.

"What about you?" asked Matthew, turning toward Tad. "Don't you have plans of your *own* for this time in Germany?"

"Oh, there are a few things I want to do. I'm going to poke around, probably in Berlin, and see what I might be able to come up with for that article. Seeing that picture in the magazine has got me wondering how I might even be able to tie that night into the conference."

"Sounds intriguing."

"But mostly," continued Tad, "I want to steep myself in my own past, in what was important in your lives."

"An unusual thing for a son to say," remarked Sabina.

"I'm only following Dad's example," rejoined Tad. "He's made it his business to honor his own father, and yours, even to the point of studying Grandpa's journals and making Grandpa's ideas and thoughts and prayers public. So I'm just following in the family footsteps— placing importance on the heritage from previous generations that has come down to me."

"You honor both your grandfather and us," said Sabina sincerely.

"I want to keep everything the two of you have taught alive for future generations, in the same way that you have kept alive your fathers' dreams and visions and the things the Lord showed them when they were alive. I suppose you would say I've bought into your vision of the importance of the ongoing generational flow of God's work in human life."

Matthew and Sabina smiled quietly. What could make their hearts swell more than to hear such words from a faithful and loving son!

"I want to spend the whole first week roaming the fields and hills and trails around Oberammersfeld," Tad continued. "I want to bring back every memory of everything I did there, not only with the two of you, but with Grandpa Thaddeus and Grandpa Heinrich. The images are sketchy, and somehow it's never seemed so important on other trips we've made back as it seems to me now to solidify those memories so they become a permanent part of me. No doubt the older you get, the more value you place on the past."

"I'm glad to hear you say that, Tad, my boy," said Matthew. "Both your grandfathers were fine men, honorable men of God, and they are worthy of remembering. Your character will be enriched from it."

"It's nothing more than what you've always taught me about revering and honoring the past and those who have come before."

Matthew smiled. "I suppose you're right. But it's nice to hear it coming from your own mouth."

It fell silent a few minutes. Matthew was the first to speak. "I tell you," he said, addressing both wife and son together, "I'm probably going to be using this whole first week stewing over what ought to be my role in this conference. If there's one thing I don't feel like, it's a so-called church leader."

"You ought to just forget all about it," laughed Sabina. "You sometimes wax the most eloquent when you're just talking spontane- ously. Why don't you just wait until the moment comes, then get up and say whatever the Lord puts in your heart to say?"

"I'm not sure I could do that this time," replied Matthew with a sigh. "There's so much going on inside this brain of mine—it's tumbling around full of ideas in a hundred directions. How should we as a body of God's people respond to these changes that have swept through the world? Or more to the point, What ought we to be giving to the world as a result? Do we have anything to offer it? Those seem to me the essential questions."

"Evangelism?"

"It's larger than just that. How do we transmit truth to the world? How is God's life communicated, passed on, spread to individuals, to nations, from father to son, mother to daughter, friend to friend? What are the spiritual implications of the generational flow you were talking about, Tad? How are the followers of Jesus to take the life he brought and give it to the world?"

"What do you think my father would say?" asked Sabina with a serious tone.

Matthew reflected for a long time before answering. "I have the feeling he might be asking some of the same questions," he answered finally.

"So do I," agreed Sabina.

Matthew nodded thoughtfully. Before he had the chance to reply further, however, they were interrupted by a flight attendant in the aisle next to Tad.

"Would you care for some dinner?" she asked.

PART IV

New Times
. . . and Old

1 9

New Age of Opportunity

• • •

Bonn

THE SKY IN BONN WAS GRAY, THE AIR CHILLY AND DANK.

This was no place from which to run a government, thought the black-suited official as he strode quickly along Goerres Straβe, then bounded up the steps two at a time into the building next to the Bundeshaus that had for years been his parliamentary home.

An aberration in the history of Germany's self-rule, that's all it had been. Notwithstanding Beethoven's birthplace and the Kurfurstliches Schloss and the Poppelsdorfer Schloss, and its two-thousand-year history, in his estimation this was a city without character, without culture, given a status it did not deserve to house the nongovernment of the postwar period.

Thank the heavens it had ended two years ago. The Bonn tenure would one day be a mere asterisk in the history books of Germany's proud Reichs—preceding the Fourth, which he fully believed would be the proudest and mightiest of all.

Hitler had been an uneducated and egotistical incompetent, he reflected, one utterly ill equipped to carry forth the grand ideas embodied within his brilliant creed. An idiot . . . but not a fool. His convictions were daring. They had simply been made public several generations before their time. The Nazis and storm troopers—they were all morons who couldn't see the limitations of militarism to achieve their ends.

Such would not be Klaus Drexler's mistake.

When his time came—and it would come very soon!—he would

take Der Führer's vision to new global heights never conceived of by Himmler, Göring, or any of the other imbecilic goons with which Hitler surrounded himself. And he would do so without so much as a single bullet being fired.

He would do so without a military at all! His destiny, the cosmic alignment of forces upon him, could not fail to bring it about. This was a new age! A new age whose time, thanks to Herr Gorbachev, was now at hand.

A time in which xenophobic fervor had to be combined with the spiritual values of the age and fueled by economic and political clout, given brawn and cohesiveness, not with tanks and weapons and missiles but with the power of *Das Geld* and the knowledge of how to use it!

With purposeful direction he strode down the deserted hall to the office he still maintained in this *provisional* capital. Not many were here by 6:00 A.M. these days. Already, though not many offices had yet been removed to Berlin, the place had begun to feel different. One day these active corridors would have no more life than a drowsy, bureaucratic, record-keeping basement.

The future was eastward. Berlin had beckoned to him all his life. How eagerly he had yearned to get out of this hole—forever! Now that reunification had come and plans were being made to move the Bundestag, notwithstanding the ridiculous construction of its massive new building right here, he would shut down the last of his offices here at the first available opportunity. They said the complete change would take till 1996 to effect, but he planned to be out of here long before that.

Given the delicacy of some of his activities, however, and the secretive nature of a number of important associations, he found it convenient to yet conduct certain discreet business arrangements from this location.

It was more private. Fewer prying eyes. Individuals such as Claymore he had to see as far from Berlin as possible. He had only to get a few final things in order before the summit in Moscow. While there he would play the loyal leader of his contingent of Bundestag members, supportive and enthusiastic of the chancellor's negotiation over aid.

But the real history to be made in Moscow a few hours from now would likely be seen by no one. He and the defense minister of that troubled conglomeration of new republics would finalize their time-table for action. They had been waiting years, and now suddenly events were lining up perfectly. The summit could not have provided a more perfect cover.

He opened a drawer and took out a file, glanced through it hastily, then tossed it into his briefcase. He sat down, made two phone calls, then glanced at his watch. Six twenty-three. He had to catch the plane in an hour and a half. He would be in Moscow three hours after that for the meetings.

He rose, then cast one last look about the small office. With any luck, this might be the last he saw of this place. Within days, a week or two at most, his plans would not have to be hidden any longer.

20
Old Times

• • •

Oberammersfeld

MATTHEW WELL REMEMBERED THE DAILY WALKS HIS father and the baron had made down to the village from their chalet up the hillside.

And though the name above the shop still read *Bäkerei Rendt,* it was not the same as it had been back in the days when the two older men had made a visit to smiling Frau Rendt a regular part of their morning routine. There had then been an exuberant sense of freedom and new life overspreading the atmosphere of their home in Oberammersfeld. He and Sabina had just been married. The baron was out of prison. He and his own father had been reunited. Suddenly, even unexpectedly, they were all together again, and life was happy and full and rich. Those past days were now but memories.

Matthew was older than his own father had then been. Thus the mist of nostalgic melancholy could not help but cling to his spirit, making his thoughts quiet and reflective, in contrast to the tinkling of the bell on the door shutting behind them, as he and his own son—a grown man now—resumed their stroll along the street and toward the edge of town.

He and Sabina and Tad had been in the village guest house now for three days. Every morning he and Tad had visited the bakery, purchasing two pastries—as much in memory of his father and Sabina's as to satisfy their own appetites—which they had then consumed in a leisurely walk out of the village toward their former home and back.

Whether the sweet rolls were as delectable as the current baker's grandfather had made in the same ovens thirty years before, Matthew was unable to determine. Certainly the good Bavarian was unaware what the daily ritual signified for both father and son in the way of solidifying memories of the past and cementing their own bonds, both between one another and with those who had come before. Even though Tad had been here several times during the years since their departure in 1970 and had heard all the old stories before, Matthew yet recounted them again, and Tad asked questions as if he were a ten-year-old.

Both sensed, though nothing was ever said, that this was the last such time they would enjoy here together. This pensive realization occasioned no sense of regret for the two men. They had steeped themselves too long in the truths passed down from father-in-law and grandfather for that. They recognized that the cycle of life illustrated so vividly by the baron's Spring Garden included human plants as well.

Matthew knew well enough that the garden of his son's life was entering the flourishing season of summer, while he was progressing steadily toward the final months of his earthly year. Inside he rejoiced and gave quiet thanks, not only for the memory of seasons left behind, but in anticipation of the new and more spectacular Spring that was soon awaiting him.

As the two walked leisurely along, Sabina, meanwhile, had renewed the acquaintance of the current owner of what for almost nine happy years in the 1960s had been the Dortmann/McCallum chalet, where she was now enjoying morning tea even as her husband and son sauntered out of the village and toward her up the edge of the mountainside.

"What have the two of you discovered, anything new this morning?" she asked as they rejoined one another half an hour later.

"We made the acquaintance of one particularly curious cow," answered Tad.

"It is remarkable how little the village has changed in all these years, is it not?" remarked Matthew, as Sabina fell into step with them.

"Even with all these political events stirring up the world," said Sabina, "there is still so much of it that *doesn't* change, it seems, no matter what goes on. That's one thing that will always be different in the States than over here. Everything is in constant flux there, always changing, always new. Yet here, the old world customs and traditions keep things the way they have been for generations."

"Especially in the country," said Matthew, "like here, away from the city."

They continued on a while in silence.

"Is this how it was when I was young?" asked Tad at length.

"What do you remember?"

"Everything looks like I *think* I remember it," laughed Tad.

"It *is* the same." Sabina smiled. "The faces have changed, a few new people come, those we knew back then who were older are gone now, the young people have grown up, like you—yet it is remarkable how much the same it really is."

"And how many people we do still know," added Matthew.

"Do they all remember you?" asked Tad.

"More than I might have thought. Your grandfathers made quite an impression on the local citizenry. The older ones still talk about them."

Again they fell silent as they walked on, approaching the village.

"What do you have planned today?" asked Tad.

"I thought we might drive up the mountain and show you the church where we were married," replied Matthew.

"You showed me last time we were here," laughed Tad.

"That was, what, eight years ago now?" rejoined Matthew. "So we'll show you again."

"Do the two of you never tire of reminiscing about the past?"

"Never!" answered Matthew and Sabina in unison.

"What did you find out this morning?" Sabina asked Matthew, in a more serious tone. "Or did you not get through?"

"Yes, I got through, but only came away from the call with another name or two they said to contact. Freedom may have come, but bureaucracy is still the same everywhere. And of course the Germans have no real say in Polish affairs. Everybody I've talked to so far is sympathetic and says they want to help, but it all boils down to the same thing—that part of Germany was given to Poland after the war when Russia took it upon itself to redraw the western border. Even the recent changes, or even the fact that Poland is supposedly democratic now, don't alter the fact that *Lebenshaus* now sits on *Polish* soil, not German. And you and your father were *German* citizens, not Polish."

"I still don't exactly understand what happened," said Tad.

"You've got to understand how things were after the war," replied Matthew. "Everyone was so tired of fighting that the Western powers pretty much gave the Soviet Union whatever it wanted. No one wanted to start up hostilities all over again. So Russia had more or less a free hand to dictate what went on in the East."

"What did happen?"

"The Soviet leaders set about to unilaterally shape the new Polish state, which included allowing Poland to annex East Germany up to the Oder–Neisse line. In other words, the Polish border of 1919–1939 was shifted 150 miles westward, and suddenly *Lebenshaus* was part of Poland."

"The United States let the Russians do that?"

"As I said, they weren't inclined to contest it, especially in that East Germany was shaping up as a Soviet satellite too. It was seen as too minor a problem to deal with."

"Minor for everyone except the Germans whose land it was. What happened to them?"

"Most were expelled to make room for Polish settlers. I suppose we are fortunate in that *Lebenshaus* was kept control of by the Communists and not just given over to vagrants, farmers, or the elements. It was still in reasonable repair when I was there in '62. But since then . . . who knows?"

Sabina sighed. "Do you think it's hopeless, Matthew?"

"Nothing is ever hopeless," he replied. "We got your father out of prison, didn't we? So we'll pursue this all the way to the end . . . and beyond if need be. I'm as determined to set eyes on the old Dortmann estate as you are. Maybe we could try to sneak in, like I did before, and right past the officials who have charge over the place."

Sabina smiled, but it was obvious the earlier optimism she had felt concerning her childhood home was being replaced by a sort of dread at what they might find.

21

Suspicions

. . .

Moscow

HE WAS ONTO SOMETHING. THAT MUCH HE WAS SURE OF.

What it was, he didn't know. But it was big—bigger than any of the old Cold War games. Russia and the U.S. may be friends now, but the world was still full of self-seeking men out to gain their own ends. And as long as politics was about power, there would be plenty of work to keep spies like him busy.

He eased out into traffic and settled in three or four cars behind the huge, black limousine.

Trouble was, he thought, now he was trying to get out of the game. How ironic that in the very process of getting out of the country for good, he should stumble upon this! He'd probably uncover the whole scheme and have no place to go with it. He had no friends, no allies, no havens anymore.

It was just as he'd feared the moment the Berlin Wall had collapsed. The change sweeping Eastern Europe was bound eventually to include him, and now it had. His worst fears had been realized. He was in danger even here in Moscow.

Yet he had to play out his hand. He'd been a KGB man too long to be able to stuff his curiosity when everything in him said something was happening. It was almost a reflex. He'd developed a sixth sense in the spy business, and he could just tell—his gut told him so.

That was the feeling he had right now about that limousine in front of him. If only he'd had time to plant a bug underneath!

Somehow or another he had to find out what this clandestine meeting between Desyatovsky and the German official was about! He could tell from the looks on their faces at the press conference that it had to do with more than the German and French aid package to the new Commonwealth of Independent States. A critical vote was scheduled in the German Bundestag the week of the seventeenth at a special session, and this little minisummit of leaders had ostensibly firmed everything up for the aid package to sail through. At least Kolter had promised to keep his coalition intact.

But something else was in the wind. Whether it had to do directly with the vote, he didn't know. It might not even be linked to the aid debate at all. Somehow he sensed something of greater import.

He'd known Bludayev Desyatovsky too long not to be able to see that he was nervous, wiping his forehead more often than could be accounted for by the mild summer day. They'd worked together for the same government for two decades. He'd even had to spy on him a time or two. So he knew Bludayev's mind was not on the aid agreement.

And the German! Too smooth—too polished. He had never trusted Klaus Drexler, and seeing him now—all smiles, but clearly hiding something—did nothing to alleviate that reaction.

All eyes had been on Yeltsin and Kolter and French president Mitterand—the star centerpieces of a mutually trusting new European community. But not Galanov's. His eyes had remained riveted on the two underlings, the Soviet defense minister and the German minority *Bundesminister*. And he had wasted no time in sprinting to his own car the moment the press conference had broken up. He would follow to see what might develop.

Who could tell? Perhaps he could parlay whatever information he gained into free passage west, or to a post in the new government without the baggage he was currently carrying as a result of his previous position. This may be the very opportunity he'd been waiting for.

No, come to think of it, he didn't want to stay—even if he could get out of this hot water. Everything had changed. Everything was upside-down, and his present predicament only typified what so many of his occupation now faced. He could have no future here. His life was in danger.

In the West he would be safer than he could ever be if he remained in his motherland. Some of his old colleagues had found ways to mainstream into the new Russian society. But he wasn't sure he wanted to chance it. An open pipeline existed to China, he knew, where many from the old Communist guard and KGB were winding up.

But that wasn't for him. He knew it would be just like the Nazis in Argentina after the Second World War—talk about the old times, always with the idealistic notion of a resumption of power. Not that there wasn't an enormous contingent left throughout what had so recently been the Soviet Union—the fifth column, silently awaiting events until the dream of 1917 could once again assert itself.

It could happen, he thought. The Gorbachev and Yeltsin eras represented but the blink of an eye in Russian history. It was no sure bet that all this democratic stuff would even stick in a nation where autocracy had been the ruling force for more than ten centuries.

But he wasn't going to hang around to find out which way the future went! It would be too dangerous. None of that was for him anymore. He had to get out. He had to find a place where he could start a new life.

The danger was real. In the topsy-turvy world of international espionage, the good guys had become the bad guys, and vice versa. Suddenly his own people were after him.

Having been a higher-up in the KGB made you a criminal in the new order. How had Bolotnikov managed to ingratiate himself with the new regime? he wondered. But now was no time to untangle that mystery. He had to worry about his own skin first. Desyatovsky was already after him, and he had probably seen him at the press conference besides. Whatever he might discover, he'd have to watch his step.

If it was information he could use to blackmail the defense minister, it still might not save him. He'd have to find out what was going on first and decide how to use the information later. And he'd have to stay out of sight. Desyatovsky would know he was snooping around if he left so much as one trace of his footsteps.

A few days, that was all he could spare. He'd already sent word through some of his old contacts in Poland and Germany that he needed to get out and would need transport and new identity papers.

When those came through, he'd have to get out of Russia for good, whether he'd unraveled this new mysterious twist or not.

But first, if at all possible, he'd dearly love to find out what was going on in that limo up ahead. After that, when his papers came, he'd resume his personal life and get out of the danger that was stalking him.

22

Dead-End Inquiries

• • •

Berlin

THIS WAS THE FOURTH OFFICE MATTHEW HAD BEEN TO IN A day and a half.

Neither the Germans nor the Americans offered much in the way of tangible hope, though everyone he spoke with promised to "look into the matter" and "see what might be done" concerning his request.

He had been writing letters and making telephone calls for over a year and following through on every State Department resource he could think of. But he found things greatly changed since the Kennedy days when a president could snap his fingers and command the government into action. Vietnam and Watergate had changed the whole complexion of things in Washington. Besides that, he was hardly on intimate terms with the president these days, nor was the U.S. held in the esteem in European affairs it once was.

Matthew had hoped actually being in Berlin might help, but so far such had been far from the case. He had discovered, however, on this side of the Atlantic as well as in Washington, that his own influence within the U.S. diplomatic service was not what he flattered himself it might once have been. What few remaining debts he had called in before the trip had resulted in little more than the scheduling of interviews in Berlin, none too hopeful.

Matthew had been pounding the pavement and making so many telephone calls that his right ear was developing a permanent ring. But thus far all he had succeeded in accomplishing was developing an extremely sore set of feet and a frustration level higher than he liked admitting to. Nor had the *Eigentumsurkunden* he had recovered from the hidden *Lebenshaus* files, which, to his satisfaction, proved Sabina's claim to the estate, been helpful.

"You see, Mr. McCallum," the most recent German official had said, echoing what he had already heard two dozen times, "since the collapse of the DDR, requests for the reinstatement of family lands and properties and houses have poured in by the tens of thousands. We have been hard-pressed to process even a fraction of them. It all takes time. It will take years to sort through all the claims. Even these old title deeds don't alter that situation."

"I'm afraid my wife and I don't have all that many years left," remarked Matthew with a tired smile.

"I understand," replied the lady as sympathetically as she could. "But even the most solid, legitimate, and confirmable of claims have involved extraordinary complexities. The lands where your property sits—"

"My wife's property."

"Yes, your wife's—in any event, these lands that were given to Poland after the war by the Soviet Union, these simply remain out of our jurisdiction. These documents appear genuine, but it is just out of our hands."

"But the land I'm investigating was German, and in the hands of a *German* noble family for generations."

"I understand that. However, as the new boundary for the DDR drawn in 1945 was situated to the west of that region, it became part of Poland."

"Yes, I know," sighed Matthew, "but *someone* must control it now."

"No doubt it has been in the hands of the Polish Communist state all this time."

"And now that Poland is becoming privatized as well?"

"I have no information on the present state of those lands in Poland, Mr. McCallum. I'm sorry. I suggest you talk to the Polish authorities themselves."

"I have tried," sighed Matthew, "but so far have not been able to get through to anyone who will give me a straight answer."

"Unfortunately, the Communist system was more deeply entrenched in Poland than here. Some of those patterns will no doubt take years to break."

An official request had been filled out through channels, which, he was told, would be processed through the Bonn government "at the highest possible levels." But until they found out how the Poles would respond, there was not much even the U.S. State Department could do.

Legally, the land surrounding and including *Lebenshaus* itself was all Polish. If there was to be any change in its status, the decision could come from only one place, the new Polish government.

If only I knew Lech Walesa personally, thought Matthew with a humorless grin and sigh as he walked toward the hotel after one more long and fruitless day. *It doesn't look like there's any other way we're ever going to have the chance to claim* Lebenshaus *again.*

23

Tracking Down an Old Photo

• • •

IN THE MEANTIME, NEITHER HAD TAD BEEN IDLE.

The moment they had arrived in Berlin, his WNS credentials had secured him access to the UPI and AP libraries in their Berlin headquarters. He had spent most of the second day questioning their Berlin operatives and photographers, to the point that he had obtained a half dozen names which, he was told, were several of the young people captured atop the Wall on film for all the world to see, which photograph had caught Tad's eye in the issue of *Time* he had read through on the plane.

Where might he contact any of them, Tad had asked.

The man didn't know. Those were the kinds of things it was difficult to keep track of, and already more than two years had passed. Most of those whose images were immortalized that fateful night in November 1989 had been thrust momentarily into the spotlight by the random fate of their presence at that historic moment and just as soon thereafter vanished back into the obscurity of their own lives.

There was a fellow, however, the man went on, whose specialty for one of the German news services was keeping track of dissidents, hotheads, revolutionaries, and terrorists. If anyone of note was in one of the pictures, Raul Schlink would be able to tell him, and if their whereabouts were known, Schlink would know that as well.

"And Schlink?" asked Tad. "Is *he* difficult to find?"

"Not at all. All the papers, even the police, use him all the time. He lives right here in Berlin."

"How can I find him?"

"I'll give you his address. I've got it right here in my file." A moment later the man handed Tad a slip of paper with the address written on it. "If any of those people in the photos are known and still in the city, Raul will be able to tell you."

"I appreciate your help," said Tad, then turned and left the building.

The fellow named Raul Schlink was a character in his own right. Had Tad not been intent on his investigation concerning the night of the Wall's opening, he might have been tempted to write the story on Schlink himself.

Entering his small apartment, one glance revealed that there was probably more information in this one place than in all the data banks of the U.S. and German governments combined. Shelves, file cabinets, stacks of books and file folders and bulging manila envelopes, several desks piled high with papers and files, two computers, three typewriters (one ancient), and an outmoded Teletype machine all met Tad's gaze in the initial four or five seconds he had to glance around the place.

He recognized the look immediately—it was the kind of hide-away where no one *else* could have possibly located one shred of usable information if given a month to rummage through and try to make sense of what was here. But with its owner at the helm, such a den—it seemed more a newshound's *lair* than what could technically be termed an office—was probably capable of accessing information more rapidly than the Library of Congress.

Tad had met people like Schlink many times—more prevalent in the news business than other professions, he thought, though he had nothing upon which to base such a conjecture. There were several on WNS's staff in Washington. People who didn't understand thought of them as hopelessly messy and disorganized.

When asked by the skeptics, "But how do you possibly keep track of anything . . . what kind of filing system do you use?" the Raul Schlinks of the world usually responded with a twinkle of the eye, a knowing smile, and an index finger tapping the side of the head. "It's all up here," came the inevitable reply.

The discerning eye of experience knew that in a crunch such a so-called filing system could be depended upon. If you wanted to explore any offbeat byways along the highways of the world's infor-mation, you had to be acquainted with any number of these kinds of individuals and had to know when to use them.

Schlink greeted Tad with casual disinterest, until learning that he was a colleague in the news service business. He knew of WNS, he said, and immediately a lively conversation sprang up between the two.

The man was shorter than Tad, thickly built, and bore the generally disheveled appearance that often went with such types. His shirt looked clean enough, though it was only half tucked into his pants—jeans not slacks—and was missing a button. The wild crop of brown hair on top of his head did not even pretend to be combed, and a full beard grew on his face. Neither beard nor moustache were of the sort that received a weekly trim.

After journalistic pleasantries sufficient to establish a level of trust and camaraderie, Tad showed Schlink the copy of the *Time* photo he had obtained.

"Ah yes," the German said, smiling, "quite a night that was."

"You recognize the picture, I assume?"

"Very well."

"You didn't take it, did you?"

Schlink laughed. "I was there that November . . . and with my camera too. But I got nothing nearly so good as this. Those fellows from *Time,* they have some great equipment."

"I was told you might be able to help me identify some of these people, even locate them."

"Hmm . . . that's a tall order. It's been a while. Still . . ." He took the photograph from Tad's hand. "Yes—that's Klapmann there, and—let me see . . . I think . . ."

He paused, then turned, picked up a magnifying glass from somewhere amidst the clutter on one of the desks, and held it to the picture and squinted into it. "Yes, I thought so," he added. "There's Horst Brandes too."

"You know these people?" asked Tad.

"A few of them—by reputation mostly. The majority of these you see are just random passersby who happened to be there. But a few stand out."

"Dissidents—is that how you know them?"

"I know most of the active revolutionary and protest groups, with a few terrorists thrown in—something of a sadistic hobby of mine, I suppose."

"So who are these two you recognize here?"

"They belong to an organization called the Freedom Alliance. I'd had some dealings with them, so I know their faces."

"Are they still active?"

"Somewhat, but most of that sort of thing has cooled down since 1989. All of a sudden everything they were protesting against quit the fight, so to speak. Reunification took away their cause."

"Are these two still active?" asked Tad.

"I haven't heard a whisper out of Klapmann," replied Schlink, "but Horst is still in Berlin."

"What about her?"

Tad pointed to another figure in the picture still clutched in the other man's hand. She was a slender, attractive young woman, with a light complexion but dark eyes and shoulder-length black hair. Tad had estimated her to be about five feet, seven or eight inches tall, based on comparisons with the other celebrants on the wall.

Again Schlink adjusted the magnifying glass to examine the photo in more detail. "Of course!" he exclaimed after a moment. "How could I have missed her the first time!"

"You know her?"

"She was in the FA too."

"Know her name?"

"No . . . no, I don't. Just the face. It always stuck with me—somehow she didn't seem to belong."

"Why?"

Schlink shrugged. "Just a sense I had—that she was out of place, that she wasn't like the others. Funny thing though," he added, "she'd been around a long time and I think was one of the leaders, along with these other two."

"What's funny about that?"

"That if she was different, what was it that made her so devoted to their cause?"

"Any idea where I could find her?"

Schlink thought for a moment. "The Alliance used to have a house in East Berlin where four or five of the women lived."

"Is it still active?"

"Don't know, but I can probably find the address around here somewhere."

"That'd be great—I'd appreciate it."

"If not, Horst would know if she's still in or near Berlin. I'm sure I could get you in touch with him. What do you want with her anyway?"

"Maybe something about her face drew me too, like you said," replied Tad.

"You mean like she didn't belong?"

"Not so much that," said Tad reflectively, then paused to ponder the question further. "Actually, I don't know what to tell you," he added. "As soon as I saw that face, something inside me was drawn to it . . . and somehow I knew there was a story inside that young lady that I had to discover."

2 4

Schemes

• • •

Moscow

"CLAYMORE?"

"That's right—who is it?"

"Your employer."

"Why are you calling me? I thought you said—"

"Shut up. Time is running short. I have to know if you've found out anything on Schmundt."

"There are some promising leads."

"What do you mean?"

Claymore's gravelly chuckle could be heard on the other end of the phone.

"What do you have?" insisted the voice.

"Potentially enough to make him do anything you want."

"I don't pay for innuendos, I need facts," barked the other.

"Then let me just say this much for now—it appears you may have been right about the man having a past."

"Everyone has a past, especially former Communists."

"Some are more damaging than others."

The phone was silent a second or two. "That is interesting . . . but not so condemning in and of itself, not nowadays," replied the German after a moment.

"Don't be so sure."

"Send me the complete file. Do you possess documentation?"

"You pay for the best, you get the best. When I submit my report, you will have what you need."

Now it was the politician's turn to laugh, though only momentarily. "What about information of a more, shall we say, *personal* nature?"

"You mean a woman?"

"If there is one."

"I can find no evidence."

"Everyone has someone."

"Not this man. He is a confirmed bachelor."

"Well, send me what you've got. It may have to be enough—usual name and post box in Berlin."

"You want me to keep digging?"

"Yes, I'll be seeing him soon. Anything on the Russian?"

"No. I'll have to go to Moscow to get the real dirt."

"That may have to wait. I want you close by for now. I'll be in touch."

Drexler hung up the phone, thought for a minute, then quickly punched in another number. He had no need to look it up. He had known it quite well from memory for several years now.

"It's me," he said, in decent but accented Russian when the voice on the other end answered. "Any further developments since I was there?"

"Not much changes in two days."

"You suspected we were being followed."

"*Ja,* a troublesome former KGB fellow. He is trying to bring me down. But I have people on him. He will be eliminated before many days."

"We cannot afford the slightest leak!"

"Not to worry, my friend. He knows nothing. He can find out nothing."

"All your other connections—everything is in readiness?"

"Not to worry, not to worry. All is ready. In a matter of days, the unions throughout the country will be clamoring for change, the railways will be crippled, financial centers in chaos, and the military firmly behind me. I have good people working very hard, even at this moment."

"It is nearly time. The vote comes in less than two weeks. That may provide my opportunity. Will you be ready?"

"I can move with forty-eight hours' notice."

"Just make sure your people are ready."

• • •

Bludayev Desyatovsky put down the phone.

That was the trouble with Germans—they worried too much. An anxious, fretful people, he thought; always nervous, always on edge.

And they could not give anyone but a German credit for doing anything right. A pompous, egocentric race—nearly as bad as the Americans.

But alas, they were his western neighbors, like them or not. History had shown that one had either to work with them or against them, and he hoped he was making the right decision for the future of *his* people to choose the former.

Bah! The fair-eyed one had only better cover his own responsibilities for this thing! More could go wrong on his end than here.

One little lapse, one vote taken for granted that went to his chancellor, one slipup with the fellow of the other party, whose support he had to woo, against the aid package—one slip, and he himself would be left out in the cold, making his bold move and then left hanging by his own rope!

Nyet, my Teutonic friend! he thought, *it is not I you need worry about, but yourself!*

He rose and strode about the room in mounting disgust at the phone call. He would have to take steps to gain complete control of the reins himself once the initial phase was completed. He didn't want to be forever at the mercy of that man. He didn't trust him.

But for the present, he was stuck with him.

PART V

Evangelism and Intrigue

25

Arrival at Conference

• • •

Berlin

"I WONDER IF JOSEPH'S CHECKED IN YET," SAID SABINA AS they walked through the doors and began walking toward the counter. Matthew started to reply, but the next sound they heard was not from his mouth at all.

"Matthew McCallum!" boomed a rousing and enthusiastic voice across the lobby.

Tad, Matthew, and Sabina all glanced up to see a man striding toward them with a huge grin to match his exuberant greeting, hand outstretched.

The three had just walked into the lobby of the Westmark Hotel from the parking basement and had scarcely glanced around long enough to locate the check-in desk when the familiar voice assailed them.

They hardly had time to turn and focus before the boisterous left hand of Darrell Montgomery landed with a friendly slap across the upper half of Matthew's back as he shook his hand with his right. "It is wonderful to see you again!" he said. "And," he added warmly, turning toward Sabina before anyone could say a word, "your dear wife looks as lovely as ever." He shook her hand now, adding, "Mrs. McCallum, I am delighted you could join your husband."

"Thank you very much, Mr. Montgomery."

"So, Darrell," said Matthew, sufficiently recovered, "how is the conference shaping up?"

"Couldn't be better! Especially since you decided to join us. I'm delighted, and so is everyone else—and looking forward eagerly to what you have to say."

Matthew threw both Sabina and Tad quick glances, with one eyebrow lifted, as if to say, "I'm glad *he's* so confident!"

"That last book of yours was a sensation," Montgomery went on. "A real thought-provoking concept. Timing couldn't have been better either, coinciding perfectly with registration for the conference."

"I don't believe you've met my son," said Matthew. "Tad," he added, "say hello to Darrell Montgomery, who's spearheading this shindig. Darrell, this is my son, Tad McCallum."

"Nice to meet you," said Tad, as the two men shook hands.

"A pleasure!" rejoined Montgomery. "Will you be joining us for the conference?"

"My son works for WNS," interjected Matthew.

"Ah, the media! I'll have to watch myself around you!"

"I'm only a translator," laughed Tad. "You have nothing to worry about, I assure you."

"A translator who's been asked to write up a news release for Germany when this is all over," added Matthew.

"So I *will* have to watch myself!"

"Nothing but the facts, Mr. Montgomery," said Tad. "I just happen to be someone who knows German, that's all, so I receive some of the European assignments."

"Well, that's wonderful, I must say," replied Montgomery expansively. "I'm so glad you have all come. It's going to be a powerful conference!"

"Have you by chance seen Aviz-Rabin?" asked Matthew.

"Ah yes, your friend from Israel—no, I'm not aware whether he's arrived yet."

"I appreciate your scheduling him on the panel with us. His perspective as a Jewish Christian is invaluable—I know you won't be disappointed."

"Well, as highly as you spoke of him, how could I refuse? Now—come, all three of you, there are some people I want you to meet!"

A small crowd had already begun to gather around them once the presence of Matthew McCallum and his mysteriously graceful and stately wife became known. They proceeded to shake several hands, as

Montgomery attempted to lead them away, while Tad tagged along at the back of the growing throng, relishing being able to see so vividly the esteem in which his two prominent parents were held within the Christian community.

Darrell Montgomery was one of the most well-known leaders in American evangelical circles. Charismatic, tall, handsome, tan, and incurably confident and outspoken, he had taken his own student evangelistic organization vastly past the bounds of high school, college, and university campuses where it had begun some twenty years before. It now boasted a publications arm, for which Montgomery had himself written several best-sellers, and a vast communications network stretching throughout the world. Reaching the lost on every continent and in every nation had long been his goal and vision, and in recent years the organization had undertaken grandiose new methods to proclaim the gospel to every creature.

With the collapse of the Berlin Wall and the disintegration of the USSR, Montgomery had turned his attention to this conference at the hub of the new nation of Germany. It was his own brainchild, which he hoped would prove the equivalent of Lausanne and Evangelism 2000 and provide a major new impetus for evangelical groups to impact what had once been the closed Eastern Bloc of Europe. Darrell Montgomery was at the apex of his sanguine personality in pulling it all together. His hopes were boundless for what would result from the two weeks of meetings.

By the time Tad, Matthew, and Sabina reached their two rooms an hour and a half later, the latter two were nearly exhausted. Matthew flopped across the bed with a mingled sigh and groan. Montgomery had kept up nonstop conversation and instructions since they had arrived.

"We should have arranged to come to the city earlier in the day," laughed Sabina. "Then we could have hidden in our room while everyone else was arriving."

"I wouldn't have minded checking in to another hotel altogether!" rejoined Matthew with a fatigued grin.

"At least that's over!"

"He's got everyone here, I'll say that much for him," said Matthew as he stretched out with a relaxing sigh.

"With you as one of his star centerpieces," quipped Sabina. "If only your father could see you now!"

"Knock it off," returned Matthew. "I'm just one in Darrell's cast of thousands."

"Come on! You saw his eyes when we walked in."

"He was starstruck from seeing *you*," kidded Matthew.

Sabina laughed. "There's not a grain of truth in that, and you know it!"

"You're as beautiful as the day I first saw you."

"Now I know you're lying. And don't try to change the subject," insisted Sabina, enjoying her husband's fame as much as Tad had earlier.

Joseph Aviz-Rabin, Matthew and Sabina's dear friend of many years, arrived in Berlin later that same afternoon. He and the three McCallums spent the evening together, renewing their friendship and catching up on the years since they had last seen one another.

The following morning, the large conference hall of the convention center across the street from the Westmark Hotel on Leitzenburger Straße was filled to capacity when Darrell Montgomery strode to the podium confidently, his face bright with smiles, one hand gesturing in greeting to the crowd as it applauded.

"I am glad to extend a warm welcome to you all," he began as the noise gradually subsided. "You church leaders who have come to Berlin will be privileged to share together like no other gathering of Christians ever before in history. For we are those who suddenly find ourselves facing days—hopefully years—of unprecedented opportunity for the taking of the gospel into whole new regions of the globe. That is why we have come together—to discuss what should be the church's response to this new world order in the midst of which we suddenly find ourselves."

As Matthew sat listening, he wondered what he could possibly contribute to those seated here. He strongly doubted that the kinds of truths he tried to emphasize in his books—those, namely, in such prominent evidence in the journals of Baron von Dortmann—were the sorts of inner and personal priorities that would be paid much attention to at such a gathering as this.

An hour later, Tad, Matthew, Sabina, and Joseph all rose together.

At the far end of the hall, Matthew spied a man he recognized and had long hoped for an opportunity to meet. As a renowned figure in both German religious and political circles, with high connections in Bonn and a solid reputation among evangelicals, Gentz Raedenburg was in curious contrast to the rousing evangelistic speech he had just heard. Raedenburg did not seem the type to fit in with the beam-the-gospel-via-satellite-across-the-world's-borders mentality.

Perhaps, Matthew reflected, *Darrell might indeed have pulled together a wider spectrum than ever before.*

Seeing Raedenburg caused Matthew to reflect further how the new politics of Europe fit in with a vision of reaching this newly structured world for Christ. *Or do they?* he wondered. To what extent did evangelism intersect with one's political worldview? Did the new world order signal a new approach to Christian strategic planning as well?

Without reaching any conclusions, but filling his bin of questions yet fuller, absorbed, reflective, unconscious of those around him, Matthew continued to file out of the hall with wife and son and the rest of the throng.

Defense Minister and KGB Boss

• • •

Moscow

THE RUSSIAN DEFENSE MINISTER HAD HAD DEALINGS WITH
the former head of the KGB before. But never on anything approaching an intimate basis. They had merely been comrades in the regime.
But now events necessitated a closer alliance.

Desyatovsky frankly didn't know if Bolotnikov was a man he
could trust. It was time he found out.

He was going to need men of his unique abilities who would be
loyal to him. He had plenty of them already. But now he believed it
was time to bring the old KGB chief into the inner circle. He had to
know, when it all came down, which side Bolotnikov was going to
land on.

In the meantime, he could make good use of his help.

"Ah, Comrade Bolotnikov," said the defense minister as the
ex–KGB chief entered his office. "How are you finding your new—
uh, position in the government?"

"Not without its adjustments," replied Bolotnikov guardedly.

"Nothing insurmountable, I hope?"

"Not at all, Comrade Defense Minister."

Leonid Bolotnikov had made a career of studying both allies and
adversaries, reading them, and discerning motives and objectives.
Without a cunning perceptiveness that came as second nature to him,
he would not have risen to the KGB's top position. Nor would he
have been one of the few to slide into the post–Soviet Union

government nearly unscathed by his past reputation. Most of his former associates had not been so fortunate.

At fifty-six, he was still a powerful man, six-foot-three, hair mostly black, with bulging strength throughout arms and shoulders and upper body. He had joined the Soviet military at eighteen. During the Hungarian uprising in 1956 he had distinguished himself, and after that his career moved into the fast track. By 1968 and the Czechoslovakian invasion, he had become a division commander, a young man for such a position, though in light of the Kremlin's propensity for filling their positions of power with octogenarians, the distinction was empty of significance. Shortly thereafter he had been elevated to membership in the Politburo, an advancement made possible by his occasional mentor, the late defense minister Dmitri Ustinov, one of Desyatovsky's predecessors. Ustinov had always considered Bolotnikov one of the motherland's future leaders, and thus when chairmanship of the KGB became available in 1978, he recommended his protégé for the post.

Desyatovsky had first encountered Bolotnikov during their mutual years in the Politburo, but this was their first private meting. He had never been exactly clear on how Bolotnikov had managed in the critical years of the late eighties when so many of the KGB's henchmen suddenly found themselves out in the cold. As top man, however, he probably had files that could bring down anyone he wanted. *He probably had enough dirt on both Gorbachev and Yeltsin,* thought Desyatovsky, *to write his own ticket during the disintegration and changeover.*

As Bolotnikov sat in his superior's office, the wheels of his mind were likewise not idle. Everyone in Russia had a motive these days, and he wondered what was Desyatovsky's. He would wait—and listen—and watch for events to develop.

"You used to have an associate," Desyatovsky continued, "one of your assistants, I believe, who is proving a bit troublesome to me."

Bolotnikov smiled. "I know precisely who you mean," he replied. "I have heard reports that he has been trying to get out of the country."

"That may be. But he remains here—and has been tailing me."

"And you think, perhaps, I may be able to help?"

"He used to be one of the KGB's best men."

"But he and I have been out of touch since—you must realize, of course, how greatly things have changed. I found my way again into the military, under the auspices of the Russian Republic, whereas the man you speak of has been, shall we say, less fortunate." Bolotnikov was feeling his way through the conversation gingerly, until he knew what Desyatovsky's game was.

"I understand," said the defense minister. "I am aware of his dilemma, that he is being sought even now by the police in connection with his past *crimes* with the KGB—meaning, of course, no disrespect to you."

"None taken."

"But as yet, he has not been found, nor has he been successful in getting out of Russia. To my knowledge he is still in Moscow itself."

"So I have heard," assented Bolotnikov.

"As long as he remains at large, he threatens certain plans and negotiations of mine that are highly delicate in nature."

"You think he is trying to undermine these—these *plans,* as you call them?"

"Of that there can be no doubt."

"Then he must be stopped."

"Precisely."

"I begin to see your point, Comrade Defense Minister. And he is being sought, you say, by the police?"

"To no effect! If I may be so bold, times have just—" Desyatovsky paused, eyeing Bolotnikov carefully. "May I speak frankly, Comrade Bolotnikov?" he asked.

"Please," replied Bolotnikov, nodding his head in assent.

"What I was going to say," Desyatovsky went on, "is that times have changed. The police today are—I hope you will forgive me for being so blunt—little more than low-level office workers from the old days. Your KGB, I must say, was considerably more effective with this sort of thing. You and your men knew how to handle problems quickly and efficiently—*if* you understand me."

Desyatovsky too was probing, feeling the man out to see where he stood.

And Bolotnikov knew it.

A thin hint of a smile cracked his lips. Perhaps he had misjudged the defense minister. It sounded as if the two might actually get along rather nicely. "I believe I do," Bolotnikov smiled. "I will take your words as a compliment."

"I do not think they know the man has two residences. Even my limited intelligence knows that much."

"They are tracking him?"

"Da, and finding nothing but cold trails."

"Why do you not put them onto the right path?"

"Don't you understand? I cannot get involved personally. Matters are too—sensitive right now. Which is exactly why I asked you to see me. Do you think . . . that is, do you still have *contacts,* as it were, whom you might call upon, men of resource and skill?"

"I could perhaps see what might be done." Bolotnikov's tone was again guarded and distant.

"You sound reticent to help me."

"Times are sensitive for us all, Comrade Defense Minister. One must walk warily in the new order. You cannot be unaware that I myself, as former head of the KGB, face certain perils if I were to stumble in the wrong direction."

"I understand perfectly. Yes, you are right—tenuous times. One must walk with caution, choosing his allegiances and friendships with discretion."

A long silence followed. The words remained heavily suspended in the air, both men clearly reflecting on their import relative to the present conversation. If an alliance were to form between them, it would not be based on trusting natures but on the fact that each saw in the other a way to gain his own objective.

"Tell me, Comrade Bolotnikov," said Desyatovsky after several long moments, "what *do* you think of the new order?"

"Your question is a broad and complex one, Comrade Defense Minister."

"Admittedly. Do you have the courage to answer?"

Bolotnikov squinted imperceptibly, then smiled. It was a bold challenge—one he could not resist. He would see what Desyatovsky had to say.

"Times have changed," he replied at length. "No one can deny that. Not even I. Yet sometimes one cannot help but wonder if the change has been positive for the motherland—or negative."

They were just the words Desyatovsky had been hoping to hear. Apparently he had not misjudged this man. "Do I gather from your words that you are *dissatisfied* with the course events are taking?"

It was a bolder challenge yet.

"Dissatisfied? It is a strong word, Comrade Defense Minister."

"Indeed. But I retain my choice of phrase. What is your answer?"

It was Bolotnikov's turn to weigh his options one last time. It did not take him long. "Let me answer you then partially. I will say that, yes, perhaps I am, as you say, dissatisfied."

It was all Desyatovsky needed. In the elusiveness of Russian double-talk, he knew what Bolotnikov meant.

"Then, perhaps you might be interested in *why* I must see that your former associate is stopped?"

"Indeed I would—most intrigued!"

"Would you care for another glass of vodka first? It is a rather lengthy story."

Variations on a Great Truth

• • •

Berlin

THE FOLLOWING MORNING, MATTHEW, TAD, AND JOSEPH participated in the full round of the speeches and workshops of the conference.

Sabina, with husband and son, attended the morning's session which offered an overview on the role of church leaders in taking advantage of newly created opportunities for reaching the world for Christ.

She found it difficult to concentrate on what was being said, however, and her mind kept drifting into other channels.

". . . *truly confident,*" the speaker was saying, "*that God is going to do many remarkable and wonderful things among us during these two weeks. I believe that we stand at one of the great watersheds of human existence, with perhaps the single greatest opportunity for fulfilling the Great Commission in history before us. How privileged we are to be among those living to witness the events of our time.*"

Sabina did not find the talk of particular interest to her and could not keep from reflecting on how much differently her father would approach the subject.

Pieces of a conversation she had had with her father as a young woman during the war came back to Sabina as she sat in the large conference hall. The Dortmann home had been full with refugee Jews at the time, as had nearly always been the case during the middle years of the war.

She had asked him one day why they were not doing more to

actively share the Christian faith with their guests. The baron had smiled thoughtfully before inviting his daughter outside for a walk in the garden.

Sabina smiled now at the memory. It was one of the most memorable talks they had ever had together. She recalled it with particular fondness in that it was one of their last such shared moments of deep spiritual intimacy at *Lebenshaus.*

"Sabina, my dear," her father had said after they were alone and had been sauntering casually down the gentle slope into *Der Frühlingsgarten,* "you have asked one of the most important of all questions for a Christian, but one which, alas, many of God's sons and daughters do not pause to reflect upon seriously and prayerfully."

Sabina waited. She knew her father would guide her gently through the pathways of thought toward the deeper understanding she sought, as he had so many times in the past.

"Do you perhaps feel, my child," said the baron at length, "that there ought to be more vocal expression given, concerning our Christian belief system, toward these who are among us?"

"It seems so, Father," Sabina replied.

"Why does it seem so?"

"Because they don't know that Jesus was God's Son, their Messiah."

"And we need to tell them?"

"God has sent them to us. Do we not have a responsibility to speak to them?"

"Is that a responsibility God lays upon us?"

"Do they not need to be told?" questioned Sabina.

"I am not so sure they need to be *told,* though of course they must come to know it eventually."

"Is it not the same thing?"

"Very different, I would say."

"If they must know that Jesus is God's Son, how will they find out if they are not told?"

"There—you have finally put your finger on the precise question," said the baron.

Again Sabina smiled, this time at the memory of her father's method of leading the progression of her conclusions by asking his own series of questions. She still, even at her age, was in the process of discovering what a wise man her father had been, and was more conscious every day that she would never uncover everything their heavenly Father had revealed to the remarkable man during his earthly life.

How she was looking forward to seeing Father and Mother again when her own pilgrimage was done!

"Therefore, I say that we—we, my friends!—stand at the very threshold. We possess the ability to carry out Christ's command to go unto all the world in a more massive way than any group of Christians ever has before. We are here because we share the vision of a world in which the gospel has been preached throughout all of its distant corners."

Sabina and her father had walked on in silence, that day so long ago, moving deeper into the lovely Garden of Spring.

"The question, it would appear," said the baron, "has to do with how we come to know truth—would you agree?"

"I hadn't thought about it in just those terms," replied Sabina, who was still a young woman and but learning to think in the ways her father had taught her, "but I can see that it may reduce to that."

Again the baron paused briefly, formulating his next question. "Tell me, Sabina," he asked after about a minute, "how do *you* know that God the Father loves you? Is it because your mother and I have told you?"

"No . . . I suppose not."

"How do you *know* it, then?"

"I would say I have learned to feel his love personally as I have grown. I have discovered what kind of Father he is."

"Your mother and I have taught you about God, but you have discovered the reality of his love yourself—is that it?"

"Yes—that's it exactly."

"And that is precisely what I would say in answer to your question—every man, every woman must make that discovery for himself."

"I have heard you say that many times, Papa."

"Any truth must be found, discovered, apprehended from *within*. Nothing coming at a person *from the outside* is capable of instilling truth inside him. Facts, intellectual data, perhaps—but not truth. That is only gained from within."

"But what about people who don't know about God—isn't it by

telling that we help them begin that process of discovering it for themselves? You told *me* about God, and then as I grew I discovered the deeper truths of what you said."

"My answer to your question would be no," replied the baron. "I do *not* think it is by telling people that we help them begin that process of discovery. I do not believe you have discovered the deeper truths of God from what I have told you."

"How then?"

"That I will leave you to discover for yourself. If you think about it long enough, it will become more than plain to you."

Again the memory brought a smile to Sabina's face. It did not take her long to know what her father was implying—that it was the *living example of his character* more than the *words from his lips* that had propelled her own spiritual journey along its lifelong pathways of discovery.

"Men and women, my brothers and sisters," the speaker was going on enthusiastically, even as Sabina drifted into reminiscence, *"can you grasp the enormity of our potential impact? With doors throughout the world open before us, vast throngs will soon be entering the kingdom as a result of our efforts. We will send teams of missionaries into the East. We will take books and tracts and pamphlets by the millions into regions where the gospel has never been heard. No longer will we smuggle them in by ones and twos, hidden in suitcases. Now we will take Testaments and materials in by the very truckload!"*

"You do think Christians can help people know God, don't you, Papa?" she had asked him at the time.

"Certainly."

"But not by telling them about him?"

"Not primarily. No doubt occasional good is done by the verbal transmission of information about God, but not a great deal. No, Sabina, the good we can do in the lives of those who do not know about the Father's love in assisting them to begin the process of spiritual discovery and growth is by another means altogether than what we *say* to them."

"You told Matthew and Thaddeus about God."

"Yes, I did."

"And that piqued their interest."

"Ah, but was it my *words* that piqued their interest?"

Sabina knitted her forehead in question.

"That they may now be seeking truth about God on their own I hope and pray is true. But if that is so, it is *not* my words that instigated the process, but something else—that very thing I told you a minute ago that I would leave you to discover. Do you know what that is?"

"I think so, Papa."

"Matthew had already noticed something about *you,* and both he and his father had noticed something about our family and our home—something different about the way we lived, something about the kind of people we are. *That* is the powerful igniting spark to faith—*what unbelievers observe in the character of God's people.*"

"I see."

"And, of course," he added, "our prayers. We have both prayed for Matthew and Thaddeus, have we not?"

Sabina nodded.

"And if the day comes when we learn that they have given themselves to become sons of the Father—which I am confident will be the case—it will be our *prayers* and our *lives* that will have been instrumental in that process most of all."

•   •   •

Meanwhile, as he sat listening, Matthew's thoughts revolved around what ought to be his own role in the events of the week. He found himself still struggling with what, if anything, he should himself attempt to contribute.

He too had been thinking of Sabina's father. He knew the thoughts and spiritual perspectives of Baron von Dortmann better than any man alive, perhaps in some ways more thoroughly even than Sabina herself. He had devoted years of his life to the attempt to make his father-in-law's insights publicly known. He had been given, he felt, the charge to pass the baron's legacy on to future generations.

Now, here he was at a gathering of influential Christians from all over the world. Was now a time for him to speak out publicly and attempt to communicate what the baron might say to all these in attendance if he had them one at a time in his rose garden?

Matthew was well aware that the baron had prayed for German unity for years and for the spiritual vitality of the German nation. What ought now to be his own role respective of his commitment to the baron's ideas? How could he act as the baron's ambassador to his own country in this new day? By the time he sensed the speech winding down, he was no nearer a conclusion than when it had begun.

"*. . . nothing has been omitted from our schedule,*" said the speaker, at last concluding his remarks. "*When you leave here a little more than a week from now, you should be equipped to carry home specific strategies with which you can immediately begin working with those men and women under your charge to fulfill what I believe is our mutual destiny in this day—carrying the Good News throughout the earth.*"

When the session was over, Sabina said little. Her thoughts were still on the past, and she returned to their room.

After a thirty-minute break, Tad attended a talk entitled: "New World Order—Friend or Foe to the Gospel," while his father listened to a symposium on "Practical Strategies in Europe in the Post–Cold War Era."

Sabina came down and met the three men for lunch, the latter looking over the conference syllabus for the afternoon's offerings.

Sabina was unusually quiet during the meal and, as her husband and son discussed their options for later, announced that she thought she would go out and perhaps see if her former home was still standing.

"Do you want some company?" asked Matthew. "I would happily forgo the conference."

Sabina smiled reflectively. "No," she replied. "I think perhaps I need some time alone."

"Are you all right?" asked Matthew, the concern evident in his tone.

Sabina nodded. "I've been thinking about my father."

"He's been on my mind too."

"I'll be fine—there's much to come to terms with. I suppose your not meeting with any success about *Lebenshaus* has been on my mind too. I must have been hoping more than I'd realized. Realizing we may never see the house again, or worse, having to accept the fact that maybe it's not even there at all, has brought a new finality somehow to the visit."

"I understand," said Matthew.

They kissed and then separated. Sabina made her way outside for a walk in the streets of Berlin. Matthew, Joseph, and Tad headed toward the Westmark's meeting rooms for the discussion they had decided to attend.

Matthew paused at the end of the corridor and glanced back after his wife, now just exiting the hotel lobby, and sent a quick prayer after her. He knew he could never completely understand what it meant to *be* a German. This was a complex land, and they were a complex people with many things to have to work through about their role and position among the world's community of peoples.

Now they were embarking upon a whole new era, he mused. It must be more difficult than he had any idea of. He supposed every German had to deal with it, each in his own way. He knew what Sabina would do—she would seek the perspective of her father, which was to seek the mind of their mutual Father. Speaking of dealing with things, he thought to himself . . . through all the years of change, he wondered how—

He stopped short before completing the question.

Where had the thought of *him* come from!

Matthew laughed to himself. His old nemesis hadn't crossed his mind in years. And he wouldn't waste any more time thinking of him now!

He turned and hurried on after his son. It was time to turn his attention to the new politics of the time, the new world order, and the opportunities presented by both for Christians.

Sabina, meanwhile, had found herself, almost at the same moment, struck with a similar wave of unwelcome nostalgia. With pleasant thoughts of her father, *Lebenshaus,* and Matthew's first visit to the estate still swirling about in the eye of her memory, suddenly another personality intruded unbidden into scenes from the past, threatening to bring a dark cloud over her spirits.

That was another consideration in her return to Berlin she had, until this moment, kept herself from facing—the disagreeable fact that this was the last place she had seen *him.*

Who could tell but that he might yet be here?

Many years had passed, but Sabina still found the thought of him unpleasant, and she shuddered to think that even the most remote possibility existed that his path might by some chance cross hers again.

28

Loyalties

• • •

IT COULD NOT TRUTHFULLY BE SAID THAT HE HAD NOT thought about her in years, for she did cross his mind more than occasionally. But the days of pining after a lost love had long since receded into the past, just as the momentary image of her face had disappeared down an empty grave into the ground nearly thirty years ago.

What dormant desires might have been aroused in his seventy-two-year-old bosom even now had he known that she upon whom he had expended such energy of misguided passion was at that moment less than three kilometers from where he stood pondering his own future.

His thoughts were on politics, however, not youthful love. The broodings of his moribund nature were preoccupied with the more recent past of his own fortunes . . . and upon what future fate might soon be awaiting him.

Things were changing rapidly on the political landscape. He had survived the advent of communism in his country and its demise. But how much longer would he be able to retain his footing in this era that was daily growing less and less friendly to former collaborators? He was not a young man. He must deal out what few cards remained in his possession with skill and cunning . . . or he knew what would be his fate.

Gustav Schmundt had been around long enough to see the handwriting on the wall. He knew the winners and losers and what came of playing on the wrong side of the political fences—fences strewn with more barbs than the slashing thick wires that used to be strung atop the Wall down the middle of Berlin.

He was certainly no historian, but he knew enough to realize it had always been so. *Loyalties and alliances are fleeting commodities on the European political landscape,* he thought as he made his way purposefully down the hall.

Funny, he mused, only a few brief years earlier these buildings were little more than empty shells. Now a new home for the Bundestag was being planned, and here he was not a stone's throw away from that part of the city that had for nearly thirty years been forbidden to him, on the way to the chancellor's provisional office in Berlin—the chancellor of a united Germany!

Yes, such was the speed with which things could change! One must be on one's toes, always sniffing the winds of fortune, guarding one's flank.

Loyalty—a fleeting commodity indeed. One didn't have to know much German history to be painfully aware of that fact. Gustav had worked too hard to let pet loyalties keep him from doing what might have to be done to ensure his own survival. It was a lesson he had learned from Korsch that he'd never forgotten. Loyalty at the wrong time could get you killed or thrown in prison, like that fool of a baron, Sabina's father.

These were times when people got shoved out into the cold for indecisiveness. Russia and Poland were full of yesterday's leaders who had become today's unemployed and imprisoned. Now it was happening with the leaders of the former DDR in East Germany too, and he had no intention of being one of the casualties like so many of his old colleagues. He would not get left behind. Sure, he owed Kolter his political life. But he'd repaid that debt by now. He'd been a loyal soldier since reunification, delivering the chancellor the votes he'd needed, just as promised. But realities were realities, and in this game—

His thoughts were interrupted by his arrival at the outer lobby of the chancellor's chambers.

"*Guten Tag, Herr Schmundt,*" the receptionist greeted him crisply. "*Wie geht is Ihnen heute?*"

"*Sehr gut, Frau Wildig, danke,*" he replied.

"The chancellor is just finishing up with the finance minister," she told him. "Please take a seat. It won't be but a minute or two, I'm sure."

Gustav nodded and complied.

As he glanced around at the chancellor's new, lavishly appointed quarters, he could not help reflecting on everything that had occurred recently. Who could have foreseen it happening so suddenly? Men like him who had come up through the bureaucratic ranks on both sides in the fifties and sixties took for granted that East and West would never meet again, in spite of the lip service paid to the goal of reunification periodically by Bonn throughout the Cold War. Nobody really believed it would happen—especially not on the side of the fence where he had spent all those years. They had not even particularly *wanted* it to happen.

Yes, he had seen a great deal. What a shambles Germany had been after the war. He remembered the rubble, the bombed-out shells of buildings, cathedrals, and apartment houses; the desolation, the quiet, the old ladies silently weeping over the fatherland.

Then had come the split that had caused the fortunes of the German people to move in two very opposite directions.

On the one side had come the economic miracle under the BRD's economic minister Ludwig Erhard. Never before had there been anything like the turnaround and growth of the Bundesrepublik Deutschland during the Adenauer era. The huge reservoir of skilled laborers had been tapped, industry rebounded in the valleys of the Ruhr and Rhine, efficiency was high, unemployment low. New industrial centers rose out of the ashes of the war's bitter defeat. A vital agricultural system energized the rural areas. Vast improvements were made in roads, airports, cities—modernizations swept through all corners of the new nation.

And all they could do on the eastern side was watch, wistfully wondering about the lot fate had dealt them, while paying their own loyal lip service, not to the notion of German reunification at all, but rather to the virtues of the Communist system.

Well, now it was their turn! Now had come the time for *East* Germany's economic miracle, and already the former DDR was being remade at an even more rapid pace than had the BRD in the fifties. They were showing the world what the German people were made of—*all* the German people!

He reflected on his own career. Though his years with the *Stasi* were not of high distinction, it had proved a singularly appropriate pathway toward the intricate and cutthroat politics of the DDR. His own political rise had followed that of his friend and colleague Erich Honecker, and he had left the *Stasi* for good in 1966, eventually rising to a somewhat rewarding degree of prominence in the East German political hierarchy.

He was not *really* one of the DDR's leading figures, of course. He was not invited to be present when Brezhnev or Gorbachev came for a visit. But the illusion was satisfying, and his role in the Moscow-controlled governmental system certainly provided him a better life with more comforts than most of his fellow countrymen.

His lack of distinction, and the fact that he was generally politically soft-spoken, in the end proved his salvation. Three weeks before the Wall had been toppled, Honecker had been replaced by another of his associates Egon Krenz, himself also a relative hard-liner against change. But even Krenz had not survived for long, and—incredibly!—it had been to *him,* Gustav Schmundt, that Hans Kolter had come on the eve of German reunification.

Somehow the West German leader had arrived at the idea that Schmundt, though a loyal Communist during the former era, was a moderate and might be someone who could help him shape the new German state. Gustav was not one to argue. There weren't many options open to one such as he, not considering his age and background. But Kolter didn't even seem to know about his *Stasi* past, and Gustav wasn't about to tell him.

The offer Kolter made was a simple one. In exchange for Gustav's support and a full renouncement of Communism on his part, the chancellor would exert his influence toward Schmundt's election to the new Bundestag of a united Germany. He needed a strong coalition, he said, made up of a few well-thought-of former DDR leaders as well. He had been watching Schmundt, he said—though Gustav wasn't sure how much of Kolter's blandishments to believe!—and felt he would be a great asset in the new government.

Gustav had gone along and suddenly found himself the duly elected head of the CSDU Party. Overnight Germany was united, and he was one of its democratically chosen leaders.

How quickly fortunes could shift!

Though the CSDU Party had not attracted a wide following, the fifty to sixty seats it garnered in representing certain of the former DDR's interests served Kolter's purposes well. This 10 to 12 percent of the vote was well in excess of the 5 percent minimum share required for a party to seat its representatives in the Bundestag. And, through the intricacies of the parliamentary system, fate had suddenly placed upon the CSDU a pivotal role in the BRD's affairs, with the potentiality upon it to make the swing vote—and determine the future.

His name would never occupy the international limelight like Kolter's. But Gustav realized that he wielded the reins of a critical cluster of votes that could make or break the very chancellor who had kept him if not from prison, certainly from ignominy.

Gustav Schmundt had become a king maker. He knew it, and he rather enjoyed the status, albeit an invisible status. His name came before the public eye every so often whenever an important vote arose or talk of a no-confidence initiative began to be bandied about by some aggressive newshound. But the rest of the time his face remained unknown.

But there was one who *did* know his face. The thought brought a smile. The very man he now sat waiting to see. The old adage was certainly true: It wasn't how many people you knew, but *who* you knew that made the difference. If power and influence were the game—and who could deny it?—then he had landed on his feet. He had become one of the game's winners. All those years working away in obscurity on the eastern side, and now here he sat about to be stroked and cajoled by one of the world's most important men.

Hans Kolter *needed* him, needed his votes, needed his support. He—Gustav Schmundt—was the man the chancellor had to turn to in order to push through this latest program upon which he had staked so much of his reputation and prestige in the new European alignment.

Power—yes, Gustav had to admit he liked possessing such influence, especially to be able to turn the tables on the egocentric and pompous West German. It had always galled him with a certain acrid bitterness to be so indebted to the chancellor. Kolter was a good enough fellow, but shallow and full of the kind of bluster and aplomb that the public ate up. The reunification of the BRD and the DDR had been the coup upon which his reputation would rest, and he had risen steadily on the wave of the world's adulation ever since, rivaling Reagan, Gorbachev, Bush, Thatcher, and Yeltsin as one of the globe's major players.

But still, Gustav could not help thinking Kolter was not as big a man inside as the largeness of his outer frame would indicate. A hero created by the times, but not a hero who made events march to the drum of his own determination and vision. A second-rate hero, he thought. Perhaps not a hero at all in the true historic sense of the word.

Yet, there he sat—chancellor of a united Germany. Who could deny that he had played his cards skillfully?

And if a shallow man like Gustav Schmundt could not quite divide the annoyance from the jealousy he harbored, who could deny him the luxury? How could a man of his lack of substance do other than envy the good fortune of one who sat at the apex and now relish the thought of turning the tables of indebtedness upon him?

Again his reflections were cut short, this time by Frau Wildig's voice.

29

Changes

. . .

SABINA FOUND HERSELF QUIET AND PENSIVE, IN STRANGE contrast to the noisy vitality of the city all about her. She remembered all those years when she had lived in the east and walked over here, and the back-and-forth emotional metamorphosis she had had to go through in each direction every day. Now the whole of East Berlin, the whole of East Germany itself, was experiencing a similar trans-mutation of its essential character.

There was no such change a pedestrian had to go through at the border these days—walking from vitality into silence. No quiet, empty, somber places were left on the other side. There were people, cars, racket, and building and pounding and shouting and urgency everywhere—even *more* in the former eastern sector, racing now at breakneck speed to close the forty-year gap in as short a time as possible.

Sabina made her way first to her former place of employment, a large dull-looking structure which, when she gazed upon it again, she found surprisingly void of any capacity to rouse feeling inside her, considering how many hours she had spent within its walls. That had been the gray period of her life, before the sun had burst out that wonderful morning in June of 1961.

Almost as if she were reliving it once more, Sabina now retraced the route she had always taken to and from work, pausing for fresh tears and memories and happy prayers of thankfulness outside the buildings that thirty years before had contained offices attached to the American consulate.

Her meeting with Matthew that day would always seem like a

miracle and a fairy tale. They still talked about it and revisited the site every time they were in Germany. The memory would never grow tiresome nor lose its capacity to make her cry. God had been so good to her . . . and her heart was full.

Sabina continued on, following the footsteps she had taken back to her home during those days, through the checkpoint into the eastern sector—the location still visible even in its absence—and on along Leipzigerstraβe, so quiet and forlorn then, so bustling with new life now.

A remaining section of the Wall was being swarmed over by tourists, hacking at it with hammers, climbing, laughing, taking pictures. Sabina walked past. There was no interest for her in the ugly thing, full of brightly painted graffiti. She knew too deeply of the pain, sorrow, and death it had caused to derive pleasure from seeing it immortalized by those chipping off souvenir relics from the past. She wished the whole thing were ground to dust.

She walked further, turning right, then left after three long blocks. She was nearly home now. It was all so familiar, yet so different at the same time, as if she had reentered a shadowy dream she had had while sleeping long ago.

She stopped and cast her gaze all about.

The house she had occupied for so long was gone.

She had half expected it not to survive the years, yet she could still not prevent tears rising to her eyes. The block was empty, though it displayed signs of recent earthmoving activity. A new high-rise apartment building or office complex or parking lot was undoubtedly going to be constructed on the site.

Everything had changed. Sabina was glad. Why then could she not keep the tears away?

Was it because a little part of *her* had passed too, along with the destruction of her former residence? Was it the mere passage of time and the recognition that her own remaining years were not many? Was it knowing she would likely never walk these same streets again?

What could account for the melancholic nostalgia that filled her?

She could not help reflecting pensively about the good life *she* had enjoyed during the years since she was here, while so many *others*— her friends and colleagues among them—had no alternative but to remain under the oppressive regime. The memories of this place were not even particularly happy ones—not until Matthew's exuberant life came to imbue the memories with fairy-tale status.

Yes, she was happy that freedom had come to the East. Why then the tears? Perhaps, she reflected, from reminders of a former life—even further back than when she had lived here—the carefree days of childhood, and with it memories of her parents . . . a life whose joys she would never be able to touch again.

Or was it, she thought further—and as she did she could not prevent a lump rising in her throat—that she feared the same sight might well meet her eyes were she to stand at the site of her childhood home again—the sight of emptiness, the sight of a building that had once contained such life but was now gone, leveled, destroyed . . . returned to the dust, as was slowly happening—one chipped-off souvenir at a time—to the Berlin Wall?

Perhaps it was just as well Matthew hadn't had any success in his efforts. She couldn't bear it if *Lebenshaus* were not still standing.

Quickly Sabina turned and began walking again.

Any more thoughts in that direction were too painful. She would have to face them, but she would do so slowly, one stage at a time.

The Alexanderplatz was about a kilometer away. She would walk there and see how the center of East Berlin life had fared under reunification. As she went, she came to a certain unremarkable street corner and suddenly found herself overwhelmed with a new memory—not of a building or a place this time, but of a face. She had more than once met Hermann at this very spot upon some network business or other.

She hadn't thought of her old colleague during the whole of her walk, and now the sight of his hard-featured and gruff face in her mind's eye brought a smile to her lips.

The dear man, she said softly. *Lord, bless him . . . wherever he is.*

How she wished she knew *where* he was!

But she had never known where he lived. Their meetings had always been at neutral locations such as this or near her home. What was he doing now, she wondered. Was he still in Berlin?

Oh, to see him again!

But how could it ever be hoped for? Except by prayer, she thought.

O Lord—do make it possible! Sabina prayed. *With you even the impossible presents no obstacle! You managed for us all to escape from here back then. Seeing Hermann again would be a far less formidable thing for you to arrange!*

She was coming to the Alexanderplatz now. Already she could see how different it was. The shops and stores teemed with people. A frenetic energy seemed to fill the place, though so different from the bustle on the other side. In the eyes of many could be detected an almost feverish impulse to *buy* and *get* and *possess,* as if the newly acquired freedom to participate in the capitalistic economic system were pleasure enough in itself, whether there was anything of worth to be bought or not. Many of the offerings were noticeably cheap and of inferior grade. The quality of West Berlin's shops had not yet extended so far. All along the sidewalks in every direction sat tables and booths where former soldiers hawked Russian army trinkets and would-be entrepreneurs peddled their T-shirts and caps and souvenir pieces of the Wall.

Surrounded by such majestic and historic buildings from Germany's past, Sabina could not help being repulsed by the tawdry commercialism of the scene. She hailed a taxi and was soon speeding away from it. There were several other places she wanted to visit. But her feet were beginning to tire, and the distance to the cemetery was too great to walk.

30

Chancellor and Politician

. . .

"AH, GUSTAV," THE CHANCELLOR GREETED HIM CORDIALLY. "Thank you for coming over so promptly."

"Your request is my duty, Herr Chancellor," Schmundt replied.

"Please, please," Kolter said, indicating a seat near his, "not so formal, Gustav. We have been through too much in recent years to reduce our friendship to platitudes."

"I am sorry, sir."

"No need for apologies. In any event, it is I who must apologize for summoning you here on such short notice like this. I must be back to Bonn first thing in the morning and I had to see you before my return."

"I assure you it is no problem."

"This is one of the difficulties of maintaining two offices," sighed Kolter, "in Bonn and Berlin. Though these are but temporary inconveniences, I look forward to the time when everything will have been moved over here."

Gustav nodded.

"Even though we represent different constituencies," the chancellor went on in a new vein, "and occasionally must debate across the aisle from one another, we respect one another and have seen too much together to allow that to stand in the way of our friendship. Would you not agree?"

"Of course," replied Gustav.

The chancellor stood and walked to the large window behind his desk. Schmundt remained silent.

"I still find myself caught up in sheer amazement at times," Kolter said after a moment or two, "when I realize what has happened in these last two or three years. Incredible times, Gustav—truly incredible! Can you believe it—we're looking out on a united, free Berlin . . . a free Berlin! Look at it out there—building and construction, cars and buses and trucks, tourists . . . why the city's bursting with life and activity—from the Alexanderplatz to the Kurfürstendam—everywhere . . . east, west . . . throughout the whole city. Life, energy, vigor, vitality! You can see it in how the people move along the sidewalk down there—"

As he spoke, still with his back to Schmundt, the chancellor pointed with animation through the window into the distance. He was altogether oblivious of the annoyance his words raised in the heart of the former East German as he spoke about Berlin's freedom. That was the trouble with the West Germans, Gustav thought silently. They thought of themselves as saviors, not partners. But the chancellor was going on with his monologue, unaware of his listener's skepticism.

"—they even walk with purpose and exuberance and bounce! It's a spirit of zest. I love our people, don't you, Gustav? There's no race like them. I have no doubt they will make your former eastern sector a powerful and invigorating tribute to the German spirit, just as we did here in the fifties."

Slowly he turned and left the window, but with a look of reflection still on his face, unaware of what responses his words were fomenting in the other. "So many changes . . . and in such a short time," he sighed. "Almost from the instant of our friend Mr. Gorbachev's ascension to power, the dominoes began to fall, but in reverse order from what the Americans always used to fear! Momentous events—new freedoms in Russia, elections . . . the waves of public demands in the East, the toppling of the Wall, the crumbling of the Soviet Union, and now the reunification of our own nation. Where is it leading? What will be next? Where does the future lie . . . and in whose hands?"

A long silence followed, during which the chancellor made his way back toward his visitor, at length settling into a chair opposite him. "It lies in our hands, Gustav," he said seriously once he was seated. "Perhaps as at few other times before, individual men have decisions before them that can truly alter the course of history. I believe you and I are in such a position—Hans Kolter and Gustav Schmundt . . . two friends and politicians brought together a short time ago by the swift changes of global events, and now thrust side-by-side into the very center of world affairs. . . ."

As he listened, Gustav kept a cautious ear tuned to the political realities underlying Kolter's cajoling words. Spreading the butter on a bit thick was the usual preparatory exercise preceding some request. He would wait before he allowed himself to feel *too* elevated in stature by the chancellor's words.

". . . rife with opportunities," Kolter was saying, "like no other time in history for Germany. Hitler was a maniacal madman. He set the fatherland back a half century or more. But now we have again reached the acme where we can step fully into our calling as one of the great nations in the history of the world. New demands now fall upon us, Gustav, as part of this heavy responsibility. Demands of leadership. New relationships must be forged throughout the world community. What is the direction of the EEC, and who will now be involved? With the breakup of the Soviet Union into its constituent republics, how will those multifaceted relationships and alliances fit into both the world picture and the European picture?

"Leadership, Gustav. Leadership! That is the key to the future. There is indeed what Mr. Bush has termed a new world order. No one denies that. But where will the leadership come from to take this new world into the twenty-first century?

"No doubt you see what I am driving at. The leadership will come from *us,* that's where. From Germany, from Berlin, from the chancellery and the Bundestag . . . from this very office, Gustav. *This* is the focal point of the future, of this new world order."

He stopped and drew in a deep breath, clearly impassioned about what he was saying. "The Bundesrepublik was a forceful entity, certainly. And similarly, and with all due respect to your former allegiance, the DDR was the leader of the Eastern Bloc in every way. But now, a united Germany possesses a might beyond what any of our predecessors ever dreamed possible. With the Soviet Union effectively out of the picture, Germany has become *the* major player in Europe. Three nations control the course of events now, Gustav—the United States, Japan, and ourselves.

"It is awesome, almost frightening in a way when you think of it, but Japan is so small . . . how long will it be capable of sustaining its present economic boom? It has nowhere to grow, no manpower resources to tap beyond its own. And eventually the energy of this burst of its creative and industrial spike will begin to wane. It is inevitable that it cannot keep pace forever.

"Do you see what I mean, Gustav—we are in the driver's seat. Even the U.S. is in a slow, protracted decline. We owe them a great deal, and it is in the interest of world stability that the U.S. and the North Atlantic alliance remain strong. But more and more in coming years will rest with us. We must steward this leadership trust with care. We must guard and protect the world's resources—natural, financial, and the resources of man's energy and vision as well.

"All this brings me to the reason I asked to see you this evening, Gustav. I need to speak with you about the situation coming up next week, to make sure I may still count on the support of your people in the CSDU. Do things still look good, Gustav?"

"As good as they could look at this preliminary juncture," replied Schmundt.

"Not so preliminarily," rejoined Kolter, with a hint of exasperation in his tone, though he quickly masked it. "A decision is scheduled next week," he went on. "This vote on aid to the Russian republics is critical, Gustav. It could well set the course for the very survival of those young, struggling nations. And it will set an example of assistance for the rest of the world to follow. I need to be sure your people are fully on board with me. The opposition is going to fight me on it tooth and nail."

Gustav nodded noncommittally.

"Klaus is determined to oppose me no matter what the cause," Kolter went on. "I think he would oppose me even if inside he favored a certain bill, just to spite me. He's determined to undermine my support. He's going to have the other minorities with him on this one, I think," he added, throwing Gustav a sly grin, "he's *probably* already been doing his best to woo you too!"

"There are no secrets in either Bonn or Berlin," replied Gustav, returning the smile. Both men knew more than they were willing to openly admit.

"In any case," the chancellor went on, "you and I have always maintained an *understanding* together. You haven't let me down, ever since I managed to pull you out of the wreckage of the DDR during those last months and get you elected to the new Bundestag. You've been the staunchest ally a man in my position could ask for, and I want you to know I am very grateful."

"Thank you, sir."

"So you see how important this particular vote is, Gustav. It's vital, not only for the republics, but for me as well, for my prestige both at home and abroad. So important that I felt it justified my calling the Bundestag back in for special session. I make no secret of it to you, my friend, you are the one holding my coalition together. My leadership is sound, and Germany's voice in world affairs is listened to largely because of you. That's why I said earlier, it's the two of us—Kolter *and* Schmundt—who jointly hold power to steer events in the right directions. That is why—"

He was interrupted by the sound of his secretary's voice through the intercom on his desk. *"Entschuldigung, Herr Chancellor,"* she said. "I am terribly sorry to interrupt. But Herr Raedenburg has just telephoned, and I know you do not like to miss his calls."

"He's on the phone now?" asked Kolter.

"Yes, sir."

"Thank you, Helga. I will speak briefly to him," replied the chancellor, rising and moving toward his desk. He picked up the receiver. "Gentz," he said, smiling. "How are you? . . . Yes. Today? . . . I see. . . . Of course I do want to see you when you are in town. Unfortunately I have to leave for Bonn in the morning. . . . Ah, good, a week—yes, I will be back while you are still here. . . . I understand. Conferences always tend to squeeze one's schedule dry—just like politics."

He went on listening a moment or two more.

"I see," he said at length, ". . . yes . . . yes, that sounds good. Set something up with Helga, and I will look forward to seeing you upon my return."

He set down the receiver and rejoined Schmundt. "Do you know Gentz Raedenburg?" he asked as he resumed his seat.

"Only by reputation," replied Schmundt. "We've never met."

"A fine man," said Kolter. "He and I go back years. As committed to his beliefs as anyone I know. He's in town for a religious convention."

Gustav nodded in acknowledgment but said nothing. In truth, he could not have cared less either about Raedenburg or the gathering of some religious fanatics.

"Getting back to the point I was making," the chancellor went on, "you and I hold the cards, Gustav, to make sure the proper things are done for these people. They've been through a rugged winter, as you know, and their economic problems are still severe. They need our help, and I am committed to leading the world community forward in providing it."

He rose abruptly, signalling that the interview was drawing to an end. "So . . . I may count on you, may I not, Gustav?" he said, extending his hand for a closing handshake, as if to seal once more the alliance that held the Bundestag coalition together.

"You have always been able to do so, Herr Chancellor," replied Gustav, rising to his feet also. He shook Kolter's hand, then exited the expansive office the way he had come and going outside the building into the breezy air of the waning afternoon.

3 1

Questions

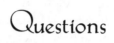

• • •

WHILE SABINA CONTINUED HER PRAYERFUL VISIT
through the great city sitting at the center of the German psyche and
so much a part of her own past, and as Gustav brooded over his
meeting with the chancellor, Matthew sat listening to a talk that had
sent his brain in as many diverse directions as his wife's.

". . . collapse of Communism has brought freedom to many," the
speaker was saying. "Yet with it there has also been a collapse of what
I might call a certain societal matrix, a fabric which, though it was
woven together with threads of fear and dictatorship and deprivation
and hopelessness, yet managed to hold together all the constituent
elements of those eastern societies in a semblance of structure and
predictability. Though there was not freedom in the sense in which
we in the West would define it, most of the people had food with
which to survive. The gulf between top and bottom stratas was not so
clearly accentuated.

"Yet almost instantly with the collapse of the U.S.S.R.'s hold, this
gulf began to widen. The streets of Warsaw, Prague, Budapest, Krakow,
Bucharest, and many others have been suddenly filled with that most
Western of blights—the homeless. These are societies and nations in
great flux. With freedom to travel has come movement. Gypsies of the
east have emerged—vagrants, wanderers, nomads, all with no place to
lay their heads. The cities have become the desert of their migrations.

"Herein, my friends, lies our greatest challenge, the greatest opportunity for evangelism of our era. These are hungry people—we
must feed them. They are thirsty—we must take them drink. They
have no shelter—we must provide them places to go. They are

cold—we must wrap blankets around their shivering frames. They live in despair—we must show them we care.

"We are the hands of the gospel!

"To us has been entrusted the challenge: 'Whatsoever you have done to the least of these, my brothers, you have done it also unto me.' This must be our charge, our banner, the clarion call of our hearts and our voices—the beacon of light toward which we point with vision and purpose. We have been charged to go into all the world with the message of hope, and to feed, clothe, visit, shelter, and give drink to those in need. Such is the core of the New Testament message, upon which our Lord based entrance into the very hereafter itself.

"We cannot, therefore, take his words lightly. Feed, clothe, and give shelter. He has pointed the way himself. Thus our pathway is also clear. And the mission field of this great endeavor is before us—walking the concrete pathways of emptiness all day and all night, in an unending drift of hopelessness."

He paused, took a drink of water from the glass in front of him, then went on after a quick glance at his watch.

As he did, Matthew could not prevent his mind drifting off. He found himself thinking about Sabina's father, as snatches of the presentation filtered through into his brain sporadically.

". . . open vast doors for us among the poor, the destitute, the homeless. . . . We must send *people* who are equipped to meet the needs I have spoken of. Individuals with language training, medical training, psychological training—people whose hands and voices can get in and penetrate and significantly *touch* the point of need. . . .

". . . *Supplies* of ministry—food, water, blankets, medicine, gloves, shirts, shoes . . . gather and send material *things* with which to carry out our commission. . . . of necessity entails food drives and fund-raising and clothing and blanket donations back home—in our parishes and churches and communities. A network of giving must be established that can provide a continuously renewing supply. . . .

". . . places from which to dispense ministry and life and food and warmth and shelter, facilities out of which to operate, in which to store the goods we will disburse, and facilities to which we may actually bring those in need. . . . the need for beds, the need for food kitchens and eating rooms. . . .

". . . key is people—men and women with Christian hearts of

compassion and charity—who are willing to lay down their comfortable lives of affluence and ease and go to these places where the need
is so desperate. People who . . ."

As Matthew glanced around at the others in the room, some were
taking notes. One or two had pocket tape recorders in their hands.
Nearly all sat spellbound. The speaker's enthusiasm was boundless and
could not help but make you want to rush up and volunteer for his
program the minute he was through.

When the talk was over, several people went forward to ask
questions and discuss further, while the rest filed out. Matthew and
Tad met afterward.

"How was yours?" asked Matthew.

"Oh, halfway as I expected," answered Tad. "Here is *the* best
approach to reaching the world that *everybody* ought to adopt."

"Which was?"

"Witness and salvation tracts, and books geared toward pressing
people to make a decision and invite the Lord into their life—that
kind of thing."

"I thought it was going to be about the new world order."

"So did I," laughed Tad. "But that was only the entrée into a
standard pitch on evangelism, with the need to get zillions of things
printed up right now in all the Eastern languages for instant giveaway
and distribution all over the place."

Matthew laughed lightly. "That's just the opposite of what I
heard."

"So tell me, what was your workshop like?"

"Actually, pretty interesting," replied Matthew as they sat down.
"Very interesting, in fact. It was so good it should have been one of
the keynote addresses before the whole conference. He's a dynamic
man, there's no doubt about that, and with lots of suggestions that
seem very practical. Important things that ought to be done—need
desperately to be done, in some cases. And yet . . . I don't know—
there's. . . ." His voice trailed off.

"A dimension missing?" suggested Tad.

"I'm not sure *missing* is the right word," replied Matthew. "Don't
get me wrong—I think what he said was good. I just found myself so
conscious of how different all this is"—he gestured widely in indication of the hotel and the conference—"from the perspective on

reaching the world—*really* impacting the world as the followers and disciples of Jesus Christ—that your grandfather espoused."

"Yeah," agreed Tad, "I can't imagine Grandpa putting together a conference like this."

"You are quite right there, Tad. The baron would have invited everyone to *Lebenshaus* to rest and explore the gardens with him, but he would never have attempted something so . . . grandiose." Matthew shook his head. "I am sure some people are getting a lot out of this conference, don't get me wrong. But I just am not sure that the help-people approach I heard *or* the get-people-saved approach you heard will turn this world upside-down."

Matthew stood up. "Let's get some coffee before the next session. I think I need to reflect on this some more. It seems that every session I attend raises more questions than it resolves."

32
Reflections

• • •

GUSTAV SCHMUNDT LEFT THE BUILDING HOUSING THE provisional chancellery office with a gnawing feeling somewhere in the region of his stomach that *Reichschancellor* Hans Kolter had been subtly toying with him.

It was probably not even intentional. As he had become more at home with the power he wielded, Hans had taken upon himself certain condescending mannerisms which were no doubt inevitable consequences of his steadily enlarging ego. He displayed the consummate German arrogance, thought Gustav. And he didn't like its being directed at him.

All that smooth talk about them sharing power together—bah! Kolter didn't believe a word of that nonsense any more than Gustav did himself! They never saw one another unless a close vote was upcoming, and then Hans always poured on the syrup.

He didn't appreciate being taken for granted. He'd been in that position for years in the DDR, and once Kolter had thrown his influence into his election here, he'd been all but forgotten . . . except at vote time. Hans knew he'd bring in the CSDU's votes on his side . . . he always did. He had to.

Like it or not, he owed Hans Kolter. Even his condescending and pompous overconfidence could never alter that fact. Without Kolter's influence in 1989 and 1990, Gustav Schmundt would be nowhere right now—maybe even in prison if his *Stasi* background were ever learned. But he'd managed to destroy all documentation leading toward him with regard to the secret police force's more questionable activities in the late fifties and early sixties, and as far as Kolter knew he had never been anything but a midlevel East German bureaucrat.

He had to keep it that way by going along with the chancellor. Even if his past secrets were never discovered, one word from Kolter and his political life would be over. He was an old and uninteresting former East German whom no one would spend the least sympathy on when it came time for him to be replaced in some future election by a younger man.

Hans Kolter had him in the palm of his hand!

Sometimes he wished things had turned out differently. He hadn't minded the Communist system so much. His life hadn't been so bad, he supposed, all things considered. But since it had changed, better his present position than anything else, so he was grateful to Kolter, even though he sometimes despised him.

Yes, he probably did owe Hans his life. And the chancellor never let him forget it. The references were always subtle, to be sure. But one way or another, whenever a critical vote was called for, he knew just where to apply a bit of pressure. It might be nothing more than his tone or the glance of the eye that let Gustav know what he really meant—that he remembered, too, and would never let him forget Honecker's fate.

Men of Kolter's kind had their way of getting their psychological clutches into you and then never letting go, tying you to them in a twisted patrimonial kind of bondage, overlaid with layers of unspoken obligations. They were not easy pressures from which to free oneself, and Hans Kolter was a master of the game. He had exerted them upon men and women all over Germany. Probably all successful politicians did. That's how they were able to stay on top—by knowing how to coerce people into doing their bidding, by the constant return of favors many times over.

How many times would he have to repay Kolter for his political survival? Gustav didn't know. Would he ever have the courage to vote against him? All Gustav knew was that he was tiring of feeling so indebted to a man he knew looked down upon him!

He resented being treated as a boy . . . especially when he was the one holding the Kolter coalition together. He'd been a good soldier. He'd delivered the vote every time. Wasn't it about time he received some respect in exchange?

But going against Chancellor Hans Kolter could be a dangerous game. If he misstepped at this late stage of his life, Gustav's career in politics—his career in anything!—would be over in an instant. Kolter was not the kind of man you wanted for an enemy, especially as high as his stock was presently riding in the world market. If he made a switch, Gustav thought to himself, he had better make sure he chose the right side!

That was why the clandestine appointment he had later this evening was so vital. The future of many people, and that of his own skin, was riding on the outcome.

33

A Talk over Dinner

* * *

SABINA RETURNED TO THE WESTMARK DURING THE FINAL hour of workshops. Matthew found her waiting for him afterward in their room.

"How was your afternoon out on the town?" asked Matthew after they had greeted.

"Pensive," Sabina replied with a quiet smile. "And yours here?"

"The same," answered Matthew.

"I want to hear about it."

"And I yours. But right now, do you feel like some dinner? Joseph and Tad are scouting out a couple of places. We're supposed to meet them in the lobby in twenty minutes."

"Oh," groaned Sabina, "my feet are so tired!"

"We could order room service."

"No—I don't want to spoil the party. What's a holiday if it doesn't leave you exhausted?"

* * *

Forty-five minutes later the four were seated around a table in the restaurant Tad and Joseph had selected. The waiter had just taken their orders, and the conversation naturally formed itself around the various activities that comprised their day.

"Where did you go on your long walk?" Matthew asked Sabina.

"All the old haunts," she answered. "You know—where I used to work, where you and I first met that day, my old house—which is gone now."

"Gone—why? . . . What's there?"

"Nothing, just an empty lot that looks like they're getting ready to build something on it. I walked from there to the Alexanderplatz, then took a taxi out to the cemetery."

"Fischer Street?" exclaimed Matthew. "You didn't!"

"I wanted to see it again," said Sabina. "It's not changed that much—except of course the Wall is down."

"I've got to see it again too," put in Joseph. "I know it's a significant place for the two of you, but you have to remember—that's where I gave my heart to the Lord, and where Ursula and I first met after our separation."

"Maybe we can all go out there together," suggested Matthew.

The others nodded in agreement.

"One thing, Sabina—," added Matthew. "Is E. Brecht's grave still there?"

She smiled. "I looked everywhere . . . but I'm afraid it's gone too."

"I'm not surprised. Still, it would have been nice to show Tad the exact spot."

"Why can't we?" said Joseph. "Whatever may be there now, I for one would be able to walk straight to the place where the good Herr Brecht's grave *used* to be. What about you, Matthew? I'm sure you couldn't forget—you were coordinating the whole thing."

Matthew burst out laughing. "The Lord was coordinating it, not me!" he said. "I was scared to death."

"You didn't show it," said Sabina. "I had full confidence in you. But," she added, "I thought about the past enough today; I want to hear about the conference. Matthew," she said, turning toward her husband, "you said your day was pensive—what did you mean?"

"A workshop I attended," replied Matthew, "where I couldn't keep my attention focused for thoughts about what your father might think of the whole thing."

"What was it about?"

Matthew explained briefly. "But you know what was almost most interesting of all was who was there as much as what was said."

"How do you mean?" asked Joseph.

"For one thing, the room wasn't even half-full—twenty-five, maybe thirty people was all. And this fellow is very well known in some circles—been written up in several of the major news magazines, a major figure on the world scene. Yet here he is, and it's as if no one knew it. I didn't see a single person I knew, and no one seemed to recognize me either."

"Your feelings hurt, Dad?" kidded Tad.

"Of course not," exclaimed Matthew. "You know better than that. What I meant was, there didn't seem to be many conservative evangelicals there. The presentation was admittedly a sort of standard liberal package—social evangelism. And a very convincing one, the kind of thing fundamentalist church leaders need to hear. But it wouldn't surprise me if the only people there listening were the ones who *already* believed along similar lines."

"That's how it was in all the meetings I attended today," remarked Joseph. "I hadn't thought of it until you mentioned it, but you're right—people go to hear what confirms positions they already have, more than to learn and be exposed to new ideas."

"Exactly," rejoined Matthew. "Christians rarely mix it up. For this thing to work there needs to be cross-pollination of ideas and methods and personalities, not just staying within one's own little clique. The people who should have been at the lecture I went to were probably all off hearing about things they're *already* doing and *already* comfortable with. Where's the challenge in that?"

"How was what he said?" asked Sabina.

"It was terrific. Good suggestions . . . important things. And yet . . . I don't know—when you hear a rousing talk like that, something remains one-dimensional. I mean, he never mentioned the gospel once—nothing about evangelism per se. No salvation, nothing about prayer, about the power of God to save lives. It was all about food and blankets and cups of cold water. All good things, things Jesus told us to do."

"What's your complaint with it then, Dad," asked Tad, "if they are things Jesus told us to do?"

"No complaint against the doing of good itself. God forbid I should speak against that. Christians don't do a fraction of what they ought in that regard, and in that light I applaud his message. My complaint, I suppose, is in calling it *evangelism*. If you're going to call that evangelism all by itself, it strikes me as a little like evangelism without any *message* of evangelism. It's doing good, and we're *supposed* to do good. It's exactly what Jesus told us to do. But I'm not sure you can automatically call it *evangelism* because it is doing good. The hands and actions of it, perhaps, but not the words, the content."

"On the other side of it, however," said Joseph, "I get so weary of listening to the evangelicals who preach nothing *but* the *content,* to use your word—the *message* of evangelism and salvation—when there's so little in the way of cups of cold water to a thirsty world to accompany it."

"Don't we all weary of it," agreed Matthew.

"That standard evangelical message goes down with great difficulty among my people," Joseph went on. "In my work with Jews through the years, that's the thing I constantly run into—negative reaction to the content of Christian preaching that is perceived to exist in a vacuum."

"It's a balanced ministry to the world's need of God's love that fully brings in both aspects," said Sabina. "That's what is needed."

"Yet you just don't hear that kind of balance articulated very often," remarked Tad.

The conversation was interrupted by the arrival of their dinner.

"I want to know about Ursula," said Sabina after they had prayed and begun eating.

"She's well," replied Joseph. "Heartsick not to be here with you," he added.

"I doubt she's all *that* heartsick," laughed Sabina, "with a new granddaughter to care for."

"Well, that is true," said Joseph, smiling. "But . . . may I let you in on a secret?"

"Please!"

"We spoke by phone earlier. Everything is going well there, so there is a chance she will be able to join us here in Berlin later."

"Oh, Joseph—that's wonderful!" exclaimed Sabina in delight.

The conversation continued about families and personal matters for a while, but by the time dessert had been served, they were once again deeply involved in a discussion of how most effectively to spread God's life in the world.

Matthew had just commented on Baron von Dortmann's influence in his own father's life, independent of any overt attempt on the baron's part to proselytize.

"Exactly. Just look at us," added Joseph, nodding in Matthew's direction. "Neither of us are Christians today primarily because of the content of some message preached at us, but because of the living example of two men—an example that was so vivid we could not ignore it. Wouldn't you agree?"

"Certainly," assented Matthew.

"That's one of the reasons nothing was going to keep me from coming to this conference—besides the chance to see you all again!"

Matthew and Sabina laughed.

"Do you mean there's a bigger draw here for you than us!" said Matthew, mimicking shocked disbelief.

"I have been praying for an opportunity to see Dieder Palacki again for all these years. I *have* to shake his hand, look into his eyes, and tell him what his compassionate ministry and his piercing words accomplished in my life."

"There is nothing so powerful to change men's lives as when one of God's people truly lays down his life for another," said Sabina.

It fell silent for a moment or two around the table as each reflected on her words. She was obviously thinking of her father and all the lives that were still being impacted from his lifetime of sacrifice.

"What do you mean by *piercing words?*" asked Tad after the pause.

Joseph smiled. "Let me simply say that Dieder Palacki is the kind of man who speaks his mind when he feels God has given him something to say. If you have the humility to listen, the effect can be life changing. I can't claim to have had much humility when he spoke to me. But I had been searching for so long that I was desperate enough to give anybody a fair hearing."

"Back to what you said a moment ago," said Matthew. "Yes, I would agree that it was the example of Sabina and both her father and her mother that drew my father and me to the Christian faith more than a specific message of salvation, per se. What they *said* made sense, of course, and rang true. But that wasn't the first thing that caused us, as non-Christians, to stand up and take notice."

"It's *life,* not words, that draws men's hearts to the Father," said Joseph. "That's what you and I need to try to communicate on that panel later this week. If my search for a rational faith is to provide any perspective on evangelism at all, it's that faith must emerge out of *life.* "

3 4

Night Meeting

• • •

NINE HOURS AFTER THE MEETING BETWEEN GUSTAV Schmundt and the German chancellor, in a seedier part of Berlin than where the former now waited for the time to pass, checking his watch and peeking outside to the street below every several minutes, another man hastened along a half-lit deserted sidewalk carrying a small parcel under his arm.

In truth, though the street-watcher knew nothing of the existence of the street-walker, the latter knew a great deal about the former. The nervous politician, in fact, was the very reason Claymore had come to Berlin, having flown in only two hours before, and Schmundt was the subject of the confidential packet he now held in his grip. He was on his way to a rendezvous with the same man, in fact, whom Gustav himself would see before the night was out.

Claymore had instructions to walk to the Brandenburg Gate in the center of Berlin, in that which had formerly been the eastern sector, then to make his way south along Grotewohlstraße, then east to Behrenstraße through the maze of tall, stone-block buildings now housing a few makeshift offices of the new joint German government, right along Friedrichstraße, until he came to the region of his own hotel.

A car would pull alongside him somewhere on his route, he had been told. He was to get in. If the car did not come, he should return to the hotel and wait.

No car came.

After thirty minutes he arrived back at the hotel from which he had recently taken a taxi to the Brandenburger Tor.

He entered the lobby, passed through without glancing at the desk clerk, then took the stairs two at a time to the second floor. The threadbare carpet on the stairs and corridors was barely enough to keep his steps from echoing his presence throughout the building.

Inserting his key in the lock, he opened the door of his room and walked inside. The accommodations were far from deluxe. He flipped on the forty-watt overhead light and sat down, irritated at the wasted hour he had just spent out walking the streets.

Two minutes later the phone in the room rang. He let it go two or three times before finally lurching himself to his feet, walking to the small desk where it sat, and picking up the receiver. He held it to his ear, but did not utter a word other than, *"Ja."*

"I see you made it to Berlin on schedule," the caller said.

"A schedule which could have included an hour's nap," snapped the occupant of the room, "if you hadn't sent me out on that wild-goose chase. Why did you tell me to go to the gate if you had no intentions—"

"Relax, Claymore," said the other, with a deep-throated chuckle. "It was all for your own good."

"My good! I don't need that kind of exercise. Why didn't you meet me out there sooner?"

"I have my reasons. I was watching you."

"Watching me? If you didn't trust me, then you—"

"Relax . . . relax! I just had to make sure you weren't being watched or followed by someone else. The stakes are high in this game, and I'm not about to take any chances. Do you have the dossier on my colleague of the Bundestag?"

"I have it," barked the undercover investigator and killer.

"His past, as you spoke of . . . the documentation?"

"It's all here."

"Good. Leave it outside the door."

"Outside the door! Are you crazy?"

"It won't be there more than ten seconds. I'm close by."

"And the money?"

"I'll leave it. I'll rap on the door, you wait fifteen seconds, and then you can open it."

"How do I know it'll be enough?"

"I'm not through with you yet. You said you were still looking and might have more later?"

"That's right."

"Then there'll be more when that time comes. In the meantime, if what you find in the packet is not sufficient, you can put me on the top of your hit list. But I think you'll find it worth the time you have spent."

Claymore did not reply.

"You remember I mentioned Moscow?" the caller went on.

"I remember."

"I want you to go there."

"To do what?"

"Just call me on my private number and let me know how I can reach you. Then sit tight. I'll be in touch."

"Will it be surveillance or a hit?"

"It might be both. Be ready for anything."

3 5

Lateness

IT WAS NOT HIS FIRST MEETING WITH KLAUS DREXLER BY any means, though certainly the most important. And never had he seen the man under quite such unusual circumstances.

Nobody exactly called him the second most powerful man in Germany, though that is what, in practicality, he was. He was actually on about the same political level as Schmundt himself, an MP and leader of his party. Drexler hadn't even been in the Bundestag a full three terms yet and had only been head of his party for one. In a sense, some people still regarded him as a relative newcomer to the national scene, and he was completely unknown outside the borders of Germany. But those who thus underestimated him had not looked deeply into his eyes. A fire burned there that spoke of larger things than one might have seen on the surface.

Gustav had seen it. Once he had he would never underestimate Klaus Drexler again. He knew that despite surface appearances and his own parliamentary seniority, Klaus Drexler was a man in the path of destiny. When his time came, Gustav wanted to be sure that he was on the right side of the fence.

It had been Drexler who had contacted him and set up the late-night interview. He had sent a car, whose driver said nothing as they threaded their way through the silent streets of Berlin. Now Gustav found himself, not without a slight sense of trepidation, climbing the stairs to the second floor, where Drexler's office was located.

All evening Schmundt had tried to prepare by telling himself that he had nothing to feel intimidated about and that he was the more experienced of the two. Yet try as he would, he could not quite succeed in removing the sense of intimidation that insisted on rising from deep within him. He walked down the long silent corridor, painfully aware of the echo of his footfall, stopped before the large closed door, took a deep breath, then lifted his closed hand.

The knock was more tentative than he had planned, but sufficient.

A commanding voice from within answered. He opened the door slowly and walked inside.

"Gustav," said his host warmly in greeting, walking toward him with outstretched hand, "so good of you to come! I am most appreciative . . . sit down, please!"

Schmundt thanked him, and did so.

"Coffee?"

Gustav nodded, and watched as the other man poured out two cups from a wet bar at one side of the office, then brought one to him. The other man stood six feet tall, perhaps six-one. His height was not extraordinary—Kolter was six feet four inches and of much larger girth. But the man before him possessed what he would call stature. He carried himself with absolute confidence in every inch of his being.

A fine, thick crop of light brown hair came down to just above his ears, neatly parted slightly off-center, dry and full and clean, not a strand out of place, and only the beginning hints of gray just above the sideburns. His healthy supply of thatch came sufficiently low so that the forehead under it did not have much room to reveal itself, though its lines that could be seen were expressive and showed no traces yet of the furrows of age. Below them, thick eyebrows—darker than the hair above—moved about in subtle expressiveness, accentuating the eyes they seemed almost to surround. High cheekbones framed the eyes below and rested calmly above chiseled, indented cheeks, whose bottommost portions revealed not a trace of excess jowl-fat, flowing into a sturdy, slightly squared, and bony jaw. The impression was of handsome strength. The lips were as full as a man's ought to be, but no more, prone to a protruding motion with German exaggeration of vowel sounds.

The voice coming from deep in the throat was smooth, not especially loud, yet authoritative, reminding the listener of the powerful Wagnerian King Wotan in *Der Ring des Nibelungen,* holding back, awaiting his triumphant entry into Valhalla, a Thoroughbred in rein. The timbre, though subdued for a time, confirmed great repositories of sinewy vigor behind it. An unmistakable magnitude of authority existed below the surface that was apparent without the pretense of volume a lesser man might have used to mask his insecurity. The overall effect would have been pleasing to a Hollywood studio as a perfect example of the hardy, well-proportioned northern European.

The eyes, however, were the most prominent feature of all, recessed into deep-set caverns of skillful expressiveness. Out of their depths shone two orbs of pale blue light, so full of the dance of fiery life that upon initial contact the unsuspecting observer found himself caught in the mesmerizing, hypnotic web of the man's penetrating and probing gaze.

Gustav Schmundt knew of the effect of those eyes, however, and thus avoided their direct onslaught as they now zeroed in on him. He let his own gaze find temporary rest on the mouth, the forehead, or even to flit momentarily about the room. He knew the eyes were seeking his, but he resisted the impulse to let them lock on to his own.

A silence followed while Drexler took a seat adjacent to Schmundt, and both men took several tentative sips from their cups. Drexler seemed to be pondering the best way to begin. His forehead and black eyebrows creased in thought. At last he looked up. "Gustav," he said, "I want to confide in you."

Schmundt sat listening attentively, cautious but intrigued.

"As you know," he went on, "I am opposed to our esteemed chancellor on the matter of aid to the Soviet republics. I have my reasons, and this is not the time to detail them now. You no doubt are well familiar with all sides of the issue, and I know you have been carefully considering it as well."

Schmundt nodded.

"However, it is not specifically with regard to the matter of the upcoming vote about which I want to speak with you, but rather of larger concerns. This particular vote will come and go, alliances will form on each side, you and I and Hans and the other party leaders will coax and cajole our people, and in the end some arrangement will come to exist between the various parties and all the members of the Bundestag, and the matter will be decided.

Perhaps Hans will win the vote and get the aid package he is requesting. Perhaps I will be able to prevent it.

"But bigger issues are at stake—in the long run, I mean, Gustav. It is a new world, a new age. I believe that over the next few years, international alliances and friendship will be very fluid. Times of great change are coming, and I for one want to be ready for them, for the sake of my constituency and for the sake of all the German people. That's why I felt that it would be useful for you and I to have an understanding between us, so that our mutual leadership—might I even be so bold as to say our mutual friendship, Gustav?—can be instrumental in helping to guide the Germany of the future in a direction that is the best for our people, our economy, and our rightful status and position in this new world order that is rapidly coming upon us. Do you hear what I am saying, Gustav?"

"Yes, I believe I do," replied Gustav. "I too am a firm believer in a strong future for our country."

"Not merely strong," Drexler went on, an orange glow almost visible in the midst of the blue of his eyes, the orange of hot embers, of coals fanning themselves to life, "but in a position in the world order to maximize that strength. We people of the German nation are a people of strength and fortitude and power and determination of skill—everyone knows it. German technology, German ideas, German education, German engineering, German theology, German literature—these have existed in the forefront of the world's progress since the ancient days of our progenitors, the Celts. This is a people, a land, a nation of great might and individuality. Would you not agree?"

"Of course."

"But it has been unrecognized, unfulfilled, always having to take a backseat to inferior peoples—the Italians in the fourteenth century, the Portuguese in the fifteenth, the Spaniards in the sixteenth, the French in the seventeenth, the Dutch in the eighteenth, the British in the nineteenth, and the Americans and the Russians in the twentieth. The Russians! Can you imagine us taking a backseat to such an imbecilic, backward culture? It's hard to conceive how such a thing could have come about. Yet—"he paused with a sigh and a thoughtful expression of pain—"our own recent history has been unkind to us, as we all know only too well."

Another pause. "But I believe a new era is coming, a new age of opportunity, where power and progress will not be measured by military might, but along other lines, where the strength of a people's belief will count more than the firepower of their arsenals, where the use of economics will direct more courses of action than armies. And where a people of vigor and energy will be required to exercise the roles of leadership required in this new order.

"Belief, Gustav! Belief in the higher values of the cosmic design, belief in man's ability to harmonize himself with the creation and with his fellows of the global creation. Belief . . . and leadership. Those are the two keys that will unlock the future, that will pave the way for what the Americans call the new world order. And both, I humbly believe, must come from outside the traditional power bases of the past, East and West.

"It is a new era. New dawns rise daily all about us. New interpretations of old beliefs must pave the way. New centers of world leadership must rise to take dominion over the affairs of man.

"So, where do you and I fit in? That is rather more interesting. I confide these thoughts with you, Gustav, because I have long been observing you. And it is my conviction that you are a man of vision, a man who shares my optimistic and bold outlook. And it is men such as yourself with whom I want to ally myself in the days and years ahead. I am not merely hoping for your support on this particular vote next week, though you can see already that the lines of the future are beginning to be drawn over such issues. But as I said, I am looking much further ahead. The panorama is larger for me. I am seeking men I can trust, men who share this radical vision, men who share a dream of Germany's future, a future of leadership in the global community of nations.

"By my assessment, you are such a man—a man of integrity and loyalty . . . and of belief in the new order, of vision, of leadership. Do I make a mistake, or do these thoughts indeed strike a chord deep within you? Do I not gauge you correctly, that you are dissatisfied also with the status quo of the past? Do you not also want to look ahead to a new time? Tell me, Gustav. How do you feel about the future?"

Schmundt could not help being bewitched by Drexler's inflating grandiloquence. Especially coming as it did on the heels of what Gustav had interpreted as one more in a long string of nettling condescensions on the part of their beloved chancellor. It felt good, naturally, to be appreciated for a change, to be recognized for what you were, to be spoken to with respect as a leader, as a man who counted for something significant in the scheme of things. Given Gustav's position and his reaction to his interview earlier in the day with Kolter, who wouldn't feel gratified by Drexler's flattery?

As Drexler sat back in his chair and waited, gazing upon his colleague with the penetrating expression of inquiry, a humble look of expectancy, he gave every impression of desiring intently to know what the other thought, almost as if he, Drexler, were the neophyte, and his guest were the seasoned mentor, the man of the world, whose experience and insights he must have or perish.

In actual fact, Drexler knew precisely what was going through Gustav Schmundt's brain. Had he not been so skilled at hiding it, the corners of his mouth might have revealed the hint of a crafty smile. He knew Gustav Schmundt because he knew men—knew their strengths and weaknesses and foibles and frustrations and tender spots, knew their secret dreams and ambitions, knew their pettinesses and secret hurts and anxieties. But more than knowing him in general, he knew Schmundt well enough in particular also to know what he was doing by the flow of his conversation and his questions. He had chosen his words like a master surgeon selecting a scalpel, and he knew exactly where to slice.

Schmundt had been set up, and Drexler had him right where he wanted him.

Looking Forward . . . and Back

• • •

THE EVENING WAS LATE.

Sabina had awakened after dozing off with a book on her lap about the same time Tad and Matthew had wandered back up to their rooms at the close of the evening's session. All three were physically and emotionally spent. Tad said good night to his parents, then walked down the hall to his room.

"How was it?" asked Sabina.

"Don't ask," replied Matthew. "I should never have gone."

"Do you want to talk about it?"

"Not tonight. It would only deepen my negative attitude."

He sat down on the edge of the bed. He let out a long sigh, glancing again over the conference syllabus.

"Have you decided yet what you're going to attend tomorrow?" asked Sabina.

"No, I'm already worn out after just one full day, wondering what we're even doing here."

"What *you're* supposed to be doing here is giving a talk that will put it all into perspective for everyone else."

Matthew groaned. "Don't remind me."

"You heard what Joseph said—you and he have a responsibility to say what's on your mind."

"Too many questions are pestering me to be able to think clearly about it."

"You have always asked hard questions. Right from the beginning, you asked me and my father questions. You followed my father's advice and learned to probe deeply into truth, beyond the surface. That's what makes you a good writer."

"Don't try to cheer me up with praise!" laughed Matthew.

"It's true—every word," rejoined Sabina. "That's why your perspective is so valuable—you have fought for it and struggled intellectually and emotionally for the ground you hold. So what are you going to listen to tomorrow?"

"Even after all you say . . . I still don't know. What about you—you're registered for the conference too."

Sabina smiled. "It's difficult to concentrate on what some speaker is saying when down inside I'm struggling—as you have been—with what all the change means . . . *for me.*"

Matthew nodded. "I *do* understand, believe me."

"I had been so optimistic that we would be able to go straight to *Lebenshaus,*" Sabina went on.

"We'll get there. I'm working on obtaining Polish visas."

"But you know what I meant—I was optimistic that, perhaps, with all the changes . . ."

Matthew nodded.

"Maybe that optimism is part of the problem," Sabina went on. "Why I'm finding it difficult."

"How do you mean?"

"Deep inside I suppose I knew I would have to make my peace with the past, and the future . . . *sometime*—but I hoped to be able to do so at *Lebenshaus.* It's beginning to sink in that this may be it, that Berlin may be as close to my old home as I'll get. When I was out walking today and saw that empty block where I used to live, it just hit me that . . . that *Lebenshaus* might not even—" Sabina stopped and began to weep softly.

Matthew rose and took a seat beside her on the couch. He placed his arm gently around her. Sabina turned her face to his chest and continued to cry for a moment or two. It was several minutes before either spoke again.

"This may be our last visit here, you know, Matthew," said Sabina softly. "As I've realized that, many emotions about the past that I'd kept at bay have started to infiltrate my thoughts, like a tide slowly coming into a harbor."

Matthew smiled at the analogy.

"It's not just *Lebenshaus*—it's *me*," she continued, "my life, my past, my heritage as a German. It's different being here in the city than down in Bavaria. Berlin itself contains so many memories as well. I spent years here before you came back into my life. When you and I left Berlin, I left part of myself behind. There's all that to think about. It's all so changed. There's a process of having to reflect on my whole life again and what it all means now. I'm nearing the end of my days, and yet Germany is starting its life all over again."

"Of course I can't thoroughly know everything you are feeling," said Matthew after reflecting on his wife's words for a few moments. "Yet in a way it's similar for me—in a spiritual rather than a national way. This conference is stirring up so many thoughts that I'm having to reflect on my life too . . . what I believe, how our perspectives about what it means to be a Christian fit into the larger picture. And too, as you said, recognizing that we are at the end of our lives, and wanting to make sure the legacy of what the Lord has given us and shown us is passed on to future generations of God's people."

"There's a lot to think about."

"Amen," sighed Matthew. "I hadn't really anticipated it."

"I had a feeling the trip might be a time of pulling the threads of life together in a sort of final way," said Sabina. "But of course you never can really prepare for the emotions that accompany such a thing. I watched my father prepare so well for the end of his earthly days, and yet it is something everyone has to go through for himself."

It fell silent between them. Slowly Matthew rose, helped Sabina to her feet, and began changing into his bedclothes. Sabina did likewise.

37

Pawn in the Hands of a Master

• • •

KLAUS DREXLER HAD BEEN HARBORING SECRET DESIGNS and aspirations for years. But things took time, and he knew he had to move slowly. He had to jump each hurdle one at a time, methodically putting the building blocks of the future in place. He would need people. He had always known that.

And thus, as he had risen slowly through the ranks of the BRD's political hierarchy, he had kept his eye peeled for those whom he might gradually begin to enlist and win over—not especially to his way of thinking (that could come later)—but to his person. Make friends of them, that was the first order of business. Win their trust. Then slowly, slowly . . . other elements would fall into line.

Long and slow.

No asinine Beer Hall Putsch tactics like his fool of a predecessor! An ignoramus who thought he was qualified to lead an empire! No, his own strategy was much more subtle and cleverly designed.

And he *had* brought them along. Many were now in his camp, many even from the opposing parties. He was garnering IOUs, developing a bevy of influential leaders throughout the country who trusted him, and, he thought, would trust him when push came to shove.

He had been watching Gustav Schmundt for some time and had had him spied on twice now. He had what he needed if Schmundt proved obstinate. He might not even have to bring in all the ugly details Claymore had unearthed. He would save whatever was necessary for future use, to make sure he retained the man's loyalty as long as he remained a viable player in the German political system.

Schmundt would do his bidding or else find himself in prison as a murderer!

The fellow had enough weak spots and character flaws that he'd be able to twist his psyche up in so many knots that he wouldn't know whether he was coming or going. But he had intentionally refrained from direct overtures for a long time. Schmundt, as head of the CSDU and one whom Kolter trusted to keep his coalition intact, was a relatively big fish, and he had to tread carefully. Alienating either Schmundt or the chancellor prematurely could set him back a good while.

The time at last seemed right.

He had seen Schmundt squirming under the pressure lately. The mole he'd planted within the inner circle of Schmundt's staff a year ago confirmed that his titular boss was annoyed with the chancellor and every once in a while could be heard commenting about what Kolter might think if "I went my own way and voted independently for a change!" He would apply no pressure, just feel Schmundt out, open a dialogue, massage his somewhat delicate and bruised ego.

Thus he had requested this meeting in his office, late enough to protect both their reputations from prematurely prying eyes.

Still he waited, gently trying to draw out the confidence of his guest with his eyes of sincerity and guilelessness.

"I appreciate your generous words," Schmundt replied after a minute's reflection. "And yes, I do share your optimism for the future and Germany's role in it. Of course, I too desire to be part of that leadership."

"You shall, Gustav," put in Drexler enthusiastically. "I am confident of it. It is men such as yourself whom I see as the leaders of the future, men who have served this land of ours for years, who know its people, which is one of the reasons I find myself personally drawn to you and want to ally myself with you. I want to follow in the footsteps of your leadership in the years ahead."

"I—I trust I will—uh, be worthy of your kindness," faltered Schmundt, not prepared for the turn the conversation had taken. "But of course it is you," he went on, "who controls a far larger block of votes in the Bundestag than I could ever hope to. My leadership is paltry beside—"

"Paltry indeed!" interrupted Drexler. "The relative size of our parties is immaterial, Gustav. I'm talking about leadership. Your party is made up of independent thinkers, of free spirits. It will never command large numbers. But it's that independent spirit of leadership I am talking about. You are an independent man, determined to stand for what you believe in. These last years you have stood firm on the principles of the CSDU, knowing that you are in the minority. Dedication! You are a man for the future, a man whose leadership will be recognized one day by the people of this nation. I would stake the future of my own career on it. As you do come into this leadership, Gustav, I want to be there with you. I want to help you achieve your dreams for this nation. I want to put all the power of my own position behind you. I believe in you, Gustav, and I see a bright future for us when we have the opportunity to work together—closely together in the leadership of the future."

"I would like to think you are right."

"Of course I am right."

"But I am not a young man."

"Age is no factor. I seek like minds to lead the world forward. You possess the wisdom of years. The age of light and destiny is approaching, drawing us into its evolutionary vortex. Peace has come to the globe, and out of recent events a new age, a new dawn for mankind, is about to emerge. Mankind's harmony with itself, with nature, with the consciousness of the universe will bring the long history of human development to its apex. I tell you, Gustav, the leaders who pave the way will come from a new generation of leaders raised up throughout the earth, men and women who perceive this purpose and harmony, and who recognize our destiny to take history to the crowning summit of its fulfillment.

"It is my conviction that we can reconstruct society along the lines of ideals only dreamed of by utopian stargazers of the past. With the dismantling of old barriers of hostility and the end of death-producing military alliances, these goals of a global society based on principles of the god-consciousness that has all this time lain dormant within man can be achieved. Toward this has man's long history been pointing.

"To this great cause I have committed myself, to enlighten this nation, and hopefully in time other nations of the world, so that we might provide a searchlight of hope to all peoples of the globe, helping to lead them out of the bondage and limited ways of thinking of the past and into the new era of peace and brotherhood and unity that is at hand. Men like you and I are the leaders who must seize the initiative when the time comes."

He paused, still eyeing his quarry with cunning observation. "So tell me, Gustav," he went on after a moment, "what are your percep-tions about the future and where the German nation is heading? How do you visualize your role as one of its leaders and spokesmen? I vitally want to know how you view these things I am speaking of because, as I said, I am committed to working with you in any way I am able."

Having laid the foundation well, Drexler now sat back and listened, seeking appropriate opportunities to further charm and inveigle the gullible Schmundt.

By the time the older man left some time later, to be driven by Drexler's car back to his home, Gustav Schmundt had been altogether seduced and could hardly have been more thoroughly or willingly ensnared into the latter's camp.

3 8

Bedtime Discussion

• • •

AS THEY LAY DOWN BESIDE ONE ANOTHER IN BED, Matthew sighed. "Wouldn't it be great to have our two fathers to talk to right now—even if it were just for ten minutes?"

Sabina smiled in the darkness. "Yes—one of my only regrets in life is that I didn't have more time to spend with my father."

"Part of growing older, I suppose."

"I doubt they would be able to clear up all our quandaries for us anyway."

"It would be nice to get their perspective, whether they could answer all the questions or not."

"You have to remember that we live in a different world than they did, Matthew. Christianity today, especially living in the States as we have, is so much broader, so intense, more involved than anything my father faced."

"He put his faith on the line more than I will probably ever have to . . . and he went to prison for it."

"Yes, but my father never faced the same issues within Christendom that you wrestle with."

"I suppose you're right. But I still wonder if I've given Tad anything like the same kind of example both your father and mine gave us."

"You know you have, Matthew," said Sabina sincerely. "He looks up to you in every way and respects your faith no less than we did that of our parents. You must be aware that he wants to emulate you."

"Sometimes I can't help having doubts."

"Comparing yourself to my father, you mean?"

"I suppose that's part of it."

"My father was an unusual man," said Sabina.

"That he was."

"You can't compare yourself with him. Besides," Sabina went on, "you are as much a man of God as my father was, and you *have* given Tad much of the same way of looking at things that my father helped give us. I see it clearly. Surely you haven't already forgotten those wonderful things he said to us on the plane ride over here."

"I suppose this conference has stirred up my thinking about everything having to do with passing on one's faith to others—and the extent to which I have done so in the life of my own son and daughter most of all."

It was silent a moment.

"Funny," said Sabina, "my thoughts found themselves in similar channels when I was out walking this afternoon."

"What? You mean about Tad?"

"Yes. Here he is a grown man, and yet I was thinking a lot of the same kinds of things we used to talk about when he and Mary were young, about how faith is planted by one generation into the soil of the next . . . remember?"

"Of course I remember. Those were special times. And Tad has turned out to be a man any father would be proud of."

"And any mother. But still you have doubts?"

"Not about Tad, or Mary either, not about the kind of young man and woman they've become . . . just about whether I've been the kind of influence on them spiritually that I wanted to be."

"I don't know what to say except that you *have*. I see your character and wisdom in Tad in a hundred ways."

"So why were *you* thinking about Tad today?" asked Matthew.

"It wasn't only Tad," answered Sabina. "But as you said—the conference, and being back in Berlin again, has caused so many things to stir up inside me. My father was on my mind too. I just found myself reflecting in many directions."

They lay in the darkness a few minutes in silence, feeling contented and close in one another's arms.

"It's funny, isn't it, to realize we're old now?" said Sabina at length.

"Yeah," chuckled Matthew. "But there's no denying it—our lives are winding down. The cycle of life continues."

"That's one of the reasons my father loved growing things so much—how the whole of life could be seen in such a short span of time. He used to talk a lot about the seasons and the progressions and the cycles. He was always looking for some new lesson nature could teach him. Now it's our turn to look beyond the end of our own cycle, just as he did twenty-three years ago."

"Tad and Mary will live on, just as we have. What have we given them of permanence? What have we passed on from our own parents that will extend on into future generations? How deeply *are* our roots planted into the soil of their characters? Those are questions that suddenly seem so much more urgent than ever before."

"Why now?" asked Sabina. "Tad's a grown man. Mary's a married woman."

"Somehow thinking about evangelism makes that question so much more real. Perhaps being at this stage in our lives makes me wonder what the next forty or fifty years of Tad's life will be like. Thinking about how we have responded to our parents in terms of the legacy they left cannot help but make me think about how Tad and Mary will respond over the rest of *their* lives to what we have tried to build into them. What have our lives meant . . . what will last . . . what is permanent . . . what will live on, not only through Tad, but through others we have known, through the books I have written?"

"Far-reaching questions, Matthew."

"That's why the issues being considered at this conference seem so pivotal. It's got to be about more than just seeing people getting 'converted' to Christianity. There has to be something of longer duration, something permanent that impacts not just the *now*, but that impacts future generations . . . that impacts *eternity*. Your father did that—he impacted eternity. Now I find myself wondering whether I have or not . . . and hoping I have in some small way."

"You have, Matthew—and not merely in small ways."

It was quiet for a long time. Sabina thought Matthew had fallen asleep. Presently, however, she heard him begin speaking again, although this time his words were not directed to her.

"O Father, we do pray that our lives will have mattered in your kingdom," he said. *"We pray that what you have taught us, that what you have shown us, that the life you have given us, will live on, in Tad and Mary, in their sons and daughters, in the generations that follow us. We pray earnestly*

for those future generations, those grandsons and granddaughters that may spring from our lives. O God, cause your life to live on through them. . . . Show us ever more and more of what it means to live for you and to pass on your life to others. Reveal truth to us through this conference, but even more through your Spirit speaking your mind into our hearts."

Musings

• • •

THE SPACIOUS OFFICE WAS QUIET. EVEN THE JANITORS HAD long since gone home. Only a security man or two sat downstairs in front of television monitors.

The building slept.

Slowly Klaus Drexler rose from his chair and walked across the room to the darkened window. He stood for ten minutes, gazing out. Even at 2:00 A.M. Berlin was alive with lights stretching as far as he could see in every direction. Truly this was the heart of the old Prussian kingdom, the domain of the Hohenzollerns—mighty, historic, proud.

The city at the heart of the fatherland—and more! The city at the heart of Europe, at the heart of the world. There was no place on earth like Berlin.

And he stood in its very epicenter! His city—his country!

How had they even imagined they could have run a government from that plebeian little outpost of Bonn? If anything gave clear signal that the hour of his destiny was approaching, the reunification and change of theater was it. He could never have done it from Bonn. That had been a makeshift apparatus at best.

But now here he stood overlooking the center of the empire from which a new global power base would emerge. The crumbling of the Wall, the vote to unite, the disintegration of the Soviet Union, and now here he stood surveying the heart of Berlin—it was all too much to have dreamed of happening so rapidly. Suddenly it was within his grasp and falling into place piece by piece with every passing day.

Klaus Drexler was a man who knew how things worked. America

was so full of its own do-good complex that it would throw money at any defeated adversary. The Americans had rebuilt both Germany and Japan after the Second World War, while watching their and Britain's own industries slowly sink down the toilet. Now their old enemies were rich and healthy beyond compare, dictating the entire world's industrial momentum, while America sank further and further into bankruptcy from incurred debt.

His own countrymen—especially the rising new affluent generation—actually resented the United States, feeling more favorably inclined toward their Eastern neighbors, even though it had been the Soviet Union who had ripped apart their nation and killed hundreds of thousands of German citizens. Yet even that misplacement of loyalty would work to his advantage in the end.

Then too, it was pitifully ironic that even seeing how its generosity had backfired with Germany and Japan, building up newly industrialized powerhouses to threaten its own industry, the U.S. continued to dish out billions in aid all over the world, propping up failing dictatorships, providing money for arms and military technology that would one day be used to kill the very Americans and allies who had supplied it. The foolish Americans seemed bent on giving, giving, giving, until the day they would discover their country bankrupt!

Even though the aid had been to his own nation's benefit and had provided the foundation for his plans, Drexler could not help but consider the Americans saps. That they should have perpetrated such a policy might have been magnanimous and even, all other things being equal, a good thing to do. But to continue doing so to the demise of their own system was nothing short of foolhardy.

Within fifty years there had been a complete reversal. The *haves* gave to the *have-nots* until the haves no longer *had* and were at the mercy of those who fifty years earlier had been plowing through the ashes and rubble of their destroyed cities. Was it some latent form of guilt that kept the Americans throwing money at their vanquished foes?

He had no doubt they would do the same thing in Eastern Europe and the Soviet republics now that they had "won" the Cold War. For fifty years they had spent billions to keep the Soviet Union down, but the moment it collapsed the aid talk began to surface. He was certain they would spend the *next* fifty years pouring money into

Eastern Europe; whether it was in cash or other forms hardly mattered. Grain credits, loan guarantees, subsidies on anything and everything, food assistance programs—the net result was the same.

Such a scenario, in fact, was exactly what he was banking on as the cornerstone of his scheme.

The nerve center of global power and economic might was in for a titanic shift. The history of the Cold War provided the forerunning example of what Drexler was certain would come next.

As Marshall Plan aid had raised the economic powerhouses of the Cold War years from the rubble of defeat, so too would the *next* economic power center emerge from this *new* defeat—Warsaw, Budapest, Bucharest, Belgrade, Prague, Moscow, Kiev, and newly renamed St. Petersburg . . . *these* would be the capitals of industry, commerce, and technology fifty years from now! Out of defeat would grow capitalistic muscle. American aid would succeed in turning Eastern Europe and Russia upside-down as it had Japan and Germany.

With democracy and capitalism in full swing in all these capitals, with the foundation of American dollars and technology and the massive manpower pool available, Poland, Hungary, Czechoslovakia, Romania, and Russia would within a generation or two be as bright and prosperous as Germany had been a few years ago—wealthy, new, rebuilt, productive, dynamic, healthy, and bursting with efficient energy, zero unemployment, multiplying GNP—to the even further detriment of the West, which would succeed in bankrupting itself all the more in effecting this latest in post-hostilities reversal.

There was the factor of national energy as well. Similarly, the new industrialized countries of Europe and the former Soviet republics would be highly motivated. All over Eastern Europe a vitality of energy was waiting to explode, just as Germany's productivity had in the last forty years.

It was in the Celtic and Slavic bloodlines—something in the native character or psyche, pent up all this time under the demotivation of communism, was now ready to burst out. True, maybe it would never match the superior ethic and determination of the Teutonic pedigree, but he had no doubt that the Slavic temperament was ready to set its corner of the world on fire too.

As industry was even then moving in massive realignments to

Korea and Taiwan and China because of the energy of their people, so too would the world's industry gradually shift toward Eastern Europe. There resided eager manpower, lusting not for exorbitant pay and excessive benefits like American workers, but simply hungry to work for the satisfaction of at last being part of a free market economy.

The future would be in the former Communist Bloc and Warsaw Pact countries. With the resources and manpower available, and the money and technology that would be thrown at them by the West, the fulcrum of the future of the world lay somewhere between Warsaw, Budapest, and Prague—heavily influenced, if he had anything to do with it, by Berlin!

And Germany, if she played her cards right, would provide the power base to direct this shift in the world balance of strength, if she didn't bankrupt herself.

That was why he opposed his own chancellor's joint aid package with the French and British and Americans to the Soviet Union's newly independent republics. For Germany to reject it would cause some international flak. But the United States would, after slapping Kolter's hand, pick up the slack, and German hesitancy would eventually be forgotten.

The aid would come. The republics and their Eastern European counterparts would get all the money they needed, and eventually they would forget where it came from.

Likely enough, thirty years from now they would all hate the United States anyway, while laughing all the way to the bank! Meanwhile, Russia's leaders would be loved and adored, everyone forgetting that they were the ones who had squeezed the world dry for fifty years.

How short was the common man's historical memory!

That was the key—let America and whoever else wanted to pick up the tab for Eastern Europe's reconstruction. Germany herself had to remain healthy financially, not give her surplus away. Germany must remain ahead of the curve of events, reserving true clout for herself within the borders of the fatherland, keeping her hands tightly around banks, financial institutions, and the centers of industry.

There were always boundaries and borders in the world, in Drexler's view, and they were always fluid and changing. With the Iron

Curtain suddenly gone, where would the next alliances be? Where would the next lines be drawn?

For centuries the struggle had been essentially between East and West, so graphically illustrated by the Berlin Wall. Drexler looked down again at the city. He imagined he could just see the course where the forty-five-kilometer no-man's-land had snaked its way cruelly through the center of Berlin. Now it was gone. Only two hundred meters of the Wall remained, fenced off as a monument. Outside it a large slab lay on the ground for tourists to hack at.

And the new global destiny would be based on a huge power block that sat right in the middle, neither east nor west, but at the very crossroads between east, west, north, and south—a convergent Eurasian alliance, a newborn twenty-first-century community of peoples!

The Iron Curtain was gone. The new demarcation would extend straight down from The Hague to Zurich, roughly marking out the French-German border. The decaying West of France, Great Britain, and the U.S.—bankrupt from their own good intentions—would be ground into the dust. The financial capitals of Switzerland and the Netherlands—it would be up to them to decide on which side of the line they chose to come.

But the center would lie to the east! In this very city. By the year 2030, he predicted, the whole world would be run from Berlin. London, Paris, Rome, New York, and Washington would be power-and-influence ghost towns. In the very triumph of the capitalism for which they had so ardently fought, they would ultimately be buried. They had given away the store. And they had given it to him!

After some time he turned from the window, returned to his desk, and sat down. Notwithstanding the hour, there was work to be done. He opened a drawer and pulled out several private files. The next week would be critical. He had to keep all the major players moving and coordinated. He flipped through the folders. . . .

Besides Schmundt, there were several lower-level bureaucrats in the Bundestag and Ministries whose roles could not be ignored—Otto Greim of the FDP, Weisskopf, and others.

And then there was Claymore—he was a loose cannon who had been invaluable thus far, but if he went off at the wrong place or the wrong time—well, you sometimes just could never tell about those kinds of people.

The Russian and all the constituent players on his side, the fellow he'd mentioned precipitating a worker revolt in a handful of auto factories, the former KGB man who was loose in the streets trying to unravel the whole thing. . . .

He exhaled deeply. There was still plenty that could go wrong.

A moment's pause more was all it took before his efficient and confident brain shook the melancholy thought away. He grabbed up a blank sheet of paper, then a pencil, and began jotting down notes of everything to be taken care of tomorrow morning.

PART VI

Disunity, Twentieth-Century Style

40

The Approach

• • •

Berlin

LISEL LAMPRECHT SAT BOLT UPRIGHT IN HER BED, BREATH-ing heavily. A nightmare had awakened her. It was not the first such dream she had experienced in the last month, and she was growing weary of them.

She glanced outside. Dawn had begun. She looked at her clock. It read five-fifteen. Slowly she lay back down, breathing more easily, though she could not prevent a few stray remaining fragments from the dream continuing to float like disconnected images in her still-hazy brain.

Lisel had not really been the same since that eventful night when, in the middle of the city, she had climbed the Wall that soon would be no more. Out of the pinnacle of the greatest triumph of her cause, a strange sense of disquiet had begun to creep into her soul. Lisel did not know it at first for what it was. Unease of soul is rarely recognized when its pangs, not unlike those of hunger, first begin to gnaw around the edges of a man's or woman's reservoir of self-sustaining content-ment.

Almost immediately things began to change. Once the euphoria of victory was past, the thrill of activism, protest, and revolution disappeared. Gradually their people began to desert the cause. It no longer drew new, young, energetic twenty-year-olds. What was there to fight for now? Freedom had come. What more purpose could the Alliance serve?

When exactly the horrifying idea first entered her head she did not remember—a year ago, six months. . . .

The thought, in its most germinal form, had stolen in unwanted something to this effect: They had been fighting—so Lisel had assumed—all this time for what they called freedom. Suddenly the Wall was gone, Communism was crumbling, freedom *had* come . . . and, perhaps, would have without their efforts at all.

What had they really accomplished all those years? What had been the use . . . if it was all going to happen anyway? The fact that so few were now even interested in their movement—half its leaders had in the last two years decided to get on with more normal lives—could not help but make one ask: *Was it possible the Freedom Alliance really had nothing of substance to offer . . . and never had?*

From out of the past of her upbringing, then came the further question: If *they* and others like them hadn't been effectual in bringing freedom . . . if, in fact, most of the efforts of half the world against Communism hadn't succeeded in uprooting it, then what *could* account for the sudden shake-up that had toppled one of the globe's two most powerful nations without the firing of a single shot?

Were *higher* forces at work . . . powers more potent than anything the Freedom Alliance could lay claim to . . . authorities and dominions more spiritual than earthly?

Thus, by a circuitous route had the single word *prayer* entered Lisel's brain, through the back door of her past, as a possible answer to her own query. She quickly dismissed the notion as nonsense.

But it was too late. The door had been wedged open a crack, and now additional speculations of a yet more disturbing nature flowed through it to haunt her.

The blitz was led by reminders of her father. She knew what *he* would say—that the freedom God gave was of a different kind, on another plane than merely earthly freedom, more eternal.

She had ridiculed his efforts to give people spiritual freedom along with helping them to the West, yelling to his face that it would never do any good. What good had *her* efforts done either? She had accused him of ineffectiveness. What about her?

Had she really helped anybody either? Was the stinging criticism of her lips now coming back upon her *own* head! Was she now finding herself judged by the same measure of judgment she had so harshly meted out?

Was it possible—she could barely force herself to formulate the notion—that it had been the efforts of people like her father, *Christians praying throughout the world,* that had done more to topple the Wall than all the Freedom Alliances throughout all of Europe?

Lately had Lisel thus felt a rapid drop of the barometer within her emotional being. The weather of change was closing in.

The interregnum when Lisel would have to confront her past was destined to be no pleasant Indian summer, no comfortably mild days in the middle of winter. Black clouds were brewing upon the horizon of her contented springtime. The distant storm had begun to gather that night on the Wall. And now as it slowly made its approach, fierce rain, and perhaps hail, sleet, and icy winds were on the way to see what they could do to awaken her and redirect her steps when she found herself again at that intersection facing her father.

The assault was under way and could not be stopped. She would not be able to keep the encroaching light of self-revelation shut out forever.

Lisel was uncomfortable and did not like it. On this particular morning she felt the inner pressure more keenly than ever.

No—it had only been a dream! she tried to tell herself. *It meant nothing.* She *would* not think about such things!

Just as she had that night on the Wall, again she forced the memory of her father from her mind.

She threw her featherbed from her and jumped vigorously out of bed. She had hardly slept but she would make the best of it. She would go out, she said to herself, thinking to combat the voices of conscience with activity. She would *not* listen to thoughts about the past. Maybe she would walk over to the western side. She would go to a park, maybe have a swim. Perhaps go shopping. She did not have to work today. She would spend the whole day having fun.

She could go out right now, in fact, even if it was only five-thirty. Have coffee and a roll somewhere. She would watch the city come awake!

Quickly Lisel dressed, feeling better already, and within fifteen minutes she was out in the chilly morning.

41

Telethon Evangelism

• • •

AN UNSEASONABLY CRISP CHILL SWEPT THROUGH THE AIR. of course, it was quarter after six in the morning, and Berlin was situated only a hundred miles south of the Baltic. It was hardly surprising that it should be nippy.

Matthew McCallum breathed in deeply.

The night just past had been a fitful one. It wasn't that the subject was unfamiliar of what it meant to transmit the Christian faith. In one sense he had given himself to that very thing for the past twenty years. His heart's desire to pass on Baron von Dortmann's teachings and life's values reduced to exactly that—transmitting faith as it had been transmitted to him. And now here he was with an opportunity to speak to a gathering of church leaders, and yet he felt so out of sync with the directions and priorities on everyone else's minds.

Last evening's video replay in the Bavarian Room of the hotel had triggered the night's round of mental gymnastics. He should have stayed in the room with Sabina. But he had decided instead to attend the video presentation.

There had been Bob MacPatrick, darling of evangelicals the world over, up on a huge wide-screen monitor, making his impassioned plea for donations for Russian and Eastern Bloc evangelism. He had brought in dozens of special big-name guests, had conducted interviews, and had shown film clips. The whole thing had resembled a secular telethon more than a religious program. The campaign that had run on his syndicated television program several months back, called "Evangelize the World 2000," had been hugely successful—raising an unbelievable thirty million dollars for the printing and distribution of gospel literature in Croatian, Serbian, Russian, and a dozen other Slavic languages and dialects. The decision to feature the video here at the conference was no doubt motivated additionally by the fact that MacPatrick was due to fly into Berlin any day and would later in the week personally present Christian leaders from the Eastern Bloc nations checks for financial assistance for their ministries.

Who wouldn't be all for taking the gospel wherever possible by whatever means possible? Matthew asked himself. Who could deny MacPatrick's worldwide impact? That was the whole point of this conference, to take advantage of changing world conditions to rush through the doors of opportunity now existing in the east. As MacPatrick had said on his show, "We cannot anticipate the duration of this tremendous opportunity. We must, therefore, do all we can immediately to send literature and radio and television messages everywhere in an all-out blitz of the gospel message."

Notwithstanding the seeming rightness of it all, Matthew could not help but detect a spirit of self-promotion in the whole thing. Most of the speakers he had heard thus far used every opportunity to plug their own vision and program and books and tapes and products. All in the name of spreading the gospel, of course. But there was such a sense of *"My* way is best so all the rest of you ought to jump in and support what I am doing."

MacPatrick had raised plenty of money, to be sure. But a good deal of it would go into his own organization to purchase new equipment and to further his own publishing and broadcasting empire. Not to mention the ever-important "administrative" expenses that always managed to require plenty off the top. How much of the thirty million dollars would actually result in hands-on evangelism?

If all for the purpose of spreading the Word, then why did Matthew have such an overpowering sense this week of men's and women's egos vying for places of preeminence? He saw the looks in their eyes. It did not take possession of the gift of discernment to realize what drove them. He could detect the faint tones, gestures, and glimpses of self-importance in the midst of the high-sounding jargon of spiritual purpose.

Over and over MacPatrick's voice replayed itself in his memory: "Send us your money; help us save the world by the year 2000!"

Help *us* save the world, thought Matthew. As if God had nothing to do with it. The messages thus far had stressed political changes and windows of opportunity and how much money it will take and who can make the pitch that will bring in the dough. Then *we* will save the world!

Most of the key players at the conference sang the same tune. Money, money, money . . . testaments . . . literature . . . tracts. Who was talking about prayer, about God's doing *his* work among men? Those on the other side of the continuum, those speaking about people's needs, weren't talking about God's role in their programs either.

Where was the balance? Get involved in people's needs but never mention God—that was the evangelism advocated by the one extreme. Arm's length evangelism was the cry of the other. Come on, everyone, send us your money. It's clean and tidy. You won't have to actually *do* any down-and-dirty evangelism yourself in and around where *you* live. Let your money evangelize the world for you. Send cash and let the professional evangelists and preachers and missionaries do it for you.

42

Berlin in Early Morning

• • •

MATTHEW HAD NOW WALKED A GOOD DISTANCE FROM
the hotel, past the huge and modern Europa-Center and beyond on
the Kurfürstendamm Straße, to Breitscheid Platz and Kaiser-
Wilhelm-Gedächniskirche, though he was scarcely paying any attention to the sights around him. He and Sabina had already taken the
time to tour the war memorial at the bombed-out cathedral and had
spent some time in prayer inside the new church next to it. But this
morning he walked on, hardly conscious of the colossal metropolis
stretching itself and coming awake all around him.

The city was truly one of the world's major conglomerations of
people, industry, business, and politics. Here in the western sector,
there was such an evidence of prosperity, and yet signs of moral
decline and seediness were everywhere mingled with the newness of
the streets and buildings.

Eccentrics of every size, shape, color, and inclination lined the
streets. Refugee families wandered about. Musical minstrels playing
the same limited repertoire, with now and then a variation on a tune,
sought handouts whether they possessed any talent or not. Some did;
others had none. Millionaire businessmen on their way to their offices
stepped over homeless beggars still asleep on the sidewalks.

Pervading the entire city was a whole series of flash points,
where opposites met. Democracy and Communism had intersected and for thirty years exchanged angry words right in the
heart of Berlin. Now that the Wall was gone, the same volatility
was present, though not so visible. The hardworking, stoic
German temperament had suddenly encountered a mass infusion

of foreigners. The promise of Western prosperity meeting the needs of the East seemed too much to hope for.

As Matthew walked, suddenly he became aware that he was alongside the very buildings that had long ago housed the U.S. governmental offices where he had been assigned in 1961. It was right here—in the next block—where he and Sabina had first seen one another on that fateful day.

He quickened his step, replaying the wonderful moment, just as Sabina had yesterday. He and Sabina had come here together the day after arriving in Berlin, but walking the sidewalk alone today in the early morning hours brought an even greater depth of thankfulness to his heart.

How good God had been to them! After all those years of separation, he was now able to look back on what seemed a whole lifetime spent with the woman he loved. God's timetables were certainly more long-reaching than man's temporal anxieties.

He continued on, his thoughts coming back once more to the present.

Everywhere he looked was contrast. Underneath all these surface appearances of health and vitality lay the stress fractures of a society suddenly finding itself squarely atop the fault line of a major political cataclysm.

To the east, only a mile or two away, the huge need for economic rebuilding had already strained the West's equilibrium. Money had come from Bonn to build up this new capital of the united nation. More was promised from other Western nations. But would it be enough to accomplish the job without rupturing the economy West Germany had preserved for so long?

Would the fall of the Wall bring harmony in the long run, or had the fault line been running beneath it too long to be healed? Were earthquakes of the spirit, psyche, and economy destined to be part of Germany's future forever? What would be the characteristic of *realpolitik* at the end of the twentieth century?

Slowly Matthew's mind took in the sights and the ambience of the city itself. It had not really changed that much in the thirty years since he'd been here with the State Department.

What would a world with Berlin as its hub be like in ten years, he wondered. A city filled with change, contrast . . . even a certain degree of chaos.

Ex–Communists, it was said, were fleeing here from all the Eastern Bloc countries, hoping in this mad, turbulent, international melting pot of millions to find corners to hide in, places to escape the new wave of democratic intolerance being sent in their direction.

Meanwhile swastikas and anti-Jewish slogans could be seen on billboards and walls, painted with spray-can haste. Every half-block or so sat a kiosk selling candy and gum and newspapers and magazines displaying nudity and pornography unimaginable in so public a setting in the States. What kind of moral value system could children possibly form when they grew up seeing such filth all around them, Matthew thought.

All the while, people walked by in clusters of tens and hundreds, impersonal looks of unconcern on their faces, painted leather jackets decorated with chains brushing against thousand-deutsche-mark suits, shouts and horns, trucks and buses . . . and everyone continuing with the business of their own private worlds.

Truly, Matthew thought, Berlin was a microcosm of the changing face of the world at this moment of climax.

What did it matter in the midst of all this that church leaders had assembled to discuss what ought to be the church's response to the changing times? What difference would their discussions and plans and agendas make?

Would that man lying on the sidewalk, or that skinhead with the earring, or that man with the briefcase walking with such a brisk, orderly tempo—would any of them really pay much attention to a Polish or German translation of some new pamphlet on the end times?

Maybe so, who could tell? But somehow pouring in planes and truckloads of literature seemed a bit removed from the streets where these people really lived.

Matthew stopped in the middle of the sidewalk and suddenly found himself praying for the people around him.

O God, he cried out silently, *reveal yourself to these people . . . save them from all this, Father! They are so in need of you, yet they don't know it. Reveal yourself to this world that needs your love so desperately. Give us, your people, eyes to see how you would have us love these poor needy children of yours with the love of your Son. Forgive our blindness, Father—give us eyes to see—*

A young lady walked by, interrupting his prayer momentarily. She looked about the age of his own Tad or Mary, and inexplicably Matthew's heart was stabbed with the pain of great love for an unknown one of his kind. Just as quickly as she had approached, she was gone.

Matthew turned and followed her retreating footfall, a tear rising into one of his eyes. *Lord, Lord . . . ,* he breathed, *draw that dear young lady whom you love to your heart.* He sighed again, then turned, drew in a deep breath, and began walking again in the direction he had been going.

Cults and every manner of cause and New Age guru were more visible in their attempt to attract followers than Christians. The mainline churches of Europe were more political than spiritual. Many of the freedom revolts had been led by so-called religious leaders. They were not going to have much of a spiritual impact. And the pervading decadent atmosphere of amorality . . . what lethal exports the West had ready to send to the newly opened nations of the East!

How was the American evangelical style going to fit in and exercise an impact in the midst of such variant forces and movements and trends?

Matthew sighed and walked on.

It was probably a little before eight o'clock by now. The streets were filling with people. Cars and trucks and buses and taxis were everywhere. Noise, the smell of diesel, the blaring of horns. A few street musicians were beginning to set up for their day of artful begging.

The kiosks were being set up, with their lewd offerings, nude magazines and postcards, suggestive items of every manner of description . . . it was disgusting, Matthew thought.

He was drawing near to the hotel. The long walk may not have solved anything, but he'd had a chance to air some thoughts and voice some prayers, and he felt somehow refreshed by the experience.

With his mind cluttered with a panorama of thoughts and bewildering questions, he reached the door of the Westmark Hotel and walked inside.

43

Journalist and Activist

• • •

AS HE ENTERED THEIR ROOM ON THE SIXTH FLOOR, MAT-
thew found Sabina just emerging from the bathroom in her robe,
toweling off her hair from a recent shower.

"Nice walk?" she asked.

"Yeah," he replied thoughtfully. "You know—more of what we
were talking about last night . . . what would Jesus do in certain
situations. Just your average, run-of-the-mill spiritual perplexities."

Before Sabina had the chance to reply further, a knock sounded
on the door, and the next instant Tad walked in. "Hey, you two about
ready for breakfast?"

"Just give me a minute or two," said Sabina, walking toward the
bathroom again, now holding her dress.

"You looked over the day's schedule?" Tad asked, gesturing with
the paper he held in his hand.

"Not much."

"Here's one that sounds right up our alley, Dad: 'Mega Fund-
Raising for Major Ministries in the 1990s'—dramatic new fund-
raising strategies for ministries committed to major evangelistic
efforts in our changing world."

Matthew groaned. "Not my alley," he said.

They sat down and looked over the syllabus together. It wasn't
long before Sabina again appeared. "I'm ready."

The three left the room and went downstairs to the dining room
for breakfast.

"You're not really going to that fund-raising workshop?" Sabina
asked Tad.

"No," he laughed. "I'm going to be gone all morning."

"Away from the conference, you mean?" asked Matthew.

"Right. I'm going to attempt to locate someone I hope will be able to give me an angle for the article I want to write."

"Something about that photograph of the Wall?"

Tad nodded. "I got a name yesterday, and what I hope is a current address. At least I'm going to see where it will lead me."

•   •   •

Lisel's morning had not been nearly as carefree as planned.

By eight-thirty she was already bored with her attempted round of activities and feeling strangely like she ought to return to the apartment. It was the last place she wanted to be. Her roommate would be gone at work all day, and in her present state of mind the place would be dreary.

Without a conscious decision, however, Lisel found herself walking up the familiar flight of stairs and inserting the key into the lock.

She walked inside and flopped down on the couch.

She was still sitting there, motionless, staring blankly ahead, wondering what to do with the day, when the knock came on the door. The sound brought her out of her melancholy reverie.

She rose and walked forward to answer it. The sight of an attractive, well-groomed young man about her own age standing in the corridor was a welcome interruption to the uneasy emotional tedium.

"Fräulein Lamprecht?" he said.

"I am Lisel Lamprecht."

"My name is Tad McCallum. I'm a journalist."

The fact conveyed nothing to Lisel in the way of explaining why he was standing there, and she waited for additional information.

"I . . . I received your name from a Horst Brandes," Tad went on. "I'm writing an article about the collapse of the Wall. It is my understanding that you are involved with an organization known as the Freedom Alliance and that you might have been there that night."

A slow nod of Lisel's head, though without accompanying benefit of a smile—she was accustomed to wariness, for the Alliance was not highly thought of in some circles—indicated permission for Tad to continue without her shutting the door in his face.

"I, uh . . . wondered if you might be willing to talk to me," Tad went on. "Maybe answer some questions, tell me what it was like being there that night—from your perspective as one who had been fighting for the cause of freedom."

"Are you a friend of Horst's?" Lisel asked, speaking at last. She knew the answer already, but it was her initial ploy to see if the fellow standing before her was in the habit of telling the truth. No one so clean and nicely dressed could possibly be a friend of her former colleague.

"No," replied Tad. "I only received his name from someone else, as one who might be able to get me into contact with you."

"Who?"

"A newsman by the name of Raul Schlink."

The thin hint of a smile broke around the edges of Lisel's lips. Everything now made sense. "And why did you want to contact me?" she asked.

"Because, as I said, I thought it would be interesting to know firsthand what that night was like."

"What makes you think I was there?"

Now it was Tad's turn to smile. "I'm not sure you'll believe me," he answered, laughing lightly.

"Try me," said Lisel.

She liked this man's countenance. Intuitively she sensed complete honesty and guilelessness from him. They were not the sort of qualities she had often encountered in her business, and seeing them now disarmed her of much of the reserve with which she usually surrounded herself as a shield of protective relational armor. She knew almost immediately that she would need no such protection with him.

Still smiling, Tad reached into his pocket for the photograph.

Lisel looked at it, now finally allowing her own smile to spread to the rest of her face. She recognized the scene instantly, though she had never before seen the photograph.

"It would appear you are right. I *was* there."

Tad did not reply.

"And," she added, "you are persistent, if you have been looking for me all this time."

"Not quite since that night," rejoined Tad. "I only ran across the picture a couple of weeks ago."

"Then you must be as much investigator as writer."

"I would never claim to be such," laughed Tad. "I only wanted to talk to you and was determined to find you."

"Well it would appear you have been successful on both counts . . . would you like to come in?"

"Do you have time?"

"As it happens—yes . . . yes, I do," replied Lisel. "Today is my day off, and I have no plans."

"In that case, I accept your invitation."

44

A Lively Talk

. . .

AN HOUR HAD PASSED AS IF IT HAD BEEN TEN MINUTES.

The American journalist and German activist had spoken of many things, including the Berlin Wall, the changes to both sides since, and the entire world situation.

Each found in the other a certain refreshing and energetic change from the ordinary relationships to which they were accustomed, and thus the dialogue between them came freely and enjoyably. Tad already had far more than he anticipated needing for the article he hoped to write, and the conversation had by now flowed into other channels. A second pot of coffee had already begun to cool.

"Your German is really quite excellent for an American," Lisel had just said. "If you hadn't told me otherwise, I would have taken it for one of the southwestern dialects, possibly Stuttgart."

Tad laughed. "That is high praise indeed coming from a native German. But I did have an advantage."

"How do you mean?"

"I lived the first seven years of my life in Germany."

"Oh—where?"

"Bavaria."

"Then I wasn't so far off! Why there?"

"My mother is German."

"East or West?"

"East, I suppose you'd say—but actually a little of both. She was raised in what is now Poland and then spent several years here in Berlin, a citizen of the DDR but working in the West."

"And your father was American?"

Tad nodded. "He was with the State Department here in the sixties. So I grew up comfortable with both languages."

"Which is how you now manage as a translator?"

"My background has opened a few doors for me all right."

"How did your mother and father meet? It is a little unusual for American diplomats to marry *East* Germans."

"It's a long story," laughed Tad. "Actually, a long and exciting one."

"I'd like to hear it."

"Perhaps you could hear it from them—you'd love my mother! They're here in Berlin with me."

"They are—on holiday?"

"We're attending a conference together—over at the Westmark. Would you like to meet them?"

"I, uh . . . yes, that would be nice," faltered Lisel, taken a little by surprise at the invitation. She was used to people being more guarded around those they had only recently met.

"It is a great story," Tad added, "and no one can tell it like my mother!"

"What kind of conference?" asked Lisel. "Politics?"

"No," laughed Tad. "Dad's been retired from the diplomatic game for eight or ten years. It's a gathering of Christian leaders, mainly about evangelism."

He half expected her, as what he assumed to be a non-Christian, to ask what evangelism was. Instead, Lisel took in the information with thoughtful expression and did not reply at all. She knew well enough what the term meant. The very idea of it was nauseating to her.

A heavy silence descended quickly over the room.

"Did I say something wrong?" asked Tad at length, laughing nervously.

Lisel did not reply immediately.

This time Tad waited.

"No," she answered at length, with noticeably tighter expression. "I'm just not interested in evangelism, that's all."

"By your reaction, it seems you're more than just passively 'not interested,'" commented Tad.

"All right—it is more than that. The very idea of Christians getting together to talk about *saving the world* both makes me sick and makes me angry at the same time. There—is that plain enough for you?" Lisel's tone had dramatically shifted from a minute earlier. By now the friendly smile had disappeared from her face and she was looking at Tad cautiously, as if he had all at once become her adversary.

"Do you mind if I ask why?" said Tad.

"No, I do not mind, if you will not be offended by my answer."

"Now it is my turn to say to you what you said to me when I was standing at your door."

Lisel cocked her head in unspoken question.

"Try me," said Tad. "I doubt you will offend me."

Lisel glanced down at the floor a moment or two, then looked up and straight into his face. "All right, then, here it is: in my view, Christians have done more harm than good throughout the world's history. They are presumptuous, arrogant, self-righteous, and hypo-critical, and the very idea of them wanting to spread their absurd beliefs, so that they can make others as hypocritical as themselves . . . the very thought of it irritates me more than I can tell you."

"You are not a Christian yourself?" asked Tad.

The laugh that came from Lisel's mouth in reply was one of scorn and derision. "That is correct," she said, punctuating her words forcefully. "I am not. How could you even ask such a question? Isn't it obvious?"

"There is not so much in your comments that would preclude your being a Christian. Frankly, I would probably agree with most of what you said."

"What—you're attending a conference on evangelism, and you're not a Christian either?"

"I didn't say that," rejoined Tad. "I am absolutely a Christian."

"But you said—"

"That I would probably agree with most of what you said," interrupted Tad. "Well," he added, "all except for the part about the beliefs of Christianity being absurd. That I deny most emphatically. But as to your other points . . . yes, I would agree with you."

"You are a Christian," said Lisel, eyeing Tad skeptically, "and yet you agree when I say that Christians are hypocrites?"

"Of course."

"I don't understand."

"Many Christians *are* hypocrites. It would be foolish for me to deny it or pretend otherwise."

Lisel's expression now displayed confusion. This was not what she had expected. She was not accustomed to hearing Christians talk like this.

"It is nice to hear someone admit it so freely," she said, relaxing her antagonistic posture momentarily.

"It might not be so nice when you hear what I would say next."

Lisel looked at him with an expression intended to convey, "Go on . . . I'm listening."

"You and I can sometimes be hypocrites too."

"I made no claim to being a Christian, remember?"

"I didn't say you were a *Christian* hypocrite, only that you can be a hypocrite too, just like me. *No one* fully lives up to his own belief system. Isn't that what a hypocrite is—someone who doesn't live up to the creed he espouses?"

"You may be right."

"I'm sure you hold to certain views and principles and standards that *you* fall short of, in the same way that I fall short of the Christian principles and standards by which I attempt to order *my* life."

"What's your point?" said Lisel, again assuming a skeptical bearing.

"That you cannot call the Christian belief system necessarily false because some Christians happen to be hypocrites. Christianity *may* be true, or it may *not* be true—every person has to weigh the evidence and make that determination for themselves. But Christians being hypocrites has nothing to do with either side of the argument."

Lisel tried to take the statement in logically, but something about it felt strangely uncomfortable. The easygoing conversation of earlier had turned disconcertingly penetrating and in directions she was not anxious to explore. On his part, Tad's upbringing and lineage had given him a strong sense of identity, which revealed itself in confidence and forthrighteousness, which he was still learning—sometimes painfully—how to walk in sensitively.

"And the rest of what I expressed," she said.

"I would again respond by saying I agree," replied Tad. "Christians *have* done great harm throughout the world's history. I do not deny it. I *could* not deny it, for it is true. It makes me sick and angry too. And yes, Christians can be presumptuous, arrogant, and self-righteous. It is unfortunate, and it upsets me as well. It especially upsets me when I am the culprit *myself*, for I am as prone to presumption, pride, and self-righteousness as the next man. It makes me sick to realize how far I have to go as a Christian before I will be anywhere near maturity."

"And I suppose you would say that I am proud and self-righteous too?" queried Lisel.

"That would not be my place to say."

Lisel did not like the suggestion, but said nothing in direct reply to Tad's words. "You do not think Christians have a worse dose of the disease than non-Christians?" she asked.

"Hmm . . . that's a good question," said Tad thoughtfully. "I would say that probably Christians do tend to be pretty seriously inflicted. *Worse?* I don't know—maybe. But that does not make all Christians more proud than all non-Christians. There are mature and selfless Christians, just as there are arrogant ones. Self-righteousness is a fairly prevalent cancer in politics, in universities, in atheism, and anywhere else you look, just as it is in Christianity. But the point I would make again is that you can't throw out the truth of Christianity because Christians haven't lived their faith perfectly, any more than you can throw out democracy as a political system because there are no perfect democracies. To do so is to be entrapped by the most elementary, yet the most blinding of logical pitfalls."

"You wouldn't call the U.S. system a perfect example of democracy?" Lisel asked.

"Not by any means. It is a dreadfully flawed system with all sorts of injustices. But it is still a more *true* form of government than human totalitarianism and dictatorship. Don't you see—the *truth* of something doesn't rest on whether it is lived perfectly. We are flawed human beings living in a flawed world. *Everything* is flawed. That doesn't mean that truth doesn't exist, only that as flawed creatures we are incapable of living it perfectly."

It was silent a minute or two. Both sat thinking.

"And when will you, as you say, consider yourself *mature* as a Christian?" asked Lisel after the pause.

"Let me just reply by saying that perhaps I will be moving toward maturity when I am *less* self-absorbed and *more* selfless than I am now.

Such is my daily prayer and constant goal, though I will never reach it—not in this life, at least."

"I might say the same thing of myself—not about *praying* to be less self-absorbed, but about the goal of becoming mature."

"Many people might make such a claim, yet Christianity is the only value system, or worldview, if you will, that offers a realistic plan toward that end."

"From *your* perspective, perhaps, though I don't happen to agree. In my own way, I am searching for truth too, but the truth I have found is very different from yours."

"What truth *have* you found?" asked Tad sincerely.

Lisel thought a moment. "That being true to myself is the most important truth there is."

"Not a very large principle to go by such a lofty name as *truth*. What happens when being true to yourself fails you?"

"It hasn't yet."

"What if it does? What then?"

"I suppose I'll have to decide at the time. For now I am content with that for a creed."

"But what if it's a hollow, empty creed. Being what is called *true to yourself*. . . . What do those words mean? There is no creed, no belief system, no *truth* in them, and might they also imply a level of self-centeredness?"

As he spoke, Lisel's face gradually reddened. It was not the color of embarrassment. "But if such satisfies me, who are *you* to say I am wrong?" she said quickly, a rising annoyance apparent in her tone.

"I do not say you are wrong. That is a potential conclusion you will have to face yourself. I am only shining a spot of light on what appears to me as a flaw in what you call your belief system, what you call truth."

"A flaw?"

"You said you were searching for truth, and I contend there is no truth in what is commonly called being true to oneself."

"Where does truth exist then, if not in being true to oneself?"

"In the Christian faith, in being true to *Truth,* not just true to yourself. Truth must proceed out of something higher than each individual's own self-motivated definition of it. Christians may be hypocrites with all the rest of the world. But that fact does not take the *Truth* out of Christianity."

"And if I said that in spite of all you say, I nevertheless *choose* to disregard Christianity and to conclude that it is absurd . . . what would you say to me then?"

"One of two things. Perhaps you do *not* care about truth as much as you think you do, and thus do not care to make honest inquiry into the claims of Christianity. *Or* perhaps you have had a bad experience at some time in the past, probably with a Christian, maybe even with one of your parents, which, because you are still responding to it emotionally, is causing you to blind yourself to what you know is the truth. If such is the case, the only way you have to perpetuate your anger is to reject the Christianity that these others hold so dear. It is your way of lashing out against them. But the person you are hurting most of all by such a response is yourself."

The rising heat of Lisel's anger as she sat listening to Tad's words at last reached a boil. She jumped to her feet, face red in fury. "How dare you accuse me of such things!" she cried, the lid at last blowing off the kettle. "You have no right to pass judgment on me. You don't even know me! I thought you were different at first. But you're just as big a hypocrite as all the rest."

Realizing he had gone much too far with his answer to her question, Tad tried to apologize. "I am sorry to have said what I did," he said, shocked by the outburst. "I meant no—"

"Don't bother!" Lisel shot back. "I don't want to hear another word!"

"Please forgive me, I honestly didn't mean to imply—"

"Just get out of here!" interrupted Lisel again.

Tad rose, sick at the sudden turn of events.

He struggled to find words that might help, but succeeded only in shaking his head back and forth a few times with mouth half open, groping for something to say, obviously grief stricken. Lisel was staring off in the opposite direction, however, and it was clear that for the present the situation had become hopeless.

Slowly Tad turned toward the door and made his way out of the apartment. No more words were spoken. Halfway down the stairway he heard the door slam shut behind him.

He continued on and outside, unaware that upstairs in the room he had just left, behind the door she had just sent crashing against its frame, Lisel Lamprecht regretted her harsh, spontaneous action. She had every right to be angry and to throw that arrogant American know-it-all out, she told herself. But now that her ire had cooled with his departure, Lisel couldn't fathom why she felt guilty for doing so. Even more, she was mystified as to why she still wanted to talk with him.

45

Differences

· · ·

THAT SAME AFTERNOON, BACK AT THE WESTMARK, A general session was scheduled at which high-ranking German Lutheran Gentz Raedenburg was to speak for the first time.

Matthew and Joseph met for lunch. About twelve-thirty they saw Tad walk into the coffee shop. Matthew hailed his son, who walked over to join them.

"Did you get your interview?" asked Matthew as he approached.

"Yeah—it was . . . *interesting*," replied Tad with a curious expression. "How about you?" he said across the table to Joseph, preempting the direction of potential conversation as he sat down beside his father. "Did you find your friend?"

Joseph shook his head, a look of disappointment evident on his face. Tad glanced at both men questioningly.

"Dieder Palacki," Matthew explained to his son, "was supposed to arrive today and offer a few words this afternoon before the Raedenburg talk."

"He's the man you were talking about yesterday, who led you to the Lord?" said Tad.

Joseph nodded. "I haven't seen him since 1962," he said. "I was hoping to get to him right when he arrived so I could set up a time to talk with him, though I even wonder if he'll remember me."

"From what you've told me," said Matthew, "I have a feeling he's not the kind of man who would forget anyone."

"I think you're right," said Joseph, smiling.

"Fill me in," said Tad. "I don't really know anything about him other than that your path and his crossed many years ago."

"You know of his reputation?" asked Joseph.

"Only that he was in prison and wrote a book called *Tortured but something*. . . . I've forgotten exactly."

"*Tortured but Undaunted: Faith in Action behind the Iron Curtain,*" added Joseph. "He managed to get the manuscript smuggled out of Poland and to Scotland, where it was eventually published."

"Well that shows how little about him I know," laughed Tad.

"For years he was imprisoned for his outspoken preaching and teaching," Joseph went on. "I don't know how soon after my visit he was put in jail, but eventually he was behind bars ten or fifteen years—beaten, tortured, solitary confinement, everything. But even there he kept up his preaching, which, knowing him the little I was privileged to, doesn't surprise me in the least. He was very outspoken and courageous, even as a young man."

"He was eventually released?"

Joseph nodded. "By the time the Communists started easing back, even from prison he was recognized as one of the leaders of the whole underground church movement. Once out, he traveled all over—through Bulgaria, Poland, Russia, Hungary, Romania—stirring up and encouraging little pockets of believers."

"Didn't he go on tour in the West too," asked Matthew, "trying to drum up support and raise money to help? I didn't follow it closely, but it seems I recall it—mideighties I think it was."

"I doubt if *tour* is what you'd call it," laughed Joseph. "I kept tabs on it as much as I was able. He traveled around in the United States, speaking in churches and wherever he could, trying, like you say, to raise enough support to get Bibles back home to his people, who had so little."

"How successful was he?" asked Tad.

"I don't think he was able to raise very much money and from what I heard ended up rather cynical about the whole experience."

"You can't deny him the right to say what he wanted, after spending those years in prison," said Matthew. "He sounds something like your grandfather, Tad."

"Having met both men," added Joseph, "I think the similarity does indeed exist, although Baron von Dortmann was certainly gentler and more soft-spoken than the man Dieder Palacki became."

"Is he still in the States?" asked Tad.

"No, he went back to Poland several years ago. I hadn't heard of him again until this conference. He dropped out of sight for a while, though the disintegration of the Soviet system ended his need to remain in hiding, and he's been fairly active and visible ever since. That's why the minute I heard he'd been invited here to Berlin, I called my travel agent immediately."

"What's the problem?" asked Matthew. "Did he arrive? Did you see him?"

Again Joseph's face fell. "Yes, but I was too late. I ran across Darrell Montgomery and asked him if Dieder had arrived."

"And?"

"He said he had, but the look on his face told me their first exchange must not have been pleasant."

"In what way?"

"I don't know exactly. All I could get from Montgomery was that Palacki was unhappy about the way the conference is shaping up and wasn't going to attend this afternoon's meeting."

"Hmm," said Matthew. "I can see why Darrell would be concerned. He has been billing Palacki and his longtime work with the underground church as one of the highlights. His presence here was the great unifying thread in it all—the underground church of the East at last meeting the free church of the West."

"Hands across the Wall, and all that," added Tad.

"Right. Palacki's quite highly thought of. Naturally if he were disgruntled, it would be disturbing to Darrell."

"When is he scheduled to speak?" asked Tad.

"Next-to-last night."

"And isn't he scheduled to receive a good-sized donation from MacPatrick's TV fund-raiser?"

"It's one of Darrell's crowning touches on the week," confirmed Matthew. "But remember what I told you, Tad," he added. "It's only a rumor at this stage, and we're not *supposed* to know. It's still being kept hush-hush. You know how these kinds of things escalate once word gets out. So don't repeat what you just said to anyone."

"Still . . . it is puzzling that he'd be disgruntled," said Tad. "Presumably *he* knows."

"Dieder Palacki is not a man who would compromise a thing he believed for any amount of money," said Joseph.

"What are you going to do, Joseph?" asked Matthew.

"I'll find some way to see him. He's the primary reason I came—present company excluded, of course!"

Matthew laughed. "Not for a moment would I think of myself on the same level as Dieder Palacki," he said. "You don't have to worry about hurting my feelings!"

Tad glanced down at his watch. "If we're going to make the general session, we'd better be heading that way."

"But what about *your* morning?" Matthew asked Tad as they rose. "You said you found the person *you* were looking for?"

"I did, though the conversation took some unexpected turns," replied Tad with a sigh. "A most interesting young lady."

"Aha!" exclaimed Matthew. "Just wait until I tell your mother!"

Tad laughed, but there was clearly not much humor in his tone.

The three men continued their discussion as they left the restaurant and walked across the street to the hotel.

46

A Call to Roots

• • •

MATTHEW RAN UPSTAIRS TO GET SABINA, WHO HAD BEEN anticipating the address by the German leader more than any other event on the schedule, while Tad and Joseph wandered about downstairs hoping to learn something more concerning the Palacki affair. The shrug of their shoulders when Matthew and Sabina rejoined them indicated they had been unsuccessful.

The four walked into the huge general meeting hall together, already filling up with the conferees, and took their seats.

At five minutes till one, several of the big names of the conference strode onto the platform and took seats along the back of it. The hall gradually quieted and Darrell Montgomery took to the microphone. Dieder Palacki was conspicuously absent from the entourage, noticeable in that he had become one of the most talked-about potential speakers present, and this afternoon had offered the first chance for everyone to get their first look at the Polish leader.

Not to be deterred, however, Montgomery had in his place an even bigger personality. The newest guest had come in next to him, full of smiles and self-satisfied ebullience, and now sat behind him with the others, clearly accustomed to and enjoying being the center of attention.

"Before we get underway," Montgomery began enthusiastically, "I just want to present to you the latest arrival in Berlin among our speakers, a man I know will require no introduction . . . Mr. Bob MacPatrick!"

A great ovation went through the hall as MacPatrick stood, beaming and waving to the huge gathering of Christian leaders. It would be difficult to imagine a more overweening expression of confidence, though it was so well disguised as to be invisible to nine out of ten of those watching. Flushed with a sense of his own renown, MacPatrick continued to wave and gesture and smile to the approving crowd, inflating more fully each second the clapping continued. He did not seem to be readying himself to teach on the truths contained in the final four words of the fifteenth chapter of Proverbs.

"Bob will, as you already know," Montgomery went on as the clapping subsided, "be addressing us and conducting some real hands-on furthering of the gospel on Friday evening, when he and our good friend Dieder Palacki will share this podium together. As leading representatives of Christ's church on earth, they will symbolically bring East and West together, as it were, in a demonstration of the unity that binds all of us here together as one. But today I wanted simply to introduce him to you and welcome him to the Berlin Church Leadership Conference."

As he spoke, Montgomery turned, shook MacPatrick's hand vigorously, then turned back to the microphone while his new marquee headliner resumed his seat. A pause followed.

"And now," Montgomery went on after a moment, "it gives me further pleasure to introduce the General Director for Budgetary Planning of the Lutheran Church here in Germany, a man highly respected both among the political and church leaders of his country, and I would have to say by the Christian community worldwide, a man who carries admirably the mantle of spiritual leadership passed down to him by many great German Christians of past eras, Mr. Gentz Raedenburg."

Behind him, Raedenburg rose, walked forward, shook Montgomery's hand, and then stood quietly behind the podium amid scattered and moderate applause. The welcome, though sincere, was notably unlike that afforded MacPatrick. Raedenburg, however, hardly seemed to take notice but stood serenely waiting, almost appearing reticent to begin. When at last he did speak, his voice was soft and methodical, though anything but timid. The power and impact of his carriage did not exude from volume of voice, public praise, nor self-approval of countenance, but rather from a reservoir of bearing and dynamism that dwelt somewhere altogether deeper inside his being.

"I so earnestly appreciate this opportunity to be with you," Raedenburg began. "This gathering is, as you all know, unusual enough simply in itself. But that uniqueness is further heightened in the variety of backgrounds and viewpoints represented. Thus I consider it a singular honor to be asked to address you, for it is not often that conservative American evangelicals and liberal German church officials interact with much depth of true meeting in the Spirit. I sincerely and prayerfully hope that can happen here.

"Frankly, I hope I am not a liberal. I do not consider myself one. Neither do I consider myself primarily a church official, though I do serve in such a capacity. I am, first of all, a Christian and, I pray, a seeker of truth and an obeyer of truth. Yet I am not so naive as to be unaware of the kinds of labels that have traditionally floated about among us, and German liberalism has been an anathema to fundamentalists in England and the United States for two centuries. And not without good reason in many cases! Yet I hope you will afford me sufficient trust to discover that I do not fit such a mold."

His voice contained just enough hints of his native German accent to spice his words with a certain flavorful ring of distinction, but at the same time reflected a flawless English fluency, striking an intriguing balance between the American and British versions of the Anglo-Saxon tongue.

"I would like to talk to you about several areas of concern to me," he went on. "First, with regard to evangelism at the national level. In the United States, among evangelicals at least, there has been an emphasis on *personal* evangelism. But from where I stand, as a German, involved in the German church and even involved to some degree with the politics and leadership of this country, from that vantage point I would say that we are rather a *nation* in deep, deep need.

"Of course I understand that spirituality must begin in each individual heart. The mass corporate baptisms and conversions that made the Roman Empire and Russia and other such lands into what we call 'Christian nations' overnight were but a religio-political gambit of history. No, I am suggesting nothing of that sort. Spirituality and conversion to the Christian faith are individual and personal.

"However, I reiterate, we as a nation, and throughout all of continental Europe and the United States, *we as nations* are in great spiritual need. My call to you as fellow leaders of Christianity is to heed and find ways to address *personal* need by recognizing our unique national needs at the same time. Right here in Berlin, we are gathered at the very core where the politics and the finances and the decision-making power of Europe is suddenly culminating. We sit at the center point of the focus of the entire world community.

"But in the midst of all this, we as a nation here in Germany—and I do not think I am speaking in too strong of terms—we are approaching spiritual bankruptcy. We are in desperate need. We need an infusion of *life!* It is not that we are without our spiritual roots. The very Reformation began within our borders. Through the years we have had spiritual giants whose voices have resounded with the cry to personal faith, even recently with the likes of Dietrich Bonhoeffer and Wilhelm Busch.

"Yet as a nation, we have been led astray by liberal theology, by money and affluence, by pride in our own success. By the very blessings that came with postwar strength has also come a certain sense of invulnerability, that we can do anything we set our minds and hands to, that we need nobody and nothing except ourselves to make a success of whatever we do. Nobody . . . not even God.

"Does this sound familiar, you Americans listening to my words? Of course it does, for I am describing your nation too. The national bankruptcy I describe as a cancer infecting Germany exists within your land as well. You could reflect similarly upon the spiritual foundation-roots of your nation and how they have been undermined by liberality and so much of the New Age humanistic thinking.

"So now here we are, we of the West, with prosperity untold. We in Germany now have our country united again. We rejoice! Yet we are dying. We are lost, spiritually suffocating and dead in our affluence.

"*We* need more than a mere tearing down of the Wall to heal the enmity that has grown in our hearts. *You* need more than an end of your cold war with Russia.

"For the enmity is at root a separation from God that modern man has allowed his prideful attitude to deepen and harden. What we desperately need is a reunification of the spirit, not merely a reunification of political entities, an end of the cold war with our Maker, not just a new truce with a political adversary. We need a revitalization of our first loves—the vibrancy of *our* German-led Reformation, the vigorous spirituality of *your* American founding fathers' faith. In both of our countries, the national fervor of Christian belief no longer exists and could spell our collective demise.

"Do not *all* the nations we represent, in fact, stand in need of just the same thing, not merely Germany and the United States?

"These may not be pleasant words for us to face, but if our Christian strategies for the future are to be of any impact whatsoever, we *must* face them.

"It may surprise, even shock, some of you to hear a man in my position speak so candidly about a subject usually reserved for fundamentalist factions. But I love my country and my Lord too much not to be willing to leave no stone unturned, no battle unfought in order to break down the barriers to spiritual truth so that the gospel can effectively penetrate the hearts and minds of men and women who need it so desperately."

47

Prayers and Reproving Thoughts

• • •

EVEN AS THE GERMAN LEADER WAS ADDRESSING THE CON-
vention of Christians, in the lonely apartment where Tad had spent
the morning the stormy atmosphere had passed. The violent bursts of
lightning and thunder had come, the rain of tears had followed, and
now a dreary fog of self-reflection had settled in.

Lisel had tried everything within her present mental capacity to
force herself to forget the incident, but without success. She could
dislodge neither Tad's words, nor her own, from her mind.

How long she remained on the couch after the expenditure of her
tears she did not know. Eventually she got up, wandered to the
bedroom, laid down on her bed, and tried to sleep, but with no more
success than she had in forgetting the incident. She lay there for hours,
almost wishing she could rouse again the anger, and thereby exorcise
the aching, silent self-reproof she felt closing inexorably around her.

But her wrath had been spent. And now all she could do was listen
to the words over and over and over in her mind's ear—against her
will, though she was powerless to stop their flow: . . . *do not care about
truth . . . worst kind of hypocrite . . . responding selfishly and emotionally . . .
blind to what you know is truth . . . lashing out . . . gaining your revenge.*

And then the words that stabbed like a cold knife into her breast:
But the person you are hurting most of all by such a response is yourself.

• • •

Meanwhile, in another part of Berlin, unaware in the least of the
conference of Christians or the high-level political machinations

swirling between Berlin and Moscow, an aging man knelt in the loneliness of the afternoon and entered into more important eternal business than now concerned any of his nation's political leaders or most of the church leaders sitting listening to the German churchman's words.

He prayed for his daughter daily. But the moment wakefulness had come on this particular morning, he had sensed that something was different. About midday the feeling had grown, taking the form that some crisis was at hand.

The more earnestly he prayed throughout the day, however, the more also his own anguish increased, as if he was bearing anew the full weight of the pain of the separation, feeling in some infinitesimal measure the grief of the Father's love at the unknowing rejection of his love by his own sons and daughters. Soon after he had given his heart to the Father and Creator, he had begun praying that he might grow—in sacrifice, in love, in selflessness, and in complete loss of his self into the will of God—to reflect the image of his Master. Little did he know that such a prayer—the ultimate relinquishment of self-will a creature can pray—would be answered by allowing him the privilege reserved but for a few in this life: the experience of knowing in small but real portion the hopeful, visionary, prayerful agony of the Father-heart . . . that central pulse of the life of the universe.

Separations of nationhood were being healed, but more personal separations were the objects of his prayers.

Indeed was the love of Christ on this man's heart as he prayed, though he would never have thought of the tears he now shed on her behalf as the quickening lubricant of the very evangelism that had sent his daughter into the rage of a few hours earlier that had opened the door to her present soul-searching plight.

•　•　•

She had to do something, Lisel told herself.

It was well into the afternoon. She could not just lie here all day.

She pulled herself up and sat on the edge of the bed. Food could not have been further from her mind. She was not hungry in the least. But she had to do *something*.

Not that she agreed with anything McCallum had said, Lisel

concluded at length. But aside from all that, she had behaved rudely. He had come on an honest errand, and once the discussion had worked around to matters of belief, he had been equally honest and straightforward in his expression.

True, he had said some things that hurt. But could she really blame him for that? At least he was plainspoken and willing to admit he was himself far from perfect. She had met few enough Christians in the last ten years about whom that could be said.

There was only one thing to do.

Slowly Lisel rose and walked across the room to the telephone.

48

A Call to Discernment

. . .

WHILE GENTZ RAEDENBURG PAUSED MOMENTARILY, taking in a breath as if preparing to move in a new direction with his remarks, most of his listeners shifted slightly in their seats.

"There are additionally," the German leader continued, "unique cultural and historical factors our approach to the future must take into account.

"Let me offer an example, citing again our two nations—the U.S. and Germany. Ungodliness pervades both lands, yet in terms of how we as Christians ought to address those mired in that ungodliness I would suggest that the approaches should be very different indeed."

Again he paused, then quickly continued. "Notwithstanding the humanism and unspirituality pervading your American society as a whole, by and large, the people in your country *know* there is a spiritual vacuum. You read about the need for a return to spiritual values. It is constantly being talked about in your newsmagazines. I have heard all three of your last presidents speak of such things.

"In general people understand what they mean. That may not imply that they want spiritual revival in their own lives, but at least there is a certain degree to which such words communicate truth to them. In other words, as I said, Americans recognize that there is a spiritual vacuum. Most don't care. They don't *want* spirituality. But at least they recognize that it is not there.

"In Germany, however, such things are rarely heard. No one is talking in a widespread way about spiritual need because so few are aware of the morass of unbelief that has swallowed our country. If I went out to people on the street and randomly asked them if they were Christians or not, probably six out of ten would look at me as if I had spoken nonsense. The question would be meaningless. Of course they were Christians . . . isn't everybody?

"You see, our two countries have gone about our loss of spiritual vitality—*our* loss of the Reformation efficacy of Luther, *your* loss of the foundation stones of your nation's spiritual beginnings—in very different ways.

"Your leaders of the last several generations have simply thrown out spirituality from your nation's heart by outlawing it in the name of equality and progress. So now prayer in your schools is against the law, while abortion is legal—an absurd aberration of right and wrong that would have probably caused your founding fathers to declare their independence from your very government all over again.

"We in Germany, on the other hand, have been ensnared by a much more subtle snare of falsehood. We have taken a different tack in our slide down into darkness. We have *institutionalized* the Christian faith. We have done the very opposite from you. Religion and prayer and the articles of the creeds are taught to our young people in school. We have not *removed* the church, we have brought the church *into* everything. The church is intrinsically linked to our whole societal and governmental system. The church, I say, not faith, not belief, not spirituality . . . the historic institution, not the sacred bride of Christ.

"As a church official, I am paid, indirectly, by the government itself. That may surprise some of you. It indicates the totality of the marriage between church and state that has taken place. I am a church official, an ordained minister of the gospel . . . and my employer is the German government. I am answerable to Hans Kolter, not Jesus Christ.

"You see, we have equally inverted the spiritual equation, yet in a completely different manner than have you Americans. There is, therefore, little *life* in the German church at all—only rote dogma . . . dogma as prescribed by the government. Religion is a subject taught in our schools just like arithmetic. Confirmation in the church at fourteen is little more than a graduation ceremony.

"You *withhold* spiritual teaching, we *give* it—in just a sufficient dosage as to inoculate our people and make them immune to the *life* and power of it.

"Now you may look at me and think, 'But you are in a position of responsibility and prestige. Why do you not tell your country's leaders these things? Surely yours is a voice that could carry far and serve to bring about revival in your land.'

"Ah, if only it were so! Yes, the Lord has blessed me by giving me a platform from which to speak. Yet my voice is so weak, and this immunization process I have spoken of has been so pervasive and lethal in our society that I feel as one shouting in the wind.

"Yes, I am on intimate terms with my nation's leaders from all the parties. Chancellor Hans Kolter is a close personal friend. In fact, I am to visit him tomorrow for lunch. And when I speak of spiritual matters, Hans is open and a willing listener. But to him the words may as well be those of another politician.

"The church is but one more faction of the government, of the country. The church has a way of expressing its perspectives, just as do the liberals, the conservatives, the Communists, and all the rest. *Christian Socialists . . . Christian Democrats . . .* we so blindly mingle the very word *Christian* with our politics. The *life* is gone, the mere hollow shell of spiritual verbiage remains.

"So tomorrow Hans is likely to ask me what I think of a crucial vote coming to the Bundestag next week on economic aid to the commonwealth of the former Soviet Union. It is an important issue. There are undercurrents of dissatisfaction with the chancellor's policies. I know Hans is concerned whether he will be able to carry the day and see the package approved.

"But he will be asking me, not in the way of wanting to discover what might be God's mind on the matter, but rather consulting me as he would any other faction or interest group with influence to perhaps sway votes in the parliament.

"Does this not have a familiar ring to you Americans? You are on your way toward just the same thing. What I believe you call your 'religious right' is on the road to becoming just another political faction of little or no *spiritual* impact. I can see it so clearly because of my own country's plight. Therefore I say to you—Beware of going too far down that road of attempting to bring about necessary change by thinking it is possible to incorporate true *spirituality* into the political arena.

"It is not.

"The point I am attempting to make is that the post–Cold War world you leaders of the church face is not one-dimensional. I exhort you to be astute in your evangelism, to attune yourselves to the realities that exist in the nations to which you would take your message so that you do more than speak into the wind."

Another lengthy pause followed. "There is one additional word of caution I would like to sound before I finish," Raedenburg continued.

"The world of the twenty-first century will be vastly different in many ways from anything we have known. The toppling of the Berlin Wall in 1989 and the remarkable events of these recent years did much more than reunify a nation and close out a fifty-year period of tension we called the Cold War.

"In the euphoria of those events, I think many throughout the world have not accurately perceived the deeper significance of what this time in the earth's history means. When your President Bush coined the phrase 'new world order,' he was speaking deeper truth than even he realized at the time. Now those three words have become buzzwords for Christian writers and secular columnists, politicians, and sociologists the world over. And let us Christian leaders not miss their true import.

"Everything has changed.

"Old alliances have suddenly crumbled. New ones will spring up in their place. In this new order of things, there is the universal feeling that we are on the threshold of seeing many evils that have plagued mankind put forever behind us as a new era of harmony dawns upon the globe. New Age and humanist thinkers and gurus and writers and speakers are putting their own gloss on world events and are swaying millions, here in Germany, in the United States, and elsewhere.

"But be not deceived, my brothers and sisters. The world has changed—man's sinful heart has not. I firmly believe we are living in the last days before the return of our Lord, and these changes are those spoken of in the Bible that would precede his coming. Great deceptions are ahead, and we must walk into the future with eyes wide open to the wiles of the enemy.

"Enmity between nations may take new forms now, but do not be lulled into the false assumption that such enmity has been eliminated. There will again be those who would rise to power to conquer nations and regions. Nationalism and greed and lust for power have not been eradicated from the human heart. But new conquerors will use the weapons of the *new* world order rather than the guns and tanks of our predecessors."

Raedenburg paused. The great hall was silent.

"Do we dismiss such fears?" he asked quietly, then paused again.

"I say no, we must not dismiss them," he continued. "I perceive the danger signs of xenophobic vanity throughout Europe and the world now as in the past. I fear no new military rise, but I do fear political and economic superiority. The new world order will be ruled no less than the old by the lusts and greeds and selfish ambitions of men. But now the specifics and the pawns in the game will change. They will become more subtle, less easy to see than invasions of tanks and explosions of bombs.

"We as Christians must heed our Master's words, now more than ever—be watchful, be vigilant, be alert, remain on guard. There will rise New-Age Hitlers and Stalins and Napoleons, intent upon conquest no less than those dictators of old, but working to achieve their ends more shrewdly, killing not men's lives but their spirits, conquering not their borders but their souls.

"Those who will bring to the world its new order will promote by altogether new and devious means new ideologies and national agendas that will, in time, take over whole nations and continents.

"As I said, everything will change—is already in the process of changing. But to most these changes remain unseen and therefore perhaps even more deadly than past methods of conquest.

"As Christians we can see that the new world order of the new age is but a prelude to an utter collapse of the earth's systems, which has been long prophesied in the last days.

"Before that time, the Lord has opened these great doors of opportunity for us to take the gospel and his life abroad unto all the world. It is a period of unprecedented opportunity for spiritual harvest. But as I said, we must not be deceived into false delusions that these doors will remain open forever.

"We are grateful for reunification. We are happy for the freedom and democracy that is coming in Eastern Europe. We praise God for these opportunities to penetrate with the gospel these areas that have only heard it scantily these last fifty years. But we must not be deceived. The enemy yet lurks about and yet is active in the world.

"The Ukrainian defector and former KGB staff officer Anatoly Golitsyn warned in 1984 of a grand Soviet deception. We have misunderstood the nature of the recent changes in the Communist world, says this former Communist. What we have seen is not the death of an ideology, but rather a new strategy that is part of the new world order. It is a strategy that remains intent on conquest in new forms. Golitsyn's words now ring with an air of prophetic truth."

Another pause followed.

"So how long will the doors of opportunity remain open for Christians? Who can tell? Our duty as God's ambassadors is to obey his commands with vigor and urgency. The Old Testament prophets tell of a day when gates and walls will be opened and torn down for a season, only to close back up in time.

"Does the prophecy speak of new cold wars and new dividing curtains that will replace those we have recently seen dismantled and destroyed? Again I say, Who can tell?

"I would not presume to interpret it, nor to myself prophesy of what the future holds. I merely sound the warning that the times are not as rosy as they seem. Christ's evangelists in this era of new thought and new orders and new worldviews and agendas and philosophies must be equipped more fully than their fellow evangelists of previous historical eras—equipped intellectually, equipped for spiritual battle, equipped with helping hands to minister to the needs of people, equipped to voice the gospel message in new times and in fresh ways—to individuals, to nations, to cultures.

"Ours is no calling merely to stand on the street corners of our cities preaching outmoded sermons to unconcerned passersby, satisfying our own need to feel important but doing little to impact those who hear us.

"Our calling is rather to take with transforming power the life of Christ to those in desperate need of it. To be astute and intellectually honed to stand on the cutting edge of today's world, to be compassionate and full of hearts that love, and to be battle-ready to face the cunning and evil resourcefulness of the enemy.

"We must prepare and equip ourselves to walk in all these ways.

The question is not, *Can* we mount to the task before us? The urgency is clear . . . we *must!*"

Raedenburg stopped, then turned and walked back to the chair he had left, sitting vacant among the row of dignitaries. The applause that followed, though slow at first, rose steadily as the listeners gradually sensed the dynamic of the message they had just heard.

Darrell Montgomery rose, went to the podium, mumbled a few words of bland praise, then closed the meeting with a prayer a bit too eloquent for the occasion.

49

A Surprising Call

• • •

WHEN TAD REACHED HIS ROOM LATER THAT AFTERNOON to take a brief break between workshops, the first thing he noticed was the light on his telephone flashing. He dialed the hotel desk. A call had come in for him. He was requested to return it. There was no accompanying message. The number itself signified nothing in Tad's memory.

He put down the receiver, thought for a moment, wondering what it could possibly be about. He picked up the phone once again and this time dialed the number he had written down on the notepad.

He recognized the answering voice on the other end of the line immediately. He identified himself.

"Yes . . . hello, Mr. McCallum—it's Lisel Lamprecht. Thank you for returning my call."

"Certainly."

"I wouldn't have blamed you if you hadn't. I half expected you to ignore the message I left."

"I would never have done that."

"I suppose maybe I knew that too." An awkward silence followed. "I . . . uh, wanted to see if you might be able to see your way clear to pay me another visit," said Lisel hesitantly after a moment. "That is, if you have time—I want to apologize for this morning and maybe have the chance to explain myself."

"Of course. Would you like me to come over?"

"Yes . . . yes, I would—if you don't mind."

"When . . . now?"

"I . . . I don't want to take you away from your conference."

"Aw, no problem," laughed Tad. "Most of it's not that interesting anyway. What time do you want me?"

"Would you, perhaps . . . consider joining me for dinner?"

"Sure, . . . but I don't want to put you out."

"It would be fun to cook dinner for someone besides my room-mate and myself. How is seven o'clock?"

"I'll be there."

Tad put down the phone, lifting his eyebrows in amused bewilder-ment. That was the fastest turnaround of an ill temper he had ever seen. He honestly had never expected to lay eyes on the young lady again.

PART VII

From Out of the Past

50

On the Run from a New Regime

• • •

Moscow

THE DARKENED STREETS DID NOT HINT THAT DAWN WAS less than two hours away.

Sounds were few, distant, muffled. The squeal of tires on pavement, the scream of a car's engine were amplified all out of proportion, as if they were the only sounds in the entire city.

Then silence once more—followed by the dull thudding of a cushioned footfall, pounding rapidly and rhythmically through the darkness.

Pursuer and prey—searching, hiding, chasing, eluding.

Even as Klaus Drexler revolved in his mind the many factors that would propel him onto center stage of the world's affairs, sixteen hundred kilometers to the east another man ran for his life through the deserted predawn streets of the Russian capital. The futures of the two men were destined to intertwine in a way neither was yet aware. Each knew *of* the other, though they had never spoken face-to-face.

Within hours Drexler's bone-crushing lackey called Claymore would be en route to Moscow to finish the job if the men now chasing him were unsuccessful. Galanov's snooping since the press conference a week ago had brought all this trouble down upon his head. All he thought about as he ran desperately through the deserted streets was to find cover before the gray of dawn began to show signs of life in the east and betrayed him.

Andrassy Galanov was older than Drexler, in his early fifties, though in the darkness it would have been difficult to tell. In his own way he had been equally powerful on his country's behalf for many years. His influence had been quiet, however, and out of the public eye, unlike Drexler, or even his own countryman, Drexler's clandestine ally, whose order had sent these neo-KGB agents after him.

But whatever influence Galanov had had, that was then, and this was now. The power he had once wielded suddenly seemed like the illusion of some dreaming fancy. He was no bureaucrat. Though had he been, he might have been safer at this moment. But he could never have taken that stifling life, and his own background had at least kept him trim and in shape, for which he was deeply grateful at this instant. The morning was about to break, and he was going to have to make a run for it, come what may.

They'd been on his trail all night, and even using all the old hideouts and routes and gimmicks, he hadn't been able to shake them. Light would expose him, and he'd be finished. How he prayed his hideaway flat was still safe. If they'd uncovered that, too, he was a dead man.

He took one last deep gulp of air, then stepped out of the alley and bolted across the wide stretch that was Vorovskovo Prospekt. With the gait of an aging marathoner well beyond the point of normal weariness, he sprinted as best he could. The imported Nikes silenced his footfall. That was some help at least, for the nearest streetlamp was over a hundred meters away.

Panting, he reached the opposite side, turned along the street, continued running half a block, then darted into another blackened alley and instantly stooped down into a crouch.

Exhaustion from a night of intermittent running was overtaking him. He closed his eyes and tried to relax, sucking in huge draughts of air. But the oxygen didn't come fast enough to ease the pain in his chest or quiet his gasping lungs.

He listened intently, trying to hear over his own breathlessness.
Silence.

He closed his eyes in relief. Maybe he *had* eluded them at last. If only he could make it back to his place and sleep for an hour or two. Then he'd be able to think about what—

The screeching of tires suddenly ended his thoughts of safety.

Curse them! They were still there!

He leapt up from his temporary hiding place, still out of breath, and ran into the depths of the darkened alleyway. Where it led he hadn't a clue, but he couldn't risk the open street again.

They would spot him instantly.

Behind him the car grew louder, its engine racing. Brakes skidded.

The tires squealed again, then headlights shone bright at his back, illuminating the alley in front of him.

How had they seen him in here! Sprinting with every ounce of fading energy, his legs felt like lead.

The car roared toward him, the headlights scattering menacing spotlights, probing the darkness in search of their prey.

Shots exploded behind him!

Still he ran.

His own pistol could do him no good. He'd run out of ammunition hours ago. Besides, there were probably four or five agents in the car.

More gunfire. A shattering series of sparks leapt off the stone building to his right, as the slug ricocheted off to the end of the alley. Another slammed into a window to his left. The sound of tinkling glass followed.

Without even realizing what he'd done, suddenly he found himself turning sharply into a narrow courtyard between two tall tenement buildings. Whether there was a way out at the other end, he didn't know. But he couldn't go back.

Behind him the car suddenly screeched to a stop.

He heard cursing and angry shouts. Two doors opened, then slammed.

The echo of footsteps in pursuit followed. Tires squealed, the car raced in reverse out of the alley.

He hesitated, listening.

A thin gray was about. Dawn was coming. But this poverty-stricken part of the city still slept.

He could hear the running steps. *Two men,* he thought. In the distance, the Mercedes tore through the streets. He could hear the occasional squeal of its tires. It was trying to cut him off at the other end.

He bolted again, wheezing in agony, chest heaving, calves tightening, arms nearly numb. His lungs stabbed with pain as he gulped for air that would not come, on—on—toward what seemed a futile attempt to escape.

But as long as he was seventy-five or a hundred meters ahead of his pursuers he would not give up.

Gradually his sleep-starved mind went numb. With dreamlike unreality, the buildings around him began to fade. The sounds of his own lungs and feet grew distant. The night's events seemed as a phantasm. Visions and illusions and mirages rose before the eye of his mind.

Yet he knew he was still awake, still running.

Is this what happens before death? his hallucinating brain asked. Was his life passing before his eyes?

Lucid again, suddenly his mind and eyes were clear. He still had a chance!

He could see the end of the narrow passageway now. It opened into another alley. There was no sound of the Mercedes. His pursuers had gained no ground. *They're probably ex-bureaucrats,* he thought cynically.

After years as the hunter, suddenly he had become the hunted—the former top KGB operative, the man Bolotnikov had depended on, all-powerful, all-feared, ruthless and cunning—now *he* was at the mercy of a carful of vindictive *bureaucrats* of old.

How quickly the tables turned! Now *they* were the *new* agents of so-called freedom.

Again his vision fuzzed. Images and faces and fragmentary glimpses of the past rose and fell in an illusory sequence of somnolent memories.

Still he ran. . . .

Feared Agent of the KGB

• • •

ANDRASSY GALANOV HAD WANTED TO BE AN AGENT SINCE before he could remember.

Born in Germany of Russian parents, he had been only four or five when the war ended. His first definable memories were of his father telling him of the encirclement and destruction of the German armies besieging Stalingrad, as the mighty Russian army moved westward to liberate Rostov, Kharkov, and the Caucasus.

He remembered little of that time personally. It was later, after they were back in Russia, that he came to know the fear, and that *had* remained vivid—hearing his parents talking, no longer about the Germans, but about the *American* threat, about the need to protect the motherland from invasion and attack.

He had been only nine when the first American spy plane had been shot down over the Baltic in 1950, and his memories of that incident were vague. But by the time the American U-2 was downed ten years later, he had decided what path his life would follow, influenced in no small measure by his uncle.

He had joined the KGB that same year, and the next had been sent to Berlin on his first assignment away from Moscow. Deporting himself well, he had thereafter gradually risen within the ranks of the Committee for State Security.

His uncle's death propelled him still higher, and for the last few years of Brezhnev's reign and the first several of the Gorbachev era, he had been KGB-head Bolotnikov's right-hand man and in all probability the second-highest intelligence man in all the Soviet Union.

The KGB was huge—with more employees in Moscow alone

than the combined numbers of the American CIA and FBI world-wide. During the Cold War years, from its headquarters at Lubyanka the secret organization extended its reach into nearly every aspect of Soviet society—protecting the country's vast borders and many leaders. It assembled dossiers on foreigners as well as its own people, from journalists to high officials, and carried out the world's largest espionage operation however it could—out of Soviet embassies, through businesses, and by using undercover agents as tourists and travelers and athletes.

He himself had been fortunate to get out in the field early in his career rather than to get stuck in the tangled web of bureaucracy. His year in Berlin, he had often said to himself since, had made a man of him and had taught him many things about the system.

It could not be denied that serving in the KGB had had its unpleasant side. Hauling old men off to the gulag, beating screaming wives until they divulged the whereabouts of their husbands' secret papers, bribing little children with candy to betray their schoolmates' parents—such requirements of the job demanded an allegiance to the state that was unquestioning.

And a ruthlessness. You just had to close your eyes to feelings. Emotions in Cold War Soviet Union didn't exist. They taught you that in training and reinforced it at every opportunity: The screams do not matter. Do not listen to them. They count for nothing.

They were not *really* the screams of anguish of a heart being ripped out of a countryman's breast. They were not screams of pain at all, only the sounds of those who didn't understand, didn't see the purpose, the necessity. Didn't see that they were *protecting* them and their interests by making the state supreme.

He had first killed at twenty-six. It had not been easy, but he had prepared himself for it. There were no emotions. You do not look into their eyes. Close your own for a moment afterward if you have to. But do not let their eyes find yours.

Killing was a necessary corollary to the protection of the people. They taught you that too.

He had killed again, with steely resolve and unflinching determination. And beaten . . . and spied upon. He had lied, tricked, double-crossed, and browbeat . . . and by thirty-five was known as one of the KGB's best and most ruthless.

His skills became so widely known in the intelligence community that attempts were made to recruit and lure him to the other side, most notably by the French. He had even been given a two-year sabbatical from his duties, had gone to Paris, lived there, and had given them completely to believe they had turned him. Thereafter he had made several forays back into the Soviet Union, ostensibly on the business of the French as a double agent, a ruse he continued for many years, even to the point of feeding Paris information of apparent intelligence value.

It was all an elaborately conceived charade, of course, contrived in Moscow and plotted out in intricate detail. He had taken such delight in all the maneuvering and posturing and secrecy with the French and their stuffy ways, stringing them along, chuckling to himself at their seriousness and pomposity. It had been like taking candy from a baby!

But even the double-agent operations with the French had not been his first love, if *love* it could be called. Hatred would more accurately describe his feelings toward the Jews and ridiculous fundamentalist believers. Where the intense antipathy had come from, he didn't know. Probably from his mother—forever praying and angering his father, who always said that kind of thing had no more place in the modern Soviet Union.

As he had grown and then moved up in his career with the KGB, no group of irritants had been more stealthy, underhanded, crafty, insidious, subtle, and outright treasonous and subversive as the Christians. His uncle Korsyakev had always said so, and his experience had confirmed it time and time again.

Something about the Christians had always enraged him more than the rest. They had seemed more determined than everyone else to thwart and resist and destroy the Communist system—meeting in secret, praying for its overthrow, distributing their Bibles and literature, smuggling *in* material and supplies, and smuggling *out* known outlaws. As a group, they had been more obstreperous and antagonistic than any other.

He had first taken a special delight in rooting them out, spying upon their unsuspecting leaders, breaking up their prayer meetings, sending their ringleaders to Siberia.

It never stopped them, of course. They *were* a determined lot! As committed to their cause as he was his, he would say that much for them.

This had been impressed upon him most graphically that night as he led the raid on their Bible factory in the small town outside Moscow.

It had been the dead of night. They had reached the place and broken in without giving a hint of their approach, and had thus discovered the lawbreakers in the very midst of their activity.

He hadn't believed it at first!

Children, teenagers, women, men, all spread out at tables or on the floor around the rooms of the house, each hand copying different sections of a single Bible that had been cut apart into its separate books. In questioning them he had learned that their laborious work went on every night.

A search of the rest of the house and attic uncovered a dozen completed Bibles, hand stitched together, representing probably several months' work. Everything had been confiscated—the whole Bibles, the portions being worked on, *and* the printed original—and promptly burned.

But he had never forgotten the lesson of that night—how tenacious and hardworking these people could be. And henceforth he kept a keen eye about for any sign of other such hidden book and Bible factories, especially those involving typewriters.

One of the worst had been an old crippled man with a broken-down typewriter who had spent every waking minute for years typing out carbon copies of Bible-teaching books, which he gave to others to bind and then circulate all over Russia.

Galanov hadn't sent the old traitor to prison. He was probably seventy-five already, so what difference did it make? But he had smashed the typewriter to bits right in front of his tear-filled eyes and kept up surveillance on the place thereafter.

Yes, they were a determined lot!

He had become known as the Believers' Worst Enemy—a nickname he had learned of after intercepting a hastily scrawled note just before a raid on a prayer meeting. He knew more of their ways, more of their secret hideouts, more of their routines than anyone in the KGB. Whenever there was a major assignment involving underground believers, it was turned over to him.

When Bolotnikov had risen to head the security organization fourteen years ago, Galanov had not had difficulty ingratiating himself and rising up still further, for the new top man was also known to despise Christians.

His nemesis, a high-up Christian leader by the name of Rostovchev—the very same man whom Galanov had himself encountered on the streets of Moscow long before either had risen in their chosen fields of endeavor—had eluded Bolotnikov for years, and Bolotnikov was consumed with a passionate vendetta to put him away permanently.

52

First Pangs of Conscience

• • •

WHEN AND WHY THE CHANGE HAD COME . . . WHO
could tell? He had never been able to figure it out. Whereas the
Christians had always enraged him, slowly Andrassy Galanov found
that they were beginning to unnerve him as well.

It might have begun early in his career, though the incident had
only recently come back to him, sowing seeds of doubt he had
ignored back then. It had been one of his first such raids. His superior
had burst into the room, with Galanov and a half-dozen others
following on his heels.

"What are you doing?" the KGB officer had demanded. From the
singing, which continued after their interruption, they knew very
well what was going on.

A man approached, and answered in a quiet, peaceful voice. "We
are worshiping God," he answered kindly.

"There is no God. You will have to stop immediately," said the
agent in charge.

"We believe there is, and we are worshiping him," replied the
man.

"You cannot!"

"Why?"

"Because it is against the law. We have been sent with orders that
say it must be stopped immediately."

"But we are *not* breaking the law," replied the man, still speaking
very politely. "Comrade Lenin himself said that citizens of our
country have the right and freedom to worship God."

He had seen his leader at a momentary loss for anything to say.

"Comrade Lenin said that every citizen of our country has the full right to exercise his belief in religious worship, or not to believe, as he chooses," the Christian went on. Then he had begun to quote the Soviet constitution, where the very words did in fact state that every citizen had the right to fulfill his religious beliefs. "All we are doing, comrade," the man had concluded, "is using the right the founder of our country and our Soviet constitution provide. We are harming no one. We simply believe in God and are worshiping him. What have we done wrong?"

At last he waited for a reply from the leader of the KGB raiding party.

But Galanov's superior could not refute what had been said. All he could do was fall back on the same argument as before. "None of what you say matters," he had replied. "You are violating the laws of our country!"

Without awaiting further discussion, he had grabbed the gentle Christian viciously by the arm, yanked him outside the house, and proceeded to beat him as if he had been a punching bag. The man never uttered a peep of protest, and three minutes later the raiding party had gone, leaving the man motionless in the snow, his face unrecognizable.

If his doubts had begun that far back, Galanov hadn't known it. Before long he was conducting raids himself, hardening himself to the reality that in truth it was *not* against Soviet law to worship the God of one's choice.

Perhaps doubts began to creep in that time he had gone to prison, accepting an invitation from the warden to see what befell the cursed believers after he brought them into *his* domain. There he had watched, silently trying to keep his stomach under control, as the prison guard had shown him tortures too horrible to imagine—red-hot pokers, razor-sharp knives, merciless beatings. He was shown specially designed pipes into various cells, through which starving rats could be released. Prisoners chosen for such torment could not sleep, but had to constantly defend themselves against the disease-infected rodents or else be literally eaten and chewed upon. Many and gruesome were the cruelties devised by the warden, whose eyes gleamed with pride in displaying his ingenuity.

Mostly the doubts had come when Galanov began to make the

mistake of looking into their eyes. Then he knew why he had been told never to do so. It undid him. He found hesitation creeping in . . . doubt—lethal to one in his position. Something was in those eyes that all his years of KGB training and experience had not prepared him to see.

When he and Rostovchev met that first time in Moscow, something about the man irritated him—the bold, soft-spoken confidence, the utter lack of fear . . . and of course all that religious humbug.

But during that madcap dash across Poland and into the DDR, after Rostovchev had eluded he and Bolotnikov that night, he found unpleasant feelings attempting to encroach into his long-secure hatred.

It wasn't that he had actually found himself stung by pangs of conscience. Yet the long furious drive had given him time to think. The idiocy of their extreme efforts to capture one man had come to his mind a time or two. He tried to tell himself that *Der Prophet* was a vital connection, a ringleader, one of the top men in the country, and that no effort to capture or kill him could be spared. At the time he had not known the Prophet and Rostovchev to be one and the same—though he should have suspected it.

Something had continued to gnaw away at him, even as he had driven recklessly toward Warsaw after him. KGB agents weren't supposed to think, to have feelings. He had squelched them sufficiently during those next few days to carry on with the assignment.

But then when he had seen Rostovchev face-to-face in that field, *that's* when he had first made the fatal mistake of looking into *his* eyes! It had momentarily unhinged him.

The man had changed, matured, deepened since their brief encounter in Moscow. Changed . . . but *not* changed. What was it—some unseen power? When Galanov came to himself, the thought of it enraged him all the more.

Yet something had begun that night, and he'd found the eyes of the Christians he persecuted more difficult to avoid ever after. He'd kept it to himself and worked doubly hard to root them out, angered all the more at their seeming capacity to twist his stomach in knots.

And he had to admit, when the orders began coming down after Gorbachev came to power to ease their investigations, harassments, and persecutions of Christian groups, down inside he felt a sense of relief. He'd be content to have nothing more to do with them.

Rostovchev's eyes had begun it!

He never should have let himself get drawn into the banter with him. He should have thrown him in the car and been off. Then that idiotic farmer wouldn't have had the chance to get in his way and louse the whole thing up!

That hadn't helped either! Getting knocked to the ground by the bumbling German fool, then Dmitri getting away in the darkness. Then accidentally shooting the girl who was running off with him . . . the whole night had ended in a dismal failure!

He was glad he hadn't seen the *girl's* eyes! In the state he'd been in right then he doubted he'd have been able to take it!

The memory of her back was hard enough to erase from his mind . . . running . . . running . . . the explosion from his pistol . . . the sound of her scream . . . then the thud of her fall.

It had replayed in his mind over and over a thousand times since. What was he turning into . . . a KGB agent feeling pangs or remorse . . . even guilt! It was not supposed to happen. They were enemies of the state. They had to be—

Suddenly his feet gave way beneath him as he stumbled over a piece of broken cement. He could not recover his balance and crashed to the ground . . . just like the girl he had killed.

Suddenly he was wide awake and alert again, his dreamlike recollections vanishing instantly.

53

Galanov's Dilemma

. . .

WHERE HE WAS HE WASN'T EVEN SURE.

He'd been running steadily, judging from the panting of his lungs and the sweat pouring from his face and shirt. How he'd summoned the energy to keep it up he couldn't imagine. He struggled to one knee. He'd fallen hard on the pavement. A shooting pain came from both hands where he'd tried to break the fall. His left knee was bleeding, though he wouldn't discover it for some time.

He listened. No footsteps followed. There was no sign of the Mercedes.

Even in his relief at having eluded his pursuers, he could not help berating them. *Stupid bureaucrats!* he thought to himself. *They are no match for the real KGB!* But their bullets were just as real. Bludayev had to know he was onto him and was scared.

It seemed *everybody* was after him!

He rose, painfully, and took stock of his surroundings. There was barely more light now than when he remembered dashing through that narrow place between the buildings. How much time had elapsed—five . . . ten minutes at the most. He didn't immediately recognize where he was.

He was alone, and that was good. And he knew the general vicinity.

He couldn't risk going home. He hadn't been there in days. They'd have had it surrounded the moment his name had been put on the list.

He wasn't far from the flat he had set up as a hideaway. *No one* knew of its whereabouts.

Not even Bolotnikov. He wondered how *he* was making out in this present purge. No doubt landing on his feet. His type always did! His old boss would no doubt find some new "position" in the current order of things. It was the second-level hatchet men—men like himself—who were now in most danger.

He began walking and now first realized how utterly exhausted his body was, from numb fingers to scraped palms, from heaving chest to bleeding knee.

The irony struck him again. A former KGB agent running for *his* life!

But Russia had had a history filled with ironies, with constant switchings and realignments. In 1917, in one masterful stroke Lenin had replaced the czarist bourgeoisie with the proletariat. Suddenly commoners ruled the empire. Yet in time, Lenin and Stalin and the Communist Party had become a brand new elite, squelching and oppressing those under them. What had he been all those years as a KGB agent but a member of an elite of sorts?

And now, just as suddenly, it was gone. The Soviet Union was dead. Lenin was in disgrace. Communism was undone.

Topsy-turvy it went. The Cultural Revolution in China. The ups were down, the downs, up. The haves were suddenly cast adrift.

Now it was *his* time, like it or not! The elite KGB agent suddenly on the underside of the realignment. Housecleaning, some had called it after 1990. The hunter had become the hunted!

He had laughed when Lithuania's black berets had complained of not being able to get out after the Baltics declared their independence, appealing for the very human rights they had denied those under them. The huge irony of it. But he was not laughing now. Now it was his time. The purge had turned on him.

Now the new democratic regime had to root out and toss the old bad guys to the wolves, and his reputation had always been as one of the KGB's worst. The very bureaucrats he had always disdained were now in power . . . and hunting him down.

Nowhere in Russia would be safe for him! Democracy . . . freedom . . . what did those words mean to people like him, caught in the web of old and new trying to sort themselves out?

This was the side of Russian "democracy" the outside world would never witness—the housecleaning. Every new set of

Russian leaders did it—Lenin purged himself of troublesome people *within* the party, as did Stalin, Brezhnev, all of them. The new democratic leaders were still Russians. A new gloss. But the old rules still applied. They always would. Russia was Russia, there was no getting around it.

He had to get out.

He would never be free here. He had to escape to the West. No matter how many democratic freedoms were given to the Russian people themselves, *he* would never be free. Those freedoms were only meant for some, but not for the hard-liners of the old regime. It would be death to remain behind.

His only hope was escape . . . and to find a new life.

As soon as he got out of this immediate fix he had to get back on track with his investigation, though it would be hard given his outlaw status. He still had plenty of contacts and friends. He'd have to conduct the investigation deep underground.

He had to find out what was going on with Desyatovsky and the German. He could smell it. He knew it was big. Hopefully big enough to deal his way out of the country with. He had a feeling it went right to the top. He had to know!

He'd been an agent too long to back away from something this big, even if his life depended on it . . . which, at this moment, he had the clear feeling it did!

Maybe he was being a fool. But he had to play out his hand . . . and then get out of Russia.

Where Does Conversion Begin?

• • •

Berlin

WHO CAN TELL, IN THE UNSEEN REGIONS OF HEAVENLY purpose, where the beginnings are to be discovered from which the arrows of truth are aimed, or when they are released in the direction of any human soul?

Likewise, who can tell why those arrows seem more decisively sent toward some than others? Why does a dawn come when suddenly a murderer beholds the light of what he is and whence comes his salvation, while millions of contented souls never in all their lives perceive that all-important revelation that leads to life?

Why do some hearts respond and allow themselves to be drawn fully into the truth, while others remain all their days in a dim spiritual stupor of listlessness?

What is the central distinctiveness between two souls that causes one to wake and choose to say *Yes!* and then rise up from his slumber and the other to glance disinterestedly about, face the light of day, and yet choose to roll over and drift lazily back to sleep?

It can only be said that the Savior came to save *all* those who are lost, and he remains about that business to this day. But it is a more lengthy affair in the case of some than others.

Yet when one of those arrows of light finds its mark, the angels rejoice—whether salvation has come to murderer, Pharisee, contented church person, or atheist rebel. The very heavens resonate with that rejoicing whenever any life—however it has been lived till that moment—is snatched from the hands of the enemy.

Such a moment was now at hand.

• • •

While the former KGB agent ran for his life, and hundreds of would-be evangelists slept contentedly in their beds, Tad McCallum lay awake in the black predawn hours replaying in his mind the events of the evening.

Many things were going through his brain.

The evening had been remarkable simply in how enjoyable he had found it.

The invitation to supper was surprising enough in itself, but even that had not prepared him for the pleasant time in store. He would never have imagined himself with the same young lady who had thrown him out on his ear that morning.

The good Fräulein Lamprecht was positively pleasant. She and her roommate had shown their guest every consideration, were friendly in every way, and had laid out an evening spread of breads and rolls, meats, cheeses, jams, and pastries such as he had not seen since arriving in Germany.

The conversation around the table had been mostly mundane. As soon as they had finished and coffee had been served, Lisel led Tad into the small sitting room, where she wasted no time jumping directly into the subject of their earlier conversation.

"As I said to you on the phone," she began the moment they were seated, "I want to apologize for this morning. I hope you will forgive me."

"Of course" Tad smiled. "Say no more—it is already forgotten."

"You are very kind to be so understanding."

"I take my Christianity seriously. Forgiveness is part of the package. You were already forgiven by the time I was halfway down the stairs this morning."

"I was still upset then. I hadn't asked for it yet."

"Forgiveness is one of many aspects of the Christian faith that is not a two-way street. The command is upon *me* to forgive, and it has nothing to do with what *you* do or do not do."

"Well, in any case, I *do* ask for your forgiveness now, and I appreciate your being so gracious in extending it."

"Don't mention it," replied Tad.

"I did behave badly, and despite the fact that I still don't agree with much of what you said, I nevertheless wanted to make it right."

"You have more than made up for it. And I sincerely thank you."

There was a brief pause.

"Do you really believe," asked Lisel after a moment, "that forgiveness is not a two-way street? It seems that without both parties forgiving, a relationship couldn't get all the way restored."

"I think just the opposite is the case," answered Tad. "I think one person is well able to see to the job being done."

"How?"

"By forgiving with no strings attached."

Lisel lifted her eyebrows, inviting him to explain further.

"If someone is waiting for another to do *his share* of the forgiving," Tad went on, "there will never be much of a solution. Forgiveness has to be complete, no strings attached, within *one* heart, in order to get the process moving. If each individual waited for the *other* person always to initiate a healing attitude and response, not much restoration would ever take place between men and women."

Lisel pondered his words a moment. "An interesting concept," she said.

"I'm not much of a believer in the old fifty-fifty adage when it comes to forgiveness. Forgiving somebody halfway is the same as not forgiving them at all, or so it seems to me."

"That's not a very modern and contemporary view in this age of equality," remarked Lisel.

"But I never claimed to be in step with the modern age. I would hope, in fact, that just the opposite is the case."

"An odd point of view."

"You find my saying I want to be out of step with the world peculiar?"

"Don't you?"

"I think it's the most sane of all possible approaches to life."

"I must admit, I don't think I've ever heard that before."

"Being in step with contemporary ways is lethal for a Christian."

"Do all Christians feel as you do about that?"

Tad laughed. "Actually, very few. Take this conference I'm attending—half the suggestions being thrown out are exactly what a marketing organization might come up with to change public opinion on some issue having nothing to do with religious beliefs at all. I have seen nothing thus far to distinguish the methods as prompted by a distinctly Christian enterprise. Which explains exactly why, as you pointed out this morning, there are so many Christian hypocrites."

"I'm not sure I follow you."

"Christians are commanded *not* to be like the world, yet most Christians expend considerable energy in the attempt to be *just like* the world. And there you have the exact recipe for making a hypocrite—not living by the precepts of the value system you espouse."

"It has always seemed to me that Christians *do* set themselves up as different," rejoined Lisel.

"I agree," said Tad. "But setting yourself up as different does not *make* you different. Down inside, most Christians have the same attitudes and values and ambitions as everyone."

"Is that so bad?"

"I didn't say it was *bad*—I only said the command is on us to be otherwise. And if, down inside, your attitudes and values and ambitions are just like everyone else's, but you spread a spiritual gloss of Christian words over the top of it . . . well, there we are again, back at the recipe for a hypocrite."

"I must admit," laughed Lisel, "you are about the plainest-speaking Christian I've ever met."

Tad laughed too. "You have to realize, I'm a little unusual. A character trait of my family, I suppose. Not many of my fellow Christians would agree with me about what I've just said."

"You mean about the hypocrisy?"

Tad nodded. "Most of my fellow Christians," he said with a sad sigh, "generally speaking, are pretty pleased with themselves. And I've got to watch constantly against that danger myself."

Again Lisel laughed lightly in spite of Tad's tone, shaking her head in something like disbelief.

"What is it?" he asked.

"I just have never talked with a Christian so willing to look at the flaws in Christianity."

"Correction—the flaws in how Christians *live* their Christianity, not flaws in Christianity itself. Concerning the latter, I don't believe there are any."

"Yes," Lisel said with a wry smile, "I believe you made that clear earlier. In any case, I do admire how you look at it all so realistically . . . I just hope you're not going to turn it back on me again," she added.

"I won't—I promise," laughed Tad.

The conversation had, by unspoken mutual consent, remained lighter and less probing than that of earlier in the day, and now drifted off into other channels.

Each felt a gradually increasing freedom to share personally how they viewed things, without either sensing that the other was attempting to change his perspective. Tad was especially nonthreatening in his half of the dialogue and avoided anything that might wrongly be construed as critical of Lisel's comments, which in truth he did not find all that objectionable.

The result for the rest of the evening was a refreshingly free-flowing yet unpressured exchange, at the end of which they both knew a great deal about the other, even though, by surface appearances, they remained poles apart in their spiritual viewpoints. They were, in reality, not nearly so far apart as it might seem.

By the time Tad left her after ten o'clock that evening, Lisel had told him of her Christian upbringing and of the explosive outburst the day she had left home.

It was with obvious feeling that she related the painful incident, though as he sat listening Tad sensed that she was still keeping the greater portion of her emotions in check. A certain dispassionate reserve could be detected in her voice. Tad realized she was sharing with him the rift with her father as a way of attempting to further explain her behavior of that same morning.

No hint of remorse entered her tone for what she had done twelve years earlier. Lisel did not tell him of her friend's death. She was not quite prepared to go *that* far in reliving that bitter time.

Tad knew there was more to the story than she had revealed, for an occasional look of pain passed through her eyes, notwithstanding the generally stoic countenance with which she spoke about the past.

He did not mind that she kept certain details to herself. For Tad also knew that in the very telling of even of a portion of what had occurred doors were preparing to open deep within her that would lead to what must always come in time: healing, restoration, and wholeness.

He began praying for his new friend, in hopes that one day he might be able to consider her his sister as well.

Slowly sleep began again to come over him.

It had been a memorable evening. Tad could hardly believe they had agreed to meet for lunch the following day. It had just seemed spontaneously to happen. Before he knew it the arrangements had been made.

All he had been hoping for was an interview for an article. Already, in less than twenty-four hours, it had turned into a great deal more.

*   *   *

Lisel likewise awoke in the middle of the night, and her thoughts were similarly directed toward the evening just past. She rolled over in her bed onto her back, staring up toward the blackened ceiling of her room, thinking to herself how unusual Tad was.

He was different from *any* young man she had ever encountered in the Alliance. He was so . . . so . . . full of enthusiasm, energy, smiles, such a keen thinker, yet sensitive too, so accepting of her, so open.

Was the difference that he was an American? Was it his personality? Or might it have to do with his being a Christian?

He had made no attempt to convert her. That was probably what drew her most of all.

He was honest and unafraid to say what he thought, but completely uncondemning in his attitude. She had told him straight to his face that she didn't believe the Christian story. Yet he seemed to accept her nonetheless for it and even seemed to like her and enjoy her company *anyway.*

It was remarkable. She could not *help* liking him. He was the most genuine and real person she had encountered in years. How different did she feel now than when they had parted in the morning. It was still embarrassing to think about what she had done, but at least it was over with.

This time she was filled with pleasant thoughts, even though the evening had touched on some deep and unresolved caverns within her own being. He had said some things that would come back to her in time, but not until the moment for their surgical work was at hand.

For now, Lisel drifted back to sleep with a smile on her face, feeling happier than she had in months.

• • •

The two young people were not alone in their nighttime wakefulness.

Down the hall from her son, while her husband slept contentedly, Sabina McCallum had been roused from her slumber by deep callings from on high.

She immediately felt upon her the urge to pray—she knew not why, she knew not for whom, she only knew prayer was required because significant things of great import in the spirit realm were nigh.

As she gave silent utterance on behalf of God's will against whatever strongholds would thwart his purposes, Sabina's thoughts came to rest upon the memory of her father.

The legacy of his presence was always with her. Every thread in the fabric of her being had been woven by the Father's hand on the loom of her earthly father's life, teaching, and character. Suddenly she was more aware than she had ever been of that legacy now passing through her, through Matthew, and on into others—not Tad merely, but many she would never know.

She began to pray for *all* those who would be touched, in whatever way and to whatever measure, by any of their lives, for those touched by all who had been part of the *Network of the Rose,* for those who would in time be touched by her son and the ongoing flow of spiritual life that would proceed through him.

And thus, in the middle of the night in the Westmark Hotel in Berlin, were more and lengthier prayer strands added to that *Rose* tapestry, which the unseen hand of the Father had been weaving with interconnected life-threads for two generations.

Wakefulness had come to mother and son because wakefulness was about to break upon the two for whom they prayed—the one knowingly, the other unknowingly.

A birthing approached, which requires *much* accompanying prayer. The Spirit had spoken to these who knew his voice, so that they might pray for readiness on the part of those who soon would come to recognize it.

Nor were they the only children of God raising intercessions at that moment to the Most High. Far in the east, interwoven into the same tapestry of life with threads connecting him to both Sabina and

Lisel, a faithful son of the Father sat in the darkness of a small room waiting . . . and praying.

For this opportunity he had prayed for many years. The Spirit was indeed readying to speak, though how different would be his voice when it entered the two hearts who had been running from him and to whom he had laid his claim.

He had sent his arrows of salvation after them . . . and they were about to find their marks.

Whence originates the salvation of men? Where does conversion begin? In the bosom of the Father, in the deepest regions of the heart of God's love.

55

A Moment of Light

. . .

Moscow

ON THE FUGITIVE WALKED.

KGB agent, persecutor of God's people, suddenly alone, adrift . . . all former reference points of life gone . . . with no friends . . . no place to turn for help but to what remained of his pride in his own self-sufficiency.

Inside many conflicts assailed him.

Visions began again to encroach upon his consciousness . . . people he had herded into waiting prison vans . . . beatings . . . screams . . . women out of whose hands he had brutally torn Bibles . . . a man he had knocked into unconsciousness for kneeling down to pray for him.

Pray for *him!*

How could those people pray for him? He hated them! He had killed them and spit on them and flogged them and imprisoned them for just mentioning the name of their so-called Savior. *They prayed for him!* The thing was logically absurd!

Their eyes were always filled with that . . . that look he could never describe.

He could still recall the man's words as he knelt down: *"O loving Father, in the name of Jesus your Son I ask you to forgive this man, and by your love to draw him one day to—"*

There had been no more. The butt of his rifle had smashed cruelly against the side of the man's head the next instant, and he had crumpled to the floor without uttering another sound.

He had never been able to forget the words. How he had tried! But they had been indelibly burned into some deep place in his own heart, and they refused to go away.

Love . . . forgive . . . what could the man have meant? How did those words bear any relation to *him!*

And the man's eyes as he had gazed upon him before closing them to utter those same words! Neither would he forget the man's eyes!

Suddenly a bright light shone in front of him, cutting short his broodings. Galanov's chest seized him in panic. They had known his whereabouts all along! Why hadn't he heard the sound of the car?

Quickly he spun around and ran in the opposite direction. Then he remembered he had been followed from behind too. He stopped, glancing around. Still no sound disturbed the gray morning air.

If the light he had seen came from the Mercedes, why was there only one light, not two? And it was far too bright to be an automobile's headlamps.

Some inner sense filled him, compelling him forward. He could not disobey. Slowly he began walking again, inching toward the origin of the great light.

A dread passed through Galanov's body. Had he finally gone over the edge into lunacy? It happened in his line of work. Had exhaustion taken over and scrambled his brain so that he could no longer distinguish fantasy from reality?

Still there was no sound . . . no footsteps . . . no car. Only the brilliance ahead of him, urging him nearer.

Something seemed to be telling him to stop. He stayed his step . . . then stood . . . still, motionless and silent . . . waiting.

Dread and expectancy mingled throughout his being.

Minutes or seconds passed—he could not tell which. Suddenly a voice spoke from out of the great light . . . or at least, he heard a voice. Whether it was audible he did not know. He only knew he *sensed* it.

"Why do you persecute me and tyrannize my people?"

Galanov was filled with terror at the sound. The voice was deep, clear, and commanding. It seemed to come from the middle of the light itself.

This is the end, Galanov thought.

He was either hallucinating or had finally gone completely mad.

Yet the voice had spoken with an authority that could not be ignored, and he found himself answering it with his own timid voice.

"But who . . . what . . . are you?" he said. To his own ears, his voice sounded small, feeble, faint. "Have you come . . . to arrest me . . . kill me?"

Still he gazed at the light.

"I come to bring you life."

"But . . . who sent you for me?" Galanov squeaked.

"I am the Sender, the Giver of life."

"I do not . . . but who . . . ?

"I am the Lord, whose people you torment and harass," came the answer, full of mingled severity, compassion, and energy. The power of the voice was not in its volume, but in its quality that commanded attention . . . and obedience.

"Now go. From this day forward, you shall serve me," said the voice finally. *"No longer shall you persecute me, but you too shall spread my Life among men."*

As he gazed, suddenly the light was gone. Silence and the gray dawn were his only companions. Andrassy Galanov stood alone on the deserted streets.

Yet a moment more he stood, then began stumbling forward. Instantly his brain cleared and he recognized his surroundings. His step gradually became more steady. He took two or three deep breaths, then quickened his pace.

A clarity of focus and a renewed sense of hopefulness infused his consciousness. He did not pause to reflect upon whether these sensations were directly connected to the extraordinary experience he had just had. He merely flowed with the feelings rising up within himself. He would sort out the implications later.

In spite of his sleeplessness and exhaustion, the former KGB agent found himself filled with a great sense of energy and well-being, and quickly he strode the remaining ten blocks to his hideout. He encountered no one and scarcely bothered to make sure he was not being followed. Somehow he knew he would be safe now. His step seemed lighter with every stride.

Out of habit rather than fear he took all the usual precautions: entering the alley two blocks away, he sat to rest deep in its darkness for five minutes, then climbed the nearby fire escape by which he entered the building beside him. It was never locked. He knew the long corridor even in the dark. The only light burning was a dim fifteen-watt bulb at the far end. Reaching it, he descended three flights of stairs and opened the door into the storage basement. Only now did he pull out his tiny flashlight. It was pitch black down here.

Stealthily he traversed the basement hallway, the end of which had been broken in to connect by a dirt tunnel only about five feet high the basement of the building across the street. Stooping down, he hurried through the passageway and within another two or three minutes was safely into the building. Up another several flights of stairs, out an open window, up the fire escape, across the roof, and across to the roof of his own building with a short leap of four or five feet. Down the fire escape, into the building, down the stairs, and at last he was nearing his own little hideaway—two rooms he'd procured years ago in an old run-down tenement building that had been used for storage longer than anybody could remember. It still said so on the door, and he possessed the only key to the lock. The outer room he still kept full of boxes and crates and broken, discarded equipment, just in case. The inner room was just large enough for a bed, a chair, a desk, and a commode.

He unlocked the door, breathing a long sigh of relief at last, and again flipped on his penlight. Everything was undisturbed.

He made his way through the cartons and refuse and into his inner lair. Without even turning on the light, he collapsed across the bed. The weak springs under the mattress had barely ceased their metallic, squeaky groaning, when the sound of someone else in the room nearly shocked him into a coronary.

"It is good to see you again at last, Herr Andrassy Galanov," said a man less than five feet away. "I have been sent for you."

Musings of a Russian Pragmatist

• • •

BLUDAYEV DESYATOVSKY WAS NOT A PENSIVE MAN, BUT rather a pragmatist.

Leave philosophy to the Chinese. Leave technology to the Japanese or Germans. Leave bluster to the Americans.

The one thing the Russian understood better than them all was power . . . raw power. The power to control and dominate world events and bend them to move according to one's will.

That's why he would come out on top in the end. That was the one thing the German fool did not grasp. They had always taken Russians for granted, thought they could have their way with them. But not now . . . not this Russian. New times were ahead. A new world order indeed! One that he, not the soft-spoken American president, would dictate.

In his early sixties, Desyatovsky was the oldest of the principal players in the drama he was himself helping to write. He had waited many years, been a good soldier, and come up slowly through the Khrushchev, Brezhnev, and Gorbachev eras, awaiting his opportunity.

Now it had come.

As he sat reflectively at his desk, slowly sipping the vodka in the glass in his hand, the bulk of his massive frame sunk low into his chair. His eyes gazed forward, not with the probing fire of vision, but rather with a contented pride in at last having reached nearly the apex of power. He would not philosophize about it, he would just move forward into it.

Again he raised the glass to his full, fleshy lips. Above them, wide-set eyes peered out from between a high forehead and multiple folds of ample cheek-skin. Thinning hair, nearly all gray, was ordinarily hidden during the day by his military hat. But now, in the privacy of his own late-night aloneness, his German counterpart would have been shocked to see how old the man appeared.

He was old and not in very good shape, for Desyatovsky's thick frame had acquired a good deal of flab over the last ten years—also skillfully kept hidden by his military uniform. But in public and over the phone where he conducted much of his business these days, the general still exerted a powerful will that did not depend on his slowly deteriorating physique.

Desyatovsky threw back his head, emptied the small crystal glass, then rose. He walked to his file cabinet, unlocked it, and flipped through masses of folders, pulling out at length a stiff cardboard packet, itself sealed by a miniature padlock and marked in bright red "TOP SECRET: For the Eyes of General Desyatovsky Only." True, he reflected, neither the padlock nor the warning would keep anyone who really wanted inside from slicing it with a sharp knife. But it would keep prying secretarial eyes from getting too curious. If he was ousted or his office broken into by force . . . well, it would be all over by then anyway. By the time they got to the file, he had already determined to make a quick exit of things by the suicidal Boris Pugo route.

And if he were greeted by Pugo on a cloud someplace bemoaning their mutual failures—Pugo's to usurp Gorbachev and his own to usurp Yeltsin—then anyone could have the packet who wanted it!

The defense minister of the Republic of Russia again closed the file drawer and walked with packet in hand back to his desk, where he opened the third drawer down and pulled out a small box, locked by combination. With deft motions of his fingers, he spun the tiny dial to the right, then left, then right again.

Flipping open the top, he reached inside and extracted a tiny brass key, by which he opened the top secret envelope lying on his desk. Replacing key and box and closing the drawer to his desk, Desyatovsky opened the file and pulled out several manila folders from within it. They were marked "Military," "Industry/Business," "Foreign Leaders," "Political/Moscow," "Political/Republics," "Media," "Transportation," and "Finance." Inside each, on the folder itself, was printed a single telephone number.

This is what Yanayev, Kryuchkov, Baklanov, Starodubtsev, and Tizyakov had never grasped. The sprawling Soviet empire had changed dramatically since 1985 and Gorbachev's ascension. The strings were more complicated to pull now. The people were more aware. They hadn't taken into account all the necessary factors, hadn't struck decisively, boldly, and quickly, hadn't seized control of enough sectors of society.

And of course they hadn't taken into account Boris Yeltsin and the huge public and international support he had behind him. He wouldn't make the same mistakes. He would have *all* the elements solidly in place. It was all in the files, Desyatovsky thought with satisfaction.

Years of work, hundreds of favors, and great patience. Luckily he'd seen the handwriting on the wall years ago. He'd disassociated himself with the party early on in the reorganizing struggle, clear back in the eighties. He'd known the futility of wedding himself to the past like the apparatchiks and defeated party stalwarts who had failed in 1991.

His was a new movement, new in the mold of Volsky and Kozyrev and Eduard Shevardnadze, but going far beyond glasnost and perestroika, going further into the future than either Gorbachev or Yeltsin or any of their own breed of rising stars could ever hope to have taken the republics.

He would make the sovereign state Russia the foundation stone of the new order that Drexler liked to call the Eurasian Alliance— strong, dazzling, prosperous, alive, energetic, and without peer on the global scene.

The Revolution of 1917 was dead, Communism was dead, the Common Market was dead, the Warsaw Pact and NATO were dead. Many of his colleagues would have had a difficult time admitting it, but capitalism had endured as the victor.

But like Communism, American capitalism was dead too! *Both* sides had lost the Cold War.

The new community of nations and peoples would emerge out of the ashes of both. No longer weighed down by the excess baggage of all the other former Soviet republics, Russia would stand tall among those of the new Eurasian community, with new might and a loud voice to proclaim the future. And *he*, Bludayev Desyatovsky, neither Communist nor American capitalist, but of a new breed of leader for the new era of mankind, he would lead the way into the twenty-first century!

Thoughtfully he thumbed through the single folder without a title. This was where it would begin, and the key was timing. Circumstances had to be just right. All the men together if possible . . . an accident . . . a limousine . . . the train . . . some mad terrorist.

The perfect situation had fallen into his lap with the so-called summit. The hit man in this file had plenty of experience in disguising his nefarious work. He trusted him completely, more than the fellow the German had told him about.

It was a good thing. If the whole plan unraveled, he'd given instructions to see to his *own* untimely end too. He didn't want to be around to face the music if something went wrong. He'd already paid the man the fee for his own head, just in case.

His thoughts flitted again to Pugo. He winced and shook the thought of an arranged suicide from his brain. Nothing would go wrong . . . nothing *could* go wrong. He had seen to everything. That's what all the other files were about.

He set the stack on his desk, took out that marked "Media," and eased back into his chair, feet propped on the edge of his desk, and began sifting through the sheets inside. This is where he had to make sure there were no slipups. Radio, television, newspaper . . . they all had to tell the same story, and simultaneously. He had the individuals who could do it. Here they were—people in high places . . . people whose friendships he had been cultivating for years. None of them knew the whole story, not yet. They didn't need to. Each just had to do his own part.

The military, that had been more difficult, he thought, setting down the one file and lifting the other from the top of the stack.

A few key individuals here were all the way in, full members and cooperators in the plan—colonels mostly. Only two other generals besides himself. Most of the generals were of the old guard and out of touch with the men. The colonels—that's where the true power lay. They could take the officers with them. That's why years ago he had begun concentrating his efforts on the substrata within the military machine, the rising stars who had yet to make their mark.

The generals of '91 had been out of touch with the realities of the new Soviet military. The army had not come with them. But it *would* come with him because he had the men the soldiers would trust and listen to.

Likewise he had recruited a bevy of sergeants from every republic, every city, every battalion, every regiment. As the colonels would bring along the officer corps, they each had a sergeant or two under them who would bring along the ranks of common soldiers. There would be no disintegration of the lines of command this time.

It was a foolproof plan, he thought with a smile, setting the military file down again on his desk and picking up that marked "Political/Republics." Here, too, he was confident in the outcome. He had to have simultaneous support from the leadership of every one of the republics and Eastern nations, at all levels—city mayors, national leaders, politicians. Flipping through the file he scanned the dozens of names, files, reports that had been accumulated for him. Budapest had raised some troubling questions . . . Donetsk was now OK . . . Riga and the Latvians—

Hmm, he thought, *it could go without them, even though here and there a few holes might exist.*

He would have to see about those. But by and large things seemed in place. He removed the letter from the Hungarian to the "Foreign Leaders" file, reflecting again on the irony of the new times.

Industry . . . worker unrest and the union strike were already in progress.

One by one, Desyatovsky went through each of the files out of the secret packet, making notes, jotting down names, thinking through last-minute arrangements, and rethinking every phase of his grand strategy for the thirteen-dozenth time.

Nothing could be left to chance!

When he had satisfied himself of what arrangements still lay before him two hours later, a list of some twenty-three contacts to make sat on a piece of paper on his desk in his own hand.

It would not do for it to be seen. Carefully he folded the paper and put it in his pocket. Then he replaced all the folders into the thick pouch, folded over its top lid, snapped together the small padlock, then rose and replaced it in the file cabinet on the other side of the room from where he had removed it earlier.

He walked to his office couch and lay down. It had been a long day. He would catch a few hours' sleep, then perhaps go out about seven for some breakfast.

Still in his uniform, Desyatovsky was asleep within ten minutes.

He did not awaken until the light of morning was streaming into his office. He rose, stretched, did his best to make himself appear presentable, and then left to find something to eat.

Crushed Eavesdropper

•   •   •

AS THE DEFENSE MINISTER EXITED HIS OFFICE, THE DRAB gray stone building was coming to life. In an outer office his own secretary sat at her desk, and a half-dozen or so assistants and midlevel bureaucrats had begun busying themselves with the morning's duties.

The wary eye of a woman in her early forties followed his moves closely as he strode across the floor. Desyatovsky cast her a quick glance as he passed, catching her eyes with his but allowing no hint of intimacy to pass his lips, only a brief smile.

She saw, and her heart thumped quickly for the next several beats. The emotions, however, were now confused and mixed up. A week ago such a look from Bludayev would have melted her heart. Today it brought anger and uncertainty along with the previous flutterings.

What was she to do?

Pretend she had never heard and hope she had misconstrued his words? Warn Yuri and tell him to undo what he had done? But they would only find out, and then perhaps even worse would come of it.

If only there was somebody to talk to, somebody to tell who could help her!

By the time Marta Repninka reached her cold, lonely apartment that evening, she was no nearer a resolution to her emotional quandary than she had been that morning. She put down her things and walked toward the small oval mirror that hung on the wall. Taking a hard look at what she saw, she unconsciously attempted to deal with several stray strands of graying black hair. Then suddenly she turned away in disgust, tears forming in her eyes. What could he have ever seen in that face!

She was a fool for believing his charming lies! She was aging, plain, and too plump even for a Russian woman. Yet he had made her believe she was beautiful. It had felt so good! She would give anything not to have found out what he *really* thought of her. But it was too late for that now. She could never go back, and now she was more miserable than she had ever been before.

Curse him! How she would love to drive a knife into that huge, strong chest of his . . . if she thought she could get away with it. But she wasn't quite ready to die yet, and she could not betray Yuri.

She opened the single unpainted cupboard in the room and scanned its meager contents. Half a loaf of dry bread, a few canned vegetables—not much to make a meal. There was some cheese in the small icebox. She hadn't had any meat for a month. From the cupboard she took a half-empty bottle and a glass.

She made her way out of the kitchen and plopped down in the only piece of comfortable furniture she owned, a threadbare, black, moderately stuffed chair. She wasn't hungry anyway. Perhaps the vodka would help her forget the misery of the day. She opened the bottle, poured the glass full to the brim, and drank half the contents with one long swallow.

Marta Repninka had worked all her adult life in various menial positions at two dozen different posts in and around the Kremlin. She had never married, never been noticed, and never allowed herself to hope for anything better in life.

The changes that had begun with Secretary Gorbachev had been full of hope at first. She and some of the other women of her level had occasionally after that been given parcels of food for special occasions and coupons allowing them to buy new clothes, even shoes, before the general public. But for most of Russia she knew the "changes" and "better times" spoken of by the secretary in all his speeches about perestroika lay somewhere off in the distant future, promises that became thinner and less tangible as the country's economy continued to decline.

She had been one of the fortunate ones. As the huge and once-invincible motherland had crumbled from within, fate had shone its light upon her. Suddenly she found herself working as a clerk and filing assistant in the new Russian defense minister's office as one of several assistants to his personal secretary. Her pay had only increased moderately. Still she lived in the same dingy flat. Still she could neither obtain nor afford meat except rarely. But hope had sprung up within her breast that better times might perhaps lay ahead.

About the same time her brother Yuri, who lived down in Kiev, had been promoted at the factory where he worked, and she had rejoiced along with his wife and son and daughter. They were the only family Marta Pavlovna Repninka had, and though seven hundred kilometers separated them, Yuri never lost hope that perhaps one day she would be able to find a position in Kiev and join them there.

How the minister had learned of her brother she had never stopped to ask herself, nor why he would be interested in either of them. But almost from the first day when he began to show subtle interest in her—smiling when he passed, paying her a compliment on her dress or her work—he also began casually inquiring about her brother in Kiev.

Now she could see—ah, what cruelty there was in hindsight!— that she should have been more cautious, asked herself such questions, questioned why she had been given the job in the Defense Ministry in the first place.

But she had been so blinded by his blandishments. A thick, slow-witted moron, that's what she was—nothing more! He had seduced her mind and emotions . . . and she had succumbed! He had used her . . . and was now preparing to throw her out like a discarded piece of trash!

But what pleasure there had been in his attentions! She had forgotten her age, forgotten her graying hair, forgotten her sinking jowls and hips. He made her feel young again with the simplest of phrases, with a wink or a smile or a kind word. And steadily, without even knowing she was doing it, she revealed more and more of herself to the minister—the hopes she harbored about bettering her life and especially about going to Kiev to live near her brother. He was interested, and she willingly confided in him.

It had all culminated in that wildly joyous day six months ago when he had actually invited her to lunch—discreetly and privately. Her heart had raced all morning in anticipation, and she even dared to whisper his first name under her breath—*Bludayev.* What sensations the mere word caused to rise up within her!

"I need your help, Marta Pavlovna Repninka," the defense minister had said sincerely.

She remembered the words like it had been yesterday. How her head had spun at the thought that the great man needed her.

Anything, Bludayev, my darling! She had said in her mind. But the words that came from her lips instead had been more modest. "How may I serve you, Defense Minister?"

"It is a highly secretive matter," Desyatovsky had replied. "No one may ever know of this conversation."

She had nodded her assent eagerly and listened as he had promised many things fantastically beyond her dreams if she would help him and could guarantee her brother's help as well, for he needed a man he could trust in Kiev. It was the most sensitive and top-secret matter of national security, even survival. There were forces, he said, attempting even now to gain control of the government. As defense minister he must stop them. But to do so he needed their help. Could he trust her? If his efforts were successful, her brother's family would be well rewarded, and she could expect a promotion and move to Kiev.

By now, what would she not have done for the man who filled her every waking thought?

She contacted her brother immediately, and a time and place was set up for him to meet with the defense minister's man there. Plans immediately began to move forward. Yuri assembled what he needed, and the countdown began toward the initial target date.

Meanwhile in Moscow, Marta took more care in readying herself for the office every day, bought some cheap fragrance to bolster the effect, and tried to eat less when she came home at night. She even began to entertain fanciful daydreams about not moving to Kiev after all.

She knew Bludayev was married. But to a lonely woman in love, what does reality matter when there are castles in the air to build! She would find ways to please him, and soon he would forget his wife altogether!

In dreamlike ecstasy she had flitted and fumbled through the routines of her job day after day, living for the chance moments when the minister would come out of his office and walk by, or else—most wonderful of all!—give her some assignment to handle *personally.*

Until yesterday . . .

As quickly as her Pushkinesque fairy-tale world had arisen, suddenly it crumbled beneath her feet like a dissolving mirage.

Foolish heart of a smitten woman, she had yielded to the awful yet irresistible urge to listen to her phantom lover in private. In the solitude of an office temporarily vacated of others, including her own boss, the minister's secretary, and seeing the red light on the secretary's desk that indicated the minister to be engaged in conversation in his office, she had stolen closer and picked up the phone line he was on.

With trembling heart she had listened as one entranced by the mere sound of Desyatovsky's voice.

Once the horrifying realization broke through that he was talking about *her,* she was too mesmerized with mingled fear and agony to be capable of removing the receiver from her ear.

"Yes, as soon as possible," Desyatovsky was saying. "I don't want there to be any possibility of his being linked to the blast. An investigation could lead straight back to his sister and my office."

"What is your preference?" asked the voice at the other end of the line, sounding impersonal and cold.

"That is your business," the defense minister had snapped. "However you people take care of these things these days—an explosion in his car, some hoodlums after work. I don't even care if it's a bullet in his head. I just want to make sure it's done."

"And the family?"

"Be creative."

"Will they all be eliminated?"

"Look, when Drexler told me to use you, he said you were the best. I don't want to have to spell out every—"

"Say no more. It will be done," came a quick reply. "You also mentioned a woman there."

"I will see to her."

"You have people?"

"I have ways. What do you think I am, a fool!" There had been a brief pause, then Desyatovsky had broken into a quiet and cruel laugh. "I may even take care of this one myself. Ha, ha, ha! I actually think the old hag is in love with me! Ha, ha! A good one, wouldn't you say . . . what's your name again?"

"My name is none of your concern. All you have to remember is that if *you* slip up, my boss may order me to put a Scottish broadsword right through *your* heart."

"Ah yes, that sounds exactly like what my melodramatic friend Herr Drexler would say. Ha, ha! But you had just better tell him to watch his *own* step! In the meantime, I'll make sure the woman never says anything to anyone again—you just do the same with her brother. I've given you all the information you need. I'll expect you to be in Kiev tomorrow."

With ashen expression as if she had looked death in the face, Marta quietly replaced the receiver and hastened to another corner of the room where she would not be noticed.

It was a good thing the day was almost over. She was trembling from head to foot in the cold panic of suffocating dread. In stunned shock she somehow managed to finish the day and stumble home that night, alternating between disbelief and terror. She had scarcely slept, but could not think clearly what to do.

Today, as the man's evil words replayed themselves in her brain for the two hundredth time and the horrifying realization sunk in that she had been but a pawn in his cruel game, whatever it was, and that she had never meant anything to him, a silent rage had gradually filled her, giving way in fits to a defeating sense of her own imbecilic blindness.

Her own life hardly mattered now. But she had to save Yuri and his family. She would call him tonight . . . immediately, and warn him.

But then, what was she to do about that despicable, hateful man she had thought she loved? What could he have been up to that he was willing to kill to achieve it? How dearly she would love to see him undone, to see him toppled from his high and mighty throne!

She may have been an idiot, but she was not such a fool that she could not find a way to turn the tables on him!

She glanced up. It was dark already. How long had she been sitting here brooding? She looked down at the clear vodka glass in her hand. It was empty. She had unconsciously drunk half the bottle. It hardly phased her.

She tried to stand, but her knees gave way and she collapsed once again into the chair. Before she could even think again about telephoning her brother or gaining her revenge against Desyatovsky, her head dropped back and the snoring in her throat began almost the next moment.

She remained sound asleep until sometime after three in the morning when she rose and stumbled to her bed.

Dan Davidson

• • •

IT WAS ADMITTEDLY A ROTTEN WAY TO MAKE A LIVING.

But he had been in the intelligence business long enough to let many of his scruples go by the boards. And one of the first lessons they had taught him in training back in Langley, Virginia, was that the quickest way to a man's secrets is through a woman.

Dan Davidson liked women fine. Even respected them, though he wasn't married himself. But they were soft, emotional creatures. And often talkative . . . if you could just find the right pressure points. It was a weakness he had exploited dozens of times already and would probably dozens more before he was either captured, killed, or put out to pasture.

And now with the Cold War over, he thought, the latter seemed the more likely scenario. He was surprised they hadn't yanked him back to the States already. A lot of his old colleagues throughout the Eastern Bloc—or what they *used* to call the Eastern Bloc (would he ever get used to the changes!)—had been shipped home and were now sitting behind desks or carrying out other trivial assignments.

He'd been fortunate and was still here. Two or three years of change wasn't that long, he supposed, and Washington still had a need to know what was going on behind the scenes, even though the Kremlin and the White House were the best of buddies.

So he supposed he would keep trying to find women to talk, keep oiling the machinery of the apparatus he had managed to develop over the years, and hope that every once in a while something turned up that his superior felt justified his continued existence over here.

He'd quit before he'd sit behind a desk eight hours a day. Even though the excitement of the old days had gone out with the toppling of the Berlin Wall, just being here was a long sight better than being relegated to the home front.

Ah, but memories of the old days, dangerous as they were, still tugged at him sometimes. Yugoslavia and the coining of his nickname . . . the chase in Leningrad . . . his underground flight from Kiev to Prague that time in '79 when he'd gotten wind of the Afghanistan invasion . . . what times they'd been!

Of course, he'd come close to buying the farm that time on the Adriatic, if not from the gunfire then certainly from the cold. But he'd survived and lived to tell about it. And done some very important work for his country to boot. If he'd just gotten to Prague two days sooner and gotten word through, he might have saved Carter's presidency.

He hadn't.

But there had been some notable successes as well. And he had saved Ronald Reagan's skin a time or two, though the old coot never knew it.

Iran-Contra. Now there was a fiasco! If it hadn't been for some quick legwork and several hefty payoffs he'd made in the right places, George Bush would never have become president.

Yeah, he'd made a difference to his country—not as a Democrat or a Republican or anything else. Just an American. A loyal, hardworking one.

That's what he'd keep being—a loyal American.

Davidson took a gulp of the lukewarm coffee in his mug, grimaced from it, and looked over the two papers on his desk. Something was here, he thought, if he could just *see* it. What was all this pointing to?

It had the definite aroma of importance . . . of something big. Or was he just fantasizing—pretending subterfuge and plot and secretive maneuverings where there really were none? Was he nothing but a worn-out agent, living in the past, hoping in vain for the old thrill of the espionage game in the new world order where there was none? Was he—death to a CIA agent!—getting senile and losing his perspective?

Still, there *did* seem to be something going on. He'd been around long enough in this country to recognize the signs. Freedom and democracy notwithstanding, Russians were Russians, and they had their peculiar ways of doing things. He could spot a ruse when he saw one . . . in any language.

That's why he had to get information from the inside. If he could just find someone to talk. Low-level people always knew something, and usually it was more important than they realized.

Finding either a man *or* a woman's weakness was harder these days. It used to be you could coax someone into betraying their own mother. Promises of freedom in the West . . . an automobile . . . furs . . . even food for a commoner—they had all worked wonders ten years ago when such things were priceless commodities in the Soviet Union. Dangle the right carrot under their nose and you had them.

Now it was all so upside-down. Travel restrictions were nearly gone. The standard of living showed hints of improvement. Democracy in the Commonwealth was a good thing, but it made his job of extracting information more difficult.

There weren't many carrots left. Although with the economy so miserable, food could still sometimes do the trick.

There was always money. That would continue to be a great motivator. Which was why he had told his superiors recently that they were going to have to cough up more dough for him to have at his disposal if they expected the ongoing flow of information.

Every person had his weak spot, which you had to discover how to exploit.

More importantly, every woman had *her* weak spot. They were often more subtle and difficult to find. But once you found a woman's soft, emotional underbelly, if you aimed your arrow true . . . you had her!

Again he scanned the sheets before him, then drained off the remainder of the contents of his mug.

It was time to call Yaschak. A little weasel if ever there was one, but a useful fellow if you paid his price. An agent needed a stool pigeon in every town where he hoped to make good, and in Moscow, Yaschak was his.

No scruples, only rubles was Yaschak's little jingle—about the only clever English he knew. It certainly was highly descriptive of the dirty parasite's character. And he knew people of all kinds, in high—and low—places.

The CIA agent picked up the phone and dialed several quick numbers. *On second thought,* he said to himself, *I'd better handle this personally.* Quickly he set down the receiver, stood up, grabbed his lightweight jacket, and headed toward the door.

PART VIII

Past Meets Future

59

A Voice from the Past

• • •

Moscow

AT THE STRANGE VOICE COMING IN GERMAN FROM THE blackness in his room, Galanov's heart leapt into his throat. Even KGB agents could be frightened when their guards were down. "In God's name, who's there!" cried Galanov, leaping forward off the bed with a start.

"One who comes in God's name," answered the voice. "You need have no fear."

"May I turn on the light?" asked Galanov, recovering himself, "so that I may at least see who has succeeded in getting the drop on me? I presume you have a gun."

"You may turn on the light," the voice answered.

Galanov rose from the bed and pulled the string where it hung down in the middle of the room. Though it was a mere forty-watt bulb, from out of the darkness the room seemed to explode into light.

A stranger sat calmly watching him from his own chair.

"But . . . but . . . I've never seen . . . who are you?" said the agent in surprise, the tiredness of his sleepless night and strange experience coming back upon him. He still could not disassociate the stranger from the men who had been chasing him.

"I am a friend."

"But . . . but how did you get in here? No one knows of this location!"

"I have many friends. There are people who want to help you."

"Help me! Bah, who could want to help me? For God's sake, you don't even have a gun! What makes you think you can sit there and tell me . . . how did you get in here? I demand to know!"

Now that he had begun to realize his danger was not so great as he had suspected, and seeing that he was not really held captive at all and that no weapon was trained on him, Galanov had begun to bluster a bit. Fatigue had frayed his nerves and brought anger nearer the surface.

His unwelcome guest continued to sit calmly, staring at him with a serious but kind look on his face, tinged with an undefined sadness and pain. He said nothing, however.

"I tell you, I will bodily throw you out of here if I don't get some answers from you—and soon!" exclaimed Galanov, now growing enraged. "If you are going to take me in, then be about your business. Though without a gun, you wouldn't have a chance. I'll kill *you* if you try!"

"I have not come to take you in."

"What have you come for then?"

"Sit down, Herr Galanov."

Galanov hesitated, still staring. The tranquility of the man's expression finally began to calm him. At length he ceased his fuming and sat down on the edge of his bed. The stranger eyed him steadily.

"I told you earlier," the man said at length. "I have been sent for you."

"Sent? By whom?"

"By One who is your friend."

"I have no friends! I have not made friends in my line of work. Who could want me but those who want me out of the way and bound for Siberia?"

"You *do* have friends. I am one of them, and so is the One who sent me."

"Who sent you then, man? Stop playing games with me!"

Placidly the stranger gazed into Galanov's face without answering. He was silent a long while, until the Russian settled into a quieter state. Finally he spoke. "Look into these eyes, my friend," he said.

Still he stared at Galanov. "Look into my eyes and tell me what you see."

As absurd as it sounded, the agent found himself powerless to disobey. "I see . . . for God's sake, man, what should I see? I see a man's face! A stranger . . . who are you?"

"Look deeply, Herr Galanov. Is there nothing more you see?"

Slowly Galanov felt himself weakening. Even in the dim light of his dingy flat, he found the same spell coming over him that he had noticed many times before.

All at once he remembered the terrifying light he had seen in the streets half an hour earlier and the voice that had been behind it. The same sense of dread suddenly came over him, and he looked away.

"Do not look away, Herr Galanov," said the stranger. "You must look into my eyes."

The same inner compelling urged the agent to do so. "Were you . . . was that you back there . . . in the street?" he asked, confused. "Did you have some spotlight shining at—"

"I have been here waiting in your room for three hours," replied the man.

"Then how did you come . . . and your voice . . . I recognize your voice. If it was not you back there, in the street . . . then why do I—"

"Look into my eyes, Herr Galanov," said the man again.

A lengthy silence ensued.

"I . . . I *do* know you, don't I?" faltered Galanov. "It's not only your voice. I . . . I know those eyes . . . I *have* seen you somewhere."

The stranger gazed at him, saying nothing.

Slowly over Galanov's face spread a look, first of recognition, then doubt, then recognition again. He seemed to be questioning within himself, reliving an old memory, perhaps painful.

A wince squinted his eyes, but only for the briefest of instants. He seemed trying to maintain his self-control, but gradually the recognition gave way to a sense of knowing, and with it came pain and grief so profound and intense as to be completely foreign to him. "You . . . you're . . ." he began, but could not bring himself to say it. At last he looked away.

"Say it, Herr Galanov. Who am I?"

"You're . . . you're the man in the field . . . the man who attacked me . . . that morning outside Berlin."

"That is correct, Herr Galanov. It was my daughter you shot in the back . . . and killed as *Der Prophet* was making his escape."

60

The Arrow Finds Its Mark

. . .

ALL HIS FORMER KGB INSTINCTS OF SELF-PRESERVATION, unfeeling nerves of steel, emotionless carelessness toward any other human being suddenly evaporated. At the shocking words, thirty years of training was gone in an instant.

At the words *"It was my daughter you . . . killed,"* something broke inside KGB agent and loyal Communist Andrassy Papovich Galanov. The man who had for years resisted emotions—who had, in fact, denied their very existence—suddenly felt vulnerable and full of unexpected feelings.

He swallowed hard, trying to still whatever it was now attempting to rise in his throat. His eyes scanned his room, now lifeless and empty. Try as he might, he could not keep them from returning to the awful presence sitting across from him in his chair.

A simple farmer was this fellow. And he . . . he had been one of the most powerful agents in the empire. Why then did he feel so intimidated? Why was he—dare he admit it?—why was he . . . afraid to look at this man?

He blinked his own eyes . . . then again. Blast them, why were they watering! He must be about to sneeze from something.

Involuntarily he glanced up. The man was still gazing at him full in the face.

"Then if that is true . . . then . . . why in God's name are you here?" he said hesitantly.

"For precisely that reason," replied the man.

"Have you come to kill me?"

"In a manner of speaking," he said with a hint of a smile. "But not in the way you think."

"Why then . . . if what you say is true, and you are . . . who you say?"

"I told you before—to help you."

"Help me—how?"

"To help you escape. Word came to us that you were in danger."

"Why should you care? Bah! I hardly know whether to believe you. The whole thing is so preposterous!"

"I care because I have not ceased to pray for you since that fateful morning. I have prayed for you daily, Herr Galanov, prayed that our paths might cross again someday and that I might look you in the eye and express my forgiveness to you."

The words might as well have been in a foreign tongue. The Russian sat as one stunned. What he had just heard did not seem to register at first.

Slowly the meaning dawned. As it did, he began to recall that other incident he had recalled an hour or so ago when running down the alley, the other man who had prayed for him, and whom he had knocked unconscious for his trouble.

"Forgive . . . ," Galanov repeated incredulously. "But . . . I do not understand. Why should you . . . why did you come here . . . you say, to *help* me?"

"We received word that you were in danger, that you were attempting to get out of your country. I had been praying, and I saw my opportunity to help you, to get you out through *Das Netzwerk* and the people of *The Rose,* the very network of believers you sought with such vehemence to destroy. I prayed and I fasted on your behalf. And then our Lord said to me in my spirit, *'Go to this man.* Go to him in Moscow. My hand is upon him. I will touch him and will speak to him myself. You must be there personally. *You must tell him of forgiveness.* You must tell him that the new life he seeks will not come from asylum in the West, but from giving his heart to me. You must tell him that I have chosen him, in spite of the blackness of his sin, to carry word of my life forth. *And you must tell him who it is that has spoken to him.'*

"And so, Herr Galanov, that is why I am here—to speak forgiveness to you, my forgiveness and the forgiveness of almighty God, your Father, the Maker of heaven and earth. For it is *he* who has recently spoken to you. I do not know how he did so or when. But he has instructed me to tell you that it was *his* voice that came to you. And you must now heed his word."

The words Galanov had heard in the deserted streets suddenly exploded in his brain. *I come to bring you life . . . I am the Lord . . . you shall serve me.*

In benumbed silence he now sat motionless, staring distantly into regions no other human can penetrate.

"But . . . but *how* can what you tell me be true?" he said at last, his voice barely above a whisper. All the fight from his spirit was gone.

"The ways of God are beyond what our reasoning and intellects can grasp," replied the German. "I am a simple man, Herr Galanov. You are perhaps more educated than me. I cannot provide you arguments satisfactory to your mind why a Communist and atheist should all at once believe in the Christian faith. The passing on of life is no mere intellectual exercise, but a birthing that takes place in the spirit of man. I come telling you, not of the Christian religion, but of a Man who brought God's life to earth, who died for our sin, through whom we can be forgiven and cleansed and made whole, and whose Spirit can dwell with us and in us and give us a permanent relationship with God, our Father and his Father. That Man is Jesus Christ. And his *life* he now offers you in your heart."

Again a long silence followed.

"But . . . why *you?* How could *you* be the one telling me of such things? You should hate me."

The German's mouth hinted at the trace of a thin smile, revealing his own prayerful struggle over the same question. "I have no answer for you," he answered softly. "Our Lord spoke of laying down our lives for one another. Through my own personal agony, I came to recognize that I had been chosen to share an intimate form of mingled love and pain with my Father—sacrifice known but to a few: giving the life of a child, in love, for the salvation of many. He gave his Son that the world might know of his love. He allowed me to give my daughter that *you* might know his love."

"But . . . but I am only one man."

"Our Savior would have offered his sacrifice on the cross had there been but *one* sinner on the planet to redeem. Had I, or you, been alone on the earth, he would still have died to save us. Perhaps it is my daughter's privilege to participate in that same truth—giving *her* life that *one other* of God's creatures might know how personal is the salvation of his Son. Though I have a strong sense that many will one day believe as a result of what God is doing here."

The German paused, thoughtfully, smiling again with a look that revealed depths unspoken of both anguish and victory. *"Why,* Herr Galanov?" he said, still speaking softly. "Such questions have answers only in the heart of God. He said that only by love will men know we are his disciples. I *am* his disciple, my friend. And through the years, as I have prayed for you he has put within my heart not only forgiveness for you, but *love.* I have come to you as one sent. I cannot answer your questions of *how* or *why.* I can only offer you what He has given me to pass on to you—my forgiveness and the transforming power of his love. I offer to you whatever help my hands can give. And I tell you, that as he loves you as a son, *so too he has caused me to love you as a brother."*

Never in all the years of his life had Galanov heard such words.

As he sat, staring vacantly ahead, within the space of but a few minutes his mind replayed fragmentary images of hundreds of scenes from the depths of his past. In poignant internal agony, the horrifying wickedness of what he had been slowly revealed itself to the newly awakening consciousness of his spirit.

Faces rose and fell . . . words . . . shouts . . . screams . . . sickening cruelties. His own voice stood out from the rest. Even as he heard himself from years before, in the very sound of his own voice he could detect the stubborn denial of truth that had always been right in front of him.

Mingled with all the rest were flashes of light and the words he had heard an hour before in that deserted alley.

Pervading everything was the life-changing and dreadful import of this huge possibility his brain could not force itself to fathom—being *forgiven* by the father of the girl he had murdered thirteen years earlier!

Round and round rang the words . . . *so too he has caused me to love you as a brother.*

Slowly the *how* and *why* he had so desperately sought only a few moments earlier faded into a blur of emptiness.

From deep within his depths, as of a rising inner spring that steadily increased and gave way to the gathering waters of rushing new life, the hardened KGB agent found words of thanksgiving and surrender escaping his lips—words he had never before uttered, words whose meaning he scarcely recognized.

The miracle of the second birth swept over him, and, unconsciously falling to his knees and bending his tear-filled face to the floor, he yielded himself in abandonment to it.

The German slowly rose, walked forward, and, placing a tender hand on the Russian's heaving shoulder, knelt at his side.

For the next thirty minutes, both men prayed, weeping freely.

61

Stool Pigeon

• • •

"YASCHAK, YOU LITTLE SKUNK!" SAID DAVIDSON IN COLLO-quial Russian, but with enough of a lightness in his tone that the other took no offense.

"Anyone else call me that, Dan," replied the little man in a high-pitched voice, "they be dead before morning."

"But you know I treat you well, do you not? Eh, Yaschak?"

"One day you may go too far."

"I doubt that," laughed Davidson. "I know your kind, and you have no more intention of cutting off the easy money I bring you than you have of slicing off your own hand."

Yaschak eyed him beadily, betraying no emotion. He was the sort of man who made a living by being able to conceal his true motives. He was dressed in a tasteless plain black suit with a white shirt frayed and dirty around the neck. Yaschak's low-level bureaucratic position at the Kremlin was of less than inconsequential significance. Yet everyone knew him, for he made a habit of hanging around where important people gathered. His hearing was preternaturally keen, and, when combined with his wit and shrewd ability to read people far better than they gave him credit for, Yaschak was a fountain of information.

No one was particularly fond of his ingratiating manner, but most put up with him as little more than a petty annoyance. His oily black hair, yellowed teeth, and persistent odor that stood out even in Russia, where deodorant was not high on the list of sought-after imports, all created a not-inaccurate impression of unrefined sloppiness and crudity.

As obnoxious as he may have been, however, Davidson had dealt with worse. And Yaschak had proved himself dozens of times. Whatever you needed, he could usually get for you. In a pinch, Davidson may even have admitted to liking him a little.

"I may be onto something, Yaschak," Davidson went on. "I need to get inside the Defense Ministry."

"You . . . personally?"

"No, not me. I mean I need a contact, a pair of eyes I can trust. If not someone I can trust, at least someone who can be bought, someone who has a gripe, someone who's angry at their boss. I need information, and I'm not particular about how I get it."

"Defense Ministry . . . that's high-up stuff. It cost you, Danny."

"Useful goods always do. I'm prepared to pay. You know anyone?"

"I might," replied Yaschak with a sly grin.

"You always do, eh, Yaschak?"

"I have my own contacts in the city and all through the Kremlin."

"In all the new republics too?"

"I work on that."

"And in the gutters?"

"Careful, Danny. You don't want to spite the hand that feeds you is, I believe, one of your sayings."

"Actually, it is 'bite the hand that feeds you,' and I believe we feed each other, so it would be best if neither of us shows his teeth. So . . . do you know someone who might help me?"

"I might. I will snoop around."

"A woman?"

"Perhaps."

"It's always a woman with you, isn't it?" said Davidson, grinning.

"They work best for our purposes. Men in high places overlook them. Women resent it. Emotions come, make eager to talk."

"Ah, you are a cunning rascal, Yaschak!"

"If she in proper place, woman make best informant. Most of time they do not realize they have revealed information to damage their man. So it safe too—they don't know what they have done."

"You know someone in the Russian Defense Ministry?"

"I know people who know people. There is someone I have in mind. Why all questions, Danny? I never disappoint you before. You tell me what you want, I deliver. I can get someone with eyes anywhere in Moscow, if you give me time. Have patience, Danny."

"I might not have a great deal of time."

"What is up? Come on, Danny, you can tell Yaschak."

"Tell you! Not on your life. I pay for what you tell me! If I told you half what I know, you'd take it elsewhere, bargain for a few extra rubles, and sell me down the Moskva River!"

"Not me."

"Besides, it might be nothing. I can't say a word till I'm sure. I just got wind of something very peculiar in a communiqué my people intercepted between Russian defense and Budapest—seemed to be from the mayor of that city to someone in the Kremlin. Very cryptic. I just want another angle on it, that's all."

"I see what I dig up."

"You find me a dissatisfied woman in defense, set up a meeting, and you'll have earned your pay. And remember, Yaschak, not a word about my involvement, as always."

"I remember. Rule one, just like you taught me."

"Just don't forget it."

62

First Instruction

• • •

SIX HOURS HAD PASSED.

The man who had brought such an unexpected thunderbolt into the life of Andrassy Galanov sat calmly on the floor of the filthy, deserted hallway, on guard so that his new brother could get some desperately needed sleep.

Before he left him, Galanov had said, "But I do not even know your name. I have it!" he had exclaimed the next instant. "I shall call you *Der Deutscher Prophet,* now that we have driven our Russian Prophet out of the land."

The visitor shook his head. "You may simply call me 'The German,' if you like," he said. "But please, nothing more."

About the time agent Davidson was meeting with his information broker, Galanov reappeared in the corridor. The German rose and greeted him with a smile. "I hope you have slept well," he said.

"Like a baby," replied the Russian. "So soundly, in fact, that for a moment after I awoke it all seemed like a dream. I half expected to open this door and find no one there."

"I told you I would not leave you for a moment."

"That you did, but . . . you must realize . . ."

"Of course I do," said the German again, smiling and placing a tender arm around the man's shoulder. "Many things will be new for you. But I have the feeling you will grow rapidly."

"Grow?"

"As I said, there is a great deal to learn. I will explain as much to you as our time together permits. But first I need to get you something to eat."

"I am sorry I have nothing to offer," apologized Galanov. "It would seem that you are my guest, but I do not spend enough time here to keep food on hand."

"Think nothing of it. Now that you are awake, I will go and buy bread or whatever I can find."

He took several steps toward the stairs, then turned back to where the KGB agent stood watching him. "And what do you feel now, Andrassy?" he asked. "That it was a dream?"

"That can hardly be, seeing you are still here."

"I mean what happened *inside* you. Is *that* still real, or does it seem as a dream?"

Galanov thought for a moment before responding. "That cannot be a dream either," he said slowly, still turning everything over in his mind, "seeing that this . . . this . . . something down inside, a peculiar sensation—I don't know how to describe it—is still with me as well."

"A *peace?*" suggested the German.

"Yes, that is something like it. But of a most unusual kind. All I can say is that it makes the tears very close again to my eyes."

"Tears of what?"

"Of . . . I don't know. I cannot keep away the grief over what I have been, what I have done, yet . . . with it is mingled a relief that it is behind me and something new, perhaps something better, awaits. I want to weep, from both joy and sorrow at the same time. Do you know this feeling?"

"Before I answer, let me ask you another question. The new that awaits—you are eager for it, or do you want to go back to how it was before?"

"Oh, no, not go back . . . not after what I have seen of myself! I do not know if I am eager. The unknown is frightening. The light I saw last night was as fearsome as the men chasing me. The voice coming from it was terrifying. But how could I not be drawn into it? I *cannot* go back."

The German smiled. "Then all is as it should be," he said. "The things you feel are very common. Yes, I do know what you mean. Tears of both joy and sorrow usually accompany the new birth."

"But how can the two opposite feelings both exist at once?"

"You will always know grief, my friend. The more the life of

God's Spirit grows and expands inside you, the deeper you will know yourself. They will not always be pleasant sights, these regions we come to see within our own hearts. You have already experienced a painful taste of that first lesson of faith. At the same time, the joy of God's life now resides within you as well and will give you a purpose for living that will make sense of all the rest."

"Why did you say that all was as it ought to be?" asked Galanov.

"Because after confessing the ugliness of their sin to the Father," replied the German, "there are those who withdraw back into themselves rather than take the offer of *life* he holds out to them. The past has become odious to you. You are eager to move forward *into* life. Many have second thoughts, after the despondency and blackness that led them to repentance no longer seem quite so dark. But you have taken the step as one not to be retreated from, and thus you will progress quickly into understanding how to walk out the life of faith."

"I hope it is so. I *pray* it is so," said Galanov sincerely. "You are right, it *is* my desire to leave the past life dead and forever behind me."

"Then there truly is much we have to talk about," said the German. "But first I must be about my errand after nourishment. The body must keep fit for the spirit to reside in. But, while I am gone—," he added, searching with his hands into the pocket of his jacket, "—take this." He pulled out a small pamphlet and handed it to Galanov. "Do you remember what I told you about Jesus being the man who brought us the Father's life?"

Galanov nodded.

"Well this is his story, his biography. It is in German."

"I will be able to read it," said Galanov.

"I marked several passages for you to look at," added the German. "Look it over and we will talk more as soon as I get back."

Galanov took the small book with almost a reverent touch. His mind could not help recalling the many now-loathsome incidents where he had confiscated and destroyed such books and materials.

Now it suddenly felt like a great treasure in his hands. At last he understood why the Christians all those years had been so willing to suffer, even die, to keep it alive.

Even as he turned and went back into his small room, his eyes were scanning the first several pages of the Gospel.

With prayers of thanksgiving rising up in his own breast, the German quickly left the building and was soon out in the streets under the warm Moscow sun.

63

An Unusual Request

• • •

THE REMAINDER OF THE AFTERNOON, AFTER THE GER-
man's return, the two men spent in the depths of the most unusual
dialogue either had ever experienced.

Upon the German steadily grew a sense of urgency, both with
respect to Galanov's safety and concerning a host of spiritual principles necessary to be built into him quickly. He was such a receptive
and humble listener, absorbing all he was told, that the effect of eight
years of intercession could almost visibly be seen. Even to compare
the hungry Russian to a spiritual sponge would have understated his
eagerness to know everything he could about this new life he had
been given.

The German could not keep himself from thinking of Acts
9:18-21 with a deep sense of humble astonishment that God was
allowing him to be part of such a remarkable conversion.

They went over many truths and passages from the Gospel
together. Even as the German returned to the hideaway with bread,
he found Galanov unconcerned with the hunger in his stomach,
engrossed instead in the tiny book with an altogether different kind
of hunger.

"Look . . . look what I found," he said excitedly, glancing up with
book in one hand and pen in the other, "here is where *Der Prophet*
got his name."

The German glanced down at the verses Galanov had noted, then
smiled. "And I suppose the same thing could be said of your Russian
prophet that Jesus said of himself—no honor in his own land."

A quick return of the painful memory crossed Galanov's face, but was soon gone as the men began to partake of food. Even as they ate, Galanov continued to ply his guest with questions, giving himself as wholeheartedly to what was opening up before him as he always had to everything he had done.

It was late in the day when the subject again returned to the circumstances of the Russian's plight. "We must get you out of here," said the German. "The Father's investment in you is too great for us to treat lightly."

"I cannot leave Moscow yet. This . . . this political trail I have been on is something I feel I must see through to the end."

"The whole concept of *Das Netzwerk* is speed and stealth," replied the German. "You should know that better than anyone."

Galanov smiled a wry smile, but without much humor in it. So much had changed in such a short time that the reminder of his past brought still again a host of conflicting memories and emotions.

"You escaped your pursuers last night. But it is only a matter of time before they discover this location as well. The people I am associated with are good, and if we can locate you, we must assume they can too."

"How *did* you find me?" asked Galanov. "I still cannot understand how you could possibly have located my hideaway."

"I don't think you have any idea how widespread the network is."

"Even now—after the easing of restrictions and all the religious freedoms that have come to my country? Surely you haven't had to help people escape in years?"

"You are right, things have changed, and our work has changed too. We are very pleased with the developments. It has been probably three years, I think, since I was personally involved in an escape such as—" he hesitated, but only briefly—"such as the one that brought us into contact together," he added. "But you must realize that such change is not overnight nor always complete. People were still being shot and killed a very short time ago. There are still many pastors and Christian teachers in prison or exile. We have had much to keep us occupied even in the new era. Our people were alerted and safe houses were in full operation during the Czechoslovakian freedom-train months. There were many dangers during those days of first openings, with even stiffer resistance from some quarters. Many lost their lives, including some of the network's people."

"But . . . *now?* Democracy has come. Look at me—I am living proof that the persecutors of old are in disfavor."

"The public hears that freedom has come to the East and to the Russian republics," replied the German. "Much freedom *has* come, for which we rejoice. But behind, where no foreign eyes see, all the old ways are not dead. Your own writers Golitsyn and Solzhenitsyn long warned that things are not always what they seem, and their words are still true in spite of political changes."

"But Christians no longer have to hide and fear for their lives?"

"In most cases, no. Though many are still wary and continue to meet in out-of-the-way places as before. Times have changed politically, yes. The age-old struggle between good and evil, however, between God's people and the enemy, the prince of this world, continues."

"The enemy . . . you mean the Communist state? How can that be now that communism is dead in Russia?"

The German laughed, but it contained no rancor, only tender love at the other man's humble ignorance. "God's people have *another* enemy, Andrassy," he replied. "An enemy in the spirit realm who has to be fought in ways and with weapons even many of his people are unaware of."

"I am already intrigued."

"And you are already engaged in the battle," rejoined the German, "though perhaps you are unaware of it. In any case, to answer the question we were discussing a moment ago, the bonds between God's body of believers have remained intact, and strongly so, for a variety of reasons. What several years ago may have been largely a pipeline for getting people out and smuggling Bibles in has in many instances now become a distribution network for dissemination of great new volumes of Christian literature that have become available. Now we just as frequently pass people along in reverse order, bringing leaders and preachers and teachers into the various countries in order to help and train local groups of believers. The need for a vital network, a supply line of God's life, has remained strong."

"Then are *you* now its leader, now that you were successful in getting Rostovchev—the man called *Der Prophet*—getting him . . . past me and into West Berlin safely?"

The other man laughed. "No, Andrassy. I am by no means its leader. I am merely one among hundreds, probably thousands."

"You did not organize this attempt to . . . to locate me?"

"Far from it! As I told you, I was praying for you and received a strong urging from the Lord to find you and attempt to help you. But I had never been to Moscow before. I speak no Russian. I am but a simple man who works with his hands. Had you not spoken such fluent German I do not know what we would have done! But you do, and thus, as he always does, God makes provision even in our deficiencies."

"So how do you come to be here?"

"I let my need to locate you be known, and the network did the rest. I found my way to Moscow, where I was warmly taken in by the believers here. They had heard of you and were very skeptical when I told them of my plan. But they agreed to help."

"They had heard of me?"

"The very mention of your name brought terror. They said you have been the church's worst enemy. But I told them I was sure the hand of God's purpose was upon you."

Galanov was silent, hanging his head in renewed awareness of the enormity of his past sin. He thought for a long time. "You know," he said at length, "there was a young fellow coming up in my footsteps. It's been so long ago I had all but forgotten about him. But now all of a sudden, with all that has happened, his face comes back to my mind. He was young, enthusiastic, and was assigned to inflict terror upon Christians in our country, which he did very well. By the time he was twenty, he was actually leading many of the attacks, and I even had secret fears that if it had continued he would one day take over my job."

"I take from your words that it did not continue."

"No, his flame in the agency, though strong, was very short-lived."

"What became of him?"

"He defected," replied Galanov. "Jumped from a naval ship off British Columbia."

"Did you hear from him again?"

"Not directly. There were reports that he had become a Christian. We heard, in fact, that he wrote a book in the United States, though of course no one ever saw it. His name was hated everywhere in the Committee. Word of his treachery even reached the Kremlin, and there were reprisals against some of my superiors at the time for their carelessness in the matter."

Again Galanov fell to reflecting. "What we heard was that he was sending messages back into Russia from Canada—messages to the Christian underground, to the very people he had once persecuted. By radio, messages smuggled in, even his book was said to contain specific words of apology to those whom he had injured, even to relatives of those who had been killed in his raids."

He paused, then looked with great sincerity into the German's face. "Perhaps you might be able to arrange for me to meet some of those whom I persecuted," he said, "some of these people you have told me about?"

"Many of them would be too afraid to risk letting you see them."

"But how else can I tell them? How can I say how sorry . . . how can I possibly begin to make up for what I have done?"

"I fear they would not trust your change of heart."

"But I *must* speak to them. I could never write a book like Sergei Kourdakov. I must go to them face-to-face and try to say what is now inside me. What if *you* told them?"

"That might help with some, but others would think I had been taken in too. You must remember, to these Muscovites I also am a foreigner. They did not know me before two days ago."

"What has become of Rostovchev? He would speak on my behalf."

"He is no longer even in Europe."

"Has harm come to him?"

"No. He is safe."

"Where?"

"Even I do not know that. Somewhere in the United States."

"What does he do?"

"Again, Andrassy, I do not know. He has been given a job, a new identity I suppose. I have heard that he is still considered a prophet by many Christians of that country and that he is involved, with others of like calling, in a ministry of attempting to alert the people of the perilous times that await the world. But beyond that I know no specifics. Perhaps he and your former associate have run across one another."

"I'm afraid that is impossible," sighed Galanov sadly.

"Why?"

"Because our people got to Kourdakov a little more than a year after he jumped ship."

"Prison?"

"No, they arranged a suicide. He was shot."

The small room was silent a long time. It was the Russian who spoke again first. "Will you try?" he said.

"Try to do what?" said the German.

"To arrange for me to meet some of your Christian friends in the city?"

"Your friends now too, Andrassy. My brothers and sisters . . . and yours. Yes, of course I will try. I only wanted to caution you about the possible response. But there is nothing I would find a greater blessing. It is the least I can do for *my* new brother."

He rose, smiled, and extended his hand. Nothing could take away the pain of having lost his daughter. But the smile now on his face gave evidence that she had not given her life in vain.

64

Initial Contact

. . .

MARTA REPNINKA PULLED HER BLACK SHAWL DOWN MORE
tightly against her ears. It was too hot a day to have her head covered
like this, but she would rather sweat than let her face be seen.

Inside she was trembling. From all she had been taught about
American spies, she was putting her life in danger to speak with one.
But the friend of the office clerk's who had come to see her a few
hours ago during midday meal had assured her this man would be
different.

"The CIA are our friends now," he said. "You can trust Dan. And
if you help him," the little man had added with a yellow-toothed
grin, "he can make it worth your while."

Maybe so, thought Marta, but she was still nervous. What if some
friend of Bludayev's saw her, or someone from the office?

She glanced out from behind the black wool that covered half
her face.

There he was! Walking toward her, with the newspaper under his
arm, just like the little man Yaschak said he would be.

For a fleeting moment, Marta considered turning the other way.
Maybe she had misunderstood the phone call! Perhaps she should go
to Bludayev himself, tell him what she had heard, and ask what he had
meant by the awful words. Surely his intent could not be so black as
it seemed!

Even as the thoughts flitted through her brain, she knew she was
deluding herself. Besides, it was too late. The man had spotted her and
was now making straight for her.

Her confused mind continued to race in a thousand directions until the very moment the American's voice broke through. "Miss Repninka, I am the man I believe you are waiting to see," he said in flawless Russian.

Startled, she looked up. There he was, right next to her! Though he wore no smile, he didn't look altogether as fearsome as the ogre she had half expected.

"Shall we walk?" he said. Marta obeyed and fell in slowly beside him.

"I understand you might be able to help me obtain some information?" he said after some moments.

"Perhaps," she replied in a timorous voice.

"You are privy to the defense minister's plans?"

"What plans?"

"I was led to believe you knew what he——"

"I know nothing," she interrupted defensively. "Only that my life is in danger."

"You are in a position perhaps to learn more?"

"I do not know. It is possible."

"If I can assure your safety, you might be able to gain access to what he is planning, certain information, perhaps from his files?"

"I do not know what it is you want."

"I will make that clear to you. Do you have access?"

"I have heard him talk about something he says is very secretive."

"What is it, do you know?"

She hesitated.

"What is it you want, Miss Repninka?" asked Davidson. "If it is money, I can arrange it. A new home in the West? That too would be possible."

"No," she said, shaking her head and putting an edge of wool to her eye to dab at a tear. "I only want a position in Kiev, to be near my brother's family. You must keep them safe too . . . if I help you."

"It can be arranged, and security for you all."

She breathed in deeply, trying to still the many emotions. Then she remembered the sense of betrayal she had felt last night, and anger once again rose up within her. "I will get you what you want," she said. "But you must tell me what to do."

They continued walking, while the American relayed to the

Russian woman the gist of the communiqué he had received from Belgrade.

"I don't know what it is we are looking for, Miss Repninka. I will have to rely on you to see what you can learn. It is very possibly linked to what you heard before. But I will need hard facts."

"If I do find out something?"

"I will arrange either to telephone you or see you in person every evening, but you will not be able to contact me. I will be watching you to make sure no harm comes and to be ready if you discover something for me."

She nodded, seemingly satisfied. She glanced down at the ground as she walked, sighed again, then looked up. She was surprised to find herself again alone.

The man had disappeared.

65

Moscow Prayer Meeting

• • •

THE BASEMENT ROOM WAS ALIVE WITH EXPECTATION.

Not every face wore a smile. Indeed, the expectancy floating in the air was about evenly split between a subdued climate of resentment and anger on the one hand and an open-minded curiosity on the other.

This was a moment none of those gathered had ever anticipated—the opportunity to meet face-to-face with one of their chief antagonists and persecutors of the past two decades.

Some were not pleased that the meeting had been opened to him. Some voiced open hostility to the notion. Others counseled restraint. Still others were positively and enthusiastically inclined, eager to do as their Master had instructed in the matter of enemies. But no one present was indifferent to the proceedings.

The room where they gathered had at one time been hidden from the house above by means of a trapdoor covering the descending stairway. But glasnost had changed many things, including the need to hide religious gatherings, and in time the once life-protecting folding floor had been joyously removed as a relic to a time now gone, hopefully never to return. The basement, however, remained one of the largest rooms available to this fellowship of Moscow believers and continued to be the site of weekly gatherings.

Some forty or forty-five were now present, with more continuing to arrive. The number was expected to reach about seventy or eighty.

The meeting had been hastily convened since Galanov and his German mentor had spoken of it the day before. When the two men—both strangers of face but neither by reputation—entered the room, led by their Muscovite contact of the network, a hubbub of whispered clamor whizzed about the room in all directions, followed almost immediately by a settling of quiet. All eyes rested upon the newcomers, and in truth Galanov's appearance did not immediately allay their suspicions. In spite of the inner peace he felt, the taxing last several days told on him, and his face bore witness to one emotionally and physically spent. The sum total of thoughts in the brains of every man and woman present whose eyes now took in the man before them would no doubt have required a thick book to contain.

The Russian who led them immediately took to the front. "My friends," he said, "I know as little as the rest of you about what we are to hear tonight. I come only to introduce to you my new friend here from Germany, whom I met but three days ago myself. But I can attest to the fact that he is our brother, and he and I have enjoyed great fellowship in the name of our Savior and have prayed together. He came to me yesterday afternoon with a story so incredible I could not believe it myself at first. But I believe *him,* so I agreed to spread the word among you to come tonight and then to translate his words into Russian for you. So I give you our German brother and comrade in the service of our Lord. I will let him tell you in his own words why he has asked you to come, and I will make his thoughts as intelligible in our language as I am able."

He stood to one side, while the German rose to his feet and took a place beside him.

"My brothers and sisters," he began in German, then paused while the man beside him repeated the phrase in Russian. The two men then continued in such a manner, speaking alternately, each in his native language.

"I come to you," the speaker went on, "as a relative stranger, yet not as a stranger, but as one of you in the communion of the saints. I come first bearing greetings from your brothers and sisters of Germany and Poland, through which I have come through the network to you.

"Secondly, I come with a story to tell you that some of you may find difficult to believe. For as you all will probably know by now, this man accompanying me tonight"—he now gestured toward Galanov, where he sat nearby—"this man is an agent of your own KGB, a name most of you already know by reputation, Andrassy Galanov."

At the name, a rustle spread briefly through the audience, though no one spoke.

"And I am here to tell you, my friends, that Herr Galanov is your enemy no longer but has, in the early morning hours of yesterday, given his heart, as have each of us, to the Son of his Maker, our Lord Jesus Christ."

Another rustle, this time louder. Some fidgeted where they sat.

"He asked me to arrange for him to speak to you, which I said I would do. However, before he does so, I want to tell you how I came to meet Herr Galanov, and thus add my own testimony to the veracity of his words. Beyond what the two of us have to say to you, you will have to determine in your own hearts what to do in the matter."

He paused, looked around, took a breath, then continued. "My path first crossed this man's some thirteen years ago in East Germany," he said. "Our first encounter, as you might imagine, was anything but pleasant. For I was a Christian engaged in the attempt of getting to safety the man you called *Der Prophet*—I was involved in the work of *Das Christliche Netzwerk* even back then—and Herr Galanov had followed the Prophet all the way from Moscow to stop the attempt. When our eyes met for the first time, we were enemies of the bitterest kind."

He paused, and the emotion was evident across his face. "Because of that encounter," he went on, "our Lord gave me to pray for this man. And pray for him I have, every day since, though I never saw him again. Recently word came to us that our old nemesis Galanov was now in trouble in his own country, being sought and hunted by the new democratic regime for what they judged his cruel hand in making the old repressive hand of Communism the terrible tool of despotism it was for so long. The same thing had been happening in my country as well—the former followers of Erich Honecker were suddenly outlaws and not safe anywhere. Many of my fellow Christians rejoiced in this news, but I found no pleasure in it. I had been praying for this man daily, and now as I heard that his life was in danger, my heart went out to him. In my prayers I asked the Lord what he would have me to do, what he would have me to pray. In answer, the Lord spoke to my spirit, telling me to come here. He said to go to Galanov, to find him, and to speak forgiveness and love of

God to him, and then to use our network of Christian believers to help him, even to protect him, and to help him out of his present danger."

He stopped. His powerful words were sinking into the minds of his listeners with widely varying impact.

"So I obeyed the inner prompting," he went on, "feeling as much trepidation as you might easily imagine. I had no idea what I might find or what might befall me. Many thoughts ran through my mind as I sat for several hours before dawn in Herr Galanov's hidden quarters, awaiting his arrival. I prayed many prayers that were not unlike the Savior's in the Garden, beseeching our Father to deliver me from my moment of trial. For I must tell you, though I had prayed for this man, I could not help being afraid. For all I knew, the moment he discovered my presence uninvited in his room he might pull a gun on me and shoot me dead. I had no reason to think he would do with me other than what I had witnessed him do with my own eyes.

"The fact that we are both before you is clear evidence that he did not shoot me, and also clear evidence of the miracle of God's restoring and redeeming power of love. For I am here to tell you, friends of the Moscow body of believers, that this man with me this evening is your brother in the family of God!"

A ripple of astonishment went through the room, accompanied by whispers and comments and shifting movement.

"Why should we believe what you say?" asked a large, gruff workingman about midway back in the gathering. His was a hardened face, toughened by years of backbreaking labor in the Soviet system, and he could be excused his apprehension on the same grounds as his spiritual predecessor the apostle Thomas. If there was one thing he had learned in this society, it was that it was best to put your trust only in things you could see with your eyes and touch with your hands. "I do not say we should do the man any harm. But I for one see no call to welcome him with a shake of my hand when he has done so much harm to so many of our people."

Slowly the Russian moderator translated his words into German. Then came the reply, through the same intermediary.

"In answer, my brothers, I will let Herr Galanov speak for himself.

When he has said what he wants to say, you may be your own judge whether you should believe what I say."

With the words, he resumed his seat.

Slowly Galanov himself rose to face the staring eyes of his countrymen. In their eyes were more questions than love.

66

Unbelievable Testimony

•   •   •

IT TOOK SEVERAL LONG MOMENTS OF HEAVY SILENCE
before the KGB agent could find his voice.

The man who had bullied and cowed thousands over the course
of his cruel career now stood intimidated by less than one hundred
commoners—awed by their very silence, knowing full well what was
in their minds and knowing that if some of them hated him, their
hatred was justified.

When at last he spoke, the voice that came forth was not what
those present would have expected. Those in back strained to hear, for
it was a quiet voice, grown suddenly chastened over the course of the
previous thirty-six hours.

"I dare call you neither friends nor brothers," Galanov began
softly. "All I can call you is my comrades, for if nothing else we share
the same Russian blood of our motherland. Yet even the word *comrade*
has suddenly grown a cold reminder of a time so quickly vanished yet
already so distant in the past, a time when we pretended that all
Russians were comrades in the Communist cause together."

He paused, reminiscing painfully. Slowly he drew in a deep breath.
"But a pretense it was," he continued, "as you have long known
much better than I. A sham. A word signifying unity where there was
no unity. A word signifying brotherhood in a society where there was
no brotherhood. A word by which those in power tried to prop up
their hopeless system with the jargon of harmony in a society of
repression and dishonest barbarity and savage mistreatment of those
whom we deceitfully continued to call *comrades*.

"So no, I cannot call you my comrades. For I too have all my life been part of that evil, crooked, inhuman system, blinded by the blindness of the evil that lay within my heart.

"But now at last my eyes are finally being opened—to what I am, to what I have been. Therefore, I pray that you will at least hear my words as your countryman, and one who desires—though I do not for a moment deserve such kindness—to be your brother and kinsman."

Again he paused and breathed deeply, glancing upward toward the ceiling as he did so. The stress told visibly on his features, and it was with great difficulty that he again met the eyes of his listeners.

"It was not until recently that I began to think about myself and what my life has amounted to. As all the old ways began to crumble, many of us who had been wedded to them for decades were forced to think for the first time in our lives, think for ourselves instead of letting the State do it for us. Many things began to come back into my memory from my many years in the KGB. Faces of people I had beaten and imprisoned began to haunt me . . . voices . . . names. . . ."

He paused, struggling to continue. "God, my past began to torment me! *God* . . . I began to find myself even saying that word, that name, more often, using it not even knowing why! It began to pop out of my mouth, though I had always professed a complete disbelief in any divine Creator or afterlife. Then I began to curse God because his name was on my lips! Cursing him as if he was real, all the time trying to convince myself he wasn't!

"Hauntings from out of my past grew more frequent and tormenting. Then the new governmental systems began to look down on those of us who had given our unquestioning allegiance to the old leaders. Suddenly the KGB was itself suspect, and we found ourselves in precarious situations.

"And then, a mere three weeks ago, what should I discover but that there was a price on *my* head. Had I not discovered it covertly, I would be in prison at this moment. But I did discover it and have been running and trying to keep in hiding ever since, trying to figure out some way to escape, to get out of the country and to the West.

"And then . . . two nights ago, they nearly had me. I ran

through the streets of the city all night until I was nearly exhausted. I—" He stopped, recalling the vivid vision he had seen after falling and the voice he had heard. But he was not ready to tell about it yet. "—I somehow reached my quarters safely," he continued. "It was only a matter of time, I thought, before they would discover my whereabouts. I didn't know what to do. I had no friends left, nowhere to turn. I walked into my darkened room, fell upon my bed, only to discover this man there waiting for me." He gestured toward the German.

"How or why he had come there, I had no idea. I was frightened out of my wits at first. All my former KGB fight was gone. I was but a man on the run and terrified for my life. I thought he was there to arrest me . . . or kill me on the spot.

"What I soon learned was that his purpose was altogether different, as he has told you. When he began to speak to me I scarcely understood a word he said, though I have spoken German all my life. For he was speaking words that refreshed my soul . . . words about forgiveness, which, without my realizing it, was exactly what I was longing for. I was so consumed by guilt over what I had done, over the people I had tormented and . . . *God forgive me!*—even killed.

"I tell you, you are looking at nothing better than a murderer before you. And yet this man . . . this man spoke to me of forgiveness and of a Father who *loved* me! Can you imagine how incredulous I was at such words? Love me! The thing was preposterous . . . absurd. How could I—the vilest, blackest individual imaginable, a killer— how could I be loved by anyone! Yet there he sat, calmly, staring into my eyes, telling me such.

"As he did, slowly began to dawn in my consciousness a recognition, something that said I had *known* this man. And gradually as my recognition grew, so did another bitter memory . . . a memory . . . of—"

He stopped, unable to continue. He looked away, rubbing at his eyes, now full of tears. "Do you hear me? . . . I *knew* the very man who had come to find me . . . to *help* me . . . the man who had *prayed* for me. I knew him, for thirteen years ago, when I was stalking your beloved Prophet from this city . . . the man who brought me here to you tonight—*this* man—" he pointed to the German sitting in front of him, also with tears in his eyes—"he stepped in front of me and threw himself in front of my loaded gun . . . endangered himself, and in so doing saved the life of your Prophet . . . only to find . . . several minutes later . . . *forgive my cruel deed!* . . . only to find his own daughter . . . *O God!* . . . his own daughter dead . . . from the bullet from *my* gun!

"And this man . . . this man who brought me here . . . and who spoke to you of me . . . *he prayed for me for all those years* . . . prayed for me—*the very murderer of his daughter!*—and then came to find me, and again risked his life to do so . . . and then he looked into my eyes and spoke to me of *forgiveness* and of a God who *loved* me!

"How could I not listen?

"How could I not believe in such a One? For this man had to either be a fool to speak to me of forgiveness—*me, a man he should have hated!*—or else he possessed a secret to life that no Communist I ever met possessed.

"The moment I saw him sitting in my hideaway I knew this man was no fool, and very soon thereafter I knew that I also wanted to possess the secret to life that gave him such power to love and forgive such a vile specimen of humanity as I."

It was all the former agent could do to get the words out. No more would come. He broke down, collapsed in a nearby chair, and wept as the roomful of stunned Muscovite Christians looked on in prayerful silence.

The German was the first out of his chair. Slowly he approached Galanov, said nothing, but merely laid his hand reassuringly on his shoulder.

Gradually one or two others rose from where they sat and came forward to join him. Within two or three minutes, Galanov was surrounded by ten or fifteen, whose hands had been gently laid upon him, and the small group prayed, some audibly, some silently, for their new brother.

This continued some thirty minutes. As one by one they began to step back, some continued to stand nearby while others resumed their seats.

After several more minutes, the large doubting Russian miner, his hands and face still blackened from the day in the coal pits, rose and lumbered forward to where Galanov still sat. He approached slowly.

Galanov looked up.

The miner extended his muscular hand. "If a German brother can believe in you, I don't see how a fellow Russian can do any less. I'd be pleased to call you my brother, Galanov, and extend you my hand of welcome into our fellowship."

Two Different Doors

• • •

Berlin

TAD MCCALLUM HAD GROWN LESS AND LESS INTERESTED in the church leaders' conference with each passing hour. He had now seen Lisel Lamprecht for each of the last three days—two lunches, a supper, and a pleasant evening's walk in the Tiergarten—and it was becoming more and more difficult to convince either of his two parents that quite so much time was necessary for "background information" for an article.

His father was continuing with the conference schedule in spite of the doubts he harbored concerning his own participation. But more and more of the meetings and workshops he was having to attend without benefit of Tad's company.

On the afternoon of the day just past Tad brought Lisel to the hotel and introduced her to his mother and father for the first time. There had not been opportunity for her to hear what Tad had called his mother's story, but he hoped for more such visits in the near future.

"Both your parents seem really wonderful," said Lisel as they left the hotel.

"They are—I couldn't ask for better."

"Your mother has such a sweet countenance," said Lisel. "I felt immediately that she cared about me."

"You felt it because she *does*," replied Tad. "I could tell she liked you, too, from the expression in her eyes."

"She looked at me . . . almost as if she *knew* me," Lisel added. "At first it was a little disconcerting."

Tad laughed. "You wouldn't find it so strange if you knew my grandfather," he said, "my mother's father. He was a Pomeranian baron."

"Why—how would knowing him explain the look in her eyes?"

"Because he was always looking *inside* things—that's the way my mother describes it."

"Meaning what?"

"That he sought to see below the surface, into deeper meanings, into roots, into what was truly significant rather than what was passing."

"Isn't everything passing eventually?"

"My grandfather wouldn't say so, I don't believe. And neither would I. In any event, I think my mother inherited her father's eyes. I have learned to detect it in her, even when she doesn't say anything—learned to detect that probing expression on her face that tells me she is gazing past what other people see."

"I'm not sure I like the sound of that," said Lisel.

"Why?"

"I don't know. It seems a little spooky. I'm not sure I like the idea of someone being able to see deeper inside me than I *want* them to see."

Again Tad laughed. "The only time it is directed at other people is in love. That's what enables some eyes to see more deeply into things—love. You can't see into what you don't love. So you see, there's nothing whatever to be afraid of."

"Are you saying that expression I noticed when your mother was looking at me was because she *loved* me?"

"That's exactly what I am saying."

Lisel was quiet a long time, pondering Tad's words. "You're fortunate," she said at length, "to have such parents. You obviously think a great deal of them."

"Yes. Yes, I do. I'm very thankful for the upbringing I had," said Tad.

Lisel was silent a few minutes. It was clear that she was thinking. "What about someone who hasn't been so fortunate?" she asked at length.

"What about them?" asked Tad.

"It seems some people have a head start in life. That hardly strikes me as fair, if there is a God, for him to have set it up like that."

"It's one of the necessary consequences of his having given us free will," commented Tad. "But that's too long a discussion for us to get into right now. I would just add, in reply to what you said, that nobody ever said life was fair. If *fairness* is your starting point, there are all kinds of things in life that will make you crazy if you think about them long enough."

"You don't think God treats people fairly?"

"I didn't say that. I do not think life *is* fair. I'm not sure it's *supposed* to be fair. To begin to truly understand anything about life and truth at all, I think you have to throw out fairness as a starting point. *Justice* will prevail in the end, but not fairness. God *will* give everybody justice. But that still doesn't make life fair."

"What's the difference?"

"They're as different as night and day. But again, that's too long a discussion to get into now. I want to go back to the question you asked a minute ago."

"Which one?"

"About people who haven't been so fortunate as maybe I have been—how some people seem to have a head start, so to speak."

"All right, what *would* you say?"

"That it's one of those factors that doesn't mean as much as it might seem."

"That's easy for you to say, being the beneficiary of such a head start."

"Everyone has to struggle to find truth for themselves," replied Tad. "My struggle may be different from yours, but that doesn't mean everything has all fallen into place for me without a price. The lines of unfairness are aligned differently in each person's life. Everyone has some things *easier* than others, and some things *harder.*"

"I suppose you are right," conceded Lisel.

"Everyone is given a completely unique set of life circumstances," said Tad. "When everything is added up, the things we are able to see as well as the things no human eye is capable of seeing, I doubt the overall equation of man's earthly existence really is as *unfair* as we sometimes think. Nevertheless, we all have to live in the midst of the circumstances in which we find ourselves and use those circumstances to discover truth and then live by it. Maybe one person *does* have a head start. Be that as it may—truth still must be found."

"Though it's harder for one than another?"

"There you are, bringing fairness into it again," rejoined Tad. "Because it's hard, maybe even unfair, is that an excuse for someone to sit back and neglect truth altogether? *Truth must be discovered,* whether a certain individual finds the process hard or easy, and whether someone *else* may have had what you call a head start or not."

Lisel did not reply immediately.

"Let me put it like this," Tad went on. "Imagine two lumps of gold sitting behind two closed doors. The lumps are free for the taking. All that has to be done is open the door and lay hold of it and it's yours! Do you have the picture?"

"I think so."

"All right. Two people walk up and turn the handles of their respective doors. One of the doors opens easily on well-oiled hinges. The person walks in, picks up the gold, and rejoices in his find.

"The other, however, discovers his door nearly rusted shut and very difficult to move on its hinges. Now my question is this: What would the wise man do, and what would the fool do? The gold is there, though the door is difficult to open. Would not the wise man set about to finding a way to get through to lay claim to the gold, notwithstanding the difficulty?"

"You have a point."

"To complain that the other door opened more easily and then turn and walk away, leaving the lump of gold there unclaimed because the door you're standing in front of is difficult to budge, that hardly seems very prudent. The wise individual would say, 'My door may be more difficult to open, but that's not going to stop me from getting through to the gold!'"

Again Lisel did not reply, and they walked on along the street for some time in silence.

She had many things to think about, and through them all continued to return to her the haunting smile of Tad's mother's eyes.

She did not know that Sabina had been praying for her. But the impact of those prayers was felt no less in Lisel's heart that she was unaware of them.

68

Out of Death . . . Life

• • •

Moscow

THE NEXT TWO DAYS WERE ONES OF UNEXPECTED pleasure for both Galanov and his German friend and spiritual father.

Welcomed wholeheartedly into the fellowship of Moscow believers whose meeting they had attended, they now found opportunity to meet many more Christians in other such fellowships. Galanov wanted to attend as many such meetings as possible, for he felt his business was urgent and he had to face as many believers as possible so as to personally make his appeal for forgiveness. The two men were well provided for in food and lodging, and Galanov did not once return to his own quarters.

Both German and Russian told their stories to different groups of believers, and they had numerous opportunities to sit in on prayer and teaching meetings within various corners of what had once been a vast underground congregation of several thousand and was now growing daily.

On his part, Galanov received a crash course in the basics of his new faith. The lessons were the more profound since the teachings came from countrymen he had once looked down upon. The tables had indeed been reversed, and he was the first to acknowledge it.

Wherever they went they were warmly received. For word about the two men had spread throughout the fabric of the fellowship more quickly than their steps. Skepticism and anger were always in supply as well, though in diminishing quantities, and usually a few words either from the German or their Russian host, a pastor by the name of Karl Medvedev, set the stage for Galanov to tell his story without hostility.

He grew gradually more at ease standing in front of his fellow countrymen, though as he spoke, tears remained always in ample supply. Forgiveness continued to be the dominant theme of his message.

"My friends," he said during a morning prayer gathering, "you cannot begin to know the impact for one like me—one who suddenly, for the first time, sees his miserable life for what it really is—of knowing that I am loved and forgiven in spite of all I have done. You cannot know the power such forgiveness brings! How desperately it makes me desire to be whole, to be clean. This is what I have experienced these recent days—the cleansing, hope-giving power of being forgiven by this man here, this man at my side . . . a man who, if ever a grudge of vengeance was justified, this man would have had it. I cannot even think of—"

Again his words were interrupted by a fresh swelling of tears. "I cannot think of that awful deed without an anguish of guilt . . . a horrible crushing weight of the evil that is in me. 'God,' I have cried out so many times in these recent days, 'O God, take my life, if such were only possible, and restore this man his daughter!'"

He paused briefly to wipe his eyes. "I have cried out for God to end my life many times! And yet . . . yet he does not do so. And here this man continues to be . . . standing at my side, on his knees with me in prayer, his hand upon my shoulder, telling me of the Father's power to wash away those multitude of stains upon my soul . . . stains of the guilt from the many whose blood I shed.

"New life is about *forgiveness,* my friends and brothers. I know something about forgiveness because daily I am being cleansed by the living example of this man's love for his Father, who told him to pray for his enemies and to do good to those who persecuted him . . . and whose Father told him to forgive."

In the middle of the day, after they had left the meeting and were waiting for an afternoon's fellowship in another part of the city to begin, in the midst of an inrush of despair, Galanov cried out yet again to be crushed and his misery and remorse ended once and for all.

"But do you not want to see my daughter again and tell her how sorry you are?" said his German friend tenderly.

"Of course, nothing could delight my heart more!"

"Then take heart. You *shall* see her."

"Let me end my life now, that I might go to her immediately!"

"Ah, my friend," said the German, following well in the footsteps of his predecessor Barnabas—whose name, *son of encouragement,* he lived out in relation to his own first-century convert's like struggle in Acts 9—"but would she not receive your gift of forgiveness with far more rejoicing were you able to bring into her presence a hundred more with you? Or perhaps a thousand . . . or still more! Brothers and sisters for whom her death opened the way into the kingdom?"

Galanov could hardly take in the largeness of the question.

The German continued, speaking words of life and hope. "Do you not see, my brother," he said gently, "that unless you offer this opportunity the Father is giving you back into his hands for him to use for the growth of his kingdom among men, then my daughter will have died to open your eyes *only.* As I told you, Jesus would have died were there only one to die for. Yet how much more wonderful for my Girdel's death to bring hundreds or thousands to our Father."

"My heart leaps at the very thought," said the Russian. "Do you mean it might be possible for me to actually present your daughter with such a gift that will make her *rejoice* upon seeing me again?"

"Not only will she rejoice, she will throw her arms around you in the gladness of unbounded delight, greeting you no longer as her adversary, but as her brother, not as one who *took* her life, but as one who allowed your mutual Father to *give* the gift of his life to thousands. She will look upon the sacrifice of her one life as the greatest and most blessed sacrifice she could make for her Savior, following his own pathway, not out of life, but *into* life. I tell you, Andrassy my brother, my daughter even now rejoices at being accorded such a great honor in the kingdom as to lay down her life for her faith, that many others may come to believe. You will be able to embrace her . . . to look her in the eye and say, 'I love you, my sister. Forgive me. Thank you for giving your life . . . that I might know the Father.'"

"What you say is . . . is too staggering. How can mortal men comprehend such enormous truths? If what you say . . . *if it could only be true* . . . if only I could truly believe that . . . some purpose . . . some higher meaning could result."

"You *can* believe it! Give your life wholly, utterly, unreservedly to the cause of the Master, and he will take it and mold with it a mighty miracle of his perfect design.

"You cannot imagine," the German went on, "how mightily our Father will be able to use your life if you place it in his hands like clay on the Potter's wheel. How can we possibly see the whys of God's larger purposes? Who can know these things? Yet it is possible that the purpose for which my daughter was given life by our Father in the first place was so that she might pour out that life, to give true life to you.

"It is a principle of the kingdom that life comes only through death. The Master said that unless a grain of wheat falls to the ground and dies, it remains alone. But when it dies, and pours out its being, its very lifeblood, new life results, and manifold fruitfulness springs forth.

"My daughter was a single seed, a grain of wheat . . . *one* life. But in her falling to the earth and dying, now new life is springing forth, and people are already hearing the Good News of God's recreative power of forgiveness—through your mouth—that they would never have heard from my own daughter. Today you are speaking to believers. But the day will come, and soon, when I believe your voice will carry far into the unbelieving world, planting seeds a hundred- and thousandfold, like the great traveling apostle of old in whose footsteps I believe you are destined to follow. Don't you see! God is *already* at work preparing the ground to bring forth the hundredfold grain out of your life because my daughter poured out hers."

"But . . . but *how* can this be? It is too incredible a thought!"

"God's ways are not man's ways. The laws of God's kingdom work upside-down, in reverse from the laws of man's kingdom."

"How do you mean?"

"Man says get and hoard and accumulate. God says, if you would truly *have,* then the secret is to give, and give, and *give* still more. It is impossible for men, whose viewpoint is only man's, to see the truth of this. To them it is nonsense. *Having* and *giving* are opposites. Only when one sees with God's eyes do they then become one and the same."

"I think I see what you mean by upside-down," said Galanov slowly. "It's not easy to learn to look at things in a whole new way. Can you show me something else like that?"

"You mean that is upside-down, in reverse?"

Galanov nodded.

The German thought for a moment. "Man says *save* your life. God says, if you would save it, you must *lose* your life. Man says *hate* your enemies. God says, *love* your enemies. It is all upside-down. To understand life in God's kingdom, we have to let go of all man's thinking. Man says *live.* God says, the road to life is through *death.* Man says *prosper.* God says, one thing still you lack—go and *give away all you have.*

"You ask *how?* I say, because God is our Father. He is the Father of my daughter. He is my Father. Now he is your Father. He does these things because we are his, and he knows all things better than we."

Galanov was silent. He had many things to ponder.

69

The Circle Is Completed at Last

. . .

Berlin

"MR. AND MRS. MCCALLUM, MAY I PRESENT MY FRIEND from long ago, Dieder Palacki. Dieder, Matthew and Sabina, also my friends for almost exactly the same length of time."

The three shook hands amid smiles and further greetings.

"Come in and sit down—please," said Sabina, still the gracious and beautifully smiling hostess, even in a hotel room. "This is as close as we have to home for the present."

"Your reputation precedes you, Mr. Palacki," said Matthew as they took seats around the small room. "We all know of your work and admire it."

"Thank you," replied the Pole. "I might say the same, for I know two or three of your books quite well."

"I must confess to surprise. I am not aware that any of my books have circulated over here in any great numbers."

"I have spent a good deal of time in the States."

"Yes, of course. Joseph told us something of your travels."

Palacki sent an inquiring glance in Joseph's direction.

"He has kept up on you through the years," Matthew added on Joseph's behalf.

Palacki smiled. "I am beginning to see that," he said, turning again toward Matthew.

"In addition to your own books," he added, "you have done considerable work, I believe, redacting some of the writings of Heinrich von Dortmann?"

Matthew smiled and nodded. "This woman beside me is the baron's daughter."

A gasp of pleasurable surprise left Palacki's mouth. "Ah, then I am more honored to meet you both even than I realized! I had not made the connection."

"We only just spoke briefly earlier," explained Joseph. "I've hardly had the chance to fill Dieder in at all."

"I am a great admirer of your father's, as well as your husband's, Mrs. McCallum," Palacki said with deep sincerity. "You are indeed a fortunate woman to have shared your life with such men."

"Yes, I am most blessed. But please, you must call me Sabina."

"Agreed, as long as we drop the formalities on both sides."

"And throughout the room!" added Matthew with a laugh.

"The three of you cannot possibly imagine how it feels for me to see you all here with me—together," said Joseph.

"How do you look to each other?" asked Matthew.

"Changed!" Palacki and Joseph said at once, then laughed.

"Would you have recognized one another?"

"Not walking down the street," replied Palacki. "But after two seconds of conversation I would have remembered the voice."

"That goes equal for me," said Joseph. "I *might* have recognized you on the street, but only because I have been hoping for an opportunity to see you again, to tell you thank you."

"It would seem the Lord has at last arranged it."

"And I am more thankful to him than you know. You are my spiritual parentage! This is a circle I have longed to see completed for thirty years. The only one missing is your father, Sabina."

"And Ursula," added Sabina.

"My wife," Joseph explained, with a glance toward Palacki.

"I see. *Well,* I am excited to hear this fantastic story you said you had for me," said the Polish pastor. "I am so thrilled to see you walking with the Lord after all this time; you cannot know what an encouragement it is to me. Of course, none of us had any idea what became of you after you left us, though we continued to pray for you."

"The Lord was truly guiding my steps and answering *your* prayers—for I fell in with *these* people—" he gestured toward Matthew and Sabina—"when I reached Berlin. By then I was ready to heed what you had told me. It was with their help, and Sabina's father's, that I gave my heart to the Lord."

"You have been walking with him ever since?"

Joseph nodded.

"The Lord truly be praised!" exclaimed Palacki. "In my particular calling, there are sometimes not so many moments when one is privileged to see the fruit of the Lord's harvest. This news not only makes my day, as the Americans say, it makes my *year.*"

The others laughed.

"I am anxious to hear all about it," Palacki added.

"Do you want the complete or the abbreviated version?" asked Joseph.

"The complete, of course. I have no more commitments for the rest of the afternoon or evening."

Joseph drew in a deep breath, glanced around at each of his three friends, then launched into the tale he had been praying for the opportunity to tell for three decades.

• • •

Four hours had passed, dusk had fallen, and they had ordered supper from room service, which had been delivered and consumed. Still the conversation in the sitting room of Matthew and Sabina's suite between the four Christians from such diverse backgrounds—a Pole, a Russian Jew, a German, and an American—showed no signs of letting up. It was the most enjoyable four hours any of them had spent since arriving in Berlin.

"I wish Tad could have been here," sighed Sabina during a lull.

"Where is he?" asked Joseph. "At the conference?"

Matthew and Sabina both laughed together.

"Not hardly!" answered Matthew. "He's out with a young lady."

"Ah . . . anything serious?"

"Who knows—it started merely as an interview, but he's seen her several times since."

"From the sound of it," added Sabina, "they talk pretty freely about things. That's always a sign two people are hitting it off— when they can discuss anything. You remember how *we* were, Matthew."

Matthew nodded. "When he starts taking her roses, *then* I'll know something's up," he laughed.

Again there was silence for a moment or two.

"Coffee, anyone?" asked Sabina, rising. "Shall I start a pot?"

A nod or two followed. Sabina went to the small kitchen counter and began the proceedings, while still listening to the conversation between the three men.

Joseph asked about Palacki's colleagues of the Brotherhood of Bialystok.

"I have not spent as much time with them in recent years as I wish were possible," replied Palacki. "I was there three months ago, however, and had a wonderful time of renewed fellowship. I still consider those men my spiritual home and root and support system. They are doing well. The older men, of course—my father and his friends who began the fellowship—are mostly gone. But there are new young believers. Kochow Rydz and Waclau Chmielnicki are two I remember for certain were there the night you were with us. To tell you the truth, I have forgotten the rest—it was many years ago."

"Yes, so have I," said Joseph. "I would probably not even remember the names if you told me. Are they still involved in underground activities?"

"More than you might think. Much has changed, but Russia is still Russia, and thus they continue in prayer to be used however the Lord wills."

A brief silence followed. Matthew was the first to break it. "Tell me, Dieder," he said, "what are *you* going to speak on when your time comes next week?"

"The inflection of your question seems to carry more meaning than the mere words would indicate," said Palacki.

"Let me simply say that I have been experiencing something of an internal crisis over what ought to be my *own* role here."

"A crisis?"

"A reevaluation of what comprises evangelism in the first place, and whether all this razzmatazz in which we engage is really what the Lord has in mind at all."

"I had the feeling from reading your books that you were probably a kindred spirit." Palacki smiled. "Now I *know* you are. You are scheduled to speak as well?"

"I made no promises, but Darrell has been exerting a great deal of pressure."

"Yes." Palacki smiled. "I have noticed that same thing in my case. I have not been altogether comfortable with what I sense he has in mind for me—playing the role of figurehead Eastern Christian leader."

"You sound as cynical as I have been lately," laughed Matthew.

"I hope I'm not a cynic," rejoined Palacki, "but—I don't know whether Joseph happened to mention it—I *do* have a way of speaking rather directly toward what the Lord reveals to me."

"Yes, as a matter of fact, he did say something to that effect," laughed Matthew. "For as long as I have known him, which is thirty years now, he has never stopped being grateful to you for your courage in speaking so forcefully to *him.*"

Palacki sighed. "I appreciate your telling me that. Bless you, Joseph," he added, turning toward him, "for being so open to the Lord's voice. As I believe I said to you, my words are not always received so humbly nor so gratefully."

"Having light shone upon one's inner cracks, as you told me back then, is not always a pleasant experience," said Joseph. "That doesn't mean it is any the less necessary. Men such as yourself, who see things more clearly perhaps than most Christians—men like Sabina's father—are vitally necessary within the body of Christ to keep truth clearly focused."

"It is a difficult assignment."

"Whether that truth is always pleasant to hear is hardly to the point if it is the Lord who is inspiring it. The words of Jesus were more often convicting and stern, even reprimanding, than warm and cozy."

Palacki nodded. "How well I know that truth," he replied with a sigh. "But you must understand that this has been my constant struggle since I first began to walk in the things of faith—what to *do* with the truths the Lord shows me. It has not been a pleasant nor an enjoyable road I have walked. Many times I have, like Paul, besought him to take my very insight from me, for it felt like a thorn in my flesh that I could endure no longer."

"And did he?" asked Sabina, rejoining the other three.

"No," replied the Polish pastor. "He only increased the clarity of my focus and said to me, 'You must learn to love my people as I love them, and give your life for them as I gave mine, and continue speaking whatever I show you.' I have prayerfully attempted to be faithful to that charge through the years."

Palacki paused, and the others waited for him to continue. "This is not to say," he went on, "that I am constantly on the prowl for imperfections in my fellows to examine and illuminate. But when God gives me insight, I submit the matter to him in prayer, and if he urges it upon me, then I will speak out. I do not speak when it will obviously accomplish nothing or create division. Sometimes division *is* created, but such is never my purpose. I speak only when I perceive it will be useful and beneficial, or when the Lord makes clear that a word of chastening is necessary for future growth."

"What is usually the reaction?" asked Matthew.

"There is a great deal of apparent openness among Christians that changes when words become pointed and personal. God has not given me to see superficialities. Therefore when I shine the light of my insight, it is often in regard to some flaw or blind spot that is hindering God's work. Therefore, there is often unpleasantness with regard to the response."

"Directed toward you?"

"Usually that is the case. If I can be discredited—taken down a notch or two is, I believe, the term—then it justifies ignoring my words."

It fell silent while everyone pondered the implications of what the pastor from the East had been saying.

"To answer your question, Matthew," said Dieder at length, "no, I do *not* yet know what the Lord would have me say. I am praying earnestly, but as yet I can only say I am feeling more and more uncomfortable in these surroundings."

Matthew sighed. He knew the feeling exactly.

"How did your father cope with the kinds of things I have been sharing?" Palacki asked, turning to Sabina.

"You mean confronting people and their reactions?"

Palacki nodded.

Sabina smiled. The question itself raised so many memories of her father afresh that she had to take a few moments before answering. "My father's way was different from yours," she replied. "He did not confront people in the ways in which God has led you to do. I would say he challenged people rather than confronted them."

"*Challenged* them—how?"

"Challenged how they thought about God, challenged them to think more of his loving Fatherhood than his stern judgeship. Wouldn't you say so, Matthew?"

"Definitely. That is the reason I am a believer today. You, Dieder, *confronted* Joseph with what you have both called his inner cracks. Baron von Dortmann *challenged* me to think differently about God just as Sabina has said—to think of his loving Fatherhood."

"If I had to reduce my father's life-priority to one thing," Sabina went on, "I would say it was to change how people view God their Father. That is his legacy."

"And it is that legacy we've given our lives to extending into the future," added Matthew. "First, to make the truths he taught us dynamic and real and practical in the way *we* live, and then to pass those truths about God on to *others.*"

"That is the calling, is it not," said Joseph, "to penetrate deeply enough into a person's heart and brain so that you really cause them to think of God in new ways. You spoke, Matthew, of the baron addressing God's *Fatherhood.* In my work I am constantly attempting—by both confrontation *and* challenge—to force people to consider the reality of God's *Sonship* as revealed in Jesus Christ. In so many aspects of his nature, men and women today simply do not grasp in any depth who God truly is."

The four continued to talk as the evening advanced. The conversation especially centered around the subject just raised—how to change the way people think about God and his character and work, and how to impact the body of Christ so that the world would be changed.

Spontaneously, a little before ten, the four aging saints of God began pouring out their hearts' desires to their mutual Father.

"*Lord, as long as we have all been walking with you,*" Matthew began to pray, "*we so desperately need your guidance in ordering our thoughts. Sometimes it seems I have come such a little distance in understanding your will. I do ask you now to continue to show me that will, and help me to walk in it.*"

"*Yes, Father,*" Sabina now joined her husband, "*we thank you for men like my father and Thaddeus who came before, who taught us and who left us a rich legacy to follow. Yet, Lord, we realize it is we who now walk in that inheritance. Help us to walk in it faithfully, so that the great miracle of your life might be passed on to others who will follow us."*

"Reveal to us the words you would have us speak at this conference," prayed Palacki. *"In the midst of these surroundings that we find difficult from time to time, give us humble spirits to hear your voice and to love our brothers."*

"We submit our questions to you, Lord," said Joseph. *"We do not know the best way to cause men to turn to you. To our minds it seems your injunction to spread your life abroad into the earth must be about more than workshops and speeches. Reveal your truth to us."*

"Give us your focus, your perspective, your eyes to see all this as you see it," said Palacki.

"And the courage to speak when you lead us, and the trust in you to be silent until you do," added Matthew.

"Yes, Lord," repeated Palacki, *"courage to speak . . . trust to remain silent."*

"O Father," prayed Sabina again, *"may our lives be such that they cause people to turn and behold you living inside us. Though we feel so incapable of living as Jesus taught us to, yet use us in ways we cannot see, so that somehow people's lives are changed because we know you. We thank you, our God, for loving us so much, for your goodness to us. We love you, our Father!"*

"Amen!" whispered several voices.

"Lord," said Joseph, *"it is our desire to impact the body of your believers, but only as you would have us. Help us to be faithful to the legacy of men like Sabina's father, but even more to that of the Master he served, your Son."*

More *"Amens!"* followed.

70

Where Does Responsibility Lie?

. . .

Berlin

TAD LAY AWAKE, REPLAYING IN HIS MIND THE CONVERSA-
tion he had had the day before with Lisel.

The illustration of the doors and lumps of gold, though he had
just thought of it as they were speaking, had come back to him several
times since. Now he found himself reflecting on what it might have
been like for him had *he* encountered a door with rusty hinges rather
than one kept lubricated by the prayerful oil of faithfulness of those
who had gone before him.

His thoughts strayed to Lisel's situation, where, he was certain,
some painful incident having to do with her father had allowed the
hinges of her heart to rust shut toward him.

Circumstances were different with everyone, it was true. But what
about *relational* rust? Who was responsible to chip it off and reoil the
hinges?

For some reason the Berlin Wall came into his mind. *What about
walls between people?* he wondered, gradually thinking back to the
conversation he and Lisel had had their first evening together in her
apartment.

Tad soon found himself pondering a question he had never before
considered. He had said to Lisel on that occasion that healing between individuals must not wait for *another* person's initiation. He had
made the comment in relation to his forgiveness of her. Now he
found himself turning the principle upon the parent–child relationship. Did the same thing hold true there as well?

The first thing to come to his mind in reply was that responsibility for change in any relationship must rest, it seemed logical, with the older, the stronger, the wiser. What if, however, Tad thought further, the weaker and younger and less mature was the one responsible for a relational break? What then *could* the stronger individual do to heal the breach? Would he not be powerless until a change was initiated within the heart of the other?

His thoughts turned again to Germany. The separation that had divided this land for so many years had been instigated in the east. The Wall had gone *up* from the east, and therefore it had had to be torn *down* from the east as well. For all its strength and prosperity, for all its desire to see unity reestablished, there was nothing West Germany could do to achieve it . . . except wait, and hope, and pray.

If the Wall was to be torn down at all, it could only come from a change of heart within *East* Germany—the smaller, the weaker, the less mature, and the one responsible for the break in the first place.

It was a dichotomy of spiritual enormity, Tad thought. For the one *most* capable of seeing truth and therefore *most* capable of doing right, is the one who is *unable* to effect a change. Change must rest with the one *least* able to institute it.

Was that not, in fact, a picture of man's rebellion against God? As strong and loving and powerful as God is, there is one thing he is powerless to do, thought Tad—tear down the walls of separation man has erected against him. They can only be pulled down, and unity between Creator and creature restored, *from within the hearts of men and women.*

Tad's thoughts returned to Lisel. He would never himself know the kind of rift she had experienced with her parents. How different had it been for him! The Lord had blessed him beyond measure with an inheritance of godliness for which he would be eternally grateful. Lisel was absolutely right in saying he had had a head start. His door toward the truth of the Christian faith *had* been easier to open.

What if it had been different? Or what if some difficulty were to develop in the future? If he ever were to find himself in such a situation, where would the responsibility lie for a change? If—God forbid—there should ever be a wall between he and his own father, upon whose shoulders would the accountability rest for tearing it down?

His thoughts, in answer to his own question, went immediately to the fifteenth chapter of Luke. It was not the *father,* Tad realized, who went seeking his son in the attempt to make amends and demolish the wall of separation that existed between them. Rather it was the *son* who at length came to his senses and said to himself, "What a fool I have been. I have sinned. *I will arise and go to my father."*

What had happened between the two Germanys paralleled the story of the prodigal exactly! The younger, weaker, smaller had gone back to its father. The *fatherland* was whole again.

It was the *son's* responsibility to see his foolishness and to go to his father. The father's heart had been full of love all along, but all he could do was wait and pray and watch down the road in loving and open-armed readiness for his son to return.

Walls of separation could only be torn down from the inside.

Tad hoped Lisel would be able one day to do that as well.

Lord, he prayed, *oil the hinges of her inner doors. Open her heart to her father . . . and to you.*

It was a simple enough prayer. But in such things, a multitude of words is not necessary.

Time to Head West

• • •

Moscow

"IT IS TIME FOR ME TO GO HOME," SAID THE GERMAN TO the former Soviet KGB agent. "And I must get you out of here as well. You are in more and more danger every day."

"Do you think that concerns me now?" said Galanov.

"We must not squander what God has given. Your responsibility is great to steward this marvelous thing he has done—steward it as a priceless gift. We must not be so careless as to throw it away."

"Perhaps you are right. Yet for so long I have harassed and tormented these people. It seems the least I can do is spend some time among them, making up for the past in the small ways that are given to me."

"The more you are around, the more people you meet, the more your story becomes known, the more likely it will be that those who are after you will get wind of your activities. I am surprised they have not already. Remember, you said yourself that there is a price on your head. Each day we tarry is another day closer to arrest."

"I fear arrest no longer."

"That may be true. Yet would you unnecessarily bring danger to your new brothers and sisters? We cannot tell what may be the repercussions. And what of the many to whom God may send you to tell of his Son? You cannot do the work that he is, I believe, giving you to do if you are behind bars or in Siberia for the rest of your life."

"You make many good points, my friend. I had not considered the wider implications of my plight."

"Which is why I urgently feel it is time we made our way West. I have been discussing the details today with Medvedev, and most everything is in place. The longer you are in Moscow, the more danger that is bound to result."

Galanov pondered his friend's words carefully. "Yes . . . yes, I see that you are right. To remain in my homeland may in the long run cut short what there might be for me elsewhere."

"Exactly. We must get you out of danger and to freedom . . . in the West."

"I place myself in your hands then, my friend."

"And we will both place ourselves in the hands of our brothers and sisters of *Das Christliche Netzwerk.*"

"They will help me, do you think? They will trust me? We will not have time to tell every person, every contact, our story."

"They will help us. Perhaps everyone need not know your identity—I should say, your former identity. The man Andrassy Galanov is dead. He exists no longer. Perhaps, for the purposes of travel, we might even give you a new name. It will solve many problems, including making you less visible and traceable for those who are after you."

"As you wish," consented Galanov. "When do you want us to leave?"

"As soon as possible."

"Tonight? I must return to my small flat to gather a few items."

"It is not so urgent we cannot get a few hours' sleep first, but most everything is arranged. What about family, friends, your other home?"

"Spies have no family," replied Galanov in a wistful tone. "My parents are both dead. Whatever other family I once had is distant. My only friends were also part of the KGB, and all that is suddenly gone. My home itself, that is part of my past life. I am certain it is being watched, and I have no need to return there. My car, furniture, clothes—I will have no more need of them. I took my money out of the bank long ago when tensions began. It is hidden at my flat and I can retrieve it. I will need nothing else."

"I am sure that is wise so that you give no appearance, should your enemies get wind of your whereabouts, of clearing out."

"When do you want to leave?"

"Go back to your place tonight. I would like to leave very early in the morning—very early, so we are well out of Moscow before daybreak. The man who drove me most of the way from Smolensk is expecting us to contact him soon. We will get word to him immediately. He will drive east to the same place he dropped me off, and there he will pick us up for the return trip."

"I will be ready," said Galanov.

72

Change of Plans

• • •

ANDRASSY GALANOV LAY ON THE BED IN HIS SMALL HIDE-away flat, staring up at the ceiling.

The hour was late, well after midnight. He would only have a couple hours of sleep before the German returned to pick him up for their flight west from Moscow.

Right here, such a short time ago, his life had been turned upside-down. It was almost as if God had reached down and forcibly yanked him out of one life and set him immediately down into another. Suddenly all these surroundings seemed so foreign, all the reminders of his many years as a KGB agent so remote and faraway and insignificant.

He sat up and glanced over at the single dilapidated chair in which his friend had been sitting waiting for him. How terrified he had been when he had heard him speak out of the darkness!

And that other voice . . . out of the bright light, preceding the German's visit. He had not had much time to reflect upon what had been said. He had been so tired and stressed. The words had faded in and out of his consciousness with the vagueness of a dream.

Yet now as he sat pondering and reflecting, both on his past behind him and his unknown future before him, the words came back into his mind with a resonant clarity they had not even had when he had heard them in the street. *"I am the Lord. . . . From this day forward, you shall serve me."*

And then the German's words of what God had spoken to him: "My hand is upon this man." And what the German himself had said:

346

"How mightily our Father will be able to use your life if you place it in his hands."

So much raced through Galanov's brain. Where would it all lead? Where was his future? He was preparing to leave this place, this piece of his home, perhaps forever.

He slipped down off the bed and onto his knees. *"God,"* he prayed, *"this is all so new. There is so much I do not know. Teach me, show me . . . help me be the man you want me to be. Show me what to do . . . what path to walk."*

Something had been on his mind for a few hours now. It had come to him this morning and had nagged more and more strongly ever since he and the German had begun making plans to leave some four hours ago. Now in the night quiet of his flat, beside his bed, praying, stronger grew the sense that he had indeed been sniffing around the edges of something with major importance earlier when he'd seen the political leaders of the two countries together. Something that maybe he was not just to walk away from.

What could it have meant . . . all the clues . . . the gut instinct that told him things were in the wind? He'd been snooping at first almost as a reflex action because spying was what he had always done. He looked into things and asked questions. He was an agent and always had been.

Suddenly he was preparing to leave all that past life behind. And yet was there something he was supposed to do, find out . . . *before* he left?

The question had been gnawing at him all day.

"Is there something more for me to do, God?" he whispered.

Still the unmistakable answer came—Yes, there was one last assignment to be completed before he could go.

But what it was, that he was not sure of. He *was* sure it had to do with the two leaders.

Suddenly a wild, incredible idea struck him! What could be the harm? He could not trust any of his *own* people or sources anymore. He was, as they used to say in the game, out in the cold. But he couldn't find out what was going on by himself. No solo flights got you very far in this business.

He would need help.

He would get in touch with his old CIA nemesis. The Americans would have no reason to harm him now. Maybe *he* had got wind of something. It was time he became friends with his old adversary of the CIA anyway.

He'd do it—he'd get in touch with Blue Doc.

Early in the darkness of morning a few hours later, a soft knock came on the door. Galanov knew it was his German friend come to retrieve him in preparation for their early morning drive out of Moscow. He let him in.

"I'm afraid I cannot leave yet," he said bluntly after closing the door. "I hope you can understand."

"Is . . . is something wrong? You're not going back on—"

"No, no, my friend," laughed Galanov. "Nothing like that. My faith is secure. It's about the thing I had stumbled onto just before you came. And something in my gut tells me I must pursue it and find out what is going on."

"You are sure? Every day you stay here I am convinced the danger grows."

"I believe you are right. I do not make this decision lightly. I have prayed, and still it comes back to me that I must see this through. I have the sense that it is important, perhaps for the people of God as well as for the politics of my country. I can say no more, for I know no more."

"If you feel the Lord would have you stay, then you must stay."

"I want *you* to return to Germany as planned, however."

"I cannot go without you."

"You must. You are also in danger the longer you remain with me."

"It was for you I came."

"And your mission was accomplished. I insist that you go ahead without me. I will be more free to do what I have to do knowing that you are safe."

His German friend thought for a few moments, then nodded in assent.

"Good," replied Galanov. "I will follow you as soon as I am able. Leave instructions with Medvedev of what I am to do when I am ready. I hope it will not be more than two or three days."

"I will pray for you night and day, my brother."

"And Godspeed to you as you return home. I will anticipate joining you soon."

They parted with a tearful embrace.

PART IX

A Different Vantage Point

How Is *Life* Spread?

• • •

Berlin

TAD AND HIS MOTHER AND FATHER HAD GONE OUT TO enjoy an American-style dinner of steak and baked potato at one of the international restaurants not far from the hotel. Joseph and Dieder Palacki were having dinner together also, and it was the first time the three McCallums had been alone together for any length of time in two or three days.

Matthew and Sabina were noticeably curious concerning Lisel, about whom Tad reported everything there was to say—namely, that he was very fond of her and that they had spoken together of many things. Beyond that, he said, they would have to wait to see what came of it . . . just like he would have to do himself.

"Do you know anything about her background?" Sabina asked.

"Not much, really," replied Tad. "Her parents are Christians, though right now Lisel is pretty antagonistic toward the Lord."

"Any sign of a change?" asked Matthew.

"The Lord is at work—I can see it clearly," replied Tad. "I think he has his sights set on her."

They left the restaurant and walked leisurely back in the direction of the hotel. A melancholy mood began slowly to come upon Matthew. His participation in the conference had continued to weigh down his spirit, and he felt like having a long walk in the nighttime city streets. It might not clear his thoughts, but at least it might stir them in new directions.

"Anyone want to join me on a visit to the Brandenburg Gate?" he said, looking at wife and son.

"Sure," said Tad.

"Sabina?"

Sabina thought for a moment, the sense coming over her that this evening might be one for father and son to share alone.

"You two go on ahead," she said with a smile. "I think I'd like to just go back to the room."

"Sure?"

Sabina nodded.

The three walked the remaining half-block to the hotel. Matthew hailed a taxi while Sabina continued on inside.

•   •   •

Ten minutes later, Matthew and Tad McCallum emerged into the pleasantly warm night air. A hundred meters away the solemnly lit Brandenburg Gate rose awesomely before them, the most recognizable symbol throughout the world of the newly united German nation.

As they walked about the expansive, wide-open area about the gate, they quietly observed the huge diversity of people, like themselves, wandering about. It was a few minutes after nine, yet from the crowd it might have seemed like noon—tourists, families, many Americans, along with a wide mixture of other foreigners, all sprinkled together with Berlin's indigenous crop of eccentric and bizarre riffraff—mostly young, with colored hair, or no hair at all, shredded trousers, leather jackets, and black boots adorned with metal, rebellion in their eyes. The smell of alcohol hung about them, and their loud, angry outbursts defied authority and declared contempt for any system of order and decency.

Everyone with a cause or a message seemed to be here roaming the streets, attempting to attract followers, some carrying placards boasting frightening slogans out of the past.

In the distance, at the edge of the sidewalk, they saw one such youth suddenly stop, loosen his pants, and relieve himself in the landscaped shrubbery. A clean-dressed man who had been following several steps behind with his daughter quickly turned her away and hurried out into the street to avoid coming any closer. A loud, mocking, masculine laugh erupted as the lawless mocker was buttoning up his pants, and he continued to throw profane, contemptuous insults after the poor man and girl.

Matthew turned from the scene with sickening disgust, and Tad followed him off a side street away from the thick of the crowd. Neither spoke for some time. It was quieter here, though well enough lit to see, and they continued on slowly.

"It's all so different now," sighed Matthew.

"How so?" asked Tad.

"It was so empty, silent, cold," answered Matthew. "When I would walk over here through Checkpoint Charlie to see your mother, even right here by the Brandenburg Gate, these same huge broad streets were empty—no pedestrians, no cars, no shoppers, no tourists. There were few stores, no souvenir shops.

"It was a bleak atmosphere, almost like being in an old movie where a guy suddenly walks into a city where space invaders have taken everybody. Especially coming from the activity of West Berlin and the intensity of my job with the State Department. It was eerie, that's how it felt. There were still buildings bombed out and desolate from the war."

"That long afterward?"

Matthew nodded. "There they sat, like the bombs had just fallen. And here in the middle of it—just back there—were the huge Brandenburg Gate and all the other landmarks, like the Reichstag building, that happened to fall on the eastern side of the Wall, standing there like silent mausoleums and sentinels to a time long past. It was . . . almost a feeling of death. Especially, as I said, in that just across a mile or two in the West it was so full of life and people and activity and energy. What contrast! I so wanted to bring your mother across to the other side for good."

"But she wanted to stay in the East?"

"The work of the network, you know," answered Matthew, "and your grandfather. We had no idea the Wall would suddenly go up."

They made their way around a large quiet block, and within ten minutes again found themselves amid voices and the noises of cars and horns.

On they walked, past booths and street vendors, tourists, taxis, buses, stands of pornography and other literature, magic acts and jugglers and musicians, and activists handing out pamphlets and preaching at anyone who chanced to look their way. Religious street preachers were represented along with any of another dozen causes, including several Christians passing out tracts in both English and German.

They continued on along the broad avenue, called Unter den Linden after the lime trees that lined the thoroughfare. This was the *centrum,* where Germany shone its brightest before the 1930s. A few of the hotels and cafés from the past still stood, but without the glamour of sixty years earlier. In the distance, black now, rose the building where until recently was located the headquarters for the *Stasi,* the notorious East German secret police force—*Staatssicherheitsdienst*—almost a modern version of the SS. Behind its walls were kept files on more than two million men and women of the West. Probably no two countries, save the U.S. and the U.S.S.R., conducted so heavy an espionage program upon one another as did the two ununited Germanys. One in five East Germans was said to have been an informer. The *Stasi* saw and heard everything.

Matthew's reflections could not help drifting toward Gustav, wondering what had become of him since that fateful day in the cemetery thirty years earlier.

Over and over in Matthew's mind, snatches of the various conference speakers he had heard replayed themselves. Was it fair of him to indict the conference because the people walking the streets in this sprawling urban colossus of multiple millions were not standing up and taking notice?

Probably not. After all, the gathering had been designed to express ideas so that they could get out into further corners of the world. Its purpose had not been to organize a citywide witnessing rally.

What would a secular newsman such as Tad write about this gathering of church leaders? Would he not see it as a mere intellectual exercise between liberal and conservative factions of a certain religion called Christianity, merely one of dozens of religions being touted as "the way" in this cross-cultural city?

What did the thing called evangelism mean in an environment like this? How could one penetrate here with the gospel? What would Jesus do had he come to Berlin in the twentieth century rather than Galilee in the first? How was God's life spread in a place such as this?

By now he and Tad had turned around and walked slowly back to the Gate area again, chatting sporadically on the surface, while each man was absorbed at deeper levels with his own thoughts.

At last, by mutual consent, they realized they had had enough. It was not a city that displayed the best of human nature. The walk had been more depressing than invigorating, and they were ready to return.

Matthew looked about and hailed the first taxi that came into view. "Westmark Hotel" was all he said.

It was enough for the German driver, who immediately sped off through the busy night streets of Berlin. The drive took ten minutes.

During that time, many wheels in Matthew's mind were turning. As he sat in the cab, gradually he found the urge to get out of the city welling up within him, to find quiet, even to distance himself for a time from the conference and all the *words* and *ideas* of evangelism.

When he and Tad walked into the room, he was glad to find Sabina still up and reading. As his wife looked up she could instantly see upon his face that something had changed.

Before she could say a word, Matthew spoke. "I've had a great idea!" he said. "How would the two of you like to get out of here for a while?"

"What . . . out of the hotel?" asked Sabina.

"No!" laughed Matthew. "Out of Berlin, out of the city! I've had enough of this conference for a while. I think the time has come to go look up some of our old friends."

Sabina did not have to be asked twice and was already out of her seat with excitement.

"All at once I'm dying to see Udo Bietmann again!" added Matthew. "What about you, Tad? Can you break away, or do your duties—"

"Sure, I can go," said Tad without waiting for Matthew to complete the question.

"What about your . . . uh, your *article?*" said Matthew with a shrewd grin.

"Well, perhaps you're right—I may need another brief interview in the morning. But I'd still like to go."

Matthew laughed, already feeling the negative effects of the walk fading into the background.

"Great. It's settled!" he said. "We'll leave in the morning, as soon as you get back."

"Then I'd better hit the hay," said Tad, heading for the door.

The Secret . . . Again

• • •

THE HOUR WAS ADMITTEDLY EARLY TO CALL. BUT TAD WAS willing to chance it.

Without realizing at first what was happening, he found that within just a few short days he had grown more attached to the intriguing young German lady than he would have thought possible. Their discussions had been so wide-ranging, so personal, and so honest and thought provoking that he found himself hardly conscious of the fact that technically Lisel *wasn't* a Christian—at least judging from what she said. The budding relationship contained more resemblance to that between his own father and mother fifty-three years earlier than he could possibly have been aware.

Tad's interaction with Lisel had progressed so far past that of their first two conversations and such a mutual respect and friendship had sprung up between them in the process that even when discussing spiritual things, the adversarial relationship had completely disappeared. In its place had grown a mutual hunger and an enjoyment of the process of growth, learning, and exploring the ideas of belief together.

Now as he stood at her door a few moments after knocking, his thoughts were only that inside lived a friend whom he could not leave town without saying good-bye to.

The look of astonishment on Lisel's face when she opened the door and saw Tad standing before her lasted only a second. Her expression quickly dissolved into a pleasant smile of gratification.

"Tad!" she exclaimed.

"I know it's early—I'm sorry."

"No . . . no, it's perfectly all right! Come in!"

"You're sure you don't mind?"

"Of course not. You can see I was up and dressed. I have to be at work in an hour. In fact, I'd just made some coffee and was wishing you were here to enjoy it with me."

"I don't know if I believe that!" laughed Tad. "But I'll take you up on your offer regardless."

"It's the absolute truth," Lisel said with a smile.

He followed her inside. "I brought you something," said Tad, pulling his right hand out from behind his back where he had been trying to keep its contents concealed.

"Oh, Tad, it's lovely . . . thank you!" said Lisel, taking from his outstretched hand the green stalk, at the end of which stood the small blossoming bud of a pale peach–hued rose.

She lifted the flower to her nose and breathed in with a contented smile.

"Not much of a smell," said Tad, with just a trace of awkward embarrassment, "but I fell in love with the color the instant I saw it. For some reason it seemed to have your name on it."

"There's just the hint of something mysterious," said Lisel. "It *does* have a smell, but faint."

"My parents are always talking about roses possessing secrets," said Tad. "Maybe this one is keeping its fragrance from us for that reason."

"For what reason?"

"For reason of its secret."

"What do they mean by the rose's *secrets?*" asked Lisel.

"I don't know. They'll never tell me. They just smile and say it's something I have to discover for myself."

"It sounds as though your mother and father have secrets, just like the rose. Sit down and I'll bring you a cup of coffee."

Tad did so. Lisel went to the kitchen, found a small vase for her gift, and returned a minute later holding two cups. She handed one to Tad, then sat down beside him.

"But what is the occasion," she asked, "for both the rose *and* the early visit?"

"I don't know. I saw the rose and thought you would like it," replied Tad. "And it's sort of a good-bye gift."

"Good-bye?"

"My folks and I are leaving the city for a day or two—to visit some old friends of theirs," said Tad.

"You frightened me. For a minute I thought—"

"No, we'll be back tonight, or tomorrow evening at the latest. But I didn't want to go without seeing you."

"I'm flattered," said Lisel with a sigh, "and appreciative. You are one of the most thoughtful people I've ever met."

Tad did not reply. In the few seconds of silence that followed, Lisel found herself staring intently into the depths of the rose. The single word *mysterious* that had fallen from her lips now returned to her, threatening to open vaults into her past she did not care to explore just now.

"I take that as a high compliment, coming from you," said Tad after a few seconds, rescuing Lisel from her reverie.

"Where are you going today?" Lisel asked, glad to move away from the direction the rose had sent her thoughts.

"South and east of the city, I think," replied Tad. "I'm not really sure about all the places exactly. My mother used to know quite a few people and hasn't seen them since she left in 1962."

"That's a long time."

"She said she expects to find many of them gone now, either dead or moved, but it's worth a try anyway."

"I still haven't heard her tell her story."

"We'll arrange something as soon as we get back. Which reminds me," Tad added, taking a last swallow from his cup, then rising to his feet, "my mom and dad are waiting for me at the hotel, and *you've* got to get to work."

"Thank you for taking the time to come by," said Lisel, walking him to the door. "And for the rose."

She looked up into Tad's face and smiled.

He returned the gaze, held her eyes just a moment, then nodded. "I'll call you in a day or two," he said.

75

Old Enemies

• • •

Moscow

DAN DAVIDSON SAT DOWN ACROSS THE TABLE FROM HIS old rival Andrassy Galanov.

"Times have indeed changed," said Blue Doc. "The CIA and KGB sitting down together out in the open."

"Not so open," replied Galanov. "There is a price on my head."

"I heard wind of that."

"Comrades have become enemies, and . . . well, here I am sitting across from *you.*"

"If not exactly as friends, at least I don't have the table bugged. Of course, maybe you have *me* bugged!"

Galanov laughed. "No, friend. No bugs. But what signifies the change most of all is in what we're trying to do—on the same side."

"One big happy family, that's us," rejoined Davidson ironically. "Who'd have ever thought the Cold War would come to this!"

"Not exactly a completely happy family," said the Russian, "if what I'm onto indicates what I think it might."

"You haven't let go of the spy game altogether, eh?"

"I couldn't help myself," replied Galanov. "Besides, if I can get to the bottom of this, I may be able to deal myself out altogether."

"So what's up? And why me?"

"No one else to turn to. The very nature of the thing puts us on the same side of the fence for a change."

"You think I can help?"

"I have nothing to lose. Two ex-spies are better than one, you know."

"OK, I'm listening," said Blue Doc. "What have you got?"

"Only a hunch so far," answered the Russian. "What do you know about a fellow named Desyatovsky?"

"The Russian minister of defense?"

"That's him."

"Not much," replied Davidson, keeping his own counsel for the moment.

"If my instincts are worth anything, there's something big about to break loose, and it's got his name written all over it."

"Why don't you follow through?"

"Because he's turned up the heat on me. One false move and I'm dead. I need help if I'm going to penetrate whatever his game is."

Blue Doc was silent, considering carefully how much to confide in this agent who had been his rival for so many years. Several long moments passed, during which his experienced eyes tried to read the sincerity in Galanov's expression. At last, seemingly satisfied, he decided to reveal his own hand.

"It wouldn't surprise me if your hunches *were* correct," he said at length.

"Oh?" Galanov raised an inquisitive eyebrow.

"Coincidentally or not," continued Blue Doc, "some information came my way recently that would seem to confirm your suspicions."

"What kind of information?"

"A peculiar communiqué . . . from out of the country."

"And?"

"I've got someone on it," said Blue Doc.

"What did the communiqué say?"

"The meaning was unclear, though with undertones that caught my eye. I hope to hear from my contact soon. I'll get in touch with you the moment I do. How can I reach you?"

"You can't," replied the former KGB agent. "I'm hot, I tell you. I'll contact you tomorrow."

He rose, then paused. "You wouldn't hold out on me, would you, Dan?"

"What do you mean?"

"You've got to play it straight with me on this one. Anything I come up with is yours. Anything you get you share with me. We're in it together. My life may depend on it."

"Straight up, Andrassy. I still owe you for that time in Kiev, when you could have taken me but let me get lost in the pandemonium after the shooting. That could have been my life. Now you tell me this could be yours. I believe you. Honor among agents, you know. I don't forget favors of that magnitude."

"Thanks, Dan," said Galanov, shaking the American's hand.

"I'll let you in on whatever I get."

Retracing Old Paths

• • •

Former East Germany

THE DRIVE SOUTHWEST OF BERLIN IN THEIR RENTED
automobile was a wonderful tonic for all three McCallums after the
increasingly stifling atmosphere of Berlin and the conference. For the
first time in days they felt as though they were breathing genuine
country air.

The only thing that could have made it better, commented Sabina,
was if they had been on their way to *Lebenshaus* instead.

The only thing that could have made it better, in Tad's estimation,
was to have had Lisel join them, though for the moment he kept his
sentiments to himself. He wanted her to become intimately acquainted with his parents, but thus far there had only been opportunity for a few brief encounters.

They passed quickly out of the city and into the farmland of what
had only a short time earlier been known ironically as the German
Democratic Republic, or DDR. Here and there they passed through
a lightly forested section of the Brandenburg Forest, where clumps of
birch and pine crisscrossed with dirt roads and paths. Most of the land
grew ripening expanses of grain, some harvested, some still growing,
some in the process of being harvested. Many of the fields were
golden in the sun, although the green foliage of potatoes and sugar
beets were also occasionally visible. The tracts of growing crops were
huge and expansive, in contrast to the small, individually owned farms
of the West, where more variety and crop rotation was practiced.

Here the endless stretches, now of wheat, now of potatoes, gave evidence of the ongoing legacy of the East's communal farming system, which did not seek to make the best use of the land. Though thousands of prior landownership claims were being sorted through by the German government, records were difficult to verify, and the process was tedious, as Matthew had discovered. Meanwhile, the collectives that had been operated by the Communist regime had to continue to function as best the Bonn–and–Berlin government could manage, while piecemeal portions of East German farmland gradually found their way back into the hands of families that had owned them, some for centuries.

If only, thought Matthew, the borders had fallen differently, they might even now be involved in the paperwork necessary to regain *Lebenshaus.*

Once leaving the city, they quickly noticed a dramatic difference in the two-lane road from those they had driven on in the West. Those had been spacious, well paved, with bright white and yellow striping and wide shoulders. Here the roads were narrow, pitted, mostly unpainted, and largely still made of cobblestones from decades earlier. Dodging potholes on the outdated and ruined roads made for a bumpy, winding ride, and passing oncoming traffic was an adventure. How well Matthew recalled such from his months trying to locate Sabina and her father . . . and elude Gustav.

In prominence too were hundreds upon hundreds of the tiny old DDR state-manufactured Trabant automobiles. Some had been parked or junked for newer Western models by those who could afford them. But many still veered along the highways, spewing out black exhaust and looking almost like large-scale toy cars. By this time, all automobile factories producing both the Trabant and the Wartburg had been closed, going the way of East Germany's only airline, Interflug, and most other such manufacturing industries—into bankruptcy from their inability to compete with the West.

With Tad at the wheel and Matthew directing him, given occasional help from his wife, they drove first through Potsdam, showing Tad the prison, now boarded up and empty, where his grandfather had been held.

They then proceeded to retrace the eastward route of their escape, as best they could reconstruct it, all the way to the village of

Grossbeeren, recounting to their son with both laughter and tears everything that had happened that fateful day.

The Brumfeld home still stood unchanged in the village, but Clara and Erich were both apparently dead and the current occupants had never heard of Willie. Neither could they glean any trace of Angela's father, Josef Dahlmann.

It was with many varied emotions that they drove along the roads and beheld again the sights from so long ago. Long silences followed words of explanation to Tad, sometimes brief, sometimes lengthy, during which Matthew and Sabina looked quietly about. Faces and incidents, sounds and shouts, tense moments of hiding, waiting in barns and cellars and forests with hearts pounding until the peril had passed . . . all these sensations and more rose and fell in the eyes of their memories.

There had been such danger then. Several faithful individuals had lost their lives. Now these roads and villages, this countryside, these woods, all wore such a different aspect—so sedate, so unconcerned with that frightful time of another lifetime ago.

At length, early in the afternoon, they realized there was but one last place where they might locate a familiar face—the face Matthew had wanted to see since the previous evening. It was time to drive to Kehrigkburg.

A great deal of roadwork was being done, the newly reunified government in Berlin making efforts to bring the East up to a par with the West as quickly as possible. In every city and village they passed through, construction equipment was at work, buildings were being both torn down and constructed, piles of dirt lay aside huge ditches where foundations were being poured and new pipes laid, bridges were being built . . . homes, factories, schools, all manner of construction! They had seen this throughout the eastern sector of Berlin as well, as if fifty years of dormancy had now to be made up for within one or two years. Everywhere was activity, bustle, life!

"It's so different from when I was here before," remarked Matthew. "Then, besides being old and run-down physically—you know, the roads, the buildings, the railroads, the cars, the streets—the people were run-down too, lethargic, listless, unsmiling, dull. It was dead everywhere, on every level. Now suddenly everything's alive. The people walk with that German vigor you see everywhere. They are smiling. Things are going on. There is bustle and activity. It must be really wonderful for them!"

Sabina was quiet. How well she understood Matthew's words. She had lived in the East for more than fifteen years.

Tad especially, never having been in East Germany before, noticed many differences in the structures of buildings they passed, many large institutional buildings, enormous plain apartment houses, with not nearly so many individual homes, all evidence of the communal nature of the society as it had been under Communism for fifty years. Half the farmhouses and barns they passed in the small villages were in dreadful repair, roofs caving in, unmaintained, equipment sitting out rusting in the fields.

The rebuilding of the country would not come overnight. Yet still could be seen, even in the midst of continuing poorer conditions than in the West, the pride in appearances, evidenced by flower boxes bright with color placed in front of hopelessly run-down homes.

"Look," said Tad, pointing to an elderly lady as they drove by. "I never get used to some of their ways. There is always such an attention to order and neatness!" The woman was carefully sweeping off the packed dirt walkway that bordered the fence in front of her home next to the street. "It's not everywhere you'll see people sweeping up the dirt! But if there's no *cement* sidewalk, in Germany they'll even keep the *dirt* neat and tidy!"

Sabina smiled at her son's comment.

As they approached Kehrigkburg, Matthew recounted again to Tad all the events leading up to his first meeting with the young man Udo Bietmann and all he had done to help them keep hidden from Gustav, at the risk of his own life.

"He was a true brother," concluded Matthew, "in the full spiritual sense of the word. I have prayed many years for an opportunity to see him again."

"Does he know you're coming?" asked Tad.

"I wrote about a month ago to let him know we would be in Berlin," replied Matthew. "All I had was his name and the village, so I don't know whether the letter will have reached him."

The Changes of Freedom

• • •

Kehrigkburg, Former East Germany

AS THEY DROVE INTO THE SMALL VILLAGE, ALL WAS SO familiar to Matthew and Sabina. How could it have changed so little?

There were so many memories!

Not many minutes later, with mingled apprehension and excitement, they found themselves approaching the front door of the house that had more than once given them refuge.

Christa Bietmann answered the door.

Recognition exploded on all three faces at once. Tears followed instantly from the eyes of the two women, while Tad looked on at the proceedings with something of the same sense of fulfilled delight his grandfather had felt at this same home in watching the fellowship between the men who had brought him there.

Truly unity in the Spirit is a wonderful thing to behold when it flows between God's men and women! Hairs of gray, wrinkled skin, and hearts to which had been added thirty more years of life to carry could not dim the sparkle of love that shone from the eyes, now being dabbed at with any piece of clothing that happened to be accessible.

"Oh, Udo will be so happy!" exclaimed Christa. "We hoped and prayed you would come!"

"You received my letter!" asked Matthew.

"Yes—two weeks ago. We have been beside ourselves ever since!"

"Where is Udo?"

"Out there—in the field," replied Christa, pointing behind them. Now for the first time, they heard the sound of a tractor in the distance. Following Christa's hand, they saw where her husband was busy plowing over a freshly harvested field of oats.

Sabina followed Christa inside, while father and son walked around the side of the red-brick barn next to the house and out across the freshly overturned earth, from which the oat-stubble stuck out in all directions. As they traipsed over the furrowed ground, at length the driver of the tractor saw their approach.

He was on the ground running toward them the next instant, hardly taking the time to switch off the rumbling engine. Udo and Matthew fell into one another's arms. Again Tad looked on in awe and wonderment as the tears flowed once more, with no less shame that the eyes producing them were masculine rather than feminine.

It was a great joy to his young heart to see how greatly his father and mother were loved by all those who knew them after the true manner of knowing—that is, knowing of the heart.

Introduction of Tad followed, with smiles and exclamations and the shaking of the farmer's dirt-stained hand.

• • •

Thirty minutes later the guests were seated around the humble kitchen table of Udo and Christa Bietmann on wooden chairs, drinking coffee and nibbling on some small sweetbread snacks. Whether well off or not, whether in the East or West, no self-respecting German *hausfrau* was without a supply of tasty treats to offer unexpected guests. And as these guests had been more than half-expected, there was ample supply.

It was indeed a joyous occasion, and the fellowship of rediscovered brotherhood rich. It was with tears and laughter working in intriguing combination that Matthew and Sabina recounted all that had happened to them once they left Kehrigkburg in the first days of September 1962. Tad had heard the story of the escape many times, but never, he thought, had he heard it told like today.

They then went on to tell briefly about their life since in the United States.

"Believe it or not," said Bietmann, "I have managed to learn a few things about you through the years."

Matthew showed an expression of bewilderment.

"One or two of your books have found their way into my possession," the farmer went on. "If I can say this, even though you are older than me, I have been very proud of you."

Matthew laughed. "You flatter me, Udo!"

The conversation continued with great gusto and feeling. After they had been together about an hour and a half, Matthew said, "We didn't intend to take up your entire day. I know you are busy with your harvest, so perhaps it is time for us—"

He was adjusting his frame in his chair, as if making ready to rise, when both Christa and Udo cut him off. "You are not possibly thinking of leaving!" expostulated Udo.

"I don't know, I—"

"Put the thought out of your mind immediately. After waiting thirty years to see you both again, you do not expect us to let you go so easily, do you?"

Matthew laughed.

"You will be our guests for the rest of the day. You will stay with us tonight and tomorrow . . . and for as long as we can encourage you to remain with us!"

"Thank you," said Matthew, still laughing. "I suppose I should have expected such hospitality, knowing you as I do. But the fields don't wait. This much about farming I do know."

"You are right. But food of the spirit is of far more importance than grain to make mere physical bread. Besides, most of my harvest is in. My brothers have seen to it after I was called away."

"You have brothers who are also farmers?" asked Tad.

"Others of our fellowship," answered the German. "My spiritual brothers. We help one another. When I was forced away for a few days, they added my fields to their own. Mostly all I have left is to plow the fields under, as you saw me doing this morning." Udo yawned as he spoke.

"But I can see you are tired," objected Matthew. "Perhaps we should come back. We will be in Berlin—"

"Nonsense," interrupted the farmer. "I would not think of allowing you to go so soon. You *will* be our guests tonight. I tell you, I have prayed many years for this opportunity!"

"I didn't know if we would succeed in finding you," laughed

Matthew. "You are the only familiar faces we have managed to locate today."

"Your Mennonite friends will be anxious to see you as well," said Bietmann.

"Do they know we are in Germany?" asked Sabina.

"Are you joking! Christa and I were on our way out there with your letter as soon as we received it. Nearly every day since, someone from the community is by asking if we have heard anything more from you. This evening, I would count it a special joy to introduce you to the others of our fellowship here in Kehrigkburg."

"The honor would be ours," replied Matthew. "I only regret it has taken us so long for a return visit to you."

"God's timing is never too slow or too fast. We have learned that lesson here in our corner of the world many times. There is a saying that I force myself to remember whenever I begin to get anxious, when something does not happen as quickly as my flesh might like. It is this: *In God's economy, you cannot go too slow.* You have come now, therefore this is the right time."

"Not a bad prescription to keep one from rash decisions," commented Matthew.

"Exactly. It is a truth with a thousand applications. God is never in a hurry with his work. His purposes are always accomplished, but rarely overnight."

"My father used to say almost exactly the same thing," said Sabina.

"God bless him," said Udo softly. "A man after God's heart."

"Amen," added Matthew.

"Is your daughter still near Kehrigkburg?" asked Sabina.

A silence followed. Herr Bietmann was slow to answer. "She . . . she is no longer with us," he answered.

Sabina did not inquire further. If there was more to be said, a time would present itself.

"What is it like now?" asked Tad, unable to keep the inquisitive newsman within him down for long. "Now that freedom has come to the East, is it better than before?"

A long pause followed, during which Bietmann was clearly deep in thought and reflection. At last he drew in a deep sigh. "I have often wondered what I would say to a Westerner if given the liberty to explain our situation in depth," he said.

"Now you have your chance," rejoined Tad.

"Many of the things I would say are not what an American such as yourself would expect," replied Bietmann.

"All the better. I wouldn't have asked if I didn't want to know what you really think. Mom and Dad have been giving me their impressions ever since we arrived. Now I'd like yours."

"A budding writer," explained Matthew with a smile, "and with all the curiosity necessary to dig past the surface."

"I can see that," replied Udo.

"And I don't want the newspaper version," added Tad, "but *your* perception."

Bietmann glanced at Matthew and Sabina. They both nodded their encouragement for him to continue. "Then I shall give it to you," he said.

There was again silence, after which Udo plunged in. "Everyone was excited at first," he began. "Excited is a tame way to say it. Euphoric! Travel, visitation to the West, freedom to buy goods there had never been before, getting land back that had been taken away—how wonderful it was for everyone! The Mediterranean seacoast, the Alps of Switzerland, France, Italy—marvels in the West that were only four and five hours away, but until a short time ago might as well have been somewhere on the other side of the planet.

"You cannot imagine what a priceless thing freedom is unless you have been denied it beyond memory. Freedom of travel, freedom of speech, freedom of religion, freedom of the press, freedom of ownership—all we of the Eastern Bloc nations have not stopped rejoicing over these freedoms from the day that wall in Berlin fell on 9 November 1989, until now."

"From the tone of your voice I sense that a great big *but* is coming," said Tad when Bietmann paused.

Their host smiled. "You're right. Yes, that's exactly it. The *but* is this—the euphoria did not last for long. Immediately after reunification doubts and even some regrets began to surface. For our brothers in the West, those doubts had mainly to do with the price tag. Of course, the deutsche mark is the strongest currency in Europe, but even though in time a strong and united Germany will profit from reunification and become for Europe what the United States now is in the Americas, for the present it is causing hardship in the West. They have had to face new taxes, and the government has had to borrow, and these things are painful for our prosperous brothers."

"What about for you?"

"The pain on this side is completely different. We received valuable West deutsche marks in exchange for our worthless Eastern currency. We were at first ecstatic. But in the end it was a blessing without substance. When the original supply was gone, there were no more marks to replace it. Which is better, our people have asked themselves over and over, to have money as we did under Communism but with little in the stores to buy, or to have stores full of Western consumer goods but with no money to purchase even the staples of life? Such is the situation throughout most of the countries of the East."

"But why is there no money?"

"Because the economies of the East have virtually collapsed. There was such a deterioration of everything under four decades of Communism—housing, industry, transportation, the environment, standard of living, everything. Some of our railroad lines, tracks, and switches date back to the late 1800s. After World War II, the Soviets dismantled the best of East Germany's factories and shipped them to Russia.

"Then they raped the land. Rivers and groundwater are horribly polluted everywhere. In some forests the leaves are gone by midsummer. Sulfur from burning coal is in the air. The Elbe is filled with lead and pesticides. All the best things have been plundered from our land and from all the countries the Soviets occupied.

"Capitalism and free enterprise sound good on paper, and all those of the East have been eager for democracy. But in reality they have caused only misery for most. With free enterprise installed, stores and merchants were allowed to set their own prices. Suddenly everything cost ten and twenty times more than it had before. People were shocked. What had once been readily available was instantly priced out of reach. In Czechoslovakia it is far worse. There they are talking of catastrophe, tragedy, and chaos. It was the same in Russia when Yeltsin lifted price controls in January of this year. All the most basic items are involved—bread, milk, meat. Luxuries like fresh fruit are far beyond the means of most people. Fuel is so expensive people cannot afford to travel, even though now they are free to go where they will."

"Is it only the price increases? Surely in time prices will stabilize to more moderate levels."

"Such is already happening. Unfortunately, unemployment is an even deeper and more widespread difficulty. There are towns where there is 70 and 80 percent unemployment. You cannot imagine how complete has been the economic collapse. Virtually every factory in the DDR has closed. They could not begin to compete with the West—especially with the BRD. The average East German worker produces only 25 percent of his West German counterpart."

"What about unemployment benefits? Did West Germany make no provision for it?" asked Sabina.

"There have been payments. But they are meager and are running out. Along with the staggering expense of trying to rebuild East Germany, the new government can't bankrupt itself supporting all the people too. People do feel fortunate to have had a West Germany with which to reunite. For all the *other* Eastern countries the recovery will be much longer—perhaps two generations, not just years or even a decade or two. They are all fighting for bare economic survival, though deterioration continues. Yes, there is freedom, but the financial hardships are enormous. The DDR was the strongest of all the Communist nations, yet we cannot begin to compete with the West. How much worse it is in Russia, Czechoslovakia, Bulgaria."

Bietmann stopped and his three guests pondered his words for a few moments. Sabina was filled with so many thoughts, for this was her homeland.

"Do you still call it *East Germany?*" asked Tad.

"Officially this part of Germany is known as *'Die funf neuen Bundesländer'*—"

"The five new federal states," mused Matthew to himself in English.

"—but yes," Bietmann added, "the designation *Ostdeutschland* is still in common use."

"How do most of the people respond to all this?" asked Matthew after a moment.

"Everything is mixed up. There remains joy in the freedom, yet coping with the hardships is a daily struggle for most. It has been said that East Germans are presently in a manic-depressive state of mind.

There is sometimes anger, even at our new government, for all the new regulations, for loss of jobs, for the new bureaucracy. The freedom that has come is mainly freedom only for those who can afford to take advantage of it. There is great disillusionment."

"It must be a very difficult adjustment," said Sabina.

"Only a third of our population lives better today than before the Wall came down," Udo went on. "I have even heard it said more than once, 'I wish the Wall was still there.'"

"You can't mean it!" exclaimed Tad.

"The pessimism and discouragement is so widespread that yes, some do feel that life, though not free, was better before. Certainly it was more predictable."

"Surely that is a small minority?"

"Of course. In general, we are all very glad for the changes. I only wanted you to know that side of it."

"What about the church?" asked Matthew. "How has it fared?"

"It is the same—mixed. There has always been a religious freedom here in the DDR. Though along with harassment and prejudice. We rejoice over the new tolerance, though many people are in such dire financial straits they cannot even think about spiritual things."

"Do you know much about how Christians are faring elsewhere?"

"Generally God's people are flourishing. It was always the farther east you went the more primitive conditions became. Here the church was allowed, in Russia the true church had to exist underground. In Czechoslovakia young people under the age of eighteen were forbidden to attend church, even though the church was technically legal. If they did, their higher education privileges were taken away. So though there was no underground church as such, there was a high price to be paid for faith nonetheless. Similar conditions have existed here in the DDR and in Poland."

"How do you see the outlook now, here in East Germany? What is it like for your fellowship?" asked Matthew.

"We have much to be thankful for," answered Udo. "God is good, and we are seeing many new people respond to the Savior now that there is no longer the fear of a sudden knock on the door with some brutal official standing on the other side of it. And too, we of this region are faring well economically. A decree in July of 1990 required that property confiscated by Communists after 1949 be returned to its rightful owners. Because many of the farms of this region, including ours, were ancestral holdings, we now have work. Our equipment is poor and money remains scarce. But we help one another, we can grow food to eat, and honest labor itself is healthy."

"But there is no national revival or anything of that kind now that freedom has come?" Tad asked.

"There is great spiritual activity, but I would not call it revival by any means. In fact, the breakneck speed with which all of society is being transformed, from Berlin all the way to Moscow, is opening the door to many undesirable things, too. You cannot imagine the flood of pornographic books, magazines, and videos that suddenly appeared everywhere! The curse of Western Europe's decadence penetrated everywhere overnight."

"That kind of thing hadn't been here before?"

"Communist censorship kept such materials out."

"Why, for moral reasons?"

"No, simply because the Communists saw them as a distraction from their socialistic goals. Even in matters of religion, political freedom does not always necessarily bring *life.*"

"How do you mean?"

"In the wake of communism's retreat and demise, a spiritual vacuum has suddenly appeared. The ideology that held all of society together is instantly gone. City fathers and governmental leaders and school officials are suddenly hungry to find substitutes with which to replace it. They are begging pastors and qualified laymen to come and teach Christianity and the Bible in the public schools."

"That sounds wonderful," said Sabina.

"But it is the cults who are primarily responding. They have been more ready and quick on the scene to move into that vacuum. So now it is the Mormons and Jehovah's Witnesses who are providing most of this teaching, and of course the former Communists have no idea of the falsehoods involved. Everywhere you look, cults and other such groups are making inroads. There is a hunger too among many people who have never been to church all these years and are eager to discover what Christianity is all about. They want to know what they've been missing all these years.

"All this is making our job of evangelism so much more difficult.

We find people who are either confused when we offer them the truth because one of the cults has already given them false teaching, or else we find that people will not even listen to us, especially when we go door to door, because they are so sick of the aggressively proselytizing sects. If we find ourselves following in their footsteps, claiming to be a *Christian* can give you a bad name in people's minds. To answer your first question, there is a hunger in the East toward spiritual things. But it is tempered with confusion and with concern for many other factors of change."

"But as far as persecution, that is over?" asked Sabina.

"Here in the DDR, yes. I have contacts in Czechoslovakia, however, who tell me in some cases it is actually worse. Hard-line and entrenched Communists continue to reverse the changes, sometimes taking their anger out on Christians, churches, and pastors. Those in power today—and this is true in all the Eastern countries—are reformed Communists. Their conversion and denial of the party was opportunistic rather than because of a change of heart. Much of the old bureaucracy and old police force is still in power—former Communist teachers, factory managers, officials.

"This is not so much true, as I say, here, but for Christians in other places life has not automatically become wonderful. Even the donations that now are flooding in from the West often do not reach those persons who need it the most. Large shipments of Christian literature and Bibles have gone into Prague and other of the large cities, only to be grabbed by church officials of the large denominations and then sold for hugely inflated prices. I have heard of paper-covered Bibles in Prague selling for the equivalent of 150 deutsche marks. We have received shipments too, for which we praise God. But usually the Westerners who donate materials show little concern for what happens to the contents of their boxes after they drop them off and go home. Yet in spite of this, there are many, many young men now eager to enter the ministry, and many people *are* coming to Christ all through the East."

"Yet you say things are going well in your own fellowship?"

"Yes. There are certainly financial concerns for many in the region, as well as the confusion and frustration that I spoke of. But spiritually our people are blessed to have the cloud of *angst* lifted from being a practicing Christian. We have a meeting of some kind several evenings a week now, even if only informally, relishing, I suppose, in the exuberance of freedom. I will begin spreading the word through the village immediately that you will be with us tonight."

Matthew glanced at Sabina.

"You will be our guests," Christa added once again.

The two glanced at one another again, then turned back to Bietmann, shrugged, and let their large smiles speak their acceptance for them.

78

The Warmth of Humble Fellowship

• • •

THAT EVENING TAD, MATTHEW, AND SABINA FOUND THEM-
selves treated like royal guests, participating in fellowship richer than
they had experienced for some time and of a distinct quality unlike
anything they had previously known.

For Sabina the memories of earlier times and reminders of her
former life before that fateful day when she saw Matthew walking
toward her on the sidewalk were filled with a poignancy in which
neither husband nor son could fully share.

During the remainder of the afternoon they had walked about the
premises, noting with great interest the differences in conditions in
the East and West. Both men had visited further with Udo and had a
tour of his fields, while Sabina had enjoyed a tearful discussion with
Christa, during which she learned of the childless couple's heartache
and opportunity.

That evening, following *Abendbrot,* the five piled as best they
could into the farmer's small car and drove two or three kilometers to
a large home where their fellowship was already gathering. The
instant they walked in, all three Americans knew they were in the
midst of something fresh and real.

"Udo!" came several voices at once.

Within seconds they were surrounded by handshakes, hugs, and
shoulder-slapping greetings, followed by many introductions and
words of welcome, more handshaking and smiles, and a steady torrent
of well-wishing. Two or three were present from the Mennonite
community where Matthew and Sabina had stayed years earlier,

which, once the connection had been made, increased the joyful greetings to an even higher pitch of enthusiasm.

In the midst of the proceedings, Tad noticed one of the men take their host aside and speak a few words of apparent question to him. A grave expression came over Bietmann's face, and Tad could make out but fragments of his soft-spoken reply. ". . . God is faithful," he seemed to say, ". . . much to pray about . . . crucial time . . ."

The other man again spoke. Bietmann nodded. ". . . perhaps soon . . ." were the only words of his reply Tad thought he understood. He didn't hear any more, for his mother and father took hold of his arm to introduce him to several of their Mennonite friends.

Most of those present were dressed in simple farming garb and other work attire. A few wore beards, caps, hats, and dresses indicating their Mennonite connections, though they mixed in with all the others without distinction. Afterward Bietmann explained to the three visitors that Catholics, Baptists, Lutherans, and a couple of Adventists were also included in the fellowship, along with ten or twelve new believers who acknowledged no affiliation whatsoever.

"We are a mixed-up, heterogeneous group of believers in Jesus," he had said. "Without a name, without ties to any church, where all are welcome, whatever they believe . . . whether they believe at all!"

"You include nonbelievers too?" queried Tad.

"Of course!" replied Bietmann. "Why else do you think there is such spontaneous enthusiasm? It is because there are always non-Christians present. Every time we come together there are new people—friends, neighbors someone has brought. The excitement of sharing our faith is positively infecting. These people you met tonight are praying all the day long for those of their acquaintance with whom they hope for opportunities to help or to bring to our times of fellowship. When we come together there is such joy in seeing these prayers answered every week . . . every day! There are small groups such as this growing and bursting out with life all around the countryside."

"You visit other such fellowships?"

"I do not travel a great deal," replied Bietmann, "but occasionally there are duties that require my presence elsewhere. I can tell you, many, many men and women are coming to know our Savior personally."

"That is wonderful to hear," said Matthew thoughtfully, "and wonderful to *see* and be part of in your group of believers."

Meanwhile, after the introductions were completed and Bietmann had informally explained who his visitors were and how they came to be present, singing had broken out, bringing a worshipful calm to the large room. As they sang, everyone found a seat, mostly on the floor, and settled themselves after the robust time of visiting.

There were no instruments or hymnbooks, and belying the joyous and even boisterous beginning, the songs were mostly older hymns, and many in a minor key. This fact took nothing from their power, however, for every voice raised itself in unison with the others, reminding Tad of an ancient monastery choir.

This was no lighthearted singfest of choruses, but deep-throated tones, somber and with intent regard for the words of worship, praise, and adoration coming from their mouths. As they sang, Tad could see the deep-etched lines of years of labor, hardship, and persecution through which their hard-won faith had been tested, deepened, and verified in the crucible of cruel life under Communist oppression.

All three McCallums found themselves moved deeply by the experience, though they could not have put into words exactly why. It would take time to put this evening into perspective.

As Tad glanced over at the man his father had come so far to see, now with his eyes closed as he quietly sang along with his fellow Christian friends, he could see that these people had paid dearly for their faith and that the freedom and joy and exuberant enthusiasm they manifested was born out of years and depths of endurance, even suffering, that he had himself never known. He now realized why his father and mother still, after all these years, had so many roots extending down into the same soil as did these Eastern believers.

Bietmann was a quiet man, that much was clear to Tad, though deep and profound of character, exactly as his father had described him from their brief encounters thirty years before. The maturity and wisdom with which he spoke and carried himself was evident immediately to one like Tad who encountered so many types of personalities in his work.

Udo looked to be fifty-eight or sixty years of age, though in just the short time he had been in the former eastern sector Tad had already discovered that people looked older here, that the hopelessness and despair of not being free had had an effect upon the spirit that told upon the countenances of people at a younger age. Bietmann was not the pastor of the fellowship. As far as Tad could tell, they didn't even have a pastor, as such. But his father's friend was clearly one of its acknowledged leaders.

As Tad found himself lost in thought, the singing ended. He glanced up to see his father being thrust forward by Bietmann and several others to the front of the room. There was not a sound from any of the twenty-five or thirty persons present as Matthew stood, awkward and embarrassed, trying to collect his thoughts and decide what to say.

"I am just at a loss for words," he began. "When we left Berlin this morning in search of my old friend here—" he gestured toward Bietmann as he spoke—"we were not even certain we would be able to locate him. It has been thirty years since we were here. Yet not only did we find Udo, we suddenly find ourselves in the midst of a whole new fellowship of friends! I know I speak for both my wife and son when I say that we are blessed beyond measure to be with you, and we thank you for opening your hearts to us as you have. I hope and pray the Lord will give us some way to express our gratitude and love in the short time we have with you."

79

The Plot Is Uncovered

• • •

Moscow

"I TOLD YOU IT COULD BE ANY DAY," BLUE DOC SAID TO his old KGB rival.

"I did not expect anything so soon," said Galanov.

"Can you meet?"

"Where?"

"You're the one who's hot. You tell me. I'll be there. You won't believe what I have to show you."

"All right then, let me think," said the Russian.

He was silent a moment, then gave the CIA man instructions.

"I'll be there in half an hour," replied Blue Doc, then hung up the phone.

He looked again at the incredible file in his hand that had just been delivered to him an hour ago. How the woman had managed it and how she had gotten it into Yaschak's hands he didn't know. He didn't need to know! He had it; that was all that mattered.

Davidson's mind was reeling, and in the midst of it he still wondered if it was the right thing to show it to the Russian. But like he'd said, he owed Galanov. And he had given his word.

Thirty minutes later the two agents sat huddled under the sheltering shadow of a little-used bridge over one of the small tributaries of the Moskva River. What they had to discuss could not be heard by inquisitive ears without bringing danger upon them both.

"Was my hunch about Desyatovsky correct?" asked Galanov.

"A jackpot," replied Davidson, "if you want to call a plot to completely overturn the governments of all the Soviet republics and bring the Commonwealth back under a single power source a jackpot."

"What?"

"It's all here—a plan to wrest control back out of the hands of the republics and straight into the hands of our friend Bludayev Desyatovsky."

"I can hardly believe it! Do you mean . . . another coup attempt? It could never work now that the Soviet Union is dead."

"He's got every angle covered. It could be nothing less than that, at least as I read the files. Have a look for yourself."

Davidson opened the file that was in his hand, stooped down to one knee, and spread out several smaller files on the ground before Galanov.

The Russian looked through the papers, turning and scanning, then moving to another, with deepening concern etched across the lines of his face. When he at last spoke again, his tone reflected the severity of the situation. "You're right. That's exactly what it looks like," he said. "Everything has changed so much with the breakup of the Union, I can't see how he could pull it off. Yet this has none of the earmarks of the *coup de farce* of earlier. Why, he's got every segment of society tied into this thing, besides top leaders in all of the republics."

"You think Desyatovsky's the mastermind?"

"Who else? You got these things from his department, didn't you say?"

Blue Doc nodded. "But look at this other file," he said.

Galanov took two or three additional sheets from the CIA agent's hand and read quickly over them. A long whistle followed.

"This is as big as I'd imagined. . . ."

"I take it you're not surprised?" said Blue Doc.

"I suspected it when I saw them together."

"I knew there must be some good reason to let you in on this thing," said the CIA man with a grin.

"This guy is high up, a leader in the German parliament."

"So," said Blue Doc, "what's Drexler's game?"

"Don't know exactly. He's a powerful man, head of the SPD Party, opposition leader of the Bundestag, second to Kolter in power."

"You've seen him with Desyatovsky recently?"

Galanov nodded. "After the summit."

"The aid package, of course," exclaimed Blue Doc. "You think that has anything to do with all this?"

"I don't know. But they were up to something. I could smell it. That's what aroused my suspicions in the first place. I've been trying to find out more ever since. But that's when things started getting hot. I'm sure they're onto me."

Now it was Blue Doc's turn to whistle. "Or maybe you should say, now that they know you're onto them."

"How did you get these files anyway?" asked Galanov. "I used to be high up in the KGB, but I would never have dreamed of getting my hands on something this explosive. We've got enough to bring the whole thing down around their ears."

"Stole them."

"You stole them . . . right from Desyatovsky's office!"

"Not exactly. I had help."

"You Americans always were more clever than we gave you credit for!"

"The help I had was pure Russian," laughed Blue Doc. "In this business, success depends on who you know and what kind of information they can buy."

"On the other hand," mused Galanov, "once you find yourself out in the cold *without* friends, you've got nothing left . . . it's over."

"Which is, I take it, your present predicament?"

He nodded.

"Well, maybe you can, like you told me yesterday, use this to bargain your way out."

"It's got to be handled with care . . . and quickly. After what I've seen, especially given my present status here, there's nobody in my country I'd trust enough to take it to."

"Kolter and the U.S. State Department seem the likely hands we ought to put these files into," said Blue Doc. "They'll know what to do. We've got to get the information out of Moscow and to Berlin and Washington."

"Don't you have a CIA hotline? Call your superiors," suggested Galanov.

Blue Doc thought a moment, many factors running through his

mind. Just when he'd thought all the tension in the world was over, here he was with dynamite sitting in his hands and him not knowing what to do with it!

Finally he spoke. "You're the one who needs to blow the whistle on it," he said.

"Why? You could get word back to your country faster than I could do a thing."

"If it comes from our end, they'll be able to claim the U.S. is trying to resume Cold War hostilities. With the media contacts they have in their pocket, they could bury anything that originated with the CIA, and world opinion would probably believe them. No, it's got to come from your end."

"Hmm . . . I see what you mean." Galanov perused one of the files again. "You're right—with Alekdanyov on his team, there wouldn't be much *anyone* could do."

"Listen, we'll go back to my office and make a set of copies of the whole thing. You'll take these. I'll have copies to give to my people in case . . . well, you know, in case you get fouled up along the way."

"Why don't you get the information to them immediately, but tell them to sit on it until I can expose it from my end?"

"Once the State Department got wind of this they would be up in arms and it wouldn't stay quiet an hour. The people back in Washington just don't have any idea of the contempt with which the United States is viewed in most of the rest of the world. No, it's a judgment call, and I'm going to sit on it for a few days at least."

"Then I've got to get out of Russia with this. But you have to be ready. They're looking for me as it is. If I'm found, I've had it."

"You want me to get you out?" asked Blue Doc. "I've got ways."

"No. I have that covered."

"How? I thought all your contacts had gone dry."

"Never mind. The less you know the better," said Galanov.

"I'll take your word for it. But are you sure you can get out?"

"I have some new associates. They're already working on it for me. But once we get two sets of these things, we have to go our separate ways. We can't take any chance of being caught together. I'm not even going to go back to my place. Time is too critical. I'll be out of Moscow before midnight."

"I won't act until I know you have done so or aren't going to be able to."

"If you see the coup starting to go down, forget about me. That will probably mean they've got me or else I'm lying dead someplace."

"OK," said Blue Doc. "But look, I'm going to give you the name of my contact in Washington."

He took out a scrap of paper and wrote down a name and telephone number, then handed it to the Russian.

"Here, take this. If you get in trouble you can't get out of, call this number. The instant you tell them that code word written there, they'll listen. It'll be my insurance too. Something could happen to me here, just as well as you. I want to make sure *one* of us gets through to Washington or Berlin."

Galanov nodded. "But I do not think it wise to go with you to your office at the American embassy. If I am wanted, Desyatovsky probably has men near the embassy waiting for me, in case I tried to seek asylum."

"Good point. And we wouldn't want to be seen together to raise any suspicions." Blue Doc thought for a moment as he replaced all the papers in their appropriate files. "I'll go back to the embassy and make copies of these files and then bring them back to you. Let's meet back here in two hours."

"Agreed."

They rose and parted with a handshake and serious expression. Both were fully aware of the irony of how much trust each had suddenly placed in such a longtime adversary.

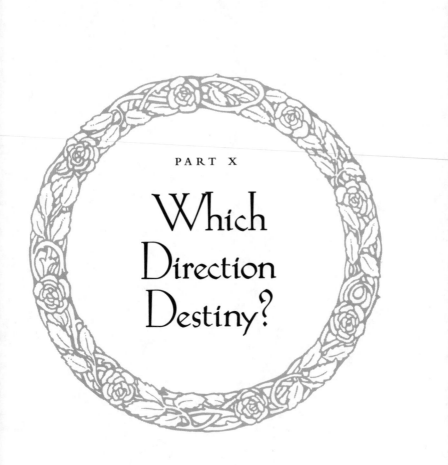

PART X

Which
Direction
Destiny?

80

Coup Review

• • •

Moscow

BLUDAYEV DESYATOVSKY WALKED THROUGH THE REMAIN-
ing staff of underlings who had not yet gone home for the evening
with a tall stride of confidence.

He hardly took the slightest note of his pawn and confidante
Marta Repninka. In truth, for the last two days she had trembled at
the very sight of him and clung to the out-of-the-way corners of the
office in hopes he would not detect the look of terror and betrayal in
her eyes.

Especially now!

She had done the horrible deed.

Within her breast pulsated, along with the fierce, quiet anger
against the two-faced beast of a man, a nearly uncontrollable feeling
of dread that he would take one look at her and know everything. If
she could just get through today and out of the office. She would
never have to come back to this place. The American had promised
safety. By tomorrow at this time she would . . . well, she didn't know
where she would be. But she wouldn't be here.

Marta needed not worry. The mind of the defense minister of the
Republic of Russia was a thousand miles away, and he strode into his
office with a smug grin of satisfaction, then closed the door behind
him.

It had been one of those days when, contrary to the usual saying,
everything had gone *right*. He could hardly believe it, in fact! Things
could not more perfectly be falling into his lap.

He had had three interviews today, all significantly in his opinion boosting not only the likelihood of his final success, but actually impelling and stimulating circumstances toward the very end he desired by the force of their own momentum. He would ultimately have to do very little to goad and prod events toward the inevitable outcome. All he would have to do would be to push the first domino, as it were, to borrow that old ridiculous analogy from the paranoid Americans, and the rest would just happen!

The very cosmos itself seemed lining itself up with his destiny, as that blowhard Drexler was always saying with his Dianetic, nonsensical flummery.

It was all bilgewater, of course, but he would never say so to Drexler's face. He would play that New Age game if he had to. It was what the people wanted to hear—at least affluent Germans and the rest who had nothing better to do than sit around and gaze at stars and crystals and talk such malarkey. He knew his own countrymen better than that, and to them the whole thing was hocus-pocus.

After today, who could tell? Maybe Drexler was right. Maybe he had prayed to one of his ridiculous crystals and said some incantation over it and that's what had caused things suddenly to fit into place so well.

Who could have hoped for better? The earthquake in Azerbaijan . . . they could not have scripted a more fortuitous prelude! Everything would flow naturally out of events without them having to artificially prod them along.

And the recent accident at the Kuybshev nuclear plant! Sure, it wasn't a fiftieth as serious as Chernobyl and actually was of little industrial significance at all. But it made worldwide headlines and had the people edgy.

That was good. A jittery populace was the perfect backdrop. And with Yeltsin and Shevardnadze and the presidents of three of the largest of the other republics scheduled to visit the reactor site in Russia and then travel together down to Kirovabad . . . it was perfect!

The first "Commonwealth crisis," they were calling it. An opportunity to demonstrate unity between the newly independent republics. A Commonwealth summit of sorts, to show the world that the leaders of the former Soviet Union still were committed to harmony between one another, and that the republics, though independent, would help and stand by one another.

The leaders would all be gone at the most critical time. He had allayed Donetsk's last-minute reservations in Budapest. Nearly all the holes of previous concern had been plugged. If two or three of the smaller republics proved obstinate, the momentum of events would pull them along. He would make his calls over the weekend, Desyatovsky thought. Then all he would have to do was wait.

Eight phone calls was all it would take! The union strike was already set in motion thanks to his sweet-talking to the old Repninka woman.

Momentum in all the other arenas would gather about him instantly. By the time anyone knew anything he would have assembled about him a committee that was in touch with leaders of all eight vital groups—intrinsic links to power—in each of the republics.

The takeover would be so quick and so complete that there would be no possibility of either failure or reprisal. He would step in, the committee would take command and assume authority in all the capitals.

No one would even use the dreaded C-word, unless it was to refer to the *Commonwealth* or a *consolidation* of power due to the crises. A sudden and shocking state of emergency, he would call it when he went on nationwide television to announce the tragic accident that had claimed the lives of several of the Commonwealth leaders. A tragedy out of which had gathered around him leaders in every sphere, dedicated to preserving the democratic principles of independence set in motion by these beloved former leaders.

He might even use the C-word, to tell the people he and those with him were taking steps, even as he spoke, to make sure there was no disruption of order, that no *coup* was possible, that everything would go on in each of the republics as before, and that he and the Committee for the Preservation of the Commonwealth were working to ensure that no nefarious forces were able to use the crisis for their own power-hungry ends.

He would tell them that he had already spoken with the American president and other world leaders by phone, assuring them that everything in the Commonwealth of Independent States was calm and orderly, that they need have no fears of unrest, violence, civil strife, or the disruption of the continued process of democratization and independence in any of the sovereign republics.

Ah, his mind soared at the thought. It was actually going to happen! And it would be easier than he'd ever imagined.

Maybe Drexler *did* have something with his talk of stars and destiny and karma and cosmic forces aligning themselves. If he'd ever felt in the middle of destiny's focus, now was the moment.

He poured himself a glass of vodka and sat down at his desk, reflecting on the events of the day.

He'd met that morning with television giant Valeri Alekdanyov. To use the term *media mogul* about a Russian would have seemed inconceivable just a decade ago. But now Valeri was as close to a Russian version of his hero and mentor Ted Turner as could be imagined. They'd been friends for years and had hashed over the plan for months.

Valeri was as thirsty for power as he was himself, Desyatovsky thought with a smile. It would work out well for them both. He would give him total control over the media, perhaps through some indirect ministry-level appointment, but the effect would be the same. Alekdanyov would control the news flow both in and out of the Commonwealth and would himself be influential in putting just the right spin on the impact of that flow. In exchange, Alekdanyov would give Desyatovsky what *he* wanted.

Desyatovsky rose and walked to the television cabinet in his room, opened it, and shoved the videotape he had received just two hours earlier into the VCR. In the silence of his own office he watched Valeri's production once again.

Genius, that's what it was. Positive genius! Valeri was every bit the media master he knew himself to be . . . and with an ego to match, thought Desyatovsky.

There it was, the news broadcast prepared *before* the fact, all ready to be played nationwide and conveniently "intercepted" by the CNN wires and shot instantly around the world.

There *he* was, Bludayev Desyatovsky, confident, in command, at the helm of the Commonwealth by the *request* of Yeltsin and other republic presidents during their mutual absences. Granted, the requests were implied and the absences, though such was not said, were forced. But Alekdanyov had put the media package together with such skill that not a speck of his adroit splicing would be visible and neither would a word of the speeches be questioned for a moment. Especially with the accompanying interviews from leaders throughout the spectrum of society giving overt support and encouragement to the temporary "consolidation" of power, as it was called.

Parliamentary leaders in all the republics had been interviewed, and all sung the praises of the new acting president of the Commonwealth, Bludayev Desyatovsky.

He couldn't imagine how Valeri had come up with all those interviews! There were a good number from people he didn't even know were with them in the scheme. Had he patched them together? Were they pure fakery? Could the splicing together of tapes really make something out of nothing?

He had asked, but Alekdanyov had only smiled and replied, "Trade secrets, my friend. It is not wise to ask too many questions. If I tell you everything, then *my* power is gone."

He was a sly one!

And the point was, in any case, that this is what millions, perhaps even billions of people would see. It was so utterly flawless and believable that they would question nothing. Especially when follow-up interviews with people he already had in place, leaders and influential every one, would confirm everything. Let CNN's Shaw interview them himself, the outcome would be the same—unanimous support for the new president of the Commonwealth, and chairman of the Committee for the Preservation of the Commonwealth.

Desyatovsky took out the videotape, laid it aside, then inserted a copy of the interview he had taped today, which Alekdanyov would splice in with the other, adding pertinent bits of current news and details when the time came. He watched himself addressing the nation and the world, a serious expression on his face, recounting the events leading up to the moment of necessary change, events that had not even happened yet, changes requested, in fact, and set in motion by Boris and Eduard and the other republic leaders.

It was good. Even he had to admit it. If he didn't know better, he would believe it all himself! Valeri could make anyone look good in front of a camera . . . and could make the final version of an interview say anything he wanted it to!

The moment of crisis . . . circumstances prompting consolidation—the time was nearly upon them. In less than a week the whole world would be watching these two videos, spliced into one, as if they had emerged out of events themselves.

They were indeed to the moment of takeover.

He had been wise to bring Alekdanyov in so early. It was inspired. The man could take the country wherever he wanted with his media genius.

Desyatovsky ejected the tape and turned off the machine. He returned to his desk and began to reflect on his second interview of the day.

He had arrived at General Fydor Shaposhnikov's office about two o'clock. He had had a long relationship with the former chairman of the Soviet General Staff and first acting defense minister for the Ukrainian Republic. The native Kievian, however, had resigned that post in favor of again taking up quarters in the Kremlin in Moscow, where he had been now for six months acting as liaison and chief military attaché between the separate military agencies of the Commonwealth. His new position kept him in near constant touch with Desyatovsky and the military leaders of the other republics. He had been selected to coordinate military affairs between the fifteen republics and was especially close to subordinate-level leaders in his native Ukraine as well as Uzbekistan and Kazakhstan—all three of whose presidents would be with Yeltsin and the others.

Those three republics, along with his own Russia, represented a population base of over 235 million, or more than 82 percent of the total Commonwealth. If Turkmenistan or Tadzhikistan with their one or two percent didn't come along, who would care? The four major republics would be enough, and Shaposhnikov would make sure their military leaders fell into step.

Having climbed slowly up the ladder during the Gorbachev era, Shaposhnikov was the perfect military ally, thought Desyatovsky with satisfaction. He had never been a hard-liner during the late-eighties' debate over the future of the Soviet Union, so when the change had come, he was all groomed and ready to step in as a moderate, well-respected in the West and one of what the U.S. Kremlin watchers liked to call a "new breed" of Russian leaders. No one knew Fydor's secret motives and ambitions like his old friend Bludayev

Desyatovsky, and he had been an intrinsic part of the plan almost from the beginning.

Shaposhnikov's preparations were just as effective and widespread in their own way as Alekdanyov's. He had every conceivable military scenario and antiscenario and counterscenario covered, from generals down to lieutenants—and with the officers leading the way, the conscript soldiers would follow—all the men in the positions to both alleviate uneasiness and move things forward. One word from Fydor and the entire military machine in every republic, from nuclear readiness down to conscripts polishing their boots, would be united behind him.

Fydor wasn't the only one behind him. He had at least two dozen influential colonels and a couple generals committed to the cause as well. Some were frustrated and dissenting conservatives who had never gone along with the reforms in their hearts, and some aggressive new bloods—all of whom were willing to put aside communism-versus-democracy idealistic disparities to participate together in a new order, a new world order.

And not merely a new *world* order, but a new *Soviet* order in which they would have—though they had to share it—power and prestige once again. The plan was genius, and its implementation sure.

The defense minister of Russia ran again through the specifics of the military details in his mind.

Granted, communicating simultaneously to all the subordinate positions at the precise moment of the coup would be vital and perhaps difficult. Then there were the practicalities of how power would be apportioned out later, again, not without its potential hazards.

And he had to keep *Pravda* and *Tass* behind them, though Alekdanyov should be able to ensure that. Nothing of this magnitude was without its intricacies . . . and its risks.

Desyatovsky fell to thinking about the other key members of his plan. The *inside putsch,* as he called it. There was Gunder Haslack of the European Community Bank and chairman of the World Banking Cartel headquartered in The Hague with a major regional center of operations in Geneva. He would swing European financial leaders in their favor and keep anxiety low.

Of course they had Carter McPherson in New York and Hawasaki Nakasone in Tokyo as hands-on liaisons to keep Wall Street and the Nikei Index from tumultuous ups or downs. Both would be the subject of live interviews from their respective scenes saying that all was calm and no major fluctuations in the markets were anticipated. Business was proceeding normally, they would say, and in fact seemed buoyed a little by the news.

Those interviews, according to Alekdanyov, had already been shot and were in the video-editing room at the moment. They would be ready within twenty-four hours to be inserted into world news telecasts the moment word came from Desyatovsky himself.

Valentin Gorbunovyev came into his mind, chairman of the Committee for Democratization and Information—a loosely assembled body linking the fifteen republics in a joint vision of the future. It was designed to keep leaders in all the former Soviet provinces in touch with one another, if not with binding formality, at least with an unofficial attempt to coordinate their tentative steps into the future. His communiqués to all the republics had already been prepared as well, ready not merely to set the various parliaments at ease, but to swing them solidly behind the new Kremlin leadership with pledges that President Desyatovsky was firmly committed to the continuing independence and autonomy of the provinces. This temporary need to consolidate, it would be explained, was merely a strengthening maneuver that would accelerate and further the democratization process.

Desyatovsky was, in fact, the documents said, planning a visit to each of the republics and their leaders very soon to reassure them of his support and encouragement with regard to their independent directions. First he would focus his attention on Russia, the Ukraine, Uzbekistan, and Kazakhstan, whose presidents had so tragically been taken from them. He would speak personally at the funerals, of course, and preside over the smooth transition of leadership. What was *not* said was that he had already hand-selected their successors.

Throughout the days of crisis, every assurance would be made— in speeches, on television, through the print media, in meetings with foreign leaders—that Desyatovsky was progressive and supportive and, if anything, would speed the move toward independence, Westernization, and a market economy. They had actually spoken with Vadim Petrikov, president of Moldava, Anatoli Dzasokhov, president of Belorussia, and Yevgeny Baramertnykhm, president of Kirghizia.

It was risky bringing such high-level leaders into the plan. But where there was no risk, there could also not be such high rewards. And all three, his informants had told him, had latent disgruntlements about the way things had gone over the last two years.

True, their constituencies were small. But with four republic presidents dead and three more lending their eager support, he doubted dissension from any of the others. He continued to hold his breath that none of them would cause a leak prematurely.

Union leader Marktov Bobrikov would have all he needed for explosive unrest once the sabotage at the factory in Kiev led to a widespread worker walkout. Tensions were already so high after recent food shortages and continued low wages that Bobrikov assured him that within thirty-six hours, the entire labor force in the Ukraine would be at a standstill.

His stepping in would, under the circumstances of that republic's suddenly incapacitated leadership, be absolutely justified.

Which reminded him, he still had to take care of the woman and her brother so there would be no traceable link back to him. He should never have used anyone so close. It was a sloppy mistake . . . but containable.

He had just left a short while ago his third meeting of the day, this with Commonwealth Minister of Transportation Nursultan Khasbulachek and Eurasian industrialist Max Harmin. Their three-way summit had not ever been secretive, for distribution of goods and foodstuffs had been one of the severest problems facing them for decades. Harmin's commitment to bring American, French, and Japanese technology and know-how to bear on the problem and to assist in the revamping of Russian transportation systems to accommodate the implementation of the sweeping reforms he said were necessary—such discussions had been well documented. No one had a hint, however, of the larger magnitude of plans the three had committed themselves to once the doors closed behind them and "official" discussions were laid aside.

He ran down the list of all the principal players in his mind, recalling the years of preparation, all the work, all the moles and circumstances put in their proper places long before, and then the waiting for events to line up, watching the rise and fall in public favor of men like Gorbachev, watching . . . waiting . . . slowly knitting together the fabric of the whole master plan at the grass roots and at the mountaintop levels.

Ah, what magnificent scope the plan contained, he thought with satisfaction, leaning his head back and emptying the last of the clear liquid from the glass on his desk.

He would make Russia great again. He would keep his people from starving. He would give them hope and purpose. The masses would love him for it!

He rose and slowly walked to the file cabinet across the room, several papers in his hands representing notes and developments from today's interviews. He pulled his keys from his pocket, inserted one into the top drawer of the oak cabinet, and slid out the deep drawer to its full extension, reaching without much concentration about two-thirds of the way back where the locked cardboard packet of secret files was kept.

His hand fell only upon the top of standard manila folders. Suddenly a cold dread swept over the huge man and his face went instantly pale.

The file was gone!

Top-Priority Assignment

• • •

FRANTICALLY, WITH SWEAT ALREADY BEADING ON HIS clammy white forehead, Desyatovsky flew through the files again, fingers trembling, back and forth through the entire drawer.

It was impossible . . . but the thing was gone!

With the cabinet drawer still hanging open and a few files strewn on the floor from his panicked search, Desyatovsky spun around and ran to the door, striding in horror into his outer office, struggling desperately to conceal the ghastly sickness that was sweeping over him.

A quick glance around revealed the entire staff gone home for the evening, except his own faithful secretary.

A hasty questioning assured him that she knew nothing. She had been with him too long and was not nearly clever enough to lie her way through something of this magnitude.

Ignoring her looks and questions of alarm over his anxiety, he turned again and retreated back into his office, closing the door behind him. Breathing heavily and feeling the thick shirt already getting wet under his arms, he sat down heavily at his desk, staring straight ahead in stupefied silence.

How was this possible! How could anyone have infiltrated his office? And . . . what to do now?

With the file missing, suddenly everything changed! If the thing hadn't been unraveled by now, it would be soon. It all depended on *who* had that file . . . and how astute they were to understand what they had stumbled into.

If they didn't act with lightning speed and decisive force, all the years of planning would be down the drain, and he would be chipping salt out of some cave in Siberia! Democracy didn't change everything.

He rose and paced around his desk, as if movement were the only escape from the terrible feeling of the walls closing in around him.

How could it have happened, he asked himself again . . . and what was he to do now?

But no . . . those questions didn't matter anymore! Who cared *how* it had been pulled off? Someone *had* penetrated the inner sanctum of his private files. It was too late to change that.

The question that mattered most now . . . was *who!*

Again he sat down at his desk, fiddling with his tie and loosening the top button of his nearly drenched shirt. *Who would have the know-how . . . the expertise . . . the daring? Who would stand to gain from such a—*

Suddenly the large palm of the big man slammed down on top of the wooden desk with a violent force of anger and instant realization.

"Of course!" he exclaimed. "How could I have been such a fool?"

Suddenly his eyes were opened. It was all so clear! Why else had the misbegotten Galanov been following him? He'd known the fellow was dangerous. He should have put more men on him immediately. Only the KGB could have gotten in and out of his office so cleanly.

The blundering fools almost had him four nights ago. How could they have possibly lost his trail?

There was only one thing to do. The former agent *had* to be found and the file recovered. Whatever it took . . . whoever got in the way!

He picked up the phone, his shaking but purposeful fingers attacking the dial with venom.

"Bolotnikov," he said after a moment, "it is time you became involved in this thing at a more personal level. Whatever you have attempted thus far, as is the case with my own contacts, it has not been enough. A serious compromise has occurred. Galanov must be found and silenced—immediately!"

The silence which followed lasted only three or four seconds.

"Of course, it's him!" exploded the defense minister.

Bolotnikov again spoke.

"That may be," said Desyatovsky, calming. "But best people or not, they haven't done the job. He's got to be put away, and I mean immediately. You're the only one I can trust at the moment, and the job has to be done without delay."

He listened at the receiver to several more questions. ". . . Good, that sounds like the lead to follow . . . good! Yes, personally. . . . How far to go? Look, do I have to spell it out for you, Leonid? This is it, the final gambit . . . checkmate! Silence him, snuff him out, put a slug through his head, that's what I mean! If you want to move up in the new regime as we talked about."

He hung up the phone with annoyance, then sat back in his chair.

Bolotnikov was a frightening man. If Desyatovsky didn't have a complete dossier on him, he'd be scared that *he'd* take over.

But he was the only kind of man to have on this assignment—ruthless and without scruples. He'd just better find Galanov or they'd all be packing their bags for Siberia!

He knew he had to make one more call. He dreaded doing so. It would be much more difficult. He sat for several minutes, trying to phrase his words and think through every possible question he would be asked.

At length he picked up the phone again. This was not going to be easy. Slowly and methodically he circled his fingers around the plastic dial, then sat back to await the voice he did not look forward to hearing.

82

Dreams of Destiny

. . .

Berlin

KLAUS DREXLER PUT DOWN THE BRIEFING PAPER HE HAD just read on the aid package, rose, and walked with slow but purposeful steps toward the window of his office, then drew in a deep breath and slowly exhaled.

The situation had nearly reached critical mass, he thought. Action would be required soon—very soon. As the paper delivered to him just hours ago by special courier from the chancellor's office made clear, Kolter was making his move. He was going ahead with his bold stratagem that had begun when he had called the Bundestag back to act without delay. Now he had requested them to vote immediately on the package.

But Drexler was ready. He had been lining up the necessary factors for a long time now, including assuring himself of Gerhardt Werner's support. He would take the fight to the floor, would use the opportunity to knock Kolter off his high horse with a vote of no-confidence, and step into the leadership void himself.

At last the moment had arrived!

The aid package should be easy to defeat simply on its own, reflected Drexler. Germany had already provided far more than it could reasonably afford in credits to the former Soviet Union. On top of 250 billion deutsche marks spent on former East Germany's reconstruction, the massive aid package proposed by Kolter would as well bankrupt Berlin's treasury. And all it would accomplish would be to prop up a grossly inefficient and now scattered and nonhomo-

geneous Soviet industry that hadn't a clue how a free-market economy really worked. Money down a sieve is all it would be—throwing
jillions at them as an expensive reward for lying down and finally
admitting that communism couldn't work.

Let the Americans give away their dollars to get Soviet industry
revamped, to put free-market reforms in place, to establish a Commonwealth stock exchange in Moscow that worked and fueled
widespread growth, and to bring foreign industry and investment into
the former Soviet republics. They were dragging their feet, but they
would do it . . . just so long as Germany didn't step in and do it for
them! They had to reserve their own efforts for strengthening a united
Germany, so that—once the Commonwealth and all the other Eastern Bloc countries were humming along smoothly to the tune of
profitable capitalism—Germany would be powerfully poised to guide
the new Eastern-looking alliance into the twenty-first century.

The time was right, the forces aligned. He would win the battle,
and within a week or two he would be the new chancellor of
Germany.

Truly the karma of a foreordained role in shaping global affairs
was his! All that now remained were a few final pieces so that when
he ascended to power everything would be ready. The alliance with
the Russian Commonwealth was the hinge pin, as well as making
sure the industrial/military syndicates in both countries were ce-
mented together and awaiting the precise moment to make their
simultaneous moves.

Kolter was strong, yes. But he had been in power more than a
decade now and was vulnerable, for that reason alone if for no other.
The Thatcher syndrome. No matter how great a politician's achieve-
ments, there was a limit to how long he could ride the favorable crest
of approval. He had accomplished a great deal, but he had been in the
public eye so long that his star inevitably had to dim in time.

That time was now! And he, Klaus Drexler, was prepared to step
forward. As long as the Russian could be prodded into decisive action
at the same time.

In his eyes burned the deep fire of self-appointed destiny, a
futuristic vision, far-reaching and cunning. Almost since the moment
Mikhail Gorbachev had succeeded Chernenko and had begun mak-
ing his noises of *glasnost* and *perestroika* seven or eight years ago, Klaus

Drexler, then barely into his second term in the Bundestag, had seen the writing on the wall. He had begun even then garnering support among businessmen and in the intellectual community, making himself agreeable to his fellow politicians, and most important, taking frequent trips to the Soviet Union to spy out the land, as it were, feeling out those on the fringes of power, assessing strengths and weaknesses, keeping an eye peeled for the next generation of up-and-coming leaders. He had known even back then that Boris Yeltsin was a force to be reckoned with. But he did not suit his particular purposes—too independent, too forceful, too much bluster and not enough craft. But he had learned a thing or two from his relations with Yeltsin, as he had from Gorbachev. Both were skilled politicians, but without the vision to truly stretch distantly into the future. Neither could hope to lead with him into the twenty-first century.

So he had continued his search, eventually in the late eighties being drawn into a relationship with the crafty Desyatovsky, discovering many mutually unspoken and mutually beneficial goals. They had learned a great deal from the Moscow Eight—most importantly, what mistakes not to make and the necessity for full and instantaneous coordination of all elements.

All the while, Drexler had fashioned his own image and reputation to dovetail into his perception of the German leader of the future—a renaissance man for a new era, subtly capitalizing on past dreams and future hopes of a people who had never quite managed to scale the heights of world prestige and power to their own satisfaction. He was foremost among a new generation of astute and savvy, highly popular German politicians, with great appeal among those who had conveniently forgotten (or had never known firsthand about) the events of the thirties and forties. Packaging his speeches in New Age rhetoric, his dedication to Germany's rise again to preeminence was viewed mostly in economic terms. In Drexler's vision, the power of the future was neither information nor industry, as many claimed, but simply money. Technology, economics, business, industrial modernization and competitiveness, productivity, communications . . . it all began with cash reserves in the world's banks. The country with the most solid currency, the highest asset-to-liability ratio, and the lowest national debt would lead all others into the future. In all these respects, Germany stood at the forefront of all the nations of the world.

The moment George Bush began talking about a new world order Drexler had seen visionary implications far beyond what he knew anyone in the West could possibly see. These new times spelled opportunity for him and for the nations of the disintegrating Eastern Bloc. He had seen the economic possibilities east of ten degrees longitude, and the sight had dazzled him with its brilliance. He was content to let Bush, Gorbachev, Kolter, Yeltsin, Mitterand, and Major bask in the limelight for now. They had moved everything in just the right direction. But now the new era had come, and his cue to step onto center stage was at hand.

He was suddenly interrupted from his reverie by the ringing of his phone behind him.

Acceleration

. . .

"DREXLER," SAID THE VOICE ON THE OTHER END, "DESYA-
tovsky. Is the line secure?"

"Of course; this line is for our ears only."

"Good, because what I have to say to you is . . ." Desyatovsky's
voice failed him momentarily.

"What is it?"

"Just this," he finally managed to get out, "the game is over."

"What!"

"My entire file on the coup and the alliance has been stolen from
my office."

"Why, you idiot!" exclaimed Drexler. "How could you let such a
thing happen?"

"It happened," rejoined Desyatovsky testily, not appreciative of
Drexler's condescension. "How they broke in I don't know, but this
file will be retrieved."

"You know who stole it?"

"A KGB agent. We're onto him."

"How can you be so sure?"

"We are taking precautions to plug other possible security
holes as well."

"My man Claymore is in Moscow. I will send him to you to assist
in cleaning this thing up."

"I have my own people," replied Desyatovsky. "We need no help.
We will handle it ourselves."

"Like letting the file be stolen out from under your nose! I want

Claymore there. If security problems exist, he will see to them quickly and efficiently."

"I resent your implication!" shot back Desyatovsky.

"If you have an objection, then I will put you at the top of Claymore's project list while he is in Moscow."

Gradually the two would-be world leaders calmed down.

"You know what this means," said Desyatovsky finally.

"We must act without delay."

"I will take steps the minute we are off the phone."

"Steps . . . which are?"

"The first domino. I will make my phone calls. The union strike will be instigated. Everything is in place to trigger the worker revolt. Then everything else will begin to happen."

"Are Yeltsin and the republic presidents still meeting at the earthquake and reactor sites?"

"This weekend. By the middle of next week, I will control the Commonwealth. You just make sure you are ready to move on *your* end."

"Don't worry, my Siberian friend. The German will make sure everything goes off as planned, *without* anyone breaking into my office."

They hung up, each man retreating into the privacy of his own thoughts.

Desyatovsky in Moscow breathed a deep sigh of relief to have the phone call over with. He had handled himself better than he had expected given the circumstances. Nervous and still sweating, he sat down and poured himself another vodka.

Meanwhile, in Berlin, a cool, confident, and eager Klaus Drexler stood for a moment behind his desk, just as he had during the call. His calculating mind spun through the upcoming scenario for the hundredth time, pausing only long enough to think what a fool the big Russian bear was.

If only I could do this without them all, he thought to himself. Alas, given the scope of his dream, he couldn't do it without help.

It was just too bad they couldn't all be as competent as Germans!

8 4

Scriptural Clues

• • •

Moscow

IF THERE WAS A UNIQUELY RUSSIAN LOOK AND PHYSIQUE, Leonid Bolotnikov carried it. Large, calculating, and cunning, he was committed to one cause, and only one—his own.

As former head of the KGB, he now had to walk a treacherous tightrope between past and future. He had to fit in with the new system and pretend to go along, without compromising his long-range, personal agenda. So far he had been reasonably successful. Not a single individual knew what he *really* thought of Gorbachev and Yeltsin and all the other reformers.

His own moment would come again. In the meantime . . . he walked the tightrope. But times were about to change. That is why he had committed himself to Desyatovsky's plan. Not that he had that much respect for Bludayev Desyatovsky. He was a reasonably competent bureaucrat. And he had vision, Bolotnikov had to give him that much. Vision *and* contacts.

Desyatovsky had the position and contacts and prestige to just possibly pull this thing off. If he didn't and the whole thing went down the toilet, well, Bolotnikov was a survivor and had been around long enough to know how to cover his own backside pretty well. He'd do his part, but if the coup unraveled, he'd land on his feet one way or another and continue to move on . . . and up.

For Leonid Bolotnikov was a man with his *own* vision. Some would call it a lust. That lust was for nothing short of power. And no one who knew him would make the mistake of thinking he had yet reached the apex of his political career.

He walked down the deserted street, his steps echoing sharply against the vacant buildings. *What a sleazy part of the city,* he thought. *The perfect part of town for a hideout.* If only his lead and suspicions proved correct.

This is just what *he* would have done under the circumstances. He had taught his subordinate well. Now here he was trying to root out the very man he had chosen . . . and with whom he had rounded up all kinds of creeps back in the old days. How things changed. The shoe was suddenly on the other foot. The fortunes of peace as well as war. Why couldn't he see that the future lay with them, instead of trying to undermine . . .

His thoughts trailed away indistinctly. It wasn't as if Galanov had had much choice. After all, Bolotnikov *himself* had turned him in to boost his own standing with the new powers of the Commonwealth. He hadn't let Desyatovsky in on that tidbit of information and had played the innocent bystander instead. But that was the only way to move up in this part of the world, making sure you always knew more than your colleagues—friends and foes alike—gave you credit for.

Bolotnikov grinned. Actually, if he was in Galanov's shoes, stealing the file would be exactly what he'd have done, too, to try to save his hide. Yes, his protégé was in some ways still his protégé. Bolotnikov was almost proud of him.

Of course that changed nothing, he thought, as he entered the run-down building whose address he'd scribbled on a piece of paper and now consulted one last time. Proud of him or not, he still had to kill him.

Down the hall he walked, now and then hearing a squeal of a rat in some distant part of the building. He used the flashlight he carried only intermittently, just in case anyone was about. Which he doubted. The place seemed deserted.

A slight breeze came through the dark corridor from the broken windows at each end. Pieces of broken plaster lay about the floor, fallen from the ceiling who could tell how many months ago. The place probably hadn't been cleaned in five years.

Around a corner, then up two flights of stairs, peering in the darkness for labels on the doors. It was not quite as filthy here, and a few signs of life were apparent. A few tenants must still live in the flea trap, he thought. He reached the third floor, then stopped. He began to tiptoe more quietly. Galanov's secret room should be right down this corridor, if his snitch had told him the truth. As hard as he'd pummeled him, he had little reason to doubt it.

Quite a nice touch, he thought, still half congratulating the man he was on his way to kill. Two completely separate living quarters, only a mile from each other. *It really was ingenious of you, Andrassy! And you even kept this place from me, your boss.* Again Bolotnikov smiled, then reached into his pocket and pulled out his high-tech automatic pistol.

As he tiptoed, gun drawn, the look on the man's face told the entire story of his character. The eyes squinted against the darkness would have been black even in broad daylight, reflecting also the color of his heart. The broad chest and muscular biceps had not been won with niceties.

Through his mind revolved the incident thirteen years ago when he and Galanov had let that no-good Rostovchev slip through their fingers. That couldn't help reminding him of all the time he'd spent trying to get his hands on the spiritual leader. Even as he replayed that earlier failure in his brain, he arrived at the door, eyes wide, flashlight off, gun ready.

Bolotnikov stopped. Then with a swift punishing blow, the door shattered under his foot. The sound exploded down the dimly lit hallway. Even as it crashed to the floor, Bolotnikov charged over it and inside, pistol poised in readiness to fire.

As the sound died away, he looked around at the room inside which he found himself. Why, it was nothing but a storage room! Boxes and crates and cleaning supplies. Slowly he stepped over the rubble, including the mess he had made of the door, which lay in four pieces splintered on the floor. He made his way to the far darkened end.

A curtain hung down. He pulled it aside with his left hand, gun poised again, and peered behind it. All was black. Still holding the gun in his right hand, with his left he flipped on his flashlight. The tiny hideaway was filled with the sudden burst of light. The next instant it was off again, but Bolotnikov had had a long enough look to see that it was empty. He flipped on the light again, located the string hanging down from a single bulb on the ceiling. He reached up and pulled. The bulb lit.

Standing still, he glanced around, taking in the small room, which was just as Galanov had left it. Slowly he put his gun away. The look, the feel, even the smell said that this room had been deserted for at least twenty-four or thirty-six hours. He looked around, searching, opening a couple drawers and a cupboard.

This was Galanov all right. He recognized some of the clothes, the style, the . . . he even thought he could faintly smell his old colleague. And now it was just the two of them, he in person and the ghostly shell of Galanov's departed spirit engaged in a battle for supremacy. And he had to win.

He *would* find something here that would betray his old protégé, the one man who stood between him and the next rung on the ladder upward. He *would* find something that would deliver Galanov into his hands!

He searched for twenty minutes, turning over every corner, every shred of clothing, every scrap of paper. At last his eyes fell upon what looked like a small pamphlet or book, partially obscured by a shirt laying on top of it. Why hadn't he noticed it before? No matter. He grabbed it up with interest. It was the only thing written he had found in the whole place, and thus potentially a clue.

It was not large enough for a book, with paper covers, and only twenty or thirty pages in length. Hurriedly he flipped through it. The script was in German. He tried to make something of it, but his German was too scanty. It appeared to be some kind of religious tract or pamphlet. Across the top of the title page were the words, *Die Gute Nachricht Nach Markus.*

Why German? mused Bolotnikov. *And why a religious document? Galanov hated religion.*

Still flipping through it semiconsciously as his mind was absorbed elsewhere, suddenly Bolotnikov's eyes fell upon several lines that had been underlined. His mind snapped back to attention. He squinted in the thin light, bringing the pamphlet closer to his eyes, trying to make something of the words that came just shortly after the large 6 to the side of the text. . . . *Aber Jesus sagte zu ihnen: Ein Prophet wird überall geachtet, nur nicht in seiner Heimat, bei seinen Verwandten und in seiner Familie.*

What was it all about? puzzled Bolotnikov. *What was so important here that it had been underlined?*

He looked at the passage again. Suddenly the word jumped at him off the page. That was a word whose German meaning he understood well enough! *Prophet!*

His mind flashed back to that day he had been thinking of as he walked down the hallway . . . that day so long ago when he had finally gotten the drop on Rostovchev, only to see him slip through his fingers. That's what they had called him—*Der Prophet!* A *German* appellation!

Galanov had been sent after Rostovchev too, all the way to the outskirts of Berlin, and likewise had failed. Was this booklet some bizarre reminder he kept for himself all this time of his failure?

No. Bolotnikov doubted that. He had a feeling . . . a hunch . . . a gut instinct that something was going on here bigger than he'd imagined. Something . . .

Hastily he grabbed up the booklet again. There were a few other underlined passages too. He saw them now as he hurriedly scanned through the pages. Here was one that seemed to be marked with the numbers 8:34, whatever that meant: . . . *Dann rief Jesus die ganze Menschenmenge hinzu und sagte: "Wer mit mir kommen will, der darf nicht mehr an sich selbst denken. Er muss sein Kreuz auf sich nehmen und mir auf meinem Weg folgen. Denn wer sein Leben retten will, wird er verlieren. Aber wer sein Leben für mich und für die Gute Nachricht verliert, wird es retten."*

He read the words over and over, trying to make sense of them from the little German he knew. ". . . *anyone . . . come after me . . . deny . . . follow . . . lose life . . . for me. . . .*"

He stopped, thinking again. Suddenly his brain was seared with a lightning bolt of realization! That was it! Of course! The fool had gone off the deep end . . . he had become one of them! The persecutor had been seduced by his prey!

The fool Galanov had become a Christian!

Bolotnikov threw his head back and roared with laughter. The idiocy of it was so ironic . . . so beautiful. The stress of finding himself out in the cold had fried the idiot's brain! *"Ha, ha, ha!"* Bolotnikov laughed aloud. It was altogether too comical.

All at once he stopped. His head jerked down, glancing at the pamphlet again. But it could not tell him the answer to the question that had suddenly slammed into his brain. Suddenly he remembered why he had come, that Galanov had the files.

His job was to find him. And now he knew how. It all had to do with that ridiculous Rostovchev and his band of Christians scattered who knew where all over Europe. That was it! Galanov was trying to escape through what they had called *Das Christliche Netzwerk!*

The next instant the former KGB chief stormed out of the small room as loudly as he had come, his hard boots crashing through the debris he had made upon his entry. Those people worked fast. There wasn't a moment to lose.

The Polish Files

• • •

LEONID BOLOTNIKOV BLEW INTO HIS OWN OFFICE WITH nearly as much fury as he had Galanov's flat an hour earlier.

He ran to his cabinet, threw it open, pulled out the second sliding drawer, nearly crashing it to the floor, and flipped back through the old "Closed" files.

Here it is! he thought. Everything he'd accumulated through the years on the Christian network, including the files of his predecessor. Twenty-five years of names, places, contacts, spies, moles . . . all the way back to the days of Nikiforov and Kourdakov, the executions at the Elizovo baptism ceremony, and Sergei's defection in 1971. It was all here!

How much in the file was still valid, he had no way of knowing. And in spite of all their research and informants and KGB efforts, they never had gotten all the way to the bottom of the vast interconnecting matrix of Christians, especially the escape network. There were still major holes.

They knew some of the connections, but certainly not all of them—a few of the handoff points, but not nearly enough to form a continuous thread of how the people worked and what they did. But he'd kept a few of his people working on it in a low-key way even after Gorbachev eased religious restrictions, for this very purpose . . . just in case. They had filled in a few more of the gaps, gathered a few more names. The border crossings were clearly the most crucial points, and upon those he had had his people concentrate their efforts in the last few years.

Galanov was probably making for the West, and the most direct route would be to Poland and then to Germany. There were dozens of other directions he could go—north through Scandinavia, south to Turkey, the Mediterranean, even perhaps into the Middle East—who could tell what he was going to do with those documents?

But if he was indeed in the hands of the Christians, their main escape network had always been due west.

If he was wrong about it this time . . . well, he couldn't cover the whole world! That was a chance he had to take.

He sat down and began digging through all the old records. He turned to the file marked "Polish Border Crossings." He hoped Galanov was still in Russia. That was the one good thing about him being in the hands of the Christians. Though they wasted no time, they tended to be overtly careful and took many precautions, which did slow them down. He might be able to intercept them this side of the border.

He grabbed a map of the northwest and spread it out on the table before him, searching through the file and alternately looking over the map.

There were three crossings where they were likely to make their break. His finger traced over the border on his map southward from Kaliningrad to L'vov. The Christians, according to the files—at least KGB sources in the past thought as much—used the borders at Brest and Przemysl, but also had ways past the border where the roads had been closed at Grodno and south of Kounas. The road was open at Brest.

He discounted the northernmost and southernmost spots. Galanov would be urging speed and therefore would take the most direct route possible. Bolotnikov would therefore concentrate on the two crossing points, fortunately nearby one another, at Grodno and Brest. Meanwhile, he would take steps to shut the entire border down.

He grabbed his telephone and called the defense minister.

Final Mission

• • •

Berlin

WHEN LISEL OPENED HER DOOR TO THE PERSISTENT knock late in the afternoon the day after Tad's visit, she half expected to see him standing there again on his return to Berlin.

Excitedly she ran to the door and threw it open. The exuberant welcome poised on her tongue died before it reached her lips. The wide smile faded to a neutral expression of recognition, which was followed the next instant by a look of surprise. "Horst," she said, half in exclamation, half interrogation.

Without smile, word, greeting, or awaiting invitation, her visitor glanced nervously about, then hastened inside, brushing past his hostess, with whom he was obviously on familiar terms.

By the time Lisel had closed the door and followed him inside, her colleague of many years was pacing back and forth across the small sitting room. "Can you get away?" he asked.

"What do you mean?" Lisel asked.

"Just what I said—can you get away, out of the city?"

"I don't know—for how long?"

"Several days . . . maybe a week."

"I have to work."

"This is more important."

"What?"

"Something's come up—an opportunity for the Alliance that will reestablish our reputation."

"I . . . I don't understand, Horst. What could possibly—"

"It's big, Lisel," interrupted Brandes. "The biggest!"

"But I told you—I am scheduled to work."

"Get the schedule changed."

"It's not that easy."

"Quit your job."

"I can't do that!"

"I'll get you a new one."

"Just like that?"

"Trust me. I need you on this one. I tell you, it's big. This is the chance we've been waiting for to put the Freedom Alliance back in the spotlight. You told me only last month you wanted the same thing."

Lisel did not reply immediately. She remembered the conversation. It seemed like a year ago now, not just four weeks. So much had suddenly changed. Horst Brandes seemed so different . . . now that she knew Tad.

Slowly she nodded. "What's it all about?" she asked.

"I have an acquaintance who called me."

"Who?"

"No one you know. He's involved in something he says is hot. He needs help and has offered to pay me four thousand marks for my trouble."

"So what's stopping you taking the job?" asked Lisel.

"He says we can claim credit once it's all over, if we want to. None of that matters to him."

"Credit?"

"For the Freedom Alliance—what's eating you anyway, Lisel?"

"Nothing's eating me," rejoined Lisel, slightly annoyed. "Is it that big, that it would make the news?"

"Guaranteed. But I can't tell you the details."

"Why?"

"Because I don't know them yet myself. My contact in Russia will fill me in."

"Russia!"

"We are to go to a small town near the Polish–Belorussian border and await his instructions. Are your passport and visa still current?"

Lisel nodded, not at all sure she liked the sound of a sudden trip away from Berlin. The eyes of her associate were wide and full of fire.

She had not seen him so agitated in more than two years. His hair was a mess, and he looked as though he hadn't made use of either a bed or a bath recently.

"Who else is involved?" Lisel asked.

"Just the two of us."

"Why do you need me?"

"I may need a driver."

Lisel looked at him with a curious expression. Something in the wild gleam in the man's eye was unsettling and told her she should say no. But she and Horst had been through a lot together, and now there was just about no one else committed to the Alliance's cause besides the two of them.

If she didn't help him, no one would.

Tragedy

• • •

Moscow

MARTA REPNINKA HAD NO INTENTION OF RETURNING TO the office. She only wanted to get as far away from Moscow as she could.

When the man Davidson had called telling her where to go and what to do, she had been packed and ready for the train to Kiev an hour later. She had waited at home all the rest of the day, hiding, fearful, waiting for every minute to creep by until time to go.

He was supposed to be outside for her at 10:00 P.M. and would take her to the station for the overnight ride south to Kiev. An associate of his would meet her, he said, and take her to her brother's. She would be reunited with her family and safely out of Desyatovsky's reach by noon the next day.

Finally she could stand the waiting no longer. At quarter till ten, Marta took one final wistful, nostalgic look around her small apartment, then turned off the lights and headed down the flight of stairs with her two bags. She would wait the last minutes on the street, just in case the American happened to be early. She didn't want to miss him.

• • •

The man his associates knew only as Claymore didn't like working for two people at once.

Drexler had always been good to him, though he was annoyingly uppity. But this Russian fellow Drexler had instructed him to get in touch with and do his dirty work for, that he wasn't so sure about. He had warned Drexler on the phone that he was stretching their previously agreeable business relationship to the limit on this one.

The German had promised to make it all worth his while when it was over. And after all, Claymore reflected, that was supposed to be the name of the game. Anyway, if something went wrong, he could always dust off both the German and the Russian.

No extra charge.

The big Russian had said to do it on the street. "There can be no ties to my office," he had insisted, "not even to her apartment. Make it look like the work of street violence, imported from the United States. A by-product of democracy. I'll make sure it's reported that way to the press."

Politicians are such a peculiar breed, thought Claymore, pouring himself another cup of coffee in the car where he sat. It would be dark soon. So much the better, though he was anxious to have it over with. He'd been sitting here most of the day. Was she never going to leave her apartment for anything?

Then he finally saw the lights go out. Perhaps she was just going to bed. But he'd better be ready, just in case. He set down the coffee cup on the dash and reached down to the floor to retrieve the implement of his wicked trade.

• • •

Blue Doc had growing reservations about his decision all day. Things were not always black and white in this business, and this was one of the murkiest he'd faced.

Not that he doubted Andrassy's motives or even his ability to get through. But he wasn't used to sitting around and doing nothing, waiting for somebody else to do a job he thought he ought to be doing.

The only thing he'd had to occupy himself with today was making the final arrangements with his people in Kiev for the woman and her family down there. It was finally all taken care of, including a place for her to stay for the first month. Now all he had to do was get her safely out of Moscow.

He probably should have put her on an earlier train, he

thought, or made arrangements with a special CIA courier. But he didn't want to risk her being seen in broad daylight. If the thing was as serious as he thought, there was no telling what the fellow Desyatovsky might try.

The overnight train would be quiet, safe, and he would see her personally on board himself, with a few hundred extra rubles in her pocket. She would be deliriously happy, and it would be the cheapest the CIA had ever paid in its history to unravel an international coup.

He rounded the corner three blocks from Marta's run-down apartment building, the beams from his car the only light or movement disturbing the silent dusk of the northern evening.

Driving slowly, he suddenly saw a car door open a block in front of him. Instinctively Davidson hit the brakes and extinguished his lights. He must not be seen picking her up. The diplomatic plates of his car would be too easily recognizable.

He sat in the middle of the street. It was a tall, thin man who emerged from the driver's side of the car on the next block. Another tenant, Doc thought. He would wait until he was safely inside whatever building he lived in, then continue on. In fact, there was Marta in the distance, standing alone with her two suitcases waiting for him.

Wait, what was in the fellow's hands! It couldn't . . . he had been watching too many old spy pictures! *God, no . . . it was a rifle!*

All the years of training and experience in his brain suddenly scrambled into disarrayed confusion. By instinct his right foot sought the accelerator to send the car screaming forward, even as his right hand flew inside his coat after his gun.

But the recent conditioning of his brain stopped them both. Low profile . . . everything is low profile these days—so had said every order and communiqué for the last two years. *No incidents . . . don't provoke so much as a sneeze . . . let this democratic revolution work itself out without our help.*

Hadn't a briefing from Langley said those very words less than four months ago?

But counterdemocracy was in the air, threatening everything. Wasn't it his business to protect American interests? Marta had stood up for democracy. Didn't she deserve his help and protection?

The conflicting thoughts battling for supremacy bounced through his mind in less than two seconds. But that was all the hesitation it took for the unknown enemy to lock onto his prey.

Even as Blue Doc finally jammed the accelerator to the floor, his eyes watched with sickening horror as the man stooped, laid the deadly weapon across the top of his car, and took aim.

Doc's car had not lurched more than twenty feet toward him before the explosive crack of a single shot shattered the night air, drowning out the squeal of his tires as its sound echoed off the tall buildings and gradually died away. As if in slow motion, in the distance Doc saw the poor woman's body slump to the pavement in a red pool of her own blood.

As used to all this as he had once been, in the recent years of the thaw Blue Doc's humanity had slowly begun to reemerge, and with awful revulsion his stomach gagged at the sight.

Accelerating forward, his hand drew out the pistol he had not used for three or four years now. He would use it now! He would kill the evil scum who had shot that innocent woman!

The blast of another shot brought him to his senses, shattering the plate glass of his windshield.

Doc slammed on the brakes. His car careened sideways to a stop. More rifle fire crashed through the metal sides of his car. In a second Doc was outside, kneeling on the street behind the protection of the open door.

Blindly he reached his hand above the hood and returned several shots in the direction of the murderer. He would have no chance against an automatic rifle unless one of his shots happened to get lucky.

Again, rifle fire exploded in his ears. Inches from his ear the side mirror exploded, the glass shattering against him.

Doc fell to the ground, protecting his face. When the echo had again faded, he rose to one knee, then vainly tried to return the fire again. It was useless. The only sound to meet his ears in return was the screeching of tires receding in the distance.

8 8

Claymore's Report

• • •

IT WAS LATE. PAST HIS CUSTOMARY TIME TO RETIRE.

But these were perilous times. He had spent many entire nights in this office of late. There would probably not be much sleep tonight. Fear and anxiety would no doubt keep him too on edge to sleep until those files were back in his own hands.

The ringing of his phone startled him. The defense minister grabbed at it hastily.

"I was assured there would be no unexpected hitches," said a voice he didn't recognize at first.

"What do you mean?" asked Desyatovsky.

"Someone else was there," said the man.

"Where?" asked the Russian, not even sure yet to whom he was speaking.

"At the woman's apartment. Where do you think, you idiot!" snapped the caller.

Now he knew him—it was the fool Drexler had insisted on using. "And?"

"I got out of there, but I don't like being seen. It's a messy complication that is not good in my business."

"A witness?"

"No. I wasn't seen."

"The woman?"

"The job is done. You need not worry about her."

"And the other person . . . what makes you think—"

"Because I was fired at, that's why!" interrupted Claymore.

Desyatovsky thought for a moment. Who else could have stumbled into the middle of this scenario?

"Were you followed?" he asked after a moment.

"What kind of fool do you take me for? Of course I wasn't followed!"

"Then how could—"

"How it happened is your business to figure out!" snapped the angry hit man.

"Did you get a look at him?"

"I was too busy dodging his bullets to look at him!"

"The car?"

"Russian make . . . different license."

"Polish, German?"

"No. I can't be sure. He was racing toward me before I fired at him. But I think they were embassy plates."

"Whose?"

"Can't be positive . . . probably American."

"Hmm," mumbled Desyatovsky, his mind spinning rapidly. "All right . . . lie low. I'll take care of it."

"You had better, my Russian friend, for your *own* sake!"

89

Evil Breed

• • •

WHEN THE DEFENSE MINISTER'S PHONE RANG AGAIN A short while later, he was still deep in thought. He was glad, however, for at least the hint of positive news.

"I think we've got him," said Bolotnikov. "Can you do what is required to close down the Polish border?"

"All of it?"

"Of course all of it!"

Desyatovsky thought for a moment. "It would be better if this had come a few days from now," he said. "An order of that magnitude will involve the Lithuanians, Belorussians, and Ukrainians and could be somewhat ticklish just before we make our move."

Bolotnikov silently swore.

Just three years ago, as KGB chief his power had been so vast he could have shut *every* border down within an hour. Now they were at the mercy of a handful of ridiculous independent republics. Fortunately, that was soon to change!

"At least we could call for everyone being stopped and being thoroughly checked," Bolotnikov suggested.

Desyatovsky continued to weigh their options. Every move they made had the chance of imperiling the coup. "Here's what we'll do," he said after a moment. "I'll call General Shaposhnikov. He's with us. He'll be able to shut down the Polish-Ukrainian border in the south. I'll shut the Russian border down in the north, hopefully discouraging him from crossing into Lithuania. Even if he does, the Lithuanian border isn't long. We'll have to hope for the best. I don't want to stir up the Lithuanians before next week. The problem is going to be the

Belorussian border. That's his most direct route. You say there are two most likely spots?"

"Grodno and Brest," replied Bolotnikov.

"Both in Belorussia. Hmm . . . no, we just can't take the chance of stirring something up there either."

"Can you put it in my hands?" asked Bolotnikov.

"Do you still have people?"

"If you put it in my hands, I will do what needs to be done."

Desyatovsky hesitated only a moment. He had come too far to turn back now. "If you fail," he said seriously, "you must understand, I would have to disavow any knowledge of your actions."

"I understand," replied the former KGB chief.

"Then we are clear on the fact that you are not acting under my direct orders?"

"Clear."

"Then do what you have to do. The Belorussian border is in your hands."

"I will intercept the traitor and have the file back in your hands before the Belorussians have any idea I have even been there."

A slight pause followed. "We have one other . . . uh, problem," said Desyatovsky.

"I'm listening," replied Bolotnikov.

"It appears the CIA may somehow have stumbled into this thing."

"Where? Here in town?"

"Yes."

"I know them all. Do you want me—"

"No," interrupted Desyatovsky, thinking through the myriad of options even as he spoke. "I'll take care of it here. We must get that file! You get to the border and after Galanov."

Bolotnikov hung up the phone. He thought a minute. Then he picked it up again. "Order my chopper!" he barked into it.

Then, gathering up the files with everything they had in the Minsk, Kiev, L'vov areas and whatever they had on the Christians of eastern Poland, he stormed from the room, grabbing only coat, hat, and gun. He needed nothing else. This was not a complicated mission. The tiny slug in his weapon was all he *really* needed!

90
Nabbed

• • •

DAN DAVIDSON, ALIAS BLUE DOC, HAD RECEIVED HIS NICK-
name from a frightening escape on the Yugoslavian coast of the
Adriatic. It had been his first serious run-in with the KGB, and the
method by which he'd managed to escape with his life had labeled
him with the sobriquet for the rest of his undercover career in the
Soviet Union and other points east.

He chuckled morosely at the thought. That's when there *were*
countries called Yugoslavia and the Soviet Union! Now there was
neither.

He'd been driving about all night, trying to make some sense out
of what had happened hours ago, trying to figure out whether to cut
his conscience some slack over the woman's death or whether to
chastise himself for letting something happen he should have been
able to prevent. Thus far he had not arrived at any solid conclusion.

He'd been lucky last night, just like he had been on the Adriatic.
But you never knew if next time fate would fall with you or against
you. Times had eased, or so they said. Last night it hardly seemed like
it! It probably was true, in spite of the incident outside the woman's
apartment. But now more than ever he still had no reason to trust the
KGB to the extent of a hairbreadth.

Thoughts of the old Communist security agency—if in fact it was
the KGB at all who had ordered the hit on the woman—sent his
mind off once more in the direction of his new ally in all this.

Galanov was different. He didn't know why exactly, but he believed him, and certainly the files didn't lie. Something had to be
done, and his own sources told him Galanov had been on the "new

KGB's" hit list for some time. So that, if nothing else, put them sort of on the same side. Although the "new KGB" was technically the U.S.'s "friend," which would make their enemy, the old-style Galanov, still his adversary.

Good grief! He couldn't keep straight all the alliances in this ridiculous new age of the changing world order! Sometimes he wished they could just go back to the *good guys–bad guys* of the Cold War. At least you knew where you stood.

In any event, he didn't trust the new people any more than he had the old. And whether Galanov was on the level hardly mattered. They both had the files in their hands.

If Galanov in fact did get through and blew the whistle on the coup, then fine. But he wasn't going to wait around to find out.

He probably should have been on the phone to the president personally within minutes of seeing what was in those papers. He shouldn't have delayed.

It had gnawed at him all day yesterday and had kept him awake the whole night. It had cost an innocent woman—the woman to whom they owed everything—her life!

What to make of all that religious stuff Galanov had said to him, Blue Doc hadn't an idea. It didn't speak particularly well for Galanov's mental and emotional state. Which was one more reason, besides last night's incident, why now thirty-six hours after they'd parted, Davidson had decided he couldn't sit on what he'd uncovered. His life could be in danger now, as well as Galanov's, and he had to get word to Washington.

True, in his opinion the whistle ought to be blown from inside the Commonwealth rather than by the U.S. for maximum believability.

As he'd reflected on it, however, he realized that was not *his* decision to make. He worked for the CIA, not himself. This was too big, potentially too explosive for him to make such a determination. He had to pass it off to higher powers. Let the Joint Chiefs and the president and the National Security Council decide whether to swoop down in high-profile fashion or whether to wait and let Galanov play out his hand.

He continued driving through the early morning Moscow streets on his way to the embassy, the stolen files beside him on the seat. He had been chastising himself for not making copies instantly and replacing them in Desyatovsky's office so he would not have discovered them stolen. But there hadn't been time, and it would have only complicated everything with Yaschak and the woman. To try to replace them in Desyatovsky's office now was out of the question. He only hoped it wasn't too late and that he hadn't yet discovered them missing. He would fax them to Washington, then follow it up with an immediate phone call.

He was six blocks from the embassy when suddenly the blare of a police siren sounded behind him. He pulled over. Glancing in his rearview mirror, he saw the policeman remain where he was at the wheel.

From the other side of the automobile, a man got out and approached him. The long trench coat, hat, and facial expression left no doubt he was a KGB agent. Blue Doc had been around long enough to spot them in an instant, whether of the new *or* old regime.

"Mr. Davidson," said the man in attempted English. "Would you please come with me?"

"I'm sorry," replied Doc, thinking that they just didn't make spies like they used to, "I'm afraid I won't be able to. I'm attached to the American embassy. I have my diplomatic papers right here."

He started to reach inside his coat, but the man reached through the car window and laid a hand on him.

"Please, Mr. Davidson," he said, sternly this time. "My boss would like to see you . . . now."

"I don't want to see your boss."

"I'm afraid I really must insist." With the words, the barrel of a gun exposed itself through his coat and then neared his head.

"Well, I suppose I could spare *some* time," rejoined Blue Doc, trying to be humorous. "By the way, do you still answer to my old friend Bolotnikov, or did he not fare too well in the recent purge?"

"Comrade Bolotnikov has been called out of town suddenly," the man replied stiffly. "I have been ordered to deliver you to the defense minister, General Desyatovsky."

Blue Doc climbed out of the car.

"Oh, and Mr. Davidson," the agent added, "please bring along the files there on the seat beside you."

PART XI

Das Christliche
Netzwerk

The Summons

• • •

Kehrigkburg, Germany

THE EVENING WAS CALM AND WARM. FROM THE STONE firepit came aromas only a German-style barbecue could produce, though the smoke went straight up through the metal grating which held two or three dozen round, spicy sausages. No breath of wind disturbed the air.

Scattered about in groups of three or four or six were some thirty or thirty-five men and women, with probably an additional dozen youngsters scampering about the nearby field. A more classically German gathering of neighbors and friends could not have been imagined—about half the men held bottles of stout beer in their hands, another half fidgeted at the ground with their walking sticks. Most were attired in cotton work shirts above and either short-cut *ledern hosen* or knee breeches below, while the women wore pinafores brightly colored half or full aprons. Everyone of both sexes was talking and laughing freely, enjoying to the full this opportunity to fellowship in the time-honored tradition of the land.

Their two days with Udo and Christa Bietmann and the Christian believers in and around Kehrigkburg had been rich beyond measure, and now the McCallums were saying their farewells to many new friends.

"Das Fleisch is gleich fertig!" called out a voice from near the fire, signalling the meat's near readiness.

It took nothing further to entice everyone to begin moving in that direction. After a hearty prayer of thanksgiving, Christa began filling plates with potato salad, while the round tubes of spicy pork instantly disappeared from the grill.

Once all the plates were full, the conversation, laughter, and good times continued uninterrupted amid hearty eating and drinking.

"A toast!" called out Udo. "We must toast our guest who has made this feast possible for us."

"Here, here!"

"I shall offer it, then," said a farmer by the name of Micka, who had enjoyed the time perhaps more than the others for reasons known only to him and Bietmann. He had, in fact, been one of the most courageous of Bietmann's fellow underground workers through the years.

Everyone fell silent. Micka, who happened to be a rare teetotaler, raised his glass of *apfelsaft,* while the others raised whatever they were drinking, and spoke out clearly. "To Matthew, Sabina, and Tad McCallum, unexpected but welcome guests of our fellowship. We thank you for your visit. We thank you for providing this opportunity of fellowship. We thank you for the *fleish* and beer!"

Cheers followed.

"Our love and our thoughts and our prayers will follow you wherever you go," added Micka. "We wish you the fullness of God's blessings, and may you return speedily to us again!"

A great cheer and applause went around the group.

"Now they will want to hear from you," said Udo, in a quiet aside to Matthew.

"But they just did last evening," objected Matthew.

"And they want to again," rejoined Udo with a great smile.

Slowly Matthew rose. Before he was able to begin, however, he hesitated slightly, seeing Christa coming from the farmhouse where she had gone a few minutes before. She had walked to her husband and was now whispering something in his ear. The look on his face was serious.

"We came to Germany," began Matthew, "both to see my wife's homeland again and to attend a conference in Berlin on evangelism. Yet I would have to say it has been here among you, speaking for myself at least, that I have observed more concerning the transmission of the gospel than in all the speeches and workshops—" Matthew stopped. Christa had turned and was now walking back to the house.

". . . and we appreciate your hospitality and friendship and spiritual example more than you can know," he added. "The three of us thank you from the bottom of our hearts and pray for the Lord's blessing upon each one of you."

Udo strode forward toward Matthew. "Excuse me, my friend," he said. "Something has come up which requires our immediate attention . . . and prayer."

"Of course," said Matthew, standing aside.

"My brothers and sisters," said Bietmann, "a call of great consequence has just come to the house. My wife is at this moment in touch with our new friends in Moscow. Herr Karl Medvedev has called to inform us that our new brother, whom I told you about and whom we have been praying for, is now on his way to us."

A noticeable rustling of whispered comments and exclamations swept through his hearers.

"He says our friend's danger is great. We must pray. I firmly believe God's hand is upon this man, whatever he has been in the past. Though I have barely recovered from the fatigue since my return only two days ago, I feel I must go to him personally and bring him the rest of the way myself. I want you to see the transforming and miraculous power of God for which our dear Girdel gave her life."

"Let someone else go, Udo," urged Micka. "I am not working and have time—"

"Thank you, my friend," said Bietmann. "However this is something that must fall to me. It is my destiny as Girdel's father. The Lord has uniquely chosen my family—my wife and myself and our daughter—as the vessels through which he has poured his Spirit into the heart of his former persecutor and now his son. It is part of what has been appointed for me also to lay down *my* life for this man . . . a destiny whose path I must follow."

Invitation of Danger

• • •

AN HOUR AND A HALF LATER, AFTER THE BARBECUE HAD broken up following a time of concentrated prayer there in the field around the fire, Matthew, Sabina, and Tad sat with Udo and Christa Bietmann, listening to one of the most remarkable stories of heartbreak, prayer, and victory they had ever heard.

As yet, neither Matthew nor Sabina could know that the man of whom they spoke had been involved as Gustav's assistant in their own escape drama from the Potsdam prison. If they had not exactly squared off against him face-to-face, their paths had certainly crossed his in life-and-death circumstances.

Tad turned to his father once Udo had completed the remarkable tale and said, "This may need to be an article one day."

He glanced over at Christa, weeping silent tears of fresh pain mingled with the joy of God's goodness to them. His mother was sitting beside her, the younger woman's hand resting tenderly inside her own. Sabina too had known suffering, and she was therefore likewise able to comfort.

"People need to hear about the evangelism of sacrifice," Tad added.

Matthew sighed with deep thoughtfulness. *"Greater love has no one than this,"* he said, *"that he lay down his life for his friends.* I was just reading that last night as I was going through John's Gospel again. This is really what it's all about, you know."

Tad nodded.

In one accord, the five joined hands and spontaneously began praying for the safety and future of their newborn brother in Christ, who, even at that moment, though they knew not where he was, was being guided and led and upheld by the new life that was in him.

Even as they prayed, an extraordinary idea began gradually to steal into Tad's brain, discounted at first as mere fancy, but then confirmed as something deeper by the next words which came from Udo's lips.

"You know," said the German, opening his eyes and glancing toward the two American men, father and son, "something has just occurred to me as we were praying."

Both McCallums waited, with looks of question on their faces. "You really are interested in what I have been telling you?" he asked.

"Yes, of course . . . I've never heard anything like it," answered Matthew.

"You want to learn more?"

They nodded. By now Sabina's curiosity was aroused as well, and she was listening intently along with husband and son.

"Do you truly think you might write what I have told you someday, Tad?"

"It's hard to say for certain," replied Tad. "But I *am* a writer—at least I'm trying to be—and as my Dad said, this *is* a pretty special story. Yes, I *do* think people would be tremendously blessed to hear it."

"You would like to help us in what God has given us to do?" asked Bietmann, turning again toward Matthew.

"Yes, of course."

"Then why do not the two of you come with me?" said the German finally.

"To Russia!" exclaimed his two guests, almost in unison.

"To the Polish border, at least. Medvedev says we should reach the border just about the same time as their people."

Father and son looked at one another in astonishment at the idea.

"Wow, that is some incredible idea!" said Matthew with a wide-eyed sigh.

"And you put it right out of your mind, Matthew McCallum," said Sabina, in a humorous tone but leaving no doubt as to her seriousness. "You led one escape already, and that is enough for one lifetime. I wouldn't dream of letting you go!"

Matthew laughed.

"You and I are too old for that sort of thing anyway," Sabina added.

Tad was silent. The same thought had already occurred to him as he'd been praying.

"I would love to," Matthew went on, "notwithstanding Sabina's protests. But with the conference, I just don't see how I could. I'm feeling rather negligent already. My sense of responsibility is weighing heavily on me."

"You are right," said Udo. "It was thoughtless of me to put such a question before you when you have prior commitments you must honor. And I would be loathe to divide you and your lovely wife on the matter."

Matthew laughed. "Little chance of that, my friend," he said. "If I agreed to go with you, she would no doubt be right at my side, with as much courage and pluck as any two men half her age!"

"How about you, Tad?" Bietmann now said, turning in Tad's direction. "You do not have to speak at the conference. What might be my chances of enlisting your help?"

"I am supposed to be covering it. That's why I was sent to Berlin, after all."

From Tad's tone, it was abundantly clear there was little enthusiasm remaining for his original assignment.

"This is ten times the story you'd get in Berlin," said his father. "If your editor doesn't understand the importance of this, then send him to me. I'll straighten him out!"

Tad laughed at the thought of Matthew squaring off with Lockhart. A moment or two of silence followed. At length Tad simply began to nod his head slowly, as a grin spread across his face. "I think perhaps it's exactly what I'm supposed to do," he said.

"*Sehr gut!*" exclaimed Bietmann.

"When do we leave?" said Tad, his excitement mounting.

"If we're going to get there in time," answered the German, "we'll have to leave tonight . . . at the soonest possible moment."

At the words, Tad's first thought was of Lisel. He had told her he would be back tomorrow. "As long as I may make a telephone call to Berlin before we leave," he said.

Strange Byways

•   •   •

Western Belorussia

ANDRASSY GALANOV WAS STILL NEW ENOUGH AT BEING A Christian that he wasn't accustomed to stopping to pray every time he turned around.

Not everyone he'd met did so. But this fellow did.

It had been a real education, meeting a new Christian man or woman every several hours as he'd been handed from one to the other across northwestern Russia, then into Belorussia; from Moscow to Smolensk to Minsk to Baranavichy.

He'd traveled in automobiles, in cars, on motorcycles, in a boat along the Dnieper between Orsa and Mogilov. Most of the connections, however, had been made on foot, in woods and on obscure trails, at some of the most out-of-the-way places imaginable.

Finally he was having the opportunity to witness firsthand how they had been so adept at keeping clear of the KGB all those years. Now his own life depended upon the very network he had tried so hard to destroy.

There had been prayers and words of spiritual greeting at every juncture, mostly between the men and women of the network. He'd felt like a mere observer most of the time. With some there had been no conversation beyond absolute essentials. Others had been quite talkative, speaking of the changes that had taken place and welcoming them. The silent ones seemed still living in the fear of the KGB finding and imprisoning them.

None, he realized, had any idea who he was. His German friend had made sure that part of the mission remained secret when the thing had been initiated in Moscow through the contact Medvedev.

"Come, my friend," his present guide said, interrupting his reverie, "we are nearly to the river where I will leave you. We must pray that we make it before daylight, otherwise our contact will return home and you will have to spend twelve hours in the woods until evening."

With the words, the slender, talkative man stopped, got to his knees, and prayed similar words to those he had just spoken to Galanov. Then he rose, seemingly satisfied, and said, "We must hurry. We still have three kilometers ahead of us."

Galanov was a strong man but was tired. He'd been at this longer than his endurance was used to, even as strenuous as his work had sometimes been.

Even after they reached the border, he still had to get across Poland. That should be easier, he thought. The KGB's access wasn't quite so free there these days, from what he understood.

How could he have ever known what was in store for him when he left Moscow with Medvedev? No wonder they'd never been able to lay hands on the network! Rostovchev had set everything up not only with painstaking brilliance, but even here and there was a stroke of flair and fun, almost daring the KGB to its face. After hours of furtive hiding, they made one contact in a bakery right next to the police station and at the very time several policemen were gathered about. Who but a confident humorist could have dreamed up such a scheme!

There were traipses through forests, long tedious automobile rides, and quick naps on couches, in backseats, or even on a floor if that was all that was available.

There was the fix they had gotten into with the taxi driver in the middle of Smolensk! There was the adventurous ride that covered many kilometers in an old, ancient biplane that seemed held together with nothing more than baling wire.

He gathered, of course, that every job the network did went differently, that different people and routes and handoff patterns were used, and that none of these people knew very much. None had any idea about the Moscow parts of it, nor even where they were taking their "captive" at the border. Each merely did his particular assignment, conveyed beforehand by some method of contact by word of mouth. Sometimes telephones were used also, but always in code, giving rise to very odd-sounding conversations indeed.

Two hours later they emerged from a clearing. His guide stopped. The half-moon gave enough light for him to see the shimmering of a river in front of them.

"It is still dark, and we have arrived," said the man. "Here is the boat."

He went to the water's edge. There, tied to a tree, was a tiny skiff with a single paddle.

"Get in, then make your way to the middle of the river," he said. "The current is not swift but you must steadily paddle across. There—" he pointed downstream—"you can see a tall tree standing alone."

Galanov looked, then nodded.

"It is one-half kilometer downriver. At that tree you will be met by another brother, who will take you to his home in the town of Mosty, where you will have a few hours' sleep. Godspeed, my friend."

With that, the slender, praying man disappeared back into the woods.

Untying the boat, Galanov climbed inside.

That was the way this went. They disappeared with as few words as they appeared. It was not a way to make lasting friends, he thought, only brief and passing acquaintances.

He gave the boat a shove with one foot, then leapt inside and sat down. In a few moments he was silently moving slowly downstream, wielding his oar as best he could toward the tree-destination in the distance.

94

Doc under Wraps

• • •

Moscow

UNDER MOST CIRCUMSTANCES BLUE DOC WAS A REASON-
ably even-tempered man. But this was not a reasonable nor usual
circumstance, and he was furious. He stormed across the small room
for the fifteenth time, letting fly a small wooden stool, which crashed
up against the wall.

He had been in confinement now for over twenty-four hours in
this small dingy apartment. He was cold. He was going stir-crazy. But
most of all he was angry.

How dare these Ruskies pull an old Cold War maneuver like this!
Someone would pay when he got out. And pay good! He would pull
every diplomatic string he had up his sleeve, even if it meant going
right to the top.

Going to the top—he didn't even know what that might mean by
now. The thought sobered him. He relaxed and sat back down.

It was probably too late to stop the coup. They'd taken the files, his
gun, even his ID, then thrown him in this makeshift cell where he'd
been under locked house arrest ever since.

At least he wasn't hungry. They were feeding him, he'd say that
much for his captors. And there had been not so much as a hint of
violence. They had just immobilized him.

He recalled his brief interview with Desyatovsky right after being
picked up. It hadn't amounted to much, only an interrogation: How
had he gotten the files, who had helped him, who else knew . . . that

kind of thing. He hadn't told them anything, and though he could tell the general was boiling and nervous inside, he'd kept his cool.

"Well, at least I have the files back, Mr. Davidson," Desyatovsky had said at length. "But I do want to assure you that whatever you may think you deduced from what you saw here, let me tell you it is not what you may have surmised. We have different methods of operation in the Commonwealth, even in this new era. Your Western minds are not able to grasp our ways. So in the interest of continued cooperation between our two nations, I would ask you to put the contents of these files out of your mind."

Yeah, yeah, sure, buddy! thought Blue Doc to himself, but only nodded in acknowledgment.

Then they had hauled him off to this dump!

His only other visitor had been a KGB interrogator, probably a lackey of that fellow Bolotnikov's, a real throwback to the old days.

He hadn't been so subtle. His anger he made no attempt even to mask. He'd come in threateningly and hadn't asked but had demanded to know who was in on it with him.

The interrogator never said Galanov's name, but it was clear he knew. Blue Doc had been intentionally vague, and had implied that he'd already passed the information along to the powers in Washington.

He only wished he hadn't been lying! It was a sure bet now that he wasn't going to have a chance to talk to *anybody*—in the CIA or in the State Department or the Pentagon or the White House or anywhere else—until these bad guys had done whatever they planned to do.

He hoped Galanov was out of the country by now.

Expanded Network

• • •

Western Poland

"IT WAS PERHAPS SELFISH OF ME TO ASK YOU TO JOIN ME," said Udo Bietmann.

"Are you kidding!" replied Tad. "What an adventure! I wouldn't miss it!" His only regret about the trip, which he did not share, was that Lisel had not been home when he'd called. He hadn't made contact as he'd promised, and now he would not see her for who could tell how long.

Even as far north as they were, the night was now black as the two made their way along the narrow two-lane road heading east. They had crossed the Polish border out of Germany about thirty minutes earlier, and in Bietmann's compact European-version Ford with the extra gas tank one of their number had installed for just such occasions, they would be able to drive easily to their Warsaw contact, where they would refuel and see if any further instructions had come. Bietmann hoped to be through Warsaw and on toward Bialystok well in advance of morning, but much would depend upon conditions they found as they drove through the night.

Their destination at the Russian border lay some five hundred kilometers ahead of them.

"You mustn't be cavalier about what we have before us," rejoined Bietmann. "It is a mistake Westerners often make about Christian work in this part of the world."

"I'm sorry. I didn't mean to take it lightly," said Tad. "I only meant that I am very glad to have the opportunity to participate with you."

"I was sure such was your intent."

"I am curious, though. What did you mean with the use of that word?"

Bietmann thought seriously for a minute. "For some time after the borders were opened," he replied at length, "it was difficult for me to understand the peculiar air I noticed when Christians from the West began filtering into East Germany in greater numbers."

Again Bietmann fell silent, staring ahead through the darkness as the car bounced along the road.

"Actually, to explain what I meant, let me tell you about two men. The first is a friend of mine, Franz Schmidt, a West German with relatives in the East. He has long been permitted to travel somewhat freely and has been visiting our fellowship, and others like it, for years, smuggling things to us that we have been unable to get. Bibles and literature sometimes, but more often items of even more practical use—a guitar or harmonica, a tape player, food, books in German, perhaps material for the women, a new pair of boots for one of the men. Sometimes even the simplest packages are so welcome—a box of fresh fruit could bring tears to many eyes. You have no idea how deprived of the simplest things we have been for many years—things you took for granted in the West. Franz has been for us a lifeline to keep us sometimes from despairing of all hope. It is through Franz that I obtained some of your father's books.

"Then the second man I would tell you about is your own grandfather, Baron von Dortmann. What a dear man! And the reason I would mention him is this—he was willing to suffer for his faith and to pray for God's people. He has all these years been almost a legend among us—in the proper sense—as an example of spirituality and godliness. That may explain to you why we think so highly of your father and mother."

Tad nodded. "Yes . . . yes it does. I appreciate your sharing that with me."

"And by extension, I would have to add your own father to the list. Perhaps I should have said *three* men."

They drove on a while more in silence.

"Your father and Franz," he continued at length, "are unusual. Since the Wall came down a few years ago, and especially since reunification, we have had many, many Christian visitors from the

West. I do not know how, but they have found out about our fellowship and other churches and fellowships like ours. There have even been those who have come seeking me out—by name. How they know of me, I have no idea. The isolation we felt for so long—that same feeling no longer is present. There has been great contact with Western Christians from America. And do you know what they all come to say?"

Tad shook his head as Bietmann glanced over at him.

"They do not come to listen to us, to share, to talk quietly, to pray. They do not want to know what we are thinking or feeling. Did you notice your father and mother around the people of our fellowship? They listened. They looked upon them with love."

"But they are *one* with you," said Tad. "My mother is German. How else would they be?"

"They could have become Americanized very easily. No, it is not your mother's German blood that accounts for the difference—it is the sort of man and woman your father and mother *are*. The others—they do not come to know us by first name, and when they leave they do not say the kinds of things your father and mother said about helping us and wanting to be part of our lives."

"What then?" asked Tad. "Why *do* they come?"

"They all come to start their *own* works, as they call them," replied Bietmann. "They come to us because they think we can provide them a local base from which they can establish a church or a ministry or, as I said, what they so proudly call a *work* of God. I must apologize if I sound somewhat disdainful. But we are nothing to them if we express hesitation. They do not see us as fellow brothers and sisters. Their only desire is to expand their own organizations. If we will join them and let them affix their label upon us, then great is their enthusiasm. Then money will come and people will come and literature will come and 'missionaries' from the United States will come to 'spread the gospel' in the East.

"But if we try to say, 'God is at work here and we too are seeking to spread the gospel. We do not want to become part of your organization, but we do have needs that perhaps . . . ,' we do not even complete such an explanation before they are gone to find some other place where they can erect their building and put up a sign to proclaim the *work* that has *their* all-important organizational name attached to it."

"Is your friend Schmidt still coming?" asked Tad.

"Yes, bless him! And still bringing needed items, and still wonderfully without some program he wants to press upon us. His love has been demonstrated through the years, and he continues to show it in such practical ways."

"There is no one else like him . . . even now?"

"I tell you the truth, Tad. I have been visited personally by twenty-one American Christians or groups of Christians since reunification. You and your parents were the twenty-second."

"That must keep Christa busy! Did they all stay with you?"

Bietmann laughed. "Tad, don't you hear what I have been telling you? *None* of them stayed with us! You are the first. There have been no fellowship meetings of prayer and sharing such as we enjoyed with you, no barbecues. Not a single one of them knows of the network or of the expansiveness of the connective links between the Christians and fellowships in the East. They came, they talked *at* us, and they left just as oblivious to our real situation as when they came. They would not have *wanted* to stay with us even if I had had the opportunity to ask."

"But I don't understand. Where *did* they stay? What did you do with them?"

"They stayed in hotels in Berlin."

"But so did we."

"It's different. You've been at a conference. They drove out in fancy cars, dressed in suits. They came with packaged speeches informing us of all the benefits of becoming part of their organizations. They came with a patronizing air that expected our people to rejoice as if the liberators had come. They came—and some even had the condescension to say so to our faces—to spy out the land for the Lord, as if now, at long last, God's work could proceed in these forsaken parts of the world now that *they* had come."

"Did they participate at all in your fellowship?"

"With some the arrogance was so thick I did not introduce them to a single one of our number. I took their leaflets, saw what they were about, and told them we would not be interested in further contact. Others were genuine in their hearts' desires, and yes, we enjoyed fellowship with some of these. But without fail, all eventually came round to pulling out their organizational agendas and asking us if we wanted the exciting opportunity to join *them* in *their* groundbreaking work of spreading the gospel in *their* particular ways. Can we establish our *Baptist* work or our *this-or-that* ministry?

"But none of it addresses our real need here in the East. What we *need* are people helping and supporting us and *our* ministries, in the schools and workplace, helping to train our new young pastors who are coming up. You came and mixed with our people on their level, and that makes all the difference in the world. Especially now, with so many of our people out of work and in desperate straits for the most basic necessities of life, the words of these well-dressed people with their talk of spying out the land—it all falls on deaf ears! Your father's providing meat and beer and treating these people to what for them is a great feast went further to strengthen the bonds of brotherhood than anything any of all the other twenty-one visitors even thought of doing."

"Did none of them offer to help you, to bring you things you might need?"

"Not one."

"Not even Bibles, Testaments, literature?"

"Well, yes, of course there has been much more available than ever in the past. We have always been able to get Bibles here in Germany without a great deal of difficulty. But in Poland and Russia and some of the other places it is opening up tremendously now. So in a way I misspoke when I said they have offered nothing. It is a blessing that the Scriptures are pouring into the East in such vast numbers. Yet even that is often impersonal. In some of the larger cities, these materials either get to the black market or make enormous profits for officials rather than feeding hungry hearts. They bring their loads of literature and Bibles, almost, I sometimes think, more for the sake of how it makes them look good at home rather than for the lives that could be changed."

"Do you honestly think that is true?"

"You see it in their eyes. Some visitors come with boxes of Testaments and books to offer us. We take what they give, and with thankful hearts. We are appreciative. But in their faces you can see the pride. It is as if they are about to say, 'Just look at what *we* brought you! Aren't you grateful to us?'

"It's not a giving of sacrifice, but a giving of pride. There is 'giving' and then there is *giving*. There is pretended sacrifice, then there is *sacrifice*. There is the appearance of servanthood, then there is *servanthood*. Appearance counts for more in many people's estimation than they even know themselves. What does it *cost*—what real personal price is there—in the way of death to an individual's *self* to serve another? That is the question.

"It used to be the same way with some of the Bible smugglers back in the old days—especially the *teams* of Americans who would come in for a two-week 'holiday' of taking literature across the Iron Curtain. They cared nothing about us as real people with real needs. They only wanted to feed their own egos by being able to tell people about their experiences out on the front lines smuggling Bibles for the Lord. Our friend Schmidt, Brother Andrew—men who risked their lives time and time again to help us, not just pad their list of spiritual credits—they were few and far between."

Both men fell silent for some time. Bietmann drove on, passing not a single car for more than five minutes.

"All this is why I said to you not to be *cavalier*," he said at length. "So many of your countrymen come here with a subtle spiritual superciliousness that does not dignify them or endear them to Christians in the East. From the moment we met you struck me as a young man of deeper substance than that. I have enjoyed your presence these last two days. I knew immediately that you were of the same spiritual fiber as your father and mother and grandfather. Therefore, I want you to see what we are on a deeper level than most of your countrymen are capable of."

"I appreciate your sharing with me as you have."

"What we are about is serious business. It could be dangerous. Quite frankly, when we were praying earlier I felt an impulse that I might need someone else on this mission, and for some unexplained reason I thought of you. I felt it was no accident that you and your parents were at our house when the summons came. I hope that impulse is indeed the prompting of the Spirit."

"There are very few accidents either of timing or circumstances for God's people," replied Tad. "This is no accident. I too believe it has been set up by the Lord for a reason only he knows."

"Perhaps you will write about the things I have spoken and the things you have seen. Christians in the West need to know the state of affairs here now just as much as they did back in the days when persecution was rampant."

"I hope that I shall have the opportunity."

"In addition, if the next couple of days are anything like what they *could* be like, I am going to need a strong prayer warrior by my side. That was my chief reason for feeling like you needed to be here, to be that warrior with me."

"I will do my best."

"Simply pray that the enemy's power will be bound, Tad. There is a new order in the world, to be sure, but the power of evil is undiminished. Men out for their own gain still play for keeps, as I believe you say."

Tad was sober. "This man we are going to help," he asked, "besides what you told us earlier, is he an important man in the government?"

"No," reflected Udo, "not in the government, no more than any ex-KGB agent running for his life. No man is more important eternally than any other. Yet this man's conversion was dynamic, and I believe his testimony will carry wide and far. We have to get him out, Tad. There are forces who would silence him. I believe God's hand is upon him to spread the gospel mightily."

"Why did he not come with you when you were in Moscow just days ago?"

"As I told you, he was a KGB agent. His conversion was sudden and unexpected. It was a privilege to be a small part of it. So sudden did the change come upon him that he was not able to instantly leave his old life. He was still in the middle of many things. He did not confide totally in me, but he said he had to stay to tie up some things that the Lord would have him finish. He was onto something political he felt he had to resolve. I knew the danger he was in in Moscow, and I did my best to get him to come with me. But he said he had to know, that there were dangers and plots afoot, and that he had to follow up on the leads he was pursuing."

"Sounds dangerous."

"The man spent his whole life as a spy, Tad. It is a far different world than you and I know."

"Do you know why there was difficulty getting him out?"

"I don't know that there was difficulty. Apparently there were many factors adding to the risk."

"Like what?"

"No details. It was an emergency message, and they are usually scant on specifics."

"Why you? Are you Mr. Big?"

Bietmann laughed. "Hardly. But I am one of those who has been involved in the network a long time. Don't you know who the real Mr. and Mrs. *Big,* as you say, are . . . or I should say were?"

"No, I guess I don't."

"You own grandfather, Tad—*he's* the one who started all this, during the war. After the war, when he was in prison, it was your mother who began expanding the *Network of the Rose.* It all goes back to those two, their prayers, their obedience . . . and their courage. Hasn't she told you all this?"

Tad took in Bietmann's words with seriousness.

"No, she never said anything quite like that," he said after a moment. "Only that she was involved."

Bietmann smiled in the darkness. "Knowing your mother as I have come to—I'm not surprised," he said. "Even I did not know who she was when first we met. I was relatively new to the network then myself. It was only after they were gone that the truth began to dawn on me about who it was whom I had been able to help."

"And since then?"

"I suppose it would be accurate to say that I have been privileged to play an increasing role as the network has expanded. And because of my proximity to Berlin, I suppose I have been rather in a prominent position in the whole thing, kind of the Western focal point as *Der Prophet* was its Moscow link. He was the start of the line, I was the end, so to speak."

"*Der Prophet?*"

"A long story. I'll tell you about him, perhaps, on our way back through Poland . . . that is, if we get back."

"That is why they contacted you?"

"There is of course the reason of my association with him."

Bietmann paused, thinking. "You must understand what a dreadful persecutor and Saul this man was," he went on. "His conversion was one of the most remarkable things I have ever witnessed. But there are others among the believing fellowships that may not be so ready to accept an old enemy. I encountered that already in Moscow. With him now in difficulty, it is doubly important that I be there with him. He may need an advocate even among believers if we do get him safely out of Russia."

"His own personal Barnabas," mused Tad. "This is certainly more intriguing than the speeches I was hearing in Berlin!"

"You ought to get some sleep," said Bietmann. "It's after midnight, and I may need you to help with the driving later on."

•   •   •

Unknown to either of the Christian men, theirs was not the only automobile driving eastward through Poland that same night. And though the destination of the two cars could be said to be the same, upon what different missions were they bound!

The one was on an errand of mercy, while the other, which carried Horst Brandes and Lisel Lamprecht, had been summoned by the angel of death.

Lisel was a pawn in the enemy's hand, an unwitting and—thankfully—more and more an unwilling one as well. She was not yet aware, however, how much stronger her conscience had already grown. She would soon have the opportunity to find out.

Many prayers were being answered, in both cars, most of all the prayers of two loving fathers in regard to their daughters. The one daughter was already with her heavenly Father, while her earthly father prayed for the man who had sent her there.

The other was nearly ready to turn her steps around and return home.

Border Lodgings

• • •

Near the Polish–Belorussian Border, South of Krynki

IT WASN'T THE MOST DELUXE OF ACCOMMODATIONS. Andrassy Galanov had slept in some of the finest hotels in Moscow, Kiev, Prague, Bucharest, and Belgrade. Even a few in Paris and London. A pile of straw and hay didn't exactly compare to silk sheets and luxurious featherbeds. But at least this barn's roof overhead seemed intact. And the straw was dry. After the night hours he'd spent getting here from Masty, he wasn't about to complain.

The sun was just coming up, and its orange rays splintered through the boards on the barn's eastern wall. Even that wouldn't keep him awake. He lay down in a soft pile of straw, leaned his back against a still-bundled bale, and closed his eyes.

They'd come down through Volkovysk by car. They were not big towns and would not be watched, his guide said, especially not these days. There had been a border crossing, he'd said, at one time between Volkovysk and Bialystok in Poland. But the fence had been erected and the road torn up for about seven kilometers on the Russian side.

Those last seven kilometers they had walked.

And now, within sight of the border fence separating the former Soviet Union from Poland, he would spend the night in this old barn, owned by the Christian brother who was supposed to know how to get him from here across the border, over the fence and into Poland.

How, Galanov didn't know. But if there was one thing he'd learned, it was to trust these people. They knew what they were doing.

And they prayed a great deal. They *had* to, they said. Too much was at stake for them *not* to pray, as they were teaching him, without ceasing.

He had a cousin, the man said, on the other side, in Poland. Because of their relation, they had been allowed to maintain some degree of contact with one another, more contact in fact than the authorities on either side knew of or would have approved of.

The huge tract of land had been in the Polish family for generations and had been farmed by their great-grandfather and grandfather prior to the Second World War when the entire region was part of Poland.

As Russia encroached ever further westward between 1940 and 1945, however, a portion of the land fell under Soviet domination. The result was that when the borders of the Soviet Union were redrawn after the war to include its areas of conquest, Poland lost more of its traditional land than Estonia, Latvia, Lithuania, Romania, or Czechoslovakia.

The family farm thus found itself sliced right down the middle. And Galanov's present guide, though a Pole by birth, heritage, and blood, found himself raised in Belorussia, a republic of the Union of Soviet Socialist Republics. His father's portion of the land was confiscated by the state and made part of the Soviet communal system, though the family was allowed to continue living on it and work a small segment of what had once been their ancestors' fields.

Somehow the brothers, fathers of the two present cousins, had contrived to keep up communication across the border, an accomplishment aided by the fact that this section of the Polish-Russian border was not as closely patrolled as certain others.

The fact that they were also Christians led eventually to the involvement of their sons in the underground network. Even as teenagers, the boys had rigged up a makeshift telegraph between their two homes by the use of underground wires. Though men of the soil by day, both had something of a flair for gadgetry (as well as for the dramatic), and thus by night they continued to fiddle with contraptions and expand their modes of communication, to the point that, though they could not visit in person, they could talk with one another nearly at will.

Their mutual delight being to outwit the system that had destroyed their farm, they eventually designed a means to cut a small hole about half a meter in diameter through the border fence, while bypassing the electrical signal that would have tripped the alarm at the guardhouse three kilometers away.

All it had taken was an hour during which the electricity was shut down for maintenance. The hole was cut, new electrical connections were soldered in place, and the removed piece was put back in place. With the aid of some transplanted wild shrubbery that grew freely in the region, the woodsy portion of fence was never seen up close and inspections were minimal.

The immediate effect was that the cousins were now able to visit one another and plan additional relatively innocent shenanigans in person. In time, however, as their faith deepened and they became more involved in underground Christian activities, dozens of Christians fleeing the Soviet Union made their way through the homes of these two Polish cousins living on either side of the border. Their activities had taken on greater importance as well with the imprisonment of their mentor.

This had been their first visitor, however, in two years.

"Why do you not simply cross at the border?" the man had asked Galanov, still confused as to why the stealth network of the past had been requested in this case. "They hardly even check papers these days, everything is so relaxed. If I want to go see my cousin, I merely drive around. I could take you into Poland by car rather than all this hiding."

"They would check *my* papers," laughed Galanov. "Unfortunately, they are looking for me, probably at every border crossing between the Black Sea and Finland."

"What did you do?" asked the man in some surprise. "Are you a criminal?"

Again Galanov laughed. "The less you know, the better, my friend. No, I am no criminal. At least not against the Soviet state," he added pensively, thinking sadly again of the crimes against God's people that were on his shoulders. "No, if I am to get out," he added, "I will have to do so in secret. I am sorry to have to put you through all this, especially after you have not had to do it for so long."

"Please, do not apologize! You cannot imagine how dull life has been. I have scarcely slept since receiving word that you were coming to us. I do not know who you are or why your escape is so important. But my cousin and I will do all we can to help you. I will always be a

Pole, and until this fence is torn down and I am reunited with my family and we can once again farm this land that is *ours,* I will dedicate myself to the work of freedom."

"I cannot thank you enough."

"I do not care if it is called the independent state of Belorussia or if it is a union or a commonwealth or if Gorbachev or Yeltsin or the president of Belorussia is in power. This land is *Polish* ground, and I will always be a Pole. I will never forget that they stole it from us, whatever talk of so-called independence they now are so free to say to the world. They are still a nation of robbers and murderers, and making it a Commonwealth of Independent States changes nothing. They are still descendants of Stalin, whose soldiers killed my grandfather."

"I am sorry," said Galanov.

"It is a time long past," said the farmer. "You can see why my cousin and I take freedom seriously. Being Christians means nothing to us unless we can give tangible help to others. This is the way he has given us to do it. And . . . here we are," he said, opening the rickety door and leading his guest inside.

"What now?" asked Galanov.

"You must sleep in the barn today. My wife will bring you supper at dusk. Get as much sleep as you can. At midnight you will make your escape into Poland."

Remembering a Time of Peace

• • •

Kehrigkburg

WHILE TAD AND UDO DROVE EASTWARD THROUGH THE night, and while the man they hoped to help lay in a bed of straw, Matthew and Sabina slept contentedly in Christa Bietmann's home.

Now, after an enjoyable breakfast with Udo's wife, they were on their way to the Mennonite community where they had spent such happy and relaxed days thirty years ago, prior to their escape to the West. The morning and early afternoon that followed were hours of great joy for Sabina and Matthew.

Not many situations in life exist where one is allowed to go back and recapture former joys without the intervening years having sufficiently altered circumstances and individuals and relationships such that the luster and glow with which one's memory retains past images and happy interludes is faded with time's passage.

This, however, proved to be one of those rare moments in which the years, however many they be, melt instantly away and all is as it was before. Great were the embracings, laughter, and tears at the reunion with many of their friends from thirty years earlier. So little was changed, except of course that *everyone* had aged thirty years, as had Matthew and Sabina. Arndt Moeller was gone, though his aging widow yet lived, whose son was now one of the three elders of the community.

On this occasion, as the afternoon wore on, it was Matthew and Fritz Moeller who could be seen out quietly walking in the fields in place of the baron and Fritz's father—quietly, except for those instances when Matthew would unexpectedly break into laughter in remembering a certain section of field he had plowed or as he paused to stoop down and plunge his hand into the earth, remembering how wonderfully special this ground had been to the three pilgrims during those dangerous days of hiding back in 1962.

The years had brought the mantle of gray to new heads. These two now discussed and pondered many things, not the least of which was the legacies of the two men in whose footsteps they walked. Relishing to discover, each in the other, another of like vision, they found themselves wondering aloud how most effectively to pass on the older men's spiritual perspectives to rising generations, as those values had been inculcated into them.

Meanwhile, the kitchen remained the center of the women's activity and conversation. Sabina felt no time had passed at all! Three generations were present, from Sabina and Frau Moeller and several others, to the mothers who had been children during Sabina's first visit, to the scampering youngsters who represented those who would carry on the fellowship and who were the chief object of the prayers of the two men outside, walking and communing together concerning the deep things of life with God.

A feast more wonderful than could be imagined was enjoyed by the entire community in the Moeller home at four o'clock that afternoon, but by seven there began to be sad and reluctant acknowledgment concerning the necessary return to Berlin on the part of their two honored guests.

"Could you not just remain the evening with us and leave in the morning?" begged Frau Moeller.

Matthew and Sabina looked at each other, then laughed. They had already been gone from the city longer than they had anticipated. What would another night away hurt? More entreaties followed, and consent was eventually given. They did not find their way to their beds in their new accommodations until past midnight.

They would have to return to Berlin, if for no other reason than to catch up on their rest!

· · ·

As they drove back to Berlin the following morning, feeling happy yet weary, Sabina unexpectedly found her thoughts returning to Hermann.

He, of all her old contacts and friends, had been most involved with her for the longest time. He was as much responsible for their freedom as anyone. He had literally risked his own life and freedom for them.

He was one of those kinds of individuals whom she never really felt she "knew" at a level of intimacy, yet whom, once he was no longer part of her life, she realized she greatly *loved*.

Her old colleague of *The Rose,* more than anyone else she had ever known, confirmed to Sabina the truth that perhaps intimacy of the spirit presented itself in a great variety of—sometimes disguised—human packages.

Some inner sense told Sabina he was yet alive and still in Berlin. If only there was some way to find him, to look into his eyes again . . . and *tell* him what he meant to her.

Dominoes Begin to Fall

• • •

Brest, Belorussia

"I THOUGHT YOU HAD HIM!" EXPLODED THE RUSSIAN defense minister into his telephone.

"I *will* retrieve your files. It will just take a little longer than I had anticipated."

"Your last words to me were that if we closed down as much of the border as possible, you would be able to intercept the traitor. Now I've involved Shaposhnikov. I've made the other calls. We picked up the CIA man and have him on ice—"

"Did he talk?" interrupted Bolotnikov.

"He's blustering about, trying to make us believe he did. But he couldn't have. He still had the file, and there's been no whisper of anything out of Washington. If he had already talked, their lines would be buzzing with it."

"If he had the file, then perhaps Galanov is a red herring."

"No, you idiot!" yelled Desyatovsky. "Davidson had a *duplicate* file. He and Galanov must've gotten together on this thing. Galanov's still the target. You *must* locate him without delay!"

"My leads at Brest were all dry. Nothing is coming through here. I have memorized every route used from here to the Lithuanian border. I am leaving momentarily and will personally inspect every known possibility. I have some of the best people who are still loyal to me tracking down every known Christian we have in our files to personally interrogate them. If something is afoot through the old network, my people will discover it."

"Time is critical."

"I will be in the air momentarily. We will work all night."

"I tell you, there is not a moment to lose. The accident en route to Kirovabad from the reactor site at Kuybyshev is all set. The details have been worked out. It's in motion, I tell you. So is everything! We're all dead if you don't get to Galanov!"

"I will get to him."

"Alekdanyov is set to roll the interviews," went on Desyatovsky, livid with combined wrath and fear. "I've been in touch with Gorbunovyev just today, and I've spoken by phone with Petrikov, Dzasokhov, and Baramertnykh. The second round of factory explosions began last night. Bobrikov called a general strike on nationwide television just two hours ago. Khasbulachek is going to seize control of the rail lines sometime tonight. The dominoes are falling!"

"What about Germany?"

"You leave Germany and that featherhead Drexler to me! He'll do what he has to do in their parliament. I'm going to call him the second I'm off the phone and tell him he'd better make his move or be left behind."

"You can count on me to do my part."

"Words, Leonid! I want results. You put that file in my hands before tomorrow's sunrise, or I'll send you down the river with the rest of them!"

Bolotnikov winced as he heard the phone being slammed down at the other end of the line. He did not like being treated like anyone's fool. The day would come when he would make even a man as powerful as Desyatovsky pay for treating him so.

Shaking off the residual effects of being dressed down by his superior, he drew in a deep breath, then left the office where he had been and ran back toward his waiting helicopter.

99

The Rose Fabric Is Woven in a Circle

• • •

Bialystok, Poland

EVEN AS MATTHEW AND SABINA WERE ENJOYING THEIR renewal of fellowship with the Moellers and other Mennonite families, their son was deeply engrossed in dialogue with one of Joseph's former acquaintances from the Bialystok fellowship.

It had taken the first hour of their visit, chatting informally, for the connection between their various paths and histories to become known. The interconnection of strands had then accelerated the conversation greatly.

The Pole was anxious after news of the wandering Jew he and his friends had befriended so long ago and was excited to learn that Tad had been with him and had even met their beloved Dieder Palacki only a few days earlier in Berlin. Thereafter, the questions flowed rapidly for some time.

"So you were imprisoned, but not for your faith?" Tad asked the man who had been their host for the last three hours.

"I was considered a dissident," he answered. "It was back even before Solidarity made strikes popular. Lech Walesa became president. I, however, years earlier was only imprisoned, beaten, and eventually released to live out my days in quiet retirement. It is what comes, I suppose, of trying to change the system before the time is right."

"How long *were* you in prison?" asked Bietmann.

"Only four years."

"But Palacki wasn't a union or labor leader and he was in prison for much longer, as I understand it."

"No, only a pastor. But he was more outspoken in matters of religious intolerance than any of us speaking out about other things. Moscow and its Warsaw puppets hated him."

"How long was he in?"

"Fifteen years."

"You say you met him in prison, after not seeing him in all the years since they took him away from his home?"

"He had already been there six years when I arrived—a pitiful sight when I first laid eyes on him. I hardly knew him. I remember thinking to myself with horror, 'What if the same fate awaits me!' I thought I would rather die than go through what Dieder had obviously endured. There were purple splotches all over him from the beatings, lumps about his head, and scabs from dried blood on his lips. It was nauseating just to see the poor man whom we all loved so dearly."

Tad McCallum and Udo Bietmann had arrived at the home of Kochow Rydz, in mid afternoon, Warsaw time. They had napped and were now conversing with their host as his wife prepared an evening supper for them. They would try to sleep again before receiving their instructions from Rydz as to their nighttime rendezvous with their final contact, his friend and network brother, Waclau Chmielnicki, a member of the Bialystok brotherhood who had been a mere lad when Joseph met him, whose farm, they were told, sat adjacent to the Russian border about forty-three kilometers to the east.

"Did you and your friend Palacki have much fellowship while in prison?" asked Bietmann.

"We were in nearby cells," replied Rydz. "But it would hardly have mattered. Everyone in the prison knew Dieder. Even in prison he was on a mission, and eventually he managed to speak to every man there."

"Mission?" repeated Tad.

"His faith. You cannot imagine how seriously he took the Lord's command to spread the gospel. Even though he received new beatings every time they learned he had been talking to someone about God, he never stopped."

"How did he survive it?"

"One look into Dieder's eyes and you could tell something burned inside him unlike other men. We here of the Brotherhood knew it from the time he was a teenager. That is why we made him our pastor at such a young age. He was a man set apart. In spite of the bruises and scars and obvious malnutrition, even in prison his eyes glowed with life, and even in the midst of that horrible place . . . a love. You knew he *loved* you with one look from his eyes."

"Did many become believers as a result?" asked Bietmann.

Rydz nodded thoughtfully. Even as he did, Tad thought of Joseph.

"I don't think any man could for long witness the sufferings of a man like Dieder Palacki," replied Rydz, "and see the love in his heart without being changed by it. It seemed that usually men gave their hearts to the Father after only two or three conversations with him. They wanted the life they saw in him. There was a good chance they would both be beaten for what they did, but Dieder lost no opportunity to pray with whomever he could."

Both listeners were silent for a moment. Then Tad asked, "Were you?"

"What?"

"Beaten when you prayed together?"

Rydz smiled. "Yes. There were a number of such occasions. We prayed together every chance we had. More often than not we were beaten or sent to solitary confinement for it afterward. I could never have endured it for a month had I not had Dieder as a constant example of faith before me. How many times I heard him pray for his tormentors!"

"And you were there four years?"

"Altogether, yes . . . four."

Bietmann chuckled. "I thought it was difficult for *me*," he said. "I was imprisoned twice, and the total was only about two and a half years."

"You didn't tell me about that!" exclaimed Tad, turning toward the man he had thought he knew.

"In this part of the world, Tad," said Udo, smiling, "we do not make so much of our badges of honor as you Americans like to. Suffering has come to us *all* for our faith. It is expected. We do not make much of it."

Bietmann turned toward Rydz. "What eventually became of Palacki?" he asked.

"He was in prison a total of fifteen years," replied Rydz. "By the time he got out, though weak in body, the man had become a saint. There were fellowships and underground churches all over Poland, Bulgaria, Romania, even in Russia, where he eventually went. Everywhere I found myself I discovered men and women who credited Palacki's love and faith and forgiving heart with their own salvation. How many spiritual sons and daughters that man has throughout the Eastern countries—it must number in the many thousands!"

"Just like our family's friend Aviz-Rabin," commented Tad.

"Exactly."

"Did he return here to his home?" asked Bietmann.

"No, he has been among us very little actually. His parents were both dead, and he feared endangering us."

The room fell silent. There were many things to think about.

"It's a pretty amazing story," reflected Tad with a sigh. "But then this whole trip has been one amazing story after another."

"We're not through yet," said Bietmann. "Hopefully before this night is out, you will meet a man with one of the most moving salvation experiences you will ever hear about."

"Who is this man?" asked Rydz.

"I hope to be able to introduce you to him as well," said Bietmann.

"I would be honored," said Rydz.

"Truly," said Bietmann, "our Father makes no distinction between men when he sovereignly chooses those who will carry forward his work in the world."

100

End of the Hunt

• • •

Polish–Belorussian Border

ANDRASSY SLEPT WELL. AS WELL AS HE'D EVER SLEPT BE-tween silk sheets. The day passed quickly. Cold dinner off a wooden plate could not have tasted better with candles and linen and silver. He slept again in the evening.

Before he knew it, a hand on his shoulder roused him. "The time has come," said the voice of the Belorussian Pole.

They crept out of the barn. His guide carried a small pocket flashlight. They walked some distance across a field and through some trees.

They stopped.

His guide signalled three short flashes toward the Polish side. A moment later, two brief flickers of light shone from amid the trees.

He sent back an answering signal of two flashes.

"That is my cousin," he said. "He is ready. The coast is clear on his end."

"Is it always the same?" asked Galanov, surprised at the seeming simplicity of the exchange.

"No, we always contrive a different signal and go at different times of the night. We used to use very elaborate systems of camouflaging our movements. But it is different now. The dangers of the past do not exist like they once did."

"I hope you are right."

"Let us go."

They moved toward the fence, walking in the darkness through a lightly wooded field of sward and shrubbery.

Suddenly above them the whirring blades of a huge helicopter thundered menacingly through the night! A giant bright spotlight roamed and scanned the ground.

It took but two or three seconds to find them, and there it zeroed in. The two stood emblazoned in a wide beam of light from which it was impossible to hide. Overhead the helicopter hovered, sending hurricane winds down upon their heads.

"Do not move! You are well covered," a voice spoke over its loud-speaker. *"Ground patrols also have you surrounded and are approaching. Any attempt to flee will be met with machine-gun fire."*

As if to punctuate the seriousness of the speaker's intent, the air split apart the next instant with a few deafening rounds of fire.

A quick volley of bullets slammed into the ground about ten feet from where they stood. Galanov made no attempt to run. It would be futile. He knew the man in the helicopter meant business. It was a voice he recognized only too well.

PART XII

Climax of the
Quest

101

Last-Minute Pressure

• • •

Berlin

A KNOCK CAME ON THE DOOR. MATTHEW ROSE AND answered it. In the hotel corridor stood conference director Darrell Montgomery.

"I heard you were back in town," he said, shaking Matthew's hand. "I thought I'd better check and see if everything was OK."

"Sure, Darrell," answered Matthew, "couldn't be better. Would you like to come in?"

"Only for a minute."

He followed Matthew inside the suite and greeted Sabina. Then both men sat down.

"Well, tonight's the big night, Matthew," Montgomery said after an awkward pause.

Matthew nodded unenthusiastically.

"You are still planning to speak tomorrow?"

"I only said I'd pray about it," replied Matthew. "I made no commitment."

"You didn't say no."

"Neither did I say yes."

"I merely assumed . . ." Montgomery's voice trailed off.

"Dieder and I were praying together several days ago," said Matthew. "We both asked that the Lord would show us when to speak and when to be silent."

"You and Palacki know one another personally?" asked Montgomery, a hint of concern showing through.

Matthew nodded. Montgomery took the information in with interest. It wasn't healthy for malcontents to spend too much time together. "And what *has* the Lord shown you?" he asked.

"I think Dieder feels he is *supposed* to address the conference."

"And you?"

"I don't know yet."

"Come on, this is the climax of the week," expostulated Montgomery. "I hate to say it, Matthew, old man, but your lack of eagerness doesn't look good for the conference."

"I'm sorry, Darrell," said Matthew sincerely, "but I have to do what I feel is the right thing."

"You can't leave me hanging like this. You'd better get your head on before you take the podium."

"Don't worry, Darrell. *If* I take the podium, I won't embarrass you."

"It might do you good to hear these guys tonight. I tell you, Matthew, seeing you wander around here at the conference with a faraway expression, it makes me wonder if you aren't slipping a bit. Take care, Brother."

"I'll watch myself."

"You'd be welcome to share the platform tonight with the rest of the featured guests."

"No thanks, Darrell. Being featured, as you say, is hardly a concern of mine. Sabina and I will be sitting well in the back somewhere."

"Come on, old boy," said Montgomery, his frustration showing through. "You just don't understand—some of us, yourself included, are in positions where we must occasionally assert our leadership gifts and callings. The flocks need shepherds."

"Speak for yourself, Darrell. As for me, all I want to do is live as God's man. As God's *child,* I should say. But *not* as God's leader and spokesman. So thanks all the same. But I don't want to be on the platform with you. We'll see about tomorrow. I'll let you know."

"All right, pal. Be careful. I don't want it to get out that you backslid while at *my* conference. Bad for my reputation, you know. Ha, ha!" He laughed, then rose and walked to the door. Matthew shook his hand again, then closed the door behind him.

Matthew turned back inside, looked at Sabina with an expression for which no accompanying words could have adequately been found, then let out a long sigh as he sat down beside her. "I think I need to go out for a long walk. I need to find some quiet place where I can walk, or maybe sit down and read, and talk to the Lord until I have a definite answer about what I'm supposed to do."

"You're feeling that you ought not to speak though, aren't you?" said Sabina.

Matthew nodded. "You do know me!" he laughed lightly. "But I've got to be sure—you understand."

"Of course."

"If the Lord wants me to, I have to be willing."

"And you are."

"I suppose. Yet I *am* feeling that this may be a time when silence is the proper response, rather than adding my own words to the multitude already spoken. But, as I said," he added, "I have to be sure."

Uncertain Allies

• • •

"GUSTAV, HOW ARE YOU?"

"Sehr gut, Herr Chancellor," replied Schmundt into the telephone.

"Please, Gustav," said Kolter, "why so formal among old friends? I thought we covered that last time we spoke. Allies *and* friends, am I not right, Gustav?"

"Yes . . . yes, of course, Hans," replied Schmundt, trying to hide his nervousness. He had hoped not to have to speak to the chancellor again personally. But at least he had called and not summoned him again to his office.

"The time has come, Gustav," Kolter went on, "for us again to put that friendship to the test, and to demonstrate to the world, as we have to our own nation, that we are dedicated to the future. Do you not agree?"

"Certainly, Hans."

"The debate has nearly run its course, Gustav. I am planning to call for a vote on the aid package this afternoon. It will no doubt be tight. Our mutual friend Herr Drexler has succeeded in being highly persuasive among some of our colleagues. It could be that the Greens and FDP will vote with him. Have you heard anything to that effect, Gustav?" queried the chancellor.

"Only that what you say is correct," replied Schmundt. "Klaus has been very active." Schmundt's tone was guarded.

"The media and international community are with us in this," rejoined Kolter. "The others, I am certain, will see their required course of action in the end. The mandate upon the German government to take the leading role in helping the new Common-wealth is clear. I do not think we have anything to worry about."

"I am sure you are right."

"Still, I was uncomfortable with some of what I heard voiced from the floor this morning. Though Drexler himself cleverly remained silent, it was clear where the arguments against me had originated."

Schmundt did not reply.

"In any case," Kolter went on, "though it would tarnish my standing somewhat, even if he does take the FDP and Greens with him, the CSDU/CDU coalition will carry the vote."

"I see what you mean," said Schmundt, sidestepping Kolter's primary point. "A strong victory would speak a firmer assurance of our position."

"Yes, but we will take what *we* can get, will we not, Gustav?" replied Kolter, deliberately emphasizing the word.

"A victory is a victory," answered Schmundt.

"Good . . . good! I just wanted to make sure we were still together on this," said the chancellor. "But I'm sure you have things to do before we reconvene, so I'll let you go."

"Very well, sir."

"I'll see you in session, Gustav."

Schmundt hung up the phone. He was sweating freely.

103

A Lucrative Offer

. . .

Moscow/Berlin

"CLAYMORE, YOU IDIOT! WHAT'S THE IDEA OF CALLING ME here? I gave you this number only for an emergency."

"This may qualify."

"Has something gone wrong?" asked Drexler.

"It's all hitting the fan."

"So I understand. Don't worry—it's controllable."

"I'm not so sure. Your Russian friend is flying loose."

"Desyatovsky?"

"Yes. This place is a powder keg. I'm coming back . . . for payment, and to get out of the way of this plan of yours before it comes down on my head!"

"Wait!" exclaimed Drexler, his mind working rapidly.

Claymore, however, was in no mood to do so. "Wait for what?" he rejoined. "Another day or two and the military will be in control around here. By then the borders may be closed. I'm coming back. I tell you, the Commonwealth is about to unravel, and it's going to get ugly. Half the republics are on the verge of anarchy."

"Relax . . . relax," chuckled Drexler at the man's anxiety. "That's all part of the script. We planned it so. Believe me, it's all under control. Desyatovsky has people pulling the strings everywhere—the military included. Even if they do close the borders and some fighting breaks out between the republics here and there, you have no need to worry. As long as you're with me, Desyatovsky will protect you."

"Hah! The man's a Russian!"

"We can trust him."

"I trust no one!"

"I tell you, everything's under control."

"And I tell you, this country's about to explode! Do you know the fellow Bolotnikov?"

"Heard of him," replied Drexler. "He's in on it with us, from what I understand."

"He's a loose wire too."

"Then follow him. If he gets dangerous, kill him. Desyatovsky would never link it with us."

"Easier said than done. Bolotnikov's a man even *I'd* not willingly tangle with. Besides, I lost track of him. He took off after someone."

"Ah yes," reflected Drexler, "the agent with the file. Is *he* still on the loose? I was assured the hole would be quickly plugged!"

"Who knows!" spat back Claymore. "Bolotnikov's still not returned to Moscow."

"Then you pick up his trail and get on it. The fellow he's after *must* be stopped dead."

"Find someone else!"

"There is no one else. Neither is there time to fool around. You get to Bolotnikov's prey ahead of him, snuff him out, and retrieve what he's carrying, and I'll triple your payoff."

The phone was silent. Suddenly it was Claymore who had gone pensive. "I had already made arrangements to secure help at this end."

"What's that to me—I told you before, just get it done."

"You've got yourself a deal," he said after a couple moments. Bringing Brandes over from Berlin had been a good move, he thought. Cheap insurance. He might even give him another couple thousand marks and let him do Bolotnikov on his own.

"Good. Get on it!" shouted Drexler into Claymore's ear. "The next time I hear from you, I expect you to be calling from inside Germany to tell me you have the file." Drexler hung up the phone.

Slowly a smile spread across his lips. If the fool Claymore *could* get to the traitor before Bolotnikov, he would then have the ultimate weapon to use against Desyatovsky in the future—proof that he had orchestrated the whole thing. It would make the Russian dolt his puppet forever. The file's being stolen from Desyatovsky's office might turn out to be the best thing that could have happened!

He rose, the smile fading. However, in one thing Claymore had been right—his concern over the volatile unpredictability of events in the Commonwealth once everything began. There was always the possibility that Desyatovsky, like Gorbachev before him, would not be able to control events once he opened the door to change. These next forty-eight hours would tell the whole story and determine the course of the world's future. If Russia and all the other republics *did* unravel or blow apart, that still changed nothing about what he had to do to ensure *his* destiny.

It was time to make his move against Kolter. He would do so this very day.

He walked from his office and down the long corridor. The vote was imminent. He needed to talk once more to Keil Weisskopf, leader of the Greens, and the FDP's Otto Greim.

He would play his final cards with each man and ensure his desired result with a bit of unexpected coercion.

104

Parting with the Past

• • •

Polish–Belorussian Border

LISEL HAD HAD AT MOST THREE HOURS' SLEEP ALL LAST
night and today, with an equally unsatisfying amount of food.

She and Horst had arrived near the Polish border, where his
contact had told them to wait, in the early hours of daylight. She
had been cramped in the car, with only an occasional walk to
stretch her legs, ever since. Horst had gone out several times but
had returned with nothing more than several bottles of warm beer,
which more than the fatigue accounted for the redness in his eyes
as the day wore on.

All Lisel managed to get into her stomach was the end of a loaf of
bread she had brought from home, which she now munched on as
she waited still one more time for Horst to return.

The all-night drive from Berlin and now this day that followed
brought many unexpected things to the surface of Lisel's consciousness. Most pressing upon her was the simple question: *What had she
ever seen in such a life?*

All at once the glamour, the purpose, the intrigue was gone. It was
a *nothing* life!

And Horst! *What had she ever seen in him?* Her eyes were
opened to his true character—shallow, self-centered, with no
goals beyond immediate self-fulfillment, possessing no values,
sloppy, ill-kempt, unmannerly, capable of thinking of no one
ahead of himself.

Simply put, he wasn't particularly pleasant to be around. He was selfish. He couldn't carry on an intelligent, rational conversation about anything other than his radical political views. Courtesy, thoughtfulness, graciousness—these concepts might as well have been from another solar system for all he knew about them.

And besides all that, today he smelled. Now that she thought about it, he always did. How could she have been so oblivious to what he was really like? How could she have been so oblivious to so *many* things? What kind of a life was this she had been living these past ten or twelve years? Pigs had it better than the people in some of the places she had lived!

Bleary-eyed, Lisel glanced up to see Horst running toward her out of the village at whose outskirts they had parked. In his wide flaming eyes was an obvious look of frenzied enthusiasm. Even as he ran, he lifted a bottle to his mouth, finished off the contents as best he could, then tossed the bottle off to the side of the street as he approached.

"I finally made contact with Claymore!" he exclaimed excitedly. "It's on! Both parties involved are on the other side where he's staked out. He gave me descriptions and told me where we should station ourselves."

As he spoke, Brandes was fumbling frantically about in the backseat of the small automobile. Lisel assumed he was rummaging for another bottle of beer.

At last he succeeded in dislodging a piece of the floorboard, which he pulled back to reveal a small hidden compartment. The next instant he was settling into the front seat beside Lisel, holding a Russian issue automatic handgun in each of his palms.

With a crazed expression that suddenly struck Lisel as frighteningly that of a maniacal wild man, he handed one of them to her.

"What are these!" exclaimed Lisel in horror.

"What do they look like?" laughed Brandes in a demented tone. "They're the tools of our trade!"

"Guns have never been the tools of *my* trade, Horst! What are they for?"

"To do the job we came here to do."

"The *job?*"

"We're going to kill a high-up KGB agent. It'll make headlines all across Europe!"

"Horst!" said Lisel in terrified disbelief.

"I told you it was big, Lisel. Don't turn soft on me now. You know the stakes." His voice had suddenly turned cold and sarcastic.

"We've never used guns before."

"Speak for yourself," laughed Brandes heartlessly.

"Horst!"

"Don't be so naive, Lisel," he spat with derision.

"Naive! I thought we had ideals," she said in a pleading, almost desperate tone. She could not believe what she was hearing. "I thought we stood for something—namely, freedom. What kind of freedom is it to take another person's life?"

"Bah! You sound like some fool of an American!" he shot back. "In this part of the world, freedom isn't won without blood being shed."

"That's not the way I want to stand for freedom."

"What—are you going to back out now! You're about ten years too late, Lisel!" Brandes laughed cruelly.

"You've never put a gun in my hand before."

"Well, I'm putting one in your hand now. And if you're with me, you're going to have to use it."

"I will *not* use it! I will have no part in killing!" Lisel jerked open the car door.

"Lisel, don't be a fool. We're in Poland. You've got no car, no money, no place to go. You *have* to stay with me!" His tone was threatening not reassuring.

"Now that I know what you are, Horst Brandes, I will not stay with you another second!"

Lisel jumped out of the car and began to run down the street away from the village, tears welling up in her eyes. It was all the more horrible that the nightmare of realization had come so suddenly.

"Lisel, come back!" shouted Brandes. "You can't get far alone. If you don't stay with me and see this thing through, Claymore will come after you. He's not as compassionate as I am."

Still Lisel ran, crying freely now, having no idea where her steps were taking her.

Brandes watched her go, the alcohol in his brain dimming both vision and judgment. She would be back, he told himself. She could not survive without him. But he was not going to chase after her. Let the vixen come crawling back herself.

In the meantime, he had better delay no longer. He turned the key in the ignition, then put the car into gear. It was time he got to the place where Claymore had told him to wait.

It would not do to keep *him* waiting.

105

At the Border

• • •

TAD MCCALLUM AND UDO BIETMANN HAD ARRIVED TWO hours after midnight at the Chmielnicki farm just over the Polish border from the former Soviet Union.

An earlier rendezvous had been planned, but at the last moment a call to the Bialystok home of Kochow Rydz informed them that strange movements and the sound of a helicopter had been detected on the Soviet side of the border. They were asked to delay their leaving a few hours. They had heard nothing more of the state of affairs until now.

Waclau quickly filled them in on the situation as it then stood with his cousin and the man they had come to escort to safety. "They were captured just on the other side of the fence," he told them. "We were so close, and then suddenly the helicopter was there, and I could do nothing."

Tad and Bietmann looked at one another in alarm.

"I cannot imagine how they knew precisely where we would be," continued Chmielnicki.

"Were they hurt?" asked Bietmann. "Have they been taken back to Moscow?"

"Nobody was hurt, and no, they are still in the area," replied Waclau in mingled Polish and German. "Luckily they did not know I was hiding in the trees. Otherwise their spotlight could have found me too. I have no doubt the man in the helicopter would not have hesitated to use his machine gun."

"They did not see you?"

"No. I crouched down and watched. The helicopter landed. A large man got out, carrying a gun. There was some talk. They loaded my cousin Jahn and your man into the helicopter, then flew off. But they did not go far. I was able to follow the light and sound of the helicopter. After they were gone, I snuck through the fence and pursued the direction they went. It was less than three kilometers to an old abandoned guardhouse where at one time the road went through. The helicopter set down there, and several cars were around. I have had someone watching it ever since, and they are still holding them in one of the detention rooms. All the old border crossings had facilities for prisoners. The helicopter flew away after a while without passengers, but all the cars remained."

"And now?" asked Bietmann.

"We are still watching the site from our side of the border. There is activity about, though how long they will interrogate them I do not know. They could transfer them back to Moscow any moment. We can assume the helicopter will be back to pick them up."

"Is there a way across the border there by the old road?" asked Bietmann.

"No," replied Chmielnicki. "The road used to go through, but was divided by a high fence with concrete footings going deep and treacherous barbed wire all along the top. They keep it well lit, as well. And especially now that they have prisoners there, it is heavily manned."

"And where you went through?"

"An opening we made years ago that bypasses their circuitry."

"What's the distance again?"

"Approximately three kilometers."

"Wooded or open plain?"

"Both. There are many trees nearby and dense shrubbery that we make sure stays healthy and growing freely. Still, it is a wonder they have not discovered it. Perhaps it is such a desolate-appearing spot that they do not think to search it. We have been blessed with safety through the years."

They all were silent a few moments thinking.

"Well, I suppose what we must do first is pray," suggested Bietmann.

"We already have the word spreading out to the Christians of the neighborhood and the men of our brotherhood," said Chmielnicki.

"In the middle of the night?"

"You are here, are you not? When it comes to God's work, there are no off-hours, either for the laborers such as yourself *or* for those who pray."

"You are right." Bietmann smiled. "Are there others we can use to help us if need be?"

"Four or five I can count on."

"Good."

"One of them is standing watch even now. Come," said Chmielnicki, turning from where they had been standing with a vantage point toward the border, "let us go inside. My wife will make something warm for us to drink. We will ourselves pray and talk about what is to be done. Then the two of you must sleep."

106

A Simple Prayer

. . .

HOW LONG LISEL HAD BEEN SITTING ON THE BROKEN AND dirty sidewalk at the edge of the village she had no idea.

It was mid to late afternoon, though she was hardly thinking of time. Her stomach was making noises, but she was as unaware of her own hunger by this time as she was the hour of the day. She did know she was thirsty, but had not yet decided to try to do anything about it.

Her face was splotched with teary traces of dust. She had sobbed and wandered about for an hour or more, heedless of direction, only trying to keep out of sight. She had enough of her wits remaining to realize that the look in Horst's eyes said that for two marks he might just as well use one of those guns on her.

As the afternoon advanced, however, concern for her own safety began to give way to the realization of just what Horst had said, that he was going to try to *kill* a man.

The very idea was too horrible to think about!

What could she do to stop him? How could she prevent this murder into which she had almost been drawn herself?

Once the questions began, however, they proceeded to get worse and worse. What *could* she possibly do? Horst was right—she was utterly alone, in a strange land. She had nothing. She could do nothing. How was she even going to eat, drink . . . or find her way home?

Horst was her only lifeline, her only link to the past—yet now she did not know where he was, and even if she did . . . she was afraid of him. How could she stop him? How could she get home?

She had never felt so alone and forlorn and without anyplace to turn in her life. All former self-sufficiency had vanished. In its place was only despair and loneliness.

At length she stopped and nearly collapsed where she now sat at the side of the street, breaking into fresh sobs.

Lisel sat weeping for a long time. Then, from some deep reservoir of desperation came to the surface three unplanned whispered words she would never, two months ago, have dreamed to hear herself utter. *"God . . . help me!"*

Unexpected Reunion

• • •

TAD AND BIETMANN HAD SLEPT AND NOW, SOME FOUR-
teen hours after their arrival, sat in the Chmielnicki farmhouse with
a half-dozen Polish Christians—including two who had been involved during the equally dangerous time when Joseph had been
making his similar escape—discussing one final time the plan that had
been formulated that morning.

It was not without a good many risks. Bietmann had insisted that
those risks fall primarily upon him, and Tad had offered to take his
own share of the danger.

Waclau had to remain where he was, Udo had said, living near the
border and above suspicion. There could be no risk of his capture
without jeopardizing the future of the escape network should it be
needed again.

Likewise, he had insisted that the rest of the local Polish fellowship
had to remain behind the scenes, where their risk of apprehension
would be small.

Even as they were speaking, Erik Gomulka, another member of
their fellowship arrived. He took Waclau aside. "On my way over," he
said, "I found a young lady, a German, sitting alongside the road. I
stopped to see if I could help, but all I could get from her was talk
about them trying to kill someone, and her getting home."

"Who is trying to kill whom?" asked Chmielnicki.

"I don't know." Gomulka shrugged. "She was hardly coherent,
and I could understand but little. She is in pretty sad condition,
obviously hasn't eaten in a long while, and absolutely fatigued."

"Where is she now?"

"I brought her here—I hope you don't mind."

"Of course not. Bring her in. My wife will bathe her and feed her and put her to bed. But what do you make of her talk?"

"I don't know. I wondered if it might have something to do with the man the German is trying to help."

Chmielnicki nodded seriously. "I think we had better find out what we can from her," he said.

"And then perhaps—depending on the extent to which she is involved—talk to the German about some way to get the young woman back to Germany."

Chmielnicki nodded again. "Bring her inside, Erik," he said. "I'll explain the situation to the others."

Gomulka returned outside to his car, while Waclau rejoined the group of men in his sitting room. Before he was even through recounting their brief conversation, Gomulka reappeared.

Tad was out of his chair the next instant.

"Lisel!" he exclaimed, hurrying forward.

"Oh . . . oh, Tad . . . but . . . but what—"

The poor, exhausted, hungry, frightened, bewildered soul could find no further words to express the enormous relief that had suddenly exploded into the midst of her confusion and despair. She fell into Tad's waiting arms and wept like a baby.

It was some time before he was able to piece together any kind of explanation to Bietmann and the others, to which, in time, were added Gomulka's fragments, and, by degrees, Lisel's side of the story.

Udo Bietmann would never have known his daughter's friend from long ago had Tad not spoken her name. As it was, he knew it was the girl his network colleague had not seen in more than a dozen years. Tears immediately filled his eyes.

All through the Galanov episode he had seen the hand of God's prayer-answering purpose. But he never dreamed that dear Hermann's prayers for *his* daughter would be thus bound up in such an unexpected way with his own for Girdel. He would have to walk carefully and prayerfully around her, however. And he must *not* reveal the full extent of his connection, or Lisel's, with the man they hoped to rescue. She would likely not be strong enough to handle that information for a good while.

Within an hour, Lisel regained coherence sufficiently to pass on her side of the affair. Even though he had changed very little, given her physical and emotional state and the utterly foreign environment in which she suddenly found herself, she did not at first know Bietmann as the father of her childhood friend.

Before Waclau's wife took her away, Bietmann made himself known. Lisel took in the news as but one more addition to the bewilderment already contained in her suddenly altered circumstances. She was too weary of brain to sort through it all, and actually she could hardly remember him.

"Get some sleep, my dear," concluded Bietmann. "Be assured that you are among friends here and that I will do everything I can to see you safely back to Berlin."

Lisel went off into the tender care of Waclau's wife, who, after giving her a bath and light meal, put her to bed. In just minutes Lisel was sleeping soundly.

Though not learning anything of specific benefit to their plans, the men, meanwhile, surmised that their own new brother Galanov was indeed the intended target of Lisel's demented colleague.

"It would appear," said Chmielnicki, "that we have even more cause for caution than we realized before."

As they returned to their planning session, Bietmann reviewed the creation of the diversion, the details of which they had been reviewing before Lisel's appearance. He himself, he said, would drive the primary target vehicle.

"They could blow the car up with one explosive missile from the helicopter," objected one of the Poles.

"That is a chance I shall have to take," replied Udo. "I do not think they will, however. They will try to take us alive."

"When they do stop you, what is to keep them from killing you?"

"Again, there is always that risk. But for one thing, I will be on Polish soil, and in this new era I doubt they will risk an incident. Secondly, I believe I will be able to convince them that I am merely an innocent German on a sightseeing trip who wandered too close to the border."

The men around the table fell silent, thinking through again the many details that would have to work with precision timing if their plan was to succeed.

"Now remember," said Bietmann at length, "the car I need must be with a large and powerful engine, preferably a Mercedes, and *not* an automatic transmission. It must have loud gears. Will you be able to locate such an automobile?"

"We shall find one."

"And soon. We must be ready to act the moment the helicopter returns."

"If the man in the helicopter does not return to the guardhouse?"

"We must hope he will. The helicopter is vital to our success."

"The car you request will be here within an hour."

"Good. Make sure your watchman informs us the instant there is a hint of the chopper. Once it lands, we will have to act speedily. His intent will probably be to start the transfer of the prisoners immediately."

Shocking Vote

• • •

Berlin

THE ATMOSPHERE IN THE GERMAN PARLIAMENT THROUGH-
out the afternoon of discussion and debate had been heated. But not
to such an extent as would have indicated the momentous course of
events that was about to be precipitated.

By day's end the 650-plus Bundestag members were tired of the
pro and con arguments, tired of this unwelcome interruption of their
summer's recess, and were ready to vote and return to their homes.
Most were inwardly annoyed at Kolter's calling of the special session.
And why in Berlin? It was inconvenient. Most of their offices were
still in Bonn, and, symbolism or no symbolism, that would have been
the logical place to have held the session. But they had gone along
with it—including the symbolism—in view of the seriousness of the
times and the issue at hand.

The vote had at length been called for and was now proceeding.
After a few predictable remarks no one in the huge hall paid much
attention to, Chancellor Hans Kolter, speaking on behalf of the CDU,
cast all of the party's 211 votes *for* the proposed aid package.

Klaus Drexler rose next, and with a smile a bit too smug in
Kolter's view, in light of his certain defeat, cast the 197 votes of the
RDP *against* the measure, without so much as a sentence spoken
besides.

Keil Weisskopf of the Greens rose and spoke briefly of the merits
of the bill and the need for the nations of the West to lend their
resources and energies to upgrading the standard of living in the

newly freed countries of the former Soviet Union. Certain reservations, however, had come to his mind about the bill very recently, he said, which was why he had felt compelled to modify his party's previous inclinations. He was therefore voting *nein* on the measure, in hopes that a more comprehensive package would emerge in the near future. He sat down, amid some noisy surprise in reaction.

Kolter was clearly shocked by the sudden reversal. He tried to relax and calm himself, however. The loss of 51 votes would not hurt him. But he would talk sternly to Weisskopf later.

Next in order came Alex Mieklin of the DHP, whose 63 *ja* votes quickly put Kolter's coalition back with a comfortable leading margin.

But just as soon as the chancellor had begun to breathe somewhat easier, he was stunned by another defection, this time the 33 *nein* votes of the FDP's Otto Greim, whose brief speech of explanation resembled Weisskopf's too much to be coincidental.

Kolter sat in his seat furious at the turn of events. He hardly heard the *ja* ballots of the CSP's 27 votes in his favor. Kolter now had 301 votes. And though the CSDU's 87 would sufficiently bury the opposition, the fact that Drexler had managed to amass 281 votes and take two of the other minor parties with him was an infuriating development. There would be recriminations; he would see to that!

Slowly Gustav Schmundt rose to his feet.

As the largest of the five smaller parties in the Bundestag, how many times had he relished the role of being the last to cast the votes of the CSDU. The CDU/CSDU/DHP coalition had survived for ten years as a result of his loyalty. He and Kolter had lost a few battles, but he had remained loyal all those years. Usually two or three of the other minority parties sided with them. But now suddenly an unsettling shift seemed occurring in the Kolter coalition.

Only he, Gustav Schmundt, knew how titanic that shift truly was. Again he felt himself perspiring uncomfortably. But he had made up his mind some days ago. His course was set. He wasn't going to look back now.

All eyes rested upon him. Gustav Schmundt, for better or worse, was suddenly the man with the fate of Germany's destiny in the new world order resting upon his shoulders. Not Kolter's, not Drexler's . . . but his.

"My colleagues and friends," he began softly, trying desperately to mask his nervousness, "this matter before us today is one of far wider import than merely momentary aid to the former Soviet republics. Were economics the sole issue, our decision would be a relatively simple one. However, what we face, whether we are fully aware of it or not, is a decision that will set us on a course for relationships with these new sovereign states to the east of our borders."

As he spoke, Schmundt's confidence grew. Kolter found himself listening in rapt attention, hardly recognizing the former East German he had rescued from oblivion and, till now, taken completely for granted.

"A destiny rises before us," Schmundt went on, "that supersedes this present moment—a *German* destiny. The questions we must ask ourselves, we of the newly reunited German nation, must focus as intently on where *we* are going and what leadership role *we* are going to play in the new realignment of the European community. Do we sacrifice our own assets, our own strengths, at this critical time when we are already stretched to our limits? Or do we perhaps take a long-range view, saying no today in order that a strong Germany of the future can offer more and deeper leadership and assistance in the future? These are questions it behooves us to consider as . . ."

If he had not already begun to divine the extent of the defection against him by the resolute timbre of Schmundt's voice and the steadfast avoidance of the chancellor's eyes as he spoke, the single word *no* of his last sentence surely alerted Hans Kolter to the danger ahead. For several moments his brain ceased to comprehend meaning from the sounds flowing from his former friend's lips.

When Kolter came to himself, it was only to hear the staggering words, ". . . for all of which reasons, my party, the CSDU, has decided to cast the entirety of our ballots *against* the measure before us." Schmundt sat down.

Immediately shouts and claps, along with astonished gasps, broke out all over the floor, while two dozen of the parliamentarians jumped up and raced for the doors. The unexpected defeat of the chancellor would make international headlines within the hour!

Kolter sat ashen and stunned. He turned and sought Schmundt's face amid the pandemonium. But Gustav was turned the opposite direction. He knew what he had done, and he would not gaze upon the victim of his treason.

Suddenly Drexler was on his feet, calling in a loud voice to be heard. *"Meine Damen und Herren!"* he cried. "Please . . . remain in your seats yet a moment more!"

Gradually he was able to restore order sufficiently to be heard. "Knowing your anxiety to be out of Berlin, I must yet ask you to remain for another day," he said, still speaking loudly. "This recent vote indicates but the last in a series of disturbing fractures in the Kolter coalition, demonstrating the inability of our chancellor to effectively govern this body. I am therefore calling upon the Bundestag to render a vote of no-confidence, so that the coalition I will be forming will be free to form a new majority in this body. I call upon you to render your decision tomorrow afternoon. At that time each of the parties will finalize this referendum upon who is to lead Germany forward in the years ahead!"

Again pandemonium broke loose. This time it did not diminish until the hall was empty an hour later.

The Wait

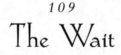

Polish–Belorussian Border

"THE CAR IS IN PLACE!" SAID A TRIUMPHANT VOICE IN POLISH as the young man entered the house.

The men gathered around Waclau Chmielnicki's table turned their eyes upon the newcomer.

"They saw it from the guardhouse on the other side?"

"Perhaps. I do not know. I backed up slowly, by degrees, while they were occupied elsewhere. By the time I snuck out and to the woods, the car sat only fifty meters from the fence."

"Excellent . . . well done! But they did not see you?"

"I made sure of that. I slipped away when the two men had returned to the guardhouse for a moment."

"Probably to report the presence of the automobile," laughed one of the men.

"If not," remarked Bietmann, whose rusty Polish was quickly returning to him, "be sure they will take note of it before long. Exactly as we wish. Still there is no sign of the helicopter?" he asked the man who had just returned.

"None," the man said, shaking his head.

"What about the man and car I described?" asked Lisel, who, after a two-hour nap, was feeling much improved and wanted to help however she might.

"I think I spotted the automobile, not far from where I parked the Mercedes," answered the newcomer, "but there was no sign of your friend."

Lisel nodded, wondering if she ought to go out looking for Horst. She thought better of it, however.

"When I left the car," he went on, "I ran to the wood and rejoined Raul and young Leeka where they were watching north of the old road. Raul said all was still quiet and that there had been no change."

There was thoughtful quiet a moment.

"And the key?" asked Bietmann at length.

"In the ignition. No one will bother the automobile."

"Anything special I should know?"

"It is a standard German Mercedes. Pull it down into first gear and it should make all the noise you want."

"How did you come by it?"

"Please, my friend," said the man, revealing a smile only half full of teeth, "do not ask. I am a mechanic with many contacts. Let me only say I borrowed it from an acquaintance who will never know."

One or two of the others laughed. This was clearly not the first time their comrade's ingenuity had been used on behalf of the network's business.

Bietmann nodded with a smile, joining in the fun. But when he spoke again, it was to return the conversation to the serious business at hand. "Timing is the key," he said. "We must act instantly. If they get them away from the guardhouse, everything is lost."

"Young Leeka is the fastest boy in our fellowship. He is but eleven, but he will cover three kilometers in ten minutes."

"Ten minutes here . . . another fifteen for us to return to the site—I fear that is too long."

"For him to run to Raul's farm and then for us to wait for Raul's wife to drive here around the roads would take much longer. Through the woods is the quickest way."

"Bicycle?" suggested someone.

"Through the woods, no bike could keep pace with Leeka's swift little legs," answered Chmielnicki.

"Hmm . . . ," mused Bietmann, thinking through the possibilities. "Perhaps we ought not to wait. We could assemble now, where the two are standing guard. Everything would be ready the moment the chopper sets back down."

"But the only way through the fence is here, three kilometers south," objected Waclau. "Most of the rescue team must be on the Belorussian side."

"Of course! How could I forget?"

"Why do we not split up now?" suggested one of the men. "Those of us going over could get through and wait in the thick shrubbery at the edge of the plain. We would only be about half a kilometer from the guardhouse. The rest of you move around and join Raul. We will await your signal and then make our move."

"What signal?" asked Bietmann.

"A grenade. Why else have we been collecting them all day but to set off?" the man asked with a grin.

Udo and Waclau looked at one another with expressions of assent.

"The explosives are all ready?" asked Bietmann.

"World War II surplus," answered Chmielnicki with a hopeful sigh mingled with a shade of doubt. "But they *are* gathered."

"And the guns?"

"Rusty, and only about half with bullets in the chambers, but we do have the three pistols we will need."

"Good. Then perhaps we should split up and get to our respective posts."

The men all rose. Chmielnicki and one of the others handed three of their number the old revolvers he had spoken of, along with several grenades and masks to cover their faces. In the meantime, Bietmann and the others were gathering up the explosives they would carry to the site on the Polish side of the border, north of the old road where the Mercedes sat in readiness.

"Remember," said Bietmann, "no grenades must get close to the helicopter. It *must* remain undamaged."

"And none close by any of the guards," reminded Waclau. "We want no injuries, only loud distractions and confusion."

"If you three men on the inside can take out any of their cars without hurting anyone," said Udo, "do so. But you must not hesitate long. Get to the back of the guardhouse quickly and back to the protection of the trees. Hopefully it will be dark by then. Do not begin making your way back southward along the border until you see the chopper in the air and after me. You must stay hidden until he is gone." He looked intently at the three men carrying the guns. "He would spot you even in the dark in an instant from the air if you make a run for it prematurely. You must delay until he is well across the border."

The men nodded.

"Then shall we go?" said Bietmann. He shook hands with the three men who would now make their way through the fence. "Godspeed to you," he said. "I will not see you again. Thank you for everything. And you, Waclau," he added, turning to Chmielnicki, "I pray I shall rejoin you either in Krynki or perhaps as I'm walking in that direction if he disables the car. Or," he added, "if he kills me, get word to Tad and get the two of them safely to Berlin."

The Pole nodded with a smile. "God will be with you, my friend. We have all prayed for the success of this enterprise and for protection. I will see you at the rendezvous point."

"Please be careful," added Lisel. "Horst is a dangerous man. I have never seen him like this. He *wants* to kill."

"The Lord will protect us, Lisel, my child." Bietmann smiled. "I must get through this so that I may get you safely home. But I will heed your advice and be very careful."

He smiled tenderly at her, then turned toward Tad. "Well, Tad," he said, shaking his young friend's hand and looking deeply into his eyes. "Yours is the most important part of the plan of all. Your father and mother may have had their adventure escaping many years ago, but it now seems to be *your* turn."

Tad nodded.

"I hope you do not have to wait long for the rest of us to carry out all of our preliminaries," Udo added.

With those words, he turned and left the house with the four who carried the bulk of the grenades and additional outdated explosives. The three others left and made their way toward the fence.

Chmielnicki, Tad, and Lisel looked at one another, smiled, then sat down to begin their wait.

The time passed rapidly. Having been rescued, as it were, from her own private hell into this paradise where so much love flowed between everyone, Lisel was in bright spirits, in spite of what she knew was a very dangerous situation and the sobering memories Bietmann's presence could not eventually help force to the surface. It had still not occurred to her to ask why Bietmann was involved in the rescue of a former KGB agent.

She had also heard enough of what had been said about the connections between all these Polish Christians, her father's friend Bietmann, and Tad's parents, to begin wondering if there was more going on here than mere coincidence could account for. She therefore asked many questions and was at last ready to listen to the answers with an open mind concerning what might be their spiritual implications.

"What did he mean," asked Lisel, "about your father and mother's escape adventure?"

"That is the story I promised to have my mother tell you," answered Tad.

"Was Udo Bietmann part of that story?"

Tad nodded.

Lisel pondered the potential significance. There seemed to be more links here, and going further back in time, than she had realized. This was far from an accidental gathering of individuals.

"Did your parents' escape have anything to do with the *Network . . . of the Rose?*" she asked after a brief silence.

"How could you possibly know that!" exclaimed Tad.

"I guess you would say that is my own *long story* that I shall tell you one day."

The conversation drifted into other channels. Within herself Lisel resolved to tell Tad everything about Girdel Bietmann and her father as soon as they were on their way home.

Come unto Me . . .
I Will Give You Rest

• • •

Berlin

MATTHEW HAD BEEN OUT WALKING FOR TWO OR THREE hours, seeing and thinking many things, but remembering only the endless string of faces, silently praying as he passed them—now the bewildered face of a small child, then the preoccupied look of a businessman talking to a colleague, then the blank stare of one of a thousand passersby or would-be revolutionaries.

Lord Jesus, he thought, *what would you do if you were walking this street right now? Would you walk by them praying as I am doing? Would you stop them all and preach to them of your Father? Would you work a miracle? Would you give them something to read or eat? How would you engage with them about life?*

Then the thought struck him, *But you are walking the street, aren't you, Lord? Of course! You are walking beside me . . . inside me . . . with me! You are here! So what would you do . . . what would you have me do? If I am your representative now, your hands, your feet, your eyes, your mouth, your ears, how do I take the life that is inside me—your life? How do I take it out among these people? How can it be transmitted to them?*

Ahead a souvenir and magazine kiosk sat in the middle of the wide walkway. An assortment of postcards were displayed on a wire rack to one side: half with photographs of Berlin, the others with lewd and suggestive pictures and sayings. Behind the counter of the booth itself two or three dozen different magazine covers shouted their indecency and erotic wantonness to all the world. A man dressed in an expensive blue suit stood in conversation with the owner of the stand, a fat, balding man with dirty shirt and a pathetic-looking grin and lecherous, coarse intent shining out of his hollow eyes. He had been holding a magazine up for his customer to see, and now with a quick movement opened it to just the right page, where fell down a tall, three-page foldout, which he brandished luridly before the man's eager, lustful eyes.

Matthew was not close enough to understand a word either man spoke. He didn't need to. The satyric glow in each man's eyes required no words for their obscene thoughts to be made clear enough.

He cast his eyes to the ground and walked quickly by, glad Sabina was not with him.

As he did, the kiosk man, not wanting his wares ignored, threw out a crude invitation, flashing the shameless picture in Matthew's direction. The man in the suit half turned around, then stepped into Matthew's path, placing his hand to one side of his mouth as he did, and making some equally suggestive comment, as if in confidence from one man of the world to another that the fellow wasn't really as bad as he seemed and he knew how to give a man a little happiness. His words were followed by a wink and knowing glance.

Matthew looked up and into his face.

It was only for an instant, but it was enough. His brain had hardly comprehended the words of the exchange, but his heart had comprehended everything. His eyes suddenly swam with tears, and he hurried on. He did not even hear the annoyed kiosk man shouting obscenities after him.

Where he went next, Matthew hardly knew. Even with a map he could not have retraced his steps. When he came to himself he was a great distance from the center of traffic and tourism and activity. He was near a small park with two or three old statues and a few benches. Paper and litter were strewn about. The few people in the vicinity were hurrying past on their way somewhere else.

Matthew walked to an empty bench, sat down, set down the book he was carrying, and cradled his head in his hands. This was not what he had expected when they had made plans to return to Germany! Had it really changed so much here, he wondered . . . or had *he* changed? Had he become more sensitive to the worldliness everywhere?

Through his brain flew thoughts of the conference and his

conversation with Darrell Montgomery. Tonight was the night, Darrell had said. MacPatrick would deliver his stirring speech congratulating them all about how they were going to join together to save the world by the year 2000.

Oh, my self-satisfied brothers! his heart cried out. *You are so caught up in your programs of what you call evangelism. . . . Can't you feel the heartbeat of the real world?*

A passage from a page of the baron's journals he had been reading came back into his mind. He had brought the thin volume with him and had all but forgotten it until now. He took the book from beside him, set it on his lap, and flipped through to locate the section. There it was—in the baron's own hand, quoting one of his personal favorites from the old Scottish writer whom he loved.

Matthew read it again, as he had this morning.

> What a breeding nest of cares and pains is the human heart! Surely it needs some refuge! How the world needs a Savior to whom anyone might go, at any moment.
>
> The words rise to mind—*Come unto me, all you that labor and are heavy laden, and I will give you rest.*
>
> Ah, the heart fills!
>
> Did ever a man really say such words? Such words they are! It is rest we want. REST—such peace of mind as we had when we were children. Do not waste time asking how he can give it. Ask him to forgive you and make you clean and set things right for you. If he will not do it, then he is not the Savior of men and was wrongly named Jesus.
>
> Come then at the call of the Maker, the Healer, the Giver of repentance and light, the Friend of sinners, all you on whom lies the weight of sin. Heartily he loves you! Call to mind how he forgave men's sins, thus lifting from their hearts the crushing load that paralyzed them. Of all words that ever were spoken, were there ever any gentler, tenderer, humbler, lovelier than these? *Come unto me all you that labor and are heavy laden, and I will give you rest. Take my yoke upon you, and learn of me; for I am meek and lowly in heart: and you shall find rest for your souls. For my yoke is easy, and my burden is light.*

Surely these words, could they but be believed, are such as every human heart might gladly hear! He wants men to have peace—HIS peace. Does it seem too far away, my friends, and very distant from the hurts and sufferings of this world, from the daily things about us?

The things close by do not give peace. Peace has to come from somewhere else. And do not our souls themselves cry out for a nobler, better, more beautiful life?

Alas! for poor men and women and their aching hearts! Come then, sore heart, and see whether his heart can heal yours. He knows what sighs and tears are.

Beloved, we MUST get rid of this misery of ours. It is slaying us. It is turning the fair earth into a hell and our hearts into its fuel. There stands the man who says he knows. Take him at his word. Go to him who says in the power of his eternal tenderness and his pity, *Come unto me, all you that labor and are heavy laden, and I will give you rest. Take my yoke upon you, and learn of me; for I am meek and lowly in heart: and you shall find rest for your souls. For my yoke is easy, and my burden is light.*

Long before he had finished reading the words over again, Matthew's eyes were nearly blinded to the page from the tears streaming down his face. With the words of the old writer in his ears, in the hand of his beloved father-in-law, mingled with distorted images from the conference, and with his mind's eye filled with the faces and voices of the two men at the kiosk, the heart of Matthew McCallum filled with the general suffering of the universal human soul.

The book slipped from his hands to the bench beside him. And there, in a lonely out-of-the-way park in a corner of Berlin, unseen by any other, the man who was hailed by many as one of the prominent Christian authors of his day quietly wept for the world his Master came to save.

• • •

When Matthew walked into his hotel room late in the afternoon, he found that Sabina had a visitor.

"Hello, Matthew," said Palacki.

"Dieder! Good to see you."

The two shook hands.

"I just stopped by," said the Polish pastor, "as I was explaining to your charming wife, to let you know that I *have* decided to take the podium tonight."

Matthew took in the information with a serious nod. "Do you know what you will say?" he asked.

"Not yet," replied Palacki. "I must still pray a good deal more. I have just seen Aviz-Rabin as well, and I asked him the same thing I now ask the two of you—to be in prayer that none of my *self* will intrude tonight and that only the Lord's word will be spoken, whether in word of encouragement or word of chastisement."

"We will be honored to join in that request."

"When I leave you," Palacki added, "I will be alone the rest of the day and evening until then—alone with him, that is. *He* will give the words that are to be spoken. And you," he added, "have you come to a decision?"

Matthew sighed. "Yes . . . yes, I think I have," he said slowly.

Both Sabina and their guest waited expectantly.

"There is a great deal on my heart," said Matthew at length. "But I feel the Lord indicating just the opposite to me—that this is a time when perhaps my own silence will most effectively enable the message from his voice to strike root."

"And what might that message be?" asked Dieder.

Matthew smiled. "For that I will have to await along with everyone else," he replied. "I honestly do not know. But I have the feeling it is a message that will proceed from life-example, not words of preaching. I pray that his leading you *to* speak and me *not* to speak will combine in a powerful way that he will be able to make use of."

"I say *Amen* to that!" rejoined Palacki.

"Perhaps the three of us might pray together now," said Sabina, "and commit these two days, and even our prayers which will follow, to the purposes of the Lord."

The two men nodded. Moments later, the three sat with eyes closed, knees to the floor, and hands joined lovingly one to the other, in that smallest yet most powerful and symbolic human circle—the threefold cord of intercession and entreaty whose agreed-upon prayers, promised the Son, *will* be carried out by the Father.

1 1 1

Through the Border!

• • •

Polish–Belorussian Border

BY THE TIME THE PANTING YOUNG LEEKA BURST THROUGH the door of the Chmielnicki farmhouse, Tad, Waclau, and Lisel had been listening to the sounds of explosions in the distance for four or five minutes.

The two men had been praying for the safety both of their brothers and their enemies since the sound of the first grenade had sounded faintly in the air toward the north.

When the helicopter had returned and set down next to the abandoned guardhouse, Bietmann's instincts had been correct.

A flurry of activity began immediately about the place as the man in charge opened the door and jumped to the ground almost before the skids of the chopper were firmly resting on the pavement.

A minute or two later, the men standing watch out by the border fence where the road had once gone through were called back inside.

Another minute yet the Poles waited.

When young Leeka was sprinting through the woods about halfway to the house to report the landing of the helicopter, the first grenade was lobbed over the fence, exploding harmlessly some twenty meters north of the guardhouse.

It was followed by another, then another, until continuous explosions were ringing the place with smoke and fire. Two of the unoccupied outbuildings were hit and were now burning.

The sudden chaos camouflaged the approach of the three armed Poles, who now made their way stealthily toward the guardhouse from the south. Bietmann's comrades had intentionally concentrated all their fire to the north of the building, toward which all the guards had directed their attention.

From inside the compound, the three saboteurs were able to make more accurate aim with the grenades they carried. Two cars were blown to bits, another outbuilding exploded into flames, and one of the rifle-towers next to the fence shattered and fell to the ground.

Yelling and pandemonium at last gave way to some attempt on the part of the Russian guards to protect the chopper. Between the explosions of dozens of grenades, which worked to a higher percentage than any of the Polish plotters had expected, rifle fire could be heard, though the guards still had no clear idea where the enemy was located.

The three insiders now donned their masks.

A terrible grenade blast ripped through the back wall of the guardhouse. Even before the dust and smoke had settled, the Poles rushed through the gaping hole, weapons poised.

"Where are the prisoners?" shouted one in the best Russian he could manage.

The single guard present, a boy of not more than twenty, threw one hand in the air and pointed with the other to a door. The man who had spoken continued to wave his pistol menacingly in the boy's face while one of the other three flew to the door, tore it open, and ran inside.

"Jahn . . . come quickly!" he cried in Polish to Chmielnicki's cousin.

In less than a minute after the liberating blast, the three Poles and two prisoners—one with a well-wrinkled parcel under his arm that he had grabbed from a table on the way out—were sprinting away from the south of the guardhouse, while the young guard shook with terror in the small room where they had placed him.

By the time other guards arrived after hearing the blast from the north side where all the previous action had been located, the five had dived beneath bushes and low-lying shrubbery some seventy-five meters away.

They lay motionless, praying that the last phase of the grand delusion would keep them from detection.

Seeing their escape from his vantage point with Raul on the Polish side of the fence to the north, Bietmann now bid his brothers a hasty farewell and inched his way toward the waiting Mercedes for the final and most dangerous charade of the evening.

"Give me two minutes," he said. "If I am not behind the wheel by then, I will be close enough. Then blast the fence to smithereens, and run for your lives!"

"Godspeed to you, German brother," said Raul, embracing Bietmann.

"I will make noise enough for ten escapes," said Bietmann. "You all get home and to your families before they can mount a search. Bless you all, my brothers!" he added, then hurried off.

Meanwhile, Leeka had delivered his message and was enjoying a glass of milk and piece of bread with Chmielnicki's wife and Lisel, while Tad and Waclau made their way to the breached section of fence to receive cousin and Russian guest.

The blast that opened a gaping hole in the fence to the north of where Raul and the others stood was so loud it was heard clearly three kilometers south where Tad and Waclau stood. It was still louder where the three rescuers and two prisoners still lay huddled in the brush. Raul had saved two or three sticks of dynamite for just such an occasion, and the TNT now accomplished its diversionary work.

The explosion was sufficiently loud to rock the entire guardhouse compound, and instantly all attention refocused itself toward where the smoke and debris now flew into the air and gradually settled. Machine-gun fire pulverized the area, even as shouts from one of the commanders shouted above the fray, "After them . . . after them!"

As the echo from the blast died down and a lull followed in the answering rifle fire, suddenly a new and unexpected sound rent the night air. An automobile engine roared to life! After several loud idling *vrooms,* its driver ground it into gear. With a screeching of tires and throttle pressed to the floor, the huge high-powered Mercedes tore off away from the border fence in the opposite direction, into Poland.

"The car! You let them get through and to the car! You idiots!" screamed Bolotnikov in white fury. "To the chopper!" he yelled to one of the rifle-bearing guards, running toward the helicopter. "We'll cut him off before he's a kilometer away!"

Thirty seconds later the helicopter was in the air and zooming at a mere twenty meters' elevation over the border into Poland, its bright spotlight focused on the once-traveled border road in the gathering dusk.

The low-whirring blades whooshed past the five concealed bodies south of the guardhouse, bending the grass and brush of their shelter toward the earth in windy turbulence. Still they lay low in their sanctuary.

A minute longer they waited. As the sound of the chopper receded in the distance after the Mercedes, and as every available guard from the compound raced through the blown-open gap in the fence to the north, and as their comrades, now scattered, made their way to their homes, at last the five rose and, with as much haste as they could summon, ran southward to the border crossing that had been so vital through the years but still was undiscovered.

Chmielnicki was there to welcome them.

Quickly he greeted his cousin, gathered up the weapons for safekeeping, placed the patch of fence back in the hole until Jahn was ready to return home, sent his three comrades back to their homes, and hurried his Russian brother to the waiting automobile that Lisel had already set idling in readiness beside his house a few hundred meters away.

They ran toward it. Hastily Waclau shoved the Russian into the backseat while Tad jumped in behind the wheel. The Pole closed both doors, spoke a few words to the driver and his front-seat passenger, punctuated with an affectionate pat on the back through the open window, and then waved them off as the small automobile made its way westward.

The three drove away from the Chmielnicki farm, then onto the road that would lead them through the woods and fields toward Wasilkow. It was not paved, but it was the shortest route to the highway. Several men were supposed to be stationed along the way to guide them at intersections of possible confusion, for the driver of the automobile had never been this way in his life.

After two or three minutes, during which, though the dusk was deepening, the lights of the automobile remained off, the driver turned and spoke to his passenger over his shoulder. "I don't know if you can understand me, Mr. Galanov," he said. "But unfortunately, German is the closest language to Russian I know. My name is Tad McCallum, and this young lady here beside me is Lisel Lamprecht."

Red Herring

• • •

MEANWHILE, AS TAD AND HIS PASSENGERS BOUNCED AS fast as they were able over the fields according to Chmielnicki's instructions, the speeding helicopter had caught the swiftly retreating Mercedes.

Boring in upon it with its beam bathing the road in light, the chopper raced past, ominously banking in a descending turn, and set down on the road a hundred and fifty meters in front of the car.

Amid the windy whirling of the blades, the Mercedes careened sideways to a stop, screeching its tires, while the former KGB chief leapt from the helicopter and ran forward with automatic rifle in hand.

"Out of the car!" he ordered.

With eyes wide open in astonished terror, Bietmann opened the door and stepped out, hands on top of his head, crying in German, "Don't shoot . . . don't shoot!"

"What are you doing here?" barked Bolotnikov.

Bietmann's answer, still in German, professed ignorance both of the words and of any wrongdoing.

"What are you doing here?" repeated Bolotnikov, attempting to communicate in Polish this time.

"Tourist . . . German tourist," replied Bietmann in a broken Polish dialect. It was sufficient for the Russian to understand.

"What were you doing back there?" he demanded, waving the rifle in Bietmann's face angrily.

"Want to see border . . . want to see Russia. . . . Please, no mean harm," stammered an apparently terrified Bietmann.

"Bah! You are lying!" he spat. "Where are the files?"

"I know not what—"

"Get out of the way, you fool!" yelled an incensed Bolotnikov.

With the rifle he shoved Bietmann forcefully to the ground and stuck half his body unceremoniously into the vehicle. With rapid, almost panicky motions, he glanced about, felt under the seat, inside the glove box, then in the back. Then tearing the key from the ignition, he got out, ran to the rear of the car, and after fumbling a moment threw open the trunk and quickly scanned its contents.

The entire car was empty.

He ran back to where the German was now struggling back to his feet. Kicking him viciously in the side with his boot, he knocked him, groaning in pain, again to the pavement,.

"Where is the file?" he screamed. "Where is Galanov? Tell me, you lying cur, or I'll kill you!"

"Please," whimpered Bietmann, covering his face in pathetic fear with his hands, "please . . . no hurt. . . . Only want to see Russian border . . . want to cause no trouble." He began to cry.

"You are lying!" Bolotnikov retreated a step, looked over the miserable heap of humanity cowering at his feet as if contemplating whether to let him live.

Suddenly he spun around, emptied several ear-shattering rounds from his gun into the car's tires, and even as the echo was resounding through the nearby countryside, ran back to the helicopter.

Knowing he'd somehow allowed himself to be duped, he cursed and swore, both at himself and the hated traitor Galanov, then revved the engine up to full and lifted the chopper off the ground, banking it steeply back in the direction of the border.

From down the street, an old rusty Trabant now came sputtering along, doing its best to catch up to the helicopter, and passed the parked Mercedes. Realizing it was hopeless, the driver finally stopped, jumped out, and emptied his handgun into the air after the retreating Bolotnikov.

It was a futile gesture, but the vacant drunken eyes that continued to stare in the direction in which he had sent the shots seemed nevertheless to have derived some faint satisfaction from the attempt.

In the distance, from a secluded vantage point on the Belorussian side about five hundred meters from the battered guardhouse compound, a solitary figure sat in his automobile of German make, watching the proceedings with interest, attempting to piece together what had transpired.

And now, seeing the helicopter's beam moving rapidly back in his direction, Claymore surmised that either Bolotnikov *had* been successful in securing the missing documents or had been suckered into a wild-goose chase.

If indeed Bolotnikov *did* possess the file, there would be little he could do. If not, then most likely his pursuit would now lead him into Poland.

So much the better, he thought. Warsaw was halfway home, and he had had more than his fill of Moscow. He would watch further and then, if necessary, pick up Galanov's trail from wherever he had escaped to.

113

Getaway

• • •

STILL FURTHER IN THE DISTANCE, TO THE WEST AND SLIGHTLY south from the escape site, another car sat under the covering of a wooded area. Its four occupants listened to the helicopter's giant blades swooshing through the night and watched with interest as its searchlight roved about up and down the border fence, panning the area for any sign of the escapees.

They knew it was looking for them.

For twenty minutes they sat, mostly in silence. The three occupants knew German, and the Pole who had joined them knew a scant amount of English, but communication was mostly carried out by signs. After two or three passes up and down the border fence for several kilometers in both directions from the guardhouse, the sound of the helicopter suddenly came nearer, circling in wide arcs in every direction from the escape site.

Holding their collective breath, the fugitives heard it slash through the air overhead and whiz by, then off further to the north.

"It safe now," said the Pole in the backseat next to Galanov. "You drive on . . . I show you."

Tad obeyed, started up the engine, and crept from the wood and continued along the road where their guide had intercepted them a short time earlier.

It was becoming increasingly difficult to see. But they would not turn on the headlights until further away from the helicopter's range. If Bolotnikov chanced to see them, he would be able to make up the distance with frightening speed.

Their route took them across several barren fields and through another wood, until the dirt road intersected with one crossing it at right angles. Tad stopped.

"You go left," pointed the man. "You go five kilometers . . . . large empty barn. Stop there . . . wait. Someone else come to you." Without further words he got out as he had climbed in, closed the door, and was gone. Tad watched as their Polish guide began the long walk back the way they had come.

Tad continued on, and ten minutes later stopped the car. Quickly he flashed on his headlights for a brief moment. Yes, there could be no mistaking it—there was the barn. He turned the lights off and crept alongside it, then stopped again.

All was still. There seemed to be no one there to meet them. "We're supposed to wait here," he said. "Shall we get out and stretch our legs?"

Galanov and Lisel agreed.

They walked around a bit, though by now it was too dark to see clearly. Even had it been broad daylight, however, Lisel would never have known that she had laid eyes on their pilgrim passenger on another day many years before—the day when her own Berlin Wall had been erected, a wall still awaiting its destruction—nor that *he* was the cause, not her father, of her own quiet inner rebellion all these years against the Father of them all.

But forgiveness was on the way and would, before the Spirit was done with it, send its healing balm in many needful directions.

"I wish I had a flashlight," remarked Tad. "I'd like to see inside the barn."

"No time for that, friend McCallum," said a voice he recognized in German. Looking up, emerging from the barn he saw two figures walking toward them. Even in the darkness he knew the form of Udo Bietmann.

"Udo!" he exclaimed, rushing forward. "Where did you come from?"

"Waclau and I have been waiting for you," replied Bietmann with a laugh. "We thought you would never get here."

Galanov now approached from behind Tad. "So, my German friend," he said, "I finally learn your name. You are called Udo!"

The two embraced.

"It is good to see you again, my brother," said Bietmann.

"Likewise," rejoined Galanov. "I must say, you have some very resourceful persons in *Das Netzwerk*. I am no longer surprised that we were not able to follow you."

"Meet the man who is responsible for engineering your escape," said Udo, bringing Chmielnicki forward. "This man's cousin was the man you were captured with."

Galanov and the Pole shook hands warmly. "Indeed it was a masterpiece of deception," said Galanov. "But how did you manage to dupe one so clever as Leonid Bolotnikov?"

"No doubt because so many were praying," replied Bietmann. "I felt his boot in my side not long ago. He is not a man I will soon forget."

"Where is he now?"

"Unless I am mistaken, he is still circling about in the helicopter. But he will find no one. All our collaborators are safely home and in their beds."

"And you four must be off," said Chmielnicki to Bietmann.

"He will not give up easily," said Galanov.

"You are but three kilometers from the highway into Bialystok," said Waclau. "There you will rest and be fed by brother Rydz."

"We must not delay long," said Galanov. He turned toward Bietmann. "You remember what I told you I was investigating?"

Bietmann nodded.

"It was far bigger than I thought. We must reach Berlin without delay."

"Then we will drive all night if need be," said Bietmann. "As you can see, you are not our only passenger—Lisel is also bound for Berlin."

"As I understand."

"All of our fellowship will continue praying," added Chmielnicki. "Now, Godspeed to you, all four!" He turned toward the barn where his car was hidden.

"Go ahead, you drive, Tad," said Bietmann, reaching for the door of the passenger side of the car. "You got our friend Andrassy safely this far." He opened the door for Lisel, then climbed into the backseat beside Galanov. Tad started up the car. "Blessings, Brother Waclau!" Udo called out toward the retreating Pole.

"How did you get here?" asked Tad, glancing back, as soon as they were underway.

"Waclau was waiting nearby the minute Bolotnikov was back in the air in the helicopter," replied Udo.

"Did he hurt you?"

"Not badly. He very easily could have killed me. Instead he took it out on the car."

"Did he destroy it?"

"No. But I hope that fellow who borrowed it knows where to come by a couple of new tires. When Bolotnikov realized I was the wrong man, he blew them to shreds!"

PART XIII

Penetrating Words of Truth

Did the Five Thousand Applaud?

• • •

Berlin

THE HUGE, PLUSH CONFERENCE CENTER WAS ALREADY buzzing with enthusiasm for the night's event when Matthew, Sabina, and Joseph walked in. The exchange tonight had been built up for several days. No one would miss this.

They made their way, as best they could without being recognized, to a row near the back, and eased into their seats. All around them, the crowd was made up of men and women who held positions of leadership and responsibility. Here were those who spoke and exhorted and taught and led millions of people throughout the world.

What are these people, these leaders, thinking? Matthew wondered.

As he glanced about, they all wore smiles and carried notebooks filled with quotes and ideas and comments. From every indication, they were buying tapes of the various sessions by the hundreds to take home for their people to hear. Had any of them walked the streets of Berlin and looked into the eyes of those who were so desperately lost? If so, what had they thought? Were any of them plagued, Matthew asked himself, with the kinds of misgivings and questions that are filling me?

Darrell Montgomery was now introducing Bob MacPatrick, amid applause from the congregation and beaming smiles from the great personality himself as he waited listening in the wings.

". . . therefore, my friends," Montgomery was saying, "I know you . . ."

Matthew's thoughts drifted in and out as he listened with one ear, while the other resounded with quieter and more eternal words from the mouth of another.

Come unto me . . .

". . . this man whose ministry and impact . . . more for the cause of Christ through the media and . . ."

. . . you that labor and are heavy laden . . .

MacPatrick was now standing and making his way forward. "Thank you . . . thank you . . ." he was saying, though the welcoming ovation kept his words from being heard. He smiled, waving to the crowd as if to quiet his admirers, but clearly relishing in the adulation which was being given him.

Take my yoke upon you . . .

As he reflected upon Jesus' tender words from the baron's journal, Matthew wondered what he was like when he addressed the crowds. Did the five thousand clap and rave when Peter introduced the Lord, prefacing it with an account of all the great things he had done?

When the four thousand gathered, did John get up and say, "Jews, heathens, lepers, and Pharisees . . . I want you to give a warm Galilean welcome today to the man who has healed thousands, and who has done more to make God's voice alive once more in our time than anyone since John the Baptist. Please join me in welcoming—we don't know his full name yet, but we call him—Jesus of Nazareth!"

Matthew chastised himself for the fleeting sarcasm. Was it sacrilege to think such a thing, he thought inwardly. Was such a comparison legitimate in view of this apparent public adulation and the willingness with which his colleagues of today basked in the glow of being praised by their followers?

God, O God! cried Matthew in his heart, closing his eyes momentarily. *Lord Jesus, when did we let go of the New Testament as our example? When did we forget to model our lives after what **you** did?*

Matthew looked up again toward the podium. The applause had died down. MacPatrick was silent a moment, but still the large smile spread across his face.

Learn of me.

"Ladies and gentlemen," he began, "you cannot know the joy it brings to my heart . . . position to further the gospel in such significant ways as . . . our organization . . . thanks to the support . . . millions of dollars . . ."

Is it really all about money? thought Matthew. *Does evangelism always have to reduce to fund-raising? Did Jesus get pledges from all the folks in Nazareth before he left home?*

". . . would like to share with you my vision for evangelism," MacPatrick continued, as Matthew's thoughts wandered in and out of attentiveness.

For I am meek . . .

". . . vision I hope each and every one of you will catch sight of . . . before 2000 . . . hope you will take this vision back . . . your own ministries and people . . . get them out there raising support . . . take them the challenge of winning the world for Christ . . . that critical year, before 2000 . . ."

. . . and lowly of heart.

". . . time is short, my friends . . . must use every means available . . . techniques you have heard in the workshops . . . good principles . . . does require money . . . so desperately need literature and Bibles and tracts . . . money to send out teams . . . beam television programs and radio . . . proposal of Christian satellite . . . opportunities made possible by today's media advances . . . staggering possibilities . . ."

What would Tad think of this? Matthew wondered, for some reason thinking of his son just then, and longing to see him again. *Or my dad, or Sabina's father. Lord . . . what do you think?*

". . . and so I am proud of what we have done . . . the Lord has called us . . . preach the gospel to every creature . . . we are taking steps toward fulfilling that . . . you are involved . . . all our ministries together . . ."

You shall find rest for your souls . . .

". . . I believe before the year 2000 . . . we will be able to make the claim that indeed every creature has heard the gospel message . . . we will be able to look the Lord in the eye . . . hear his words, 'Well done, good and faithful servant' . . . because . . ."

Bob, thought Matthew incredulously, *don't you hear what you are saying! Listen to yourself, Bob! I am **proud, we** are taking steps, **we** will be able to make the claim, **we** will be able to, **we** are working together to fulfill the great commission, it takes **money, we've** got to use every means available, **my** vision, **my** vision. Bob, listen to your own words. They're all about you and about money and about **our** efforts. Where is God's hand in it, Bob? Where is* *the room in it for the Holy Spirit convicting people and drawing them to himself?*

". . . which is why I am so proud to be able . . ."

For my yoke is easy . . .

". . . what we are going to do this evening . . . after I share more fully with you . . . my own personal vision . . . such a fulfillment after all my years . . ."

Lord, Lord, whispered Matthew silently, *I do pray most urgently for my brother Dieder up there awaiting his time. Speak to him deeply, Lord, even now. Speak into his heart as he listens. Give him your word, your perspective to communicate to these, your people. And help me, God. Protect my own thoughts, lead me into truth, lighten this burden I feel, Lord. Keep my heart pure, O Father . . . help me to discern your heart!*

. . . and my burden is light.

115
Whose Responsibility?

•   •   •

Across Poland

THEY HAD BEEN DRIVING FOR ABOUT AN HOUR.

Gradually the interaction between the four gave way to separate conversations between the occupants of the front seat and those in back. Even as he engaged in dialogue with Galanov, however, deep inside, Udo Bietmann was holding up the daughter and son of his friends in prayer.

Undergirded in such a manner did Tad McCallum unknowingly step into the footsteps of his own grandfather. In the same way that the baron had explained clearly, to the curious and searching youth that had once been his own father, concerning the character of God's Fatherhood, Tad now spoke similar truths into Lisel's budding young life.

Thus did the son of the one and the grandson of the other carry on, in a new generation, Baron von Dortmann's vision of spreading the love of the Father among men. And through him, therefore, did the fragrance of the rose continue to spread its scent in ever-widening circles among those who loved its blossoms.

Some moments had gone by in silence. The night was black. No other cars were on the road. With full tanks of petrol, they would be able to make it all the way to Berlin. From the sound of it, Bietmann and Galanov had begun to doze behind them.

As they talked, by degrees the subject of Lisel's past arose. At length she related to Tad the whole story of her friend, Udo's daughter, and the terrible events that had scarred her so deeply and caused her to leave home. Tad listened incredulously to the tale—he had only heard Bietmann's side of it the night before—realizing that even Lisel herself did not know the whole story yet: that the man at this moment sleeping in the backseat was the very same who had taken her friend's life thirteen years earlier.

After Lisel was through, a long silence followed.

The stillness of the night, and having fully shared for the first time with someone she felt understood and would neither blame her for doing wrong nor automatically take her side in the affair either, had worked a sort of preliminary healing within Lisel's heart. Communication, in and of itself, is often enough to begin opening many doors, and such was the case on this night.

She felt strangely and newly relaxed and at ease afterward, simply in realizing that Tad knew her on a much more intimate level than before. She had exposed herself, however—she knew that. It was one of the reasons she felt good. Yet there *was* another side. Tad wasn't someone you wanted to be vulnerable around if you weren't prepared for the consequences, if you weren't prepared to take what he might say in response. And he *could* be honest!

Still, Lisel wasn't afraid. At long last something inside her realized that she too was ready to face whatever might come with honesty.

"Have you seen your parents since?" asked Tad at length.

"No," she answered. For the first time in all the thirteen years of separation, there was no trace of defiance and almost a hint of regret in her tone.

"Do you *want* to see them again?"

"I don't know. I never thought about it before now."

"Surely you don't hate them so much you never want to see them again."

"No . . . no, I don't hate them."

"Do you *love* them?"

"I don't know that either. I don't suppose I do, or I wouldn't still be angry and bitter with them, would I?"

"Why *are* you angry at your father, Lisel?"

She waited some time before answering. "At first it all had to do with Girdel's death. I blamed him for it. Now that I think about it, I suppose it would have been more rational to blame Udo," she added.

"But then my papa was the one I was around every day, and so it was natural to blame him."

"We always blame those closest by when things go wrong," remarked Tad.

"Are you saying he was blameless?"

"Maybe not—I can't answer that. I only said that we tend to blame those closest by when things become uncomfortable in our *own* lives. They provide easy, though perhaps illogical, scapegoats so that we don't have to look inside our own hearts. I think we do that no matter what the circumstances . . . no matter *who* is to blame for things that happen."

"But what if they *are* to blame?"

"I don't know," mused Tad. "I'm not sure blame has much to do with anything—I mean in terms of the actual responsibility for *why* such-and-such happened."

"Responsibility must surely rest with who's to blame."

"Not if what you're after is a solution," interposed Tad.

"What? You're saying that responsibility for a solution rests with the person who's *not* to blame?"

"Maybe not always, but many times."

"I don't see how that can be. That seems exactly backward."

"Most things in the Christian life *are* upside-down to how the rest of the world would look at it."

Lisel nodded and sighed. "I suppose you're right. Still, I don't see how what you just said could possibly make sense."

"Let me try to explain it," said Tad. "Blame doesn't matter nearly so much as *who is doing the blaming.* That's where you really begin to get down to the roots of why there is a rift between two individuals. Not that wrong is done, not that things happen that shouldn't, but that one person uses an injury to blame another. The minute they do, they have begun to erect a wall between themselves and the other. *The doing of the wrong* is not what has built the wall, rather the anger, the bitterness, the unforgiveness, the sense of injury that has followed no matter where blame happens to lie—*those wrong attitudes have erected the wall."*

"But what if they are justified?"

"The wrong attitudes, you mean?"

"Yes. What if anger is warranted?"

"So what? Things happen all the time that are hurtful and insensitive between people. People hurt other people; that's part of life. What do you expect—never to be hurt? Has anyone *else* ever hurt you?"

"I suppose."

"I hurt you myself by something I said not long ago, and you became angry. But you didn't build up a permanent barrier between us. You forgave me almost immediately."

"I see what you mean."

"We *choose* when to allow hurts to erect walls between ourselves and other people and when to forgive and overlook them. *Blame,* whether we're *justified* or not, doesn't matter. It's our *choice* whether to allow a wall to go up or not."

"And when a wall does exist between two persons?" asked Lisel slowly, as if part of her wanted to know what Tad thought, while the other part already did know and didn't particularly like the idea.

"It's obviously the person's responsibility who put it up in the first place to initiate tearing it down."

Lisel took in the words without an immediate response.

"That's why I said the affixing of specific blame doesn't matter," Tad added, "but rather *who is doing the blaming.* That's where you have to look for responsibility for a solution."

"In other words," said Lisel, "all this is my fault, not my father's?"

"The word *fault* implies blame," replied Tad. "No, I cannot say it is your *fault.* I say tearing down the wall is *your* responsibility, *no matter who may have originally been to blame.*"

Lisel laughed lightly in the darkness. "I told you before that you were the most plain-speaking Christian I had ever met."

"I just never saw much good to be gained by fooling around with partial truths and looking at only the comfortable places within ourselves. If something is amiss, why not go after it?"

"Now you're at it again—and getting personal again, too."

"You tell me to stop, and there won't be another word."

"No—I won't get angry this time. Perhaps these are things I finally need to hear."

"I'm only trying to tell you what I consider the truth. I'm trying to help."

"I know you are, Tad. As much as it may hurt, I think I'm ready for it." Lisel paused. "No, I would go further than that," she added. "I think I finally *want* it, even if the unpleasantness is pointed at me."

"That's a big step to come to," said Tad. "It takes a mature person to be able to arrive at that point and make such an admission."

"I can't say I like it. But I don't want to run from the truth anymore. If that's what I've been doing, it's time I stopped and faced it. I don't want to be an incomplete woman—I want to be complete, full, whole. Maybe what I'm saying is that I want to finally grow up and put my self-centeredness and my motives of self behind me."

"Why now?" asked Tad.

Lisel smiled, wondering the same thing herself. "I don't know," she said. "I suppose the time just finally came when I faced myself, faced who I really was, faced what I had allowed myself to become, faced all the years of self-motivated choices I had made, faced the hurt I had caused others, faced the kinds of attitudes I had allowed to fester and live in my deepest character, faced what kind of miserable life lay ahead of me if I continued on the same way."

Lisel sighed, obviously unaccustomed to such a candid opening of her soul. "I tell you, Tad," she continued, "after I left Horst yesterday afternoon and wandered around that village, I have never known such despair and disconsolation. All my life, like they say when you are about to die, passed through my memory, and for the first time I saw the ugliness and selfishness of what I had unknowingly allowed myself to become. I suppose I thought I *was* going to die. And when I sat down on that street, I cried like I have never cried before. I felt so alone and so miserable—"

Lisel stopped, choking back tears again as she remembered. But she didn't want to cry again now, not in front of Tad. She took a deep breath to steady herself. "I prayed yesterday," she went on. "It was the first time in years. I guess you would say I hit bottom. I finally saw the sewer I had been living in. Maybe that's why I'm ready to listen to what you have to say, no matter how painful. I want the truth, too. I told you that once, and you challenged me on it. I did get mad then, but maybe at last I'm ready to say that I want the *whole* truth . . . especially about myself."

It was quiet for a long time.

"So . . . *continue*," said Lisel. "I *want* what you have to say to me. I *ask* for you to tell me what your eyes see down inside me."

Again it was quiet.

Finally Tad spoke. "May I ask you another question?" he said.

"Of course."

"Do you think your father is angry with you?"

Lisel thought a moment. "Two days ago I probably would have quickly answered yes. But that would have only been my way of shifting some of my own anger onto his shoulders so that I could blame *him* instead of myself. But if I am going to really be honest with myself, and if I know my father . . . no, he's probably very hurt over what I did to him and the things I said. But not angry."

"What do you think he feels toward you?"

The silence that followed was pregnant with introspective emotion. When Lisel answered, the words had clearly cost her something in her deepest regions. "I know that he loves me," she said softly.

"What have you felt toward him all these years?" Tad now asked.

"Anger . . . bitterness . . . unforgiveness," replied Lisel.

"Is love a *good* thing or a *bad* thing when it exists between two people?"

"A good thing."

"What about bitterness and unforgiveness—are they healthy or unhealthy?"

"Unhealthy."

Lisel's voice was soft. She was staring down into her lap. The knife edge of Tad's words cut deep.

"Is your father harboring wrong feelings toward you by *loving* you?"

"No."

"Are *you* harboring wrong attitudes toward him?"

"Yes—yes, in all honesty . . . I am."

"Did *he* cause those wrong attitudes?"

"No."

"Was it *you* who allowed them to take root?"

Lisel nodded.

"Who *is* responsible, then, Lisel," said Tad, in as compassionate a voice as he could, "for the breach between you and your father?"

"I am," she whispered.

"No matter what the specifics from long ago, *who* allowed them to form negative feelings?"

"I did."

"Your father didn't let those kinds of attitudes take root in his heart, did he?"

She shook her head.

"He continued to love you?"

"Yes."

"Do you think he has forgiven you?"

"Yes."

"Who built the wall between you, then, Lisel?"

"I did."

"If the wall is ever to be torn down, whose responsibility is it?"

"It is *my* responsibility," she answered.

116

Approaching Bombshell

• • •

Berlin

". . . AND SO, MY FRIENDS AND FELLOW BELIEVERS IN Christ's injunction to send the gospel abroad into every land . . . it is with great pleasure . . ."

In Berlin to the west, where the night was still young, Bob MacPatrick was at last winding down his speech and coming to that part of the evening for which many of the people had been waiting all week and that would represent the culmination of all Darrell Montgomery's planning and the greatest feather in his own personal cap.

". . . that I want to present to our beloved brothers and sisters in the church behind what we have called the Iron Curtain these last fifty years, a check from money raised by faithful believers across America . . . money we hope you will use joyfully and fruitfully in building up the body of believers and churches you have so faithfully maintained during these long hours of darkness under the shadow of Communism."

MacPatrick paused, then glanced behind him, then turned again, smiling, toward the audience. "Ladies and gentlemen," he went on, "I now want you to meet a man I know you are eager to hear, from a man who has carried the standard of the cross bravely, as you know . . . imprisoned and tortured, he never gave in to those who would destroy his faith. And so now, Dieder . . . Dieder Palacki, won't you please come . . . accept this money on behalf of Christians behind the Iron Curtain everywhere. I have here a check for three million dollars—"

At the words, sighs and gasps and a few low whistles could be heard, all of which gave way to a round of applause, with many *Praise the Lords* and *hallelujahs* sprinkled throughout.

"—to give you!" He turned, expecting Palacki to stand, come forward, and shake the outstretched hand that awaited him.

But instead Palacki remained seated where he was, until the clapping died down. At last he rose, came forward, took the check, shook MacPatrick's hand unaggressively, but still said nothing. Slightly unnerved, but still not losing his cool, MacPatrick resumed his own seat with the other dignitaries.

Slowly Palacki made his way toward the podium. He appeared not even to notice the applauding reception that broke out again, and in his eyes was not a look of warmth.

Reaching the center of the platform, he did not lift his head to scan the faces of his listeners. Instead he stood still, looking down at the lectern before him. He had no notes.

Gradually the clapping died down and the hall fell silent. Still Palacki stared downward in front of him, while the delegates waited expectantly.

It was several long moments before he at last spoke. "It has been a curious past several days," he began, speaking softly. "I have been listening with great interest to the many discussions and suggestions and exhortations, all with the end in view of promoting the Christian faith in a region of the world where one might conclude never before had a single soul heard the name Jesus of Nazareth.

"Indeed, if I were newly arrived on this planet and had come to this conference as an angel whose assignment it was to report back to our Father on the state of his people on the earth, I would have reason to conclude that a huge segment of the world's population had just been discovered of whom no one had ever heard before and who therefore had no Christian tradition whatsoever. As I have listened I have found myself wondering if any Christians have ever existed outside the United States or Great Britain.

"So as I say, it has been with great interest that I have attempted to absorb the perspectives represented among you. I must admit that when the invitation came to join you, and even to address this gathering, I found myself seized with a certain trepidation. As you know, large assemblies of Christians such as this have not been customary where I come from, and thus most of my work among Christians has been in small groups of less than one hundred. Addressing several thousand I found a very intimidating prospect.

"In the end, however, I decided to join you, for we pastors and Christians from the regions formerly behind the Iron Curtain are certainly excited about the new possibilities for evangelism in our nations too.

"But as I listened to more and more talk of money and pamphlets, of missionaries being sent and books being shipped, of teachers and pastors coming to *help* and train us in spreading the gospel, and of your gospel TV and radio stations and your gospel trains and gospel trucks full of your Western-style gospel paraphernalia—your badges and tracts and stickers and music and gaily written happiness-books with their joy-filled, razzle-dazzle Christianity—a knot has steadily risen in my stomach.

"Do not forget, I have spent much time in your countries. I have been in your churches and bookstores. I have witnessed with my own eyes the trappings of your so-called spiritual prosperity, which is really no prosperity at all, but a hollow empty shell.

"Something within me wants to shout and say to you all, *'Go home to your contented and wealthy homes and communities and churches. The Good News of Jesus Christ is alive and vibrant and is fully capable of carrying itself abroad into the hearts of hungry men and women without the benefit of your expensive and lavish commercial efforts on its behalf.'*"

Palacki stopped a moment to wipe his forehead, which had begun to sweat.

117

Is It Hard or Easy to Be a Christian?

• • •

Across Poland

THE AUTOMOBILE BEARING THE AMERICAN, THE RUSSIAN, and the two Germans had continued for a good while without further discussion. No sounds came from the backseat. The Russian and one German now slept soundly. It was approaching midnight.

From the stillness next to him, Tad assumed Lisel had dozed off as well. When she suddenly spoke, her voice startled him. "What *about* my father?" she asked, still wrestling with the discomforting implications of their earlier conversation. "He did plenty of things wrong, too. Doesn't he share any of the blame?"

"I thought we weren't going to talk about it in terms of blame," replied Tad. "Sure, as much as ninety percent of the blame might rest on his shoulders. I can't say. I don't know him. I don't know what kind of father he was to you. He might have been horribly insensitive. He might have said and done things that hurt. None of that *blame* changes the *responsibility* that lies on *your* shoulders."

"You really don't give a person much room to maneuver," said Lisel with an uncomfortable laugh.

"If we're after solutions, if we're trying to figure out how to dismantle walls," replied Tad, "we oughtn't to care about maneuvering. We ought to care only about learning how to pick up the hammer and where to strike the blows within ourselves."

Lisel nodded.

"What your father may have done did not cause *your* wrong attitudes. *You* allowed them to take root, not him. Therefore, *you* are responsible for getting rid of them. Your father cannot get rid of unforgiveness in *your* heart, only in his own. I am responsible for *my* attitudes; you are responsible for *yours.*"

"You don't make it sound very fair."

"We talked about that one other time. Christianity *isn't* always fair. It's a hundred percent deal. God wants *all* of us. Bits-and-pieces commitment, selectively giving Christ what we choose but retaining for ourselves what we don't want to relinquish, keeping our own independence alive but nicely contained so it keeps up a presentable image—there's none of that in the Gospels."

"You're not much of an advocate," Lisel laughed, "if you want to make Christianity sound appealing."

"I have no interest in making it sound appealing. As far as I can see, neither did Jesus. When men asked to follow him, he told them to leave behind all they had. When men wanted to be his disciples, he said if they wanted to be worthy to be called by the name they had to be prepared to be rejected, hated, and then to die. There wasn't the slightest quarter given to the retaining of an independent spirit at the same time as being his disciple. It was one or the other. One hundred percent. All the way in one camp or the other. Jesus could say that his joy was full because he had yielded all claims to independence and self. The two are intrinsically linked."

Lisel sighed. It *didn't* sound very appealing when he put it like that!

"I'm just trying to tell you what looks like truth to me," Tad continued. "And when problems exist, you can't look to the *other* person to deal with them. You can't even look to the other person to go fifty percent of the way. It's *all* up to you. Whatever walls exist between people are the responsibility of the people who are *carrying* the anger or the unforgiveness in their heart. They are the *only* ones who can effect a change. And, if the truth be known, usually other people aren't as much to blame as we want to think. When *we* have attitudes that have built up walls, usually it's mostly our *own* doing. You admitted the same thing just a little bit ago."

"You don't make it easy."

"No one ever said being a Christian was easy."

"What about my yoke is easy and my burden light?"

"After we've utterly relinquished *self,* that is true. But as long as we continue to try to *hold on* to a piece of our own independence, we're going to be in for a pretty rough time of it."

"What do you mean, relinquish *self?* Doesn't God want us to be ourselves? Didn't he give us an individuality?"

"Yes *and* no. If by individuality you mean your uniqueness, your personality and temperament, and all the gifts and attributes that God put into you in order that you might reflect his divine nature, then there is nothing he desires so much as that we emerge in that individuality and personhood. But I use the word *self* differently."

"What *do* you mean by it, then?"

"That part of us that is motivated only by self-interest. Call it *independence* if you like—they're the same thing. The *self* that resides down inside each one of us is dead set against God's interests. *Independence* does not want anyone else interfering with the course it sets for itself. *Independence* is its own god. That's the *self* that has to be relinquished. When the *self* is denied decision-making power and control, then the true individuality that God gave us is able to emerge—but not before.

"In other words, I would say that no, God does *not* want us to be ourselves, at least not in the way *we* mean it. *He wants to kill the self,* not give it a comfortable home in which to go its own independent way. Only after *independence* is yielded will individuality truly emerge."

"How do you do that?"

"I suppose it's something everyone has to discover the mechanics of himself. The Bible talks about 'dying to self' and 'putting the self to death,' but those phrases have never really been that helpful to me. I've been a Christian all my life, but my *self* is *not* dead and never will be in this life. It is loud and obnoxious and constantly interfering with my desire to live a godly life by putting in its two cents worth about what I should do and how I ought to behave. Its voice is *independence*—telling me I have a right to be my own master, which is a lie. I have no such right at all. No one does. It is one of the great lies of the universe that *independence* is a good thing and that we have a right to it. If I gave in to all the garbage and nonsense my independent *self* tells me, I'd be a mess and not worth a plug nickel as a Christian."

"Do you *ever* do selfish things?"

Tad laughed. "Of course," he said. "I give in to my *self* and hold selfish attitudes all the time. But usually without realizing it at first. Once I see that *independence* has gotten the upper hand and has suckered me again, I do my best to oust him from control. That's a struggle in itself because in a sense you are fighting against yourself—one part of you is fighting against another part of you for control. And even when you do succeed in getting rid of him temporarily, he'll always be back."

"If what you call your *self* is so alive and vocal, then what do you do? I'd think the struggle would be too exhausting."

"My way of looking at it is this: I don't give my *self* a vote in my affairs. I accept that *independence* is going to make a pest of itself. But it has no vote. It's not a member of the board of directors of my life. It may come in and talk and fuss and try to sway the board's vote. And as I said, I may listen from time to time. I'm as self-motivated as the next man. But when time for a decision comes, I have to do my best to kick it out of the room."

"Who is on the board?" asked Lisel.

Tad laughed. "I'm not sure how far to carry this analogy," he said. "But to answer your question—hmm, let's see . . . *God's Will* would be chairman of the board. Then *Scripture,* and *What Would Jesus Do?* and *Putting Other People First* . . . oh, and *Servanthood* and the *Fruit of the Spirit* . . . and I would add *First Corinthians 13*—those would probably be the main seven voting members . . . oh, and maybe a fellow I might call *Relinquishment of Self* or *Yielding of Independence,* whichever you want to call it, who always votes exactly the opposite of what *self* itself has proposed."

He laughed again. "I'm afraid that imagery has about been stretched to the limit!"

"You do have a very practical, yet at the same time very hard, way of talking about being a Christian."

"I think it *is* hard, until you grasp God's purpose. As long as you try to retain *self* as a voting member of your own personal board, it is going to be a battle. For *God's Will* and *Putting Others First* will always clash with *independence* in the end, and then you will be in for a rough time of it. God's only purpose is to kill *self* and *independence* altogether so that we might in the end be his perfect sons and daughters, just like Jesus. Once we recognize that purpose, relinquishing *self,* banishing him from the boardroom, *firing* him, if you want to put it like that, is the most natural next step in the world. That does not make walking as a Christian ever afterward *easy,* but it does mean many of the stress points most people find difficult are predetermined. Once that decision has been made to banish *self* and yield *independence* into the hands of another, it's not all that hard to place what comes along into God's care. Christians who don't understand that such is God's aim will always either be miserable or stagnant. As long as *independence* is allowed to continue voting, things are not going to be as they should."

"What if you don't *want* to be made into a perfect son or daughter?"

"Of course we don't want it. Our *selves* don't at least. How could they? It means they will have to die. Everyone *wants* to be independent. It feels good. But what *we* want for *ourselves* hardly matters. The only question of significance is what he purposed when he made us and whether he intends to have his way in the end. That is why it has always seemed most prudent to me that we allow him to get on with *his* business posthaste. The sooner we get our *selves* killed off and silenced and banished from the boardroom the better. The longer we delay, the more painful is going to be the divine surgery in the end."

Lisel thoughtfully took in Tad's penetrating words. "What if you only want to be an average, OK, good person—you want to be nice, but not necessarily a saint?" she asked after a moment.

"Wanting to be just 'good enough' is another way of saying you don't want to give God your all, you don't want to let him have his way with you. It's only a disguised attempt of *independence* to keep fully alive and in control, but wearing a nice face to present to the world."

"Aren't you being rather hard on nice, good people?"

"There are nice people, and then there are *nice people,*" replied Tad. "Some are nice because their *independence* is in control, others are nice because they have *relinquished* their independence altogether. Looking at someone on the surface doesn't tell you very much about which of the two happens to be the case. Two individuals may look the same to outward appearance . . . they may both be equally *nice,* but be moving in two very opposite directions—the one toward *abandonment of self,* the other toward *complete self-motive* in all he does; the one toward sainthood, the other toward something much worse.

"No, God is not in the business of making average, nice people. He *is* going to make saints out of us. And he *is* going to call us his sons and daughters. The sooner we relinquish any idea that something less than the full treatment of transformation will do, the happier we'll be."

Lisel was thoughtful. This was an altogether new perspective on being a Christian than she had ever confronted.

"Independence," Tad went on, "is the cancer of the human soul. It is every man or woman's worst enemy. It is *the* most serious spiritual and emotional disease of the personality with which we can be afflicted. And it is just like physical cancer in that it attacks silently and invisibly, sometimes working away for years, even decades, before we become aware of it. By then it is too late. It has spread throughout our entire being. We have been making choices that have contributed to its growth for our entire lives. Eradication becomes increasingly difficult with each passing year because the cancer grows ever larger and larger within us, its tentacles stretching into more and more aspects of our being."

"You do make it sound rather awful!" shuddered Lisel. "What's to be done, then?"

"The surgery will come," answered Tad. "Independence *will* be cut out of us all. But the longer we wait to get the process underway, the more excruciating will be the knife once we finally do submit to it."

"I don't ever remember hearing my father and mother talk quite like this. The whole thing sounds horribly unpleasant."

"It is only awful to one who resists the divine imperative, which is banishment of *independence* to the outer darkness so that the true personhood for which we were created—the personhood of *unself*, the personhood of yielded relinquishment, the personhood of God's divine Self living in us instead of our own—might emerge."

"But I still come back to the question I asked earlier—how do you do it?"

"By denying the *self* what it is clamoring for a hundred times a day, by turning a deaf ear when *independence* speaks its lies about your rights, by relinquishing the *self* its power to determine what ought to be your attitudes and actions. I suppose after some time doing this—denying the independent spirit ten thousand times—you begin to recognize *self's* voice. Its whisperings are subtle, but you learn, as I said, to recognize them. You train yourself to see the subtle masks *independence* and *self* wear to make you think you're behaving selflessly when actually all you're doing is feeding the independent spirit within you. It takes years of practice, but once you begin seeing these things with the kind of inner eyes my grandfather used to talk about, you get to the point where you begin automatically trying to do the opposite of what *self* says you should."

"Do you always succeed?"

"Are you kidding!" laughed Tad. "Maybe five percent of the time, if I'm lucky. I said *try* to do the opposite of what *self* wants me to."

"Do you never indulge yourself?"

"I indulge myself, sure," replied Tad. "But I will never knowingly indulge my *self.* That's one of the most dangerous things in the world to do. It has lethal consequences."

"I'm not sure I understand the difference."

"The difference can only be understood, as I said, by the ten thousand relinquishments of *self's* desires and demands and wants. In the very relinquishment of *self* are one's inner eyes opened to *self's* wiles. Obedience opens the door to understanding."

"How can you obey before you understand?"

"That's the easy part—just do what Jesus said."

"Did he say to relinquish the *self?*"

"In a thousand ways he said it," replied Tad.

"Give me an example."

"He said that the man or woman who would follow him must be last of all and servant of all. If that isn't a simple prescription for the yielding of *independence,* I don't know what is."

118

An Imperfect Vessel?

• • •

AGAIN THEY DROVE ON A LONG WHILE IN SILENCE. TAD'S thoughts had come back to Lisel's father. He knew that the piece of *self* Lisel had to oust from *her* seat of control was unforgiveness.

Now that he had heard the whole story, it was clear enough that she would not be capable of opening herself fully into relationship with her heavenly Father until she had retraced her steps back through the doorway of her anger toward her earthly father and relinquished the independent spirit that had given rise to it.

"Would you mind doing something?" he asked.

"I don't think I'd mind—what do you want me to do?"

"This is something I learned from my own dad. He's been a great father. He and I share a wonderful friendship. But he sat me down one time and told me that if I expected him to perfectly reflect God the Father, I would always end up disappointed. Then he put me through a little imaginary exercise that I've never forgotten. He made me promise I would pass on these same truths to my own children and tell them to likewise pass them on, in the same way that he had learned them from both my grandfathers. Since we've been talking about your father, I think you might benefit from it."

"Then tell me what to do," said Lisel.

"Close your eyes," said Tad. "Now bring the image of your father into your mind."

Lisel did so, but found it neither easy nor pleasant. She had persistently kept the face of her father from intruding too personally into her thoughts since the night atop the Wall three years ago.

She and Tad had already spoken of so many things on this night, however, that she was able to quietly contemplate her father now without a return of the anger that usually accompanied the memory. The face that came into the view of her mind's eye, however, was stern and disapproving, as she remembered him the last time she and he had spoken harshly to one another.

"Focus on that face," Tad was saying. "Earthly fatherhood and motherhood are the foundational means God established to give mankind pictures of himself so that we would know what he was like. To do that he gave every human being a father and a mother.

"That man you are visualizing is the man God chose for you—you personally, Lisel. That is the man through whom God specifically chose to transmit his own self—to *you,* to start you on the pathway to knowing what his perfect Fatherhood is like. He wants to be a Father to you, just as he does to me. So he began the process of showing us how to relate to him by giving us earthly parents.

"Yet all human fatherhood is flawed. A few individuals have wonderfully understanding and loving and sensitive parents, but most don't. *All* earthly parenthood is incomplete. God chose to use imperfect vessels to transmit the highest of all truths to us—the truths of what he is like. It's a mystery why he did, but it was the method he chose.

"The plain fact of the matter is—earthly parents don't do a very good job of it. They are weak and flawed. *My* father didn't do a perfect job of conveying a picture of God's Fatherhood to me, and neither did *yours,* Lisel. Even though both your parents and mine were Christians, they were still imperfect vessels for this enormous responsibility that was given them. That man whose face you see, Lisel—he failed at the most important task he was ever given."

Tad continued to speak as they drove, while Lisel sat calmly with eyes closed, listening to his words.

"Yet in spite of this imperfection, fatherhood is still able to be nurtured through them. Perhaps their failures reflect failures in us too. Perhaps *we* have not allowed the true fatherhood that *was* in them (however much or little it may have been) to nurture us in the ways of *God's* Fatherhood. Perhaps *we* have stood in God's way of allowing that process to occur just as much as they have.

"Therefore, might there yet be nurturing that God still wants to accomplish within *our* hearts through the forgiveness process? As a child can nurture the blossoming of Fatherhood in his own heart, you and I can take a share in the development of God's character within ourselves by forgiving our fathers their imperfections.

"Yes, they were imperfect vessels. But they could not help that. Your father didn't understand, Lisel. He had no idea of the high and holy calling that was upon him when you came into the world."

Tad paused briefly. "Do you still see his face?" he said.

Lisel nodded.

"Try to imagine it the first time he laid eyes on you after you were born. Do you see the great smile on his face, maybe even a tear or two that he wipes quickly away before anyone sees it. He is looking down with the great, tender, silent love of a man upon you—his very own daughter! And then the name he and your mother have chosen rises silently onto his lips . . . *Lisel, my own Lisel!* If only you could know how much he loved you in that moment!"

A lonely tear at last found its way out of one of Lisel's eyes and began its solitary journey down her cheek, unseen by any but the One who feels all our tears in his heart.

"You grew," Tad went on, "and still he loved you, though on his face was not always a smile. You remember happy times . . . you remember hurtful times. Do you see your father's face as you grew? What is on that face now? He didn't know all about God's Fatherhood, did he? He didn't know that such was his primary calling in life—to show you what God, your Maker and heavenly Father, was like.

"Then hurts began to come into your young life, things perhaps your father did that turned you away from wanting to look at God. Then you left home . . . you said things . . . your father said things.

"Oh, Lisel, imagine how God hurts in his great infinite heart from seeing the pains and misunderstandings and agonies that your father caused—either directly or indirectly—in your life. But *your poor father did not know what he did.* Despite those agonies, he was still God's chosen instrument. And yet, Lisel . . . you pushed him away.

"Your forgiveness of your father is the key, Lisel, the key that will unlock in your heart a fuller blossoming of the fatherhood of God. It really has nothing to do with your father at this point. Your father could even be dead—it wouldn't matter. *That forgiveness is between you and God and must come in your own heart.* The key is in *your* hands, not mine, not your father's, not even God's. You can't hold imperfection against your father. You can't hold mistakes against him.

"We are *all* imperfect vessels. So are you and I, Lisel. But God intended for those vessels that were our parents to carry the water of life into our spirits. And we are foolish indeed if we refuse the water God would give us because the pot is ugly and broken and some of the water may have spilled on its way to us. Our earthly parents provide an incomplete view. We are equally foolish if we limit our view of God to our broken earthly picture.

"Oh, Lisel, just imagine what forgiveness might do!

"They were dreadfully imperfect vessels. Yet God's purpose was and still is to reveal aspects of himself *through those broken pots of clay.* Even if they are but tiny fragmented glimpses, and however diligently we might have to search to find them, they are true glimpses of God himself.

"Draw your mother's face into your mind now, Lisel. All the same things still apply. God designed for her motherhood to reveal aspects of his Fatherhood and to nurture them in your life. She is also a chosen vessel to transmit God's life into your heart.

"She is equally imperfect. A vessel full of holes. She may not have known to what she was called either. She didn't understand God's Fatherhood. How could she transmit it to you?

"But the full story has not yet been told."

It became quiet. Tad had given Lisel much to think about. But the most important portion of the image was yet to be considered.

"Will you imagine one more thing?" asked Tad.

Lisel nodded in the darkness, wiping unconsciously at her eyes now filling with moisture in earnest.

"Picture your father's face after he has been taken from this earth. He is dead. You will never see him again in this life. He is now with God. He has become a child again. Suddenly his eyes are opened to all the things he didn't understand while he was on this earth.

"Imagine him standing before God. Suddenly *you* come into his mind.

"Tears fill his eyes. Do you see them, Lisel? Do you see the expression of childlike innocence upon his countenance?

"Your father is crying before the Lord because all at once he sees clearly how incomplete was his love for you. Suddenly he realizes what a mess he made of it. Suddenly he sees how woefully short he fell. It rips at his heart to realize he gave you such an inadequate picture of the heavenly Father. He is filled with a greater love for you than he ever knew possible, yet there is nothing he can do to show you that love. He wants so desperately for you to know God the Father as he now sees him, yet in agony he realizes that many of your mistaken and hurtful notions he himself caused . . . and he cannot go back and undo them.

"Your father loves you, Lisel. But now it is too late. He went to his grave with the wall between you still—"

"Stop!" Lisel suddenly cried, bursting into passionate sobs of bitter remorse. "Please, Tad . . . please stop!" she faltered in a barely audible voice, "I . . . I can't take any more."

She broke down weeping, head cradled in her hands. *"God . . . God, forgive me!"* she sobbed. *"Forgive me for blaming my poor papa . . . God . . . O God, please forgive me!"*

He Chastens Those He Loves

• • •

Berlin

WHILE THESE MOMENTOUS DISCUSSIONS WERE UNDER-way, at the Westmark Hotel in Berlin not a sound was to be heard throughout the huge room where Tad's parents and the other church leadership conferees were gathered.

"Why do you think," Palacki was saying, "that those of us such as my brothers Wurmbrand and Duduman and Vins and others have been risking our lives for all these years? Each of us has been imprisoned, beaten, tortured, humiliated because of our preaching of Christ's gospel.

"For thirty years we have smuggled and traveled, taught, preached, gone hungry, organized, yes, and even spoken and written to you of the West as well. Thousands upon thousands of our fellow Poles and Russians and Slavs and East Germans have laid their lives on the line for the sake of their faith and in order to share that faith with others.

"I tell you, my friends, God's church is alive and well in the areas you represent as lost and in such desperate need. Small, perhaps, it may be, but it is alive and thriving because in our corners of the world there is a *price* to be paid to call yourself a disciple of the Lord Jesus Christ. A price that cannot be measured as you seem to measure all things—by money. No, you who hear my words who I hope and pray are my brothers and sisters, it *costs* to believe in the East. It costs *all you have* to be a Christian. So there are very few lukewarm, halfhearted souls among us. To be halfhearted can cost you your life!

"For years we have tried to alert you Christians of the West to the true state of affairs behind the Iron Curtain. We have written, we have traveled, we have spoken, we have prayed, we have wept.

"How many of you listened to us?

"My brother and friend Alexandr Solzhenitsyn attempted for a decade to be heard, as have so many others. We asked for your prayers, for Bibles, for help in teaching and training our people. And some help did come, for which we were grateful.

"But the rest of you continued to feed your own mammoth religious systems, building yet bigger and bigger transmitting stations and more television stations and publishing more books—all in the name of proclaiming the gospel.

"But did you ever give of *yourselves?* Did you come help us? Did you pray for us? Did you suffer and die and starve with us? How much did you really care about the people you now so pompously think you will *save* for the kingdom?

"Where have you been all the time? We needed your help and prayers and support and Bibles when times were hard! We have been beaten and imprisoned and even killed for the gospel's sake. Where were you when it counted? We lived our faith behind the Iron Curtain, and now that it is down, who is to say we even *want* you coming with your pompous egoism and self-reliance?

"Come now! Did you seriously expect a huge outpouring of goodwill and gratefulness from those of us representing the East for all these grandiose plans you would make for our people?

"Did you really envision a great unity of working together in this time when you say opportunity for harvest is so great? To listen to you, all that we have been pouring our lives out for these last four decades of repression counts for naught. Do you truly expect us to share your enthusiasm and welcome you and your wealthy brand of capitalistic Christianity with open arms?

"Think again, my friends, those I would still call my brothers and sisters in spite of your blindness. Pause and consider the egotism of your presumption and the worldliness of your method."

By now the auditorium was filled with the heaviness of shocked silence. No one dared move a muscle or so much as shift in his seat. But Palacki's chastening diatribe was not over yet.

"How dare you well-fed, contented, prosperous Christians of the West," he went on bitterly, "come here now and think you can throw your money and your technology at us poor unfortunates and suddenly 'save the world' with all the gadgets and inventions and high-tech wizardry of electronic spirituality! You with your multi-million-dollar architecturally imposing churches, you with your computer Bibles and preprogrammed Bible studies, you with your posh cars and soft, upholstered pews, your grand libraries of Christian books, your leather-bound reference Bibles, you who have all the answers to the world's ills nicely at hand to spout off when asked.

"How many of you have been hauled away at gunpoint for attending a spiritual discussion? When was the last time you were beaten for uttering a sentence of prayer? Do you think you can spread the gospel with a conference, with programs, with satellites, with your television and music, with your preaching?

"Have we Christians of the East been idle all this time? What would you have us do, go off quietly somewhere so you can come in and pat yourselves on the back before your watching congregations and claim credit for saving all the souls who would be lost without you?

"No, my shallow brothers and sisters of wealthy, contented Western evangelicalism! Build a prayer tower or a glass church somewhere, but think not that your money can save lost souls. Go back from whence you came . . . and spend your evangelistic self-gratifying mammon elsewhere!"

Suddenly he stopped, stood another two or three seconds gazing at his listeners with calm countenance, yet flaming eyes. Then, with decisive motion he ripped the check he was still holding into several pieces and let it drop to the floor.

Palacki turned and strode off the platform and out of sight, leaving his hearers gaping in stunned silence.

120

Safe in Berlin

• • •

MATTHEW AND JOSEPH HAD GONE OUT EARLY FOR A WALK and coffee. Upon their return through the lobby, Matthew spotted Gentz Raedenburg, apparently waiting for someone.

Matthew walked toward him and introduced himself. "I have been hoping for an opportunity to personally express my appreciation for your remarks the other day," he said.

"Thank you very much, Mr. McCallum," replied the German churchman. "That means a great deal coming from you."

"Yours were not quite so explosive as last night's."

Raedenburg smiled. "I understand we will be privileged to be hearing from *you* this evening."

"I'm afraid not," said Matthew.

"Oh, what happened?"

"Let's call it a change of plans," answered Matthew. "Be that as it may, I thought your insights regarding our two countries were very illuminating. I found it especially interesting in that my wife is German and our son, therefore, has grown up in both cultures, so to speak."

Raedenburg nodded, though with serious expression.

"What is it?" asked Matthew.

"Oh, I was just thinking about it all now," Raedenburg replied, "wondering how the German landscape might change."

"What do you mean?"

"Haven't you heard?"

"Apparently not," said Matthew, glancing questioningly at Joseph. "Heard what?"

"Our chancellor is suddenly in a great deal of trouble—I am hoping to meet with him later in the morning."

"What kind of trouble?"

"He suffered a devastating and unexpected defeat in the Bundestag last evening. He was, I am afraid, as stunned in his own way as were most of the conferees at Mr. Palacki's words. A no-confidence referendum has been scheduled for sometime later this afternoon. The chancellor is beside himself."

"What does it mean?"

"A no-confidence vote means he would be ousted as chancellor. A new coalition government would be formed out of the parties. It hasn't happened since 1982 when Helmut Schmidt was ousted in just the same way by a vote of no-confidence. The whole country is in an uproar since the news broke last night."

The three men spoke a few more minutes. Raedenburg then spied the man he had been waiting for. "Excuse me," he said, "I am scheduled to have breakfast here with an old colleague from Sweden who just arrived in the city last night. It was a pleasure to meet you both."

They shook hands and parted.

• • •

It was only some twenty or twenty-five minutes later that Joseph accompanied Matthew into the McCallum suite to personally deliver the news that Ursula was scheduled to arrive by plane from Jerusalem at the Berlin-Tempelhof airport at five-thirty that same afternoon.

"The four of us will be having dinner together this evening!" he concluded.

"That's wonderful!" exclaimed Sabina. "Oh, I can hardly stand it—this is *so* exciting!"

Suddenly the door of the room swung open, almost crashing onto the wall behind it.

Matthew glanced up from the chair where he was sitting. Sabina turned around with a start. Notwithstanding thoughts of his wife, Joseph suddenly found his brain spinning off in new directions.

There stood Tad. Behind him two other men were entering the room, along with a very sleepy-looking young lady.

Matthew and Sabina both recognized Udo Bietmann and Tad's new friend Lisel, though the other man was a perfect stranger. They had not even two or three seconds to attempt to gather their thoughts about what it could all mean, however, before Tad spoke.

"We've got to find Gentz Raedenburg!" he exclaimed, without so much as a greeting to his father and mother. "And fast! Do you know if he's still in the hotel?"

"Joseph and I just saw him—," said Matthew, rising and shaking Bietmann's offered hand.

Tad was too agitated even to allow him to finish. "Where . . . do you know where he is now? The guy down at the desk said he had seen you together this morning."

"Just half an hour ago," said Matthew.

"We have to find him!"

"He's probably still downstairs at the hotel restaurant."

At the words, Tad turned and was already moving again toward the door and out into the hallway. Matthew hurried after him, followed by the others. On the way down the elevator, Tad quickly filled his father in.

"Let me go find him," said Matthew, as the elevator stopped at the lobby and he suddenly realized what the troop of seven of them must look like. "I'll tell him to get up to our room as soon as possible."

"Immediately!" both Tad and Udo urged.

"I will convey your sentiments precisely," rejoined Matthew, half running off through the lobby and to the restaurant.

He returned in less than three minutes, nodding his head as he approached the entourage clustered about the bank of elevators.

"He will be right up," said Matthew.

As the general mood began to calm, Tad made what introductions were necessary, then he and Bietmann began to fill Matthew, Joseph, and Sabina in on the situation. They were full of more questions than it was possible to answer quickly.

"You've been driving all night?" asked Sabina as they reentered the suite.

"Since ten o'clock last night, Polish time. What time is it here, anyway?" Tad said, glancing down at his watch.

"Quarter past nine."

"Hmm . . . we gained an hour."

"It might be a good thing," said Matthew. "From what you say, time is urgent, and Raedenburg just told Joseph and me earlier that there was a big explosion in the German parliament yesterday and that the chancellor may be ousted."

Galanov let out with an exclamation. "The dominoes have begun to fall in Germany too!" he said.

"You must all be exhausted," said Sabina.

"Actually, Andrassy and I managed to sleep some," said Udo, "but Tad and Lisel talked nonstop the whole way!"

A round of laughter erupted from the other three, albeit the laughs were sleepy ones.

"We stopped once and catnapped for a couple hours," added Tad. "It was a good thing too, otherwise we might not have discovered the tail we had picked up!"

"You were being followed?" said Joseph.

Tad nodded. "And not by some impartial observer. The first thing we knew of it we heard a shot and one of our windows blew out."

"What did you do!" asked Sabina in alarm.

"We woke up and drove off in a hurry!"

"Who was it?"

"I've been wondering if it may have been a friend of mine," said Lisel, speaking now in a very downcast tone.

The looks of confusion from Tad's two parents invited further explanation.

"That's another long story," sighed Lisel.

"Did whoever it was keep after you?" asked Matthew.

"Yeah, but then we had one advantage he didn't know about."

"He probably did know," interrupted Bietmann. "You remember what Andrassy said, that the fellow was after him."

"Right," said Tad. "Anyway, we still had the advantage of a shrewd ex–KGB man in our car." He chuckled at the thought.

"What happened—did you shake him loose?" asked Joseph.

"That's *another* long story," laughed Tad. "It cost us about an hour, and then afterward it took Andrassy *two* hours to tell us everything he'd done between the time he told us to let him off and when we met up again. I still don't know exactly how he did it, but we never saw the other car again."

"I want to hear every detail," laughed Matthew. "This sounds like the kind of thing that is right up my alley!"

But even as he spoke the words, he was interrupted by a knock on the door. "Perhaps on the plane home," he added to Tad as he rose.

"Come in, Gentz," said Matthew. "I'm sorry to so summarily interrupt your breakfast."

"You said it could not wait."

"I do not think I was exaggerating. I want to introduce you to three men."

Handshakes and introductions spread about the suite, which suddenly seemed very, very small.

"They are going to tell you the wildest story you ever heard," Matthew added. "I think you'd better sit down."

121

Untoward Meeting

. . .

THE SCENE WAS AGAIN AN UNDERGROUND PARKING
garage, although in Berlin this time rather than Bonn. The fact that it
was broad daylight as well contributed to Drexler's infuriation nearly
as much as the news he had just heard.

"How could you have let them give you the slip?" he exploded. "I
pay you top mark to not make infantile mistakes!"

"Careful, my powerful friend," seethed Claymore. "I may have
failed temporarily in my assignment. But I will not be insulted—not
by you or anyone!"

"Bah! What do I care for your sensitivities! How did it happen?"

"How do I know? I had them dead, even got a shot off. I may have
wounded one of them. But then suddenly the trail went ice cold."

"*One* of them . . . how many were there?"

"Four."

Drexler was silent a moment, wondering what the implications
could be of there being three others in the car besides Galanov.

"Whoever this guy is," added Claymore, "he is a pro. Once I
played my hand, they split up—the car went one way, your fellow the
other."

"On foot!" exclaimed Drexler.

Claymore nodded.

"And you let him elude you. . . . I don't believe what I'm hearing!"

"Their route clearly indicates Berlin as the destination. Something
will turn up here. I will find them. How much time is there?"

"Time . . . there is *no* time, you idiot! If that file surfaces before we silence Galanov. . . ." The German politician paused momentarily, his busy mind spinning rapidly. "Never mind," he added. Then, almost to himself as if he were thinking aloud, "I'll have to make sure the vote goes through today."

Another brief pause. "Listen, you get back to Moscow," he said to Claymore. "Get on the first plane and—"

"Are you crazy! I've been driving all night!"

"Sleep on the plane."

"Not for you, I won't! Tonight I sleep in a hotel! I make no more moves until I'm paid."

"For what? You came back to me empty-handed!"

"You forget, Herr Drexler, I know your face now. I know everything. I killed for you in Moscow. I watched, I listened, I learned more of your little game than you gave me credit for. You pay me today, seventy thousand D-marks—"

"Seventy thousand!"

"Forty for the hit, ten for the attempt, ten for expenses, and ten for the aggravation you have caused me. You pay me today, or you will be the next hit. If you want me back in Moscow, it will be half in advance . . . and I will not go until tomorrow."

"Look, the thing's already happening in Moscow. If it unravels and Desyatovsky's found out, I can't take the chance he'll implicate me. I need you there so that at a moment's notice he can be taken out."

"How does that help you?"

"I've seen the file on his plan. It's all Commonwealth stuff, nothing to connect it to me."

"It will be a minimum of an additional seventy thousand to remove someone of Desyatovsky's stature, especially with the heat on and such an urgency."

"You are venom, Claymore!" spat Drexler. "But I will pay your price."

"One hundred thousand or I go nowhere," shot back Claymore. "Seventy for services rendered, thirty as down payment on the Russian."

"Agreed. Meet me back here in two hours. In the meantime I will do what I can to ensure that your failure in the matter of the file does not change the outcome of the vote in the Bundestag. If it surfaces, chances are it will take too long to sift through the channels of whatever embassy or official he tries to show it to. It will be too late to hurt me, and I will already be chancellor."

"Two hours. You will have the money?"

"You will have it. Find me the file by that time and I will double the amount. Whatever you do, make arrangements to get to Moscow later today."

"Tomorrow, my friend . . . tomorrow. I go nowhere before then, file or no file, for *any* amount of money!"

"Bah!" said Drexler, cursing. "For half the price I could get twice the cooperation!"

"There is only one Claymore. And if you insult him again, the next hit will not be against the Russian!"

The hit man grinned with malice, then turned and left the basement.

122

Top-Level Conference

• • •

THE SCENE WAS THE OFFICE OF GERMAN CHANCELLOR Hans Kolter.

Two hours and several very high-placed telephone conversations later, the unlikely assembly settled themselves into their chairs. Now that they possessed the undivided attention of one of the world's most powerful men, suddenly all the anxiety of the past thirty-six hours seemed to give way to timidity.

"Well, Gentz," said Kolter, "what is this about? It's more than just highly irregular, and if it weren't for my regard for you, I would never have consented to such an interview."

"I know, Hans," replied Raedenburg. "I realize this is a dreadful time for you. I was planning to come see you anyway, if we could schedule it, to pray with you about the crisis you're facing. Unfortunately, there is an even more urgent crisis afoot of which you are yet unaware."

"What are you talking about?"

"I only ask you to hear them out."

"What are they, anyway? An East German, a Russian, and two Americans. Quite a conglomeration!"

"When you hear what they have to tell you, Hans, you will be very glad you made the time."

"I had to cancel an extremely important—"

"Believe me, sir," interrupted Tad, hardly realizing what he had done, "this is more important than anything you could have going on today. Please, just listen to us. It's not only important . . . it is *very* urgent. It may change everything, even what I understand you may face later today."

Kolter was half shocked by the interruption. But the ludicrousness of the situation suddenly seemed to strike him humorously. If he was going to lose his job anyway, why not spend his last day in office listening to these kooks!

Almost as if ready to enjoy a good joke, he finally sat down in his chair behind his large desk, looked deeply into all the faces before him, then said, "All right, gentlemen. I don't know what you're all about. But you have my attention. Now proceed with this story you have to tell."

The four looked around at one another. Both Bietmann and Galanov nodded at Tad, as the logical one to begin. Tad hesitated a moment more.

"Go on, young man . . . go on," said Kolter impatiently.

Tad drew in a deep breath, then plunged in, telling first in brief what had brought him and his parents to Berlin, how they had run into Bietmann, and then how he had been drawn into the rescue of Galanov at the border.

"I see nothing that involves me in all that," interrupted Kolter. "It is a fascinating story, but tell it to the newspapers."

"Please, sir, it's why Mr. Galanov was escaping Russia and why they were trying to kill him—that's what *does* involve you."

Kolter settled back again, and Tad went on.

"Mr. Galanov discovered a plan, sir, that is more widespread than any of us at first believed. Just hear us out before you pass judgment on what you are about to hear.

"There is, even as we speak, another coup attempt in progress in the former Soviet Union."

"What! I don't believe it!" exclaimed Kolter.

"Surely you are aware that the presidents of four of the Commonwealth republics, including Russia and the Ukraine, are gathered this very day at the nuclear reactor in Kuybyshev to inspect the damage. They are scheduled to leave tomorrow morning to travel together by what is being called the Summit Train down to Kirovabad in the Caucasus Mountains. We believe an attempt will be made en route to kill them all, thus triggering a massive takeover."

"It can't be! Nothing of such a magnitude could ever succeed in this new day. It's all changed, haven't you heard!"

"Not everything sir," replied Bietmann softly. "With all due respect to your position, men in high places still lust for power."

"They could never pull it off," replied a slightly flustered Kolter.

"It is already begun," said Bietmann. "You are surely aware of the labor unrest and union strike that has been called."

"Isolated incidents."

"Not isolated, sir. All planned from *within* the Kremlin."

"It just could never succeed," repeated Kolter. "That's been proven."

"Unlike the previous attempt," said Tad, "every element of society has been drawn in—leadership from all the provinces, from the military, from finance, from industry, all parts of the Commonwealth are involved, even a number of foreign leaders. There are documents, sir. Would you like to see them?"

"Yes, of course I would," said Kolter, beginning to pay more serious attention.

Galanov rose, stepped forward, and laid out the files on the chancellor's desk.

For several minutes Kolter studied them, then he barked into his intercom. Three minutes later the door opened and a man entered whom the chancellor introduced as his top Russian linguist and security and intelligence analyst for all Russian and Soviet affairs.

"Max," said Kolter, "what do you make of these?" He indicated the sheets spread out across his desk.

The other scanned them silently for several minutes, flipping through and back and forth.

"If these documents are reliable, what I make of them is as explosive as uranium 235. Are they reliable?"

Kolter glanced at Galanov. "Stolen from Desyatovsky's personal file," answered the Russian in German.

Kolter gave a low whistle. "Have you had wind of anything of this magnitude brewing, Max?" Kolter asked.

"Not a whisper."

A silence pervaded the room.

It was Galanov who broke it. "This is not all," he said. Slowly he pulled out several additional sheets from an envelope he had kept back, waiting to see how the chancellor would respond to the Moscow half of the plot. Now it was time to fill him in on the rest of it. "Working along with Desyatovsky has been a member of your own parliament who plans simultaneously with the coup in the republics to topple *your* government as well."

"A coup here . . . a takeover? Impossible! We have no military to speak of, and the parliamentary system would never produce a coup."

Even as he spoke, however, the eyes of the chancellor's mind were opening to the depth and scope of the events of the last twenty-four hours.

"I do not mean a coup as such," replied the former KGB agent, "but whatever sort of takeover your democratic system permits."

"There is only one man who could possibly . . . who would dare such a thing," said Kolter with a sigh, and sagging back in his chair. Suddenly everything became clear.

"Is his name Drexler?" asked Tad.

Kolter nodded. "Klaus Drexler, head of the RDP and my sternest opposition," said the chancellor. "Just last evening he rallied three of the smaller parties of the Bundestag to vote down my aid package. It undid my coalition, and he has called for a no-confidence vote against me—today. I had no idea of the magnitude of his scheme. I've been on the phone all day trying to call in old debts and gather back my support. From the looks of it though, Drexler's had this all figured out long enough to have every angle covered."

"Perhaps as a Russian," Andrassy went on, "I do not understand all your ways in the West. I have only been out of my own country a short time. But even if what we call a *coup,* you call something else, Drexler's plan is much larger than merely a desire to take your job, Herr Chancellor. If he gets away with it, it would amount to nothing less than a coup, by *any* name. Look at these."

He produced three single sheets from the envelope he had been holding apart from the others, which he laid on the desk in front of the chancellor. Both the fellow called Max and the chancellor stared at them intently.

"As you can see, Drexler and Desyatovsky are planning nothing short of a full-scale military, financial, industrial, economic, and societal axis between Berlin and Moscow. Drexler intends to cast the lot of the future of Germany with the East, eventually as much as cutting off ties with the West. After the United States, Britain, and France have poured billions into the rebuilding of the nations of the former

Eastern Bloc, they would establish a new currency, whole new military and nuclear alliances, a completely restructured financial and industrial and transportation foundation, pulling out of the EEC and NATO."

Several minutes passed during which they read over the papers in front of them.

"I never trusted Klaus a centimeter," exclaimed Kolter at length, "but . . . this . . . this is just too unbelievable! Where did you . . . how did you obtain these documents?"

"They came with the rest, from out of Desyatovsky's private file."

"If I may speak to what might be somewhat of the spiritual dimensions, Hans," said Raedenburg, "from everything I have heard and seen in the last two hours, it is my conviction that our colleague Herr Drexler is a New Age Nazi. He has obviously succeeded very well in masking it from all of us. But it now seems all too clear."

"As secretive as it has been," said Galanov, "I firmly believe that his sole goal is the supremacy of a new German state, with ties looking Eastward rather than Westward."

"Do you realize what the two of you are saying?" replied Kolter.

"Of course," said Raedenburg. "But thanks to these intrepid men, you ought to be able to stop him before any further damage is done."

Suddenly the chancellor appeared to come to attention again. His active brain awoke and began to fill with thoughts of decisive action. "Max," he said to his analyst, "get ahold of Helmut, Wolfgang, and Ralf. Get them over here immediately. Then do whatever you have to do to get Yeltsin on the phone. Wherever he is, whatever you have to do. Say anything you have to, just get me on a secure line with him. In the meantime, I'll phone the American president. But the instant you have Yeltsin, you break in."

Max left the room.

The others continued to watch, suddenly feeling very much out of place.

"I'll have to gather all my facts and the people I can trust," Kolter was saying. "I must have a foolproof strategy. Klaus has more behind him than I had any idea of. He's probably over in the parliament building right now rallying support behind him for my downfall."

"When is the vote scheduled, Hans?" asked Raedenburg.

"Debate is this afternoon. The vote will probably be later. The session might last into the evening." He rose and warmly shook each man's hand. "If there was just some way to thank you all enough for what you have done," he said. "It took courage. And now, it appears I have my work cut out for me!"

Even as he said the words, Matthew's mind was suddenly spinning with a wildly hopeful new idea! On their way out of the building, he asked Raedenburg what he thought.

The German nodded with a smile. "Hans is a most resourceful man," he said. "He's pulled off longer odds than this in his time."

"Do you think he would be offended by such a request?" asked Matthew.

"If he weathers the crisis this afternoon, I think he would do almost anything to help you that lay in his power."

"Then I suppose we must wait to see how he fares."

"If all goes well, I will be happy to call him again on your behalf. I will contact you later today at your hotel."

"Thank you," said Matthew.

The two men shook hands and parted.

New Friends of the Heart

• • •

NEITHER LISEL NOR SABINA WENT WITH THE MEN TO Chancellor Kolter's office. They remained behind at the hotel, and after Lisel took the opportunity to clean up and Sabina ordered tea and croissants from room service, they sat down to a long talk together.

Lisel began by asking about Sabina's story, which, she explained, Tad had withheld from her in the promise that it would be better heard from Sabina's own lips.

Sabina laughed. Lisel thought she had never heard such a melodic, contented, and carefree sound from a human mouth.

Sabina complied and began her tale. But it was not long before the unknown connections between the two women's pasts began to become clear. Revelation followed revelation, and many were the tears of disbelief when Sabina at length realized she was sitting with none other than dear Hermann's daughter.

Suddenly they were in one another's arms weeping as if they had known one another for years.

Lisel's story followed, clearly one with more melancholy tones throughout its telling, though as she described Tad's influence the heart of the mother could scarcely contain the swell of thankfulness to see the hand of God, as well as her own father's influence, emerging through the life of her son.

Their hearts flowed in love, one into the other. Then truly did they talk and share, as only women can—deeply and personally.

Long before they were done, Sabina had added her own loving and gentle balance to all Lisel had gained from Tad. The searching young lady felt closer to God than ever before in her life and had begun to realize that the years away from her father and mother had been years of trying to hide from God's face as well. It was clear that she had *two* fathers to whom she must go.

When she and Sabina prayed together, Lisel knew a loving Father was in the room with them. It was a morning Lisel would never forget.

She left the hotel before the men returned. She knew where her footsteps must take her before the day was through.

• • •

Lisel walked into her small house, glad her roommate was not home. The preparations she had to make were best carried out alone.

She was in no hurry. Slowly she undressed and enjoyed a leisurely bath. Then she crawled into bed and slept for an hour and a half. When she awoke she felt greatly refreshed.

The time had come to get ready. It took some time to dress. She wanted to look nice, but not to overdo it. Unconsciously, without planning, she opened the drawer and found her hand drawing out the small box that contained the few items of jewelry she possessed. There were not many. She had hardly worn a piece of any of these in years.

Lisel opened the lid. She reached in. Her fingers gently laid hold of the simple gold-plated locket her father had given her on her eighth birthday.

Considering all that had happened, she was surprised she still had it at all. Why had she kept it after leaving home? She had never worn it since, never even looked at it again . . . until now.

Slowly she unfastened the tiny latch. Inside, just as she remembered them, sat the two little rose seeds, unchanged in twenty years.

Quietly, in the heart of the woman who was at last ready to step into the maturity of becoming a child again, Lisel's memory recalled the conversation between father and daughter that had accompanied the gift and had been lovingly replayed many times afterward between them.

Her eyes filled with tears. At last, however, they contained no bitter sting, only the cleansing waters of sorrow . . . and newfound decision.

Lisel smiled. It was a pleasant memory, in spite of its poignancy.

She drew in a deep breath, then fastened the locket around her neck. It was the only possible thing she could wear.

Now, she realized, the seeds of her father's words, like those in the locket, had been planted within her in preparation for this very day.

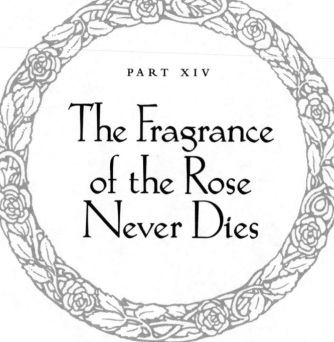

PART XIV

The Fragrance
of the Rose
Never Dies

Calling Drexler's Bluff

• • •

THE SCENE IN THE GERMAN PARLIAMENT THAT AFTER-
noon was much different than the previous evening. The air in the
Bundestag was charged with a current of energetic expectation as it
convened in Berlin for the second day of its special session.

The debate had not been as heated as expected.

Throughout the day, Chancellor Hans Kolter had scarcely been
seen. Reports were circulating through the building that he would
address the assembly before the day was out, though Klaus Drexler
was not worried. He had spent the entire day shoring up support and
was extremely confident that when he went to bed for the night, he
would himself be the new chancellor of Germany.

In the seeming absence, therefore, of a last-minute effort to save his
crumbling coalition, the debate had been more perfunctory than
necessary, and now the vote had been called for.

Kolter, however, was still not present. Out of deference for their
chancellor of so many years, the German MPs awaited his arrival,
though with growing annoyance at the delay, before voting him out
of office.

At long last Hans Kolter, Chancellor of the United Republic of
Germany, strode into the hall he had ruled so long with an iron hand.
His step was as confident as ever, and in his eye was not the look of
anticipated defeat. He walked confidently to the rostrum and immediately took up a position from which to address his colleagues of the
Bundestag. It was some time before the general buzz died down and
the MPs had returned to their seats.

"I apologize for the tardiness of my arrival," Kolter began. "These are more momentous times than any of you realize, and I do not refer to the impending vote with which you are awaiting to dismiss me from my post."

A low murmur swept through the parliament.

"Yes, I am more than aware of the plots and schemes against me which have run through this building most of today after last evening's resounding defeat of my aid bill. However, those of you who have already put your signatures on my obituary will, I am afraid, have to wait yet a while longer. And some of you—" as he spoke, he glanced in the direction of Gustav Schmundt and then over toward Keil Weisskopf—"who have been seduced into participating in this clandestine plot, will rue the day you allowed such treachery to poison old friendships and loyalties."

Schmundt could not return his gaze but looked away with mortification.

"My day has been spent attempting to avert nothing short of an international incident . . . indeed, an international crisis. I have been on the phone with the American president, the British prime minister, and President Yeltsin of Russia, of a matter, as I said, more momentous—"

He was interrupted in the midst of his discourse by a voice he knew only too well. "Come, come, esteemed Chancellor," said Klaus Drexler, who had risen to his feet. "The defeat of your ill-advised aid package hardly qualifies as an international crisis, for which, to save your political skin, you need to begin telephoning all the leaders of—"

"I do not refer to the defeat of the bill!" boomed Kolter.

"Then what, pray tell, *do* you refer to?" asked Drexler. His tone dripped with oily sarcasm.

"You know well enough, *esteemed* Herr Drexler!" shot back Kolter. "I should invite you up here with me to explain to your colleagues the details of what I am speaking."

Still Drexler had no hint of just how thorough Kolter's knowledge of the plan was. Nothing in the chancellor's words indicated to him the danger that lay ahead in his path. He was beginning to grow angry at Kolter's bravado.

"Enough, enough!" he said, and now his voice had grown icy and demanding. "A vote has been called for. We have awaited the moment of truth long enough. Your coalition has collapsed. We, your col-leagues, judge you unfit to lead and demand that you step aside or else face an immediate vote of no-confidence."

"Hear, hear!" called out scattered voices from the RDP.

"Your reign has ended, Kolter. Resign or be ousted!" said a loud voice.

"Do you hear them, Hans?" said Drexler. "You can stall no longer with your tactics of magniloquence and trying to manufacture a so-called incident as if to puff yourself up to vaunted importance on the world's stage one more time. It will not work! The Kolter dynasty is over. Resign or be humiliated by a vote! The future lies with the coalition led by the RDP!"

Love-Blossoms from Long-Planted Seeds

•   •   •

SHE HAD LIVED IN THIS CITY ALL HER LIFE. BUT SHE HAD not once returned to the street of her childhood home . . . until now.

As Lisel Lamprecht now made her way along the sidewalk on an errand that was long overdue, she recalled that day when, at sixteen, she had looked down one of these side streets at the Wall and wondered what the rough-textured stone would feel like against her soft palm.

That day she had beheld *Der Mauer* was another lifetime ago, thought Lisel. She had touched the Wall since then, and now the Wall was down and gone. Germany was reunited.

Another wall had remained, however. She hoped by day's end it would be demolished as well.

What she had to do would not be easy. Apologies rarely were. But if she wanted to be whole, this was the required first step.

Do you remember about the rose? a voice came into her mind saying.

Yes, Papa. I could never forget that, came words from a young girl.

Do you still wear the locket?

Lisel knew the reply came from her own lips: *Of course, Papa. It is the most special thing I have. I am wearing it now.*

Her eyes were wet, and unconsciously her steps increased their pace.

•   •   •

Hermann Lamprecht was aware of a strange sensation almost from the moment he had awakened.

He knew of no reason he should feel such a thing, but a keen anticipation filled him as the morning went on. By afternoon it had turned into the peculiar sense that some journey was nearly done.

What it could mean he hadn't an idea. He hadn't been out of the city in more than a year and wasn't planning a trip anytime soon. By midafternoon he found himself occasionally glancing out the window or wandering to his front door, opening it, and peering outside with his large palm on his forehead to shield his eyes. He wasn't looking for anything. He expected no visitors. The action came almost as a reflex, as a way to relieve the sense that something unexpected was at hand.

By late afternoon the restlessness had become severe. Hermann could scarcely keep from constant motion. Once again, for the two-dozenth time that day, he found himself at the window peering out along the street in both directions.

A lone figure in the distance caught his eye. Hermann's heart leapt into his throat! *It couldn't . . . God, O God . . . can it . . . O Lord—*

The poor man's thoughts and prayers turned into a jumble of incoherent words of fearful hope as he turned and stumbled toward the door.

A great cry went up to his wife, but he could not wait for her reply from inside the house.

Already he was out the door and lumbering to the sidewalk as best his aging legs and knees—quivering from what he thought he had seen—could carry him.

•   •   •

The moment Lisel saw her father hurrying out of the house and toward her, she broke into a run.

The very sight of the dear man brought a great lump to her throat. *How could she not have loved him! How could she have grown blind to his love for her!*

But there was no time for more questions, reflections, or recriminations now. There he was, and suddenly she was swallowed up in the great arms of her father once again, just as when she was a child.

"Oh, Papa . . . Papa, I'm so sorry!" cried Lisel, her face crushed against his great heaving chest. "I'm sorry, Papa . . . please forgive me."

"Oh, my child . . . my child," whispered the big man as great tears of joy fell from his cheeks, "you were always forgiven."

"Thank you . . . thank you, Papa," wept Lisel.

"I love you, child. . . . I love you."

For several long trembling moments they stood thus in one another's arms on the sidewalk.

"Do you remember about the mystery of life, Papa?" whispered Lisel.

He nodded. "It is found in the seeds," he said.

"It has taken me this long to understand what you were trying to teach me, Papa—that when seeds are planted with prayer, blossoms of love will grow."

"My heart rejoices that you remember."

"The seeds you planted in me, Papa, have finally, I think, begun to grow in earnest. At last I am ready to thank you for them."

"You make my heart proud, Lisel," said Hermann.

"I do not think I shall forget them ever again."

126

Foiling of a Coup

• • •

NOT FAR FROM THE QUIET STREET WHERE EVENTS OF eternal significance were playing themselves out, a raucous scene of great temporal importance was in progress. Clapping and cheers had by now burst out from Klaus Drexler's allies and Hans Kolter's longtime political adversaries.

But even six hundred MPs could yet be silenced by Hans Kolter's loud and towering presence. "Silence!" reverberated his huge baritone voice through the great hall, accompanied by his hand slamming down onto the rostrum with angry finality. "You, Klaus Drexler, are a traitor! I call you what you are to your face. A traitor to this body and to your nation!"

As he spoke, he turned and strode angrily forward onto the floor where his colleagues sat. "I will resign at the time the membership of this body indeed deems me incapable of holding together a coalition. But not," he thundered, "until the full truth is known!"

"Truth!" spat Drexler. "Spare us your sermons, Hans!"

"I will preach no sermons, Klaus," said Kolter, now approaching Drexler and standing face-to-face before his accuser, "but your colleagues will know the truth of your treason if *you* do not resign immediately."

"Have you lost your senses? I have not the slightest intention of resigning! It is I who shall be chancellor by this time tomorrow."

Kolter did not reply. Instead, he calmly pulled from the inside pocket of his coat a single piece of paper and laid it face up on Drexler's desk in front of him. Drexler glanced down at it and scanned it quickly.

"Now perhaps," said Kolter in a low voice, "I might be able to persuade you to have a few words with me in private?"

Drexler met his eyes with his own, squinted in narrow hatred, then nodded. Kolter led the way along the aisle and out the nearest door. Drexler followed.

An immediate uproar of wonder burst through the parliament.

In the corridor, Kolter wasted no time. "We know everything, Klaus," said the chancellor. "We know the entire scope of the plan. All of the principals in the Commonwealth are being rounded up even as we speak. The leadership and military are in safe hands, as is the CIA agent who helped to uncover this plot. President Yeltsin is on his way back to Moscow. All the other presidents are likewise safe. Your friend Desyatovsky is under arrest and is being held awaiting further orders from Yeltsin."

"What has all this to do with me?" said Drexler coolly. "Why should events in the Commonwealth concern me?"

"Come, Klaus, it's all over. The coup has failed. Desyatovsky has revealed everything and has sung an interesting tune regarding his chief accomplice."

"Why that no good—"

"Klaus, please, such anger does not become you. Even without Desyatovsky telling us all about you, about your friend Claymore, about things you have done, both here and there—even without all that, Klaus, we have his complete file. He was never able to recover it. No, and I understand your man was on it too, but he likewise failed."

"I have no idea what you are talking about, Hans," said Drexler, trying to regain his calm.

"Of course, Klaus. But you see, the file, almost by a miracle, found its way to my office this very morning. Don't you see the irony of it? *Your* scheme found its way to *my* office!"

"Whatever Herr Desyatovsky might have been trying—"

"Klaus, Klaus! Do not continue the charade. Your Russian friend kept meticulous notes. He documented everything—every conversation, every phone call. Did you know he tape-recorded most of his talks with you? We have the transcriptions—word for word. Klaus, don't you understand? It's over. You have nothing left to do but resign."

Drexler's face turned ashen. "Proof . . . I demand to see proof!" was all he could say. His voice came in a gasp, barely above a whisper.

"You shall see it all," replied Kolter. "But in the meantime—" he pulled several more papers from his pocket—"this should give you a fair idea that I am not bluffing."

Drexler grabbed them hastily. As his eyes roved down the page, his face grew whiter still. "What do you want me to do?" he whispered at last.

"For the good of the country, none of this will be made public. Mr. Yeltsin has agreed that such a course would be best for the sake of his Commonwealth also. Therefore, you will be allowed to resign your post in parliament with dignity—*if* you do so immediately, without explanation. If you do not, or if you delay, I cannot save you from the consequences. It could go very badly for you if all this leaked to the press."

Drexler sighed deeply, then looked into his chancellor's face with resolve. "My resignation shall be on your desk in the morning. You may make it public any way you see fit." He turned and walked briskly down the corridor and out of the building.

Kolter watched him go, full of his own thoughts, then turned, not without a sense of sadness, and reentered the temporary Bundeshalle. Seeing him alone, a renewed round of noise and question and exclamation filtered loudly through the room.

Kolter walked straight to the front of the hall, up the steps, and to the rostrum, where he stood awaiting quiet. On his face was not a look of victory but of grief. His colleagues seemed to sense it and quieted quickly. No more heckling came, even from the RDP side.

"My friends and colleagues," he said simply. "I ask you to postpone your referendum on your confidence in my coalition for at least twenty-four hours. Tomorrow, I request you, Gustav, and you, Keil, to see me in my office. Despite what you have done, I still consider you my friends. If the three of us are unable to hold our coalition together, then I will resign by this time tomorrow. All I ask for is twenty-four hours."

He paused, then continued, looking around to the entire assembly as he spoke. "Our colleague Klaus Drexler of the RDP has informed me of his intention to resign as a member of the German Bundestag effective tomorrow."

Exclamations and a buzz of shocked question and excitement burst out from the floor.

"Please," said Kolter. "I am nearly through. I trust this news may alter the position some of you may have been going to take on the no-confidence vote. In any case, you will have twenty-four hours to decide whether you indeed want me to continue as your chancellor or not. I would ask the president of the Bundestag to excuse my presence for the remainder of the session."

Without awaiting a reply, Kolter left the rostrum and strode as quickly as he could from the hall, looking neither to the left nor the right. He hated the black spot in his nation's past and loved his country for the democratic principles it now stood for too much to relish in this victory over a man who had nearly succeeded in taking it down.

A near roar of astonished disbelief followed him from the hall.

127

A Bold Request

• • •

ONCE AGAIN MATTHEW AND TAD MCCALLUM, ALONG WITH
Sabina this time, and their new friend Gentz Raedenburg found
themselves in the presence of German chancellor Hans Kolter.

The circumstances on this occasion, however, were far different
than they had been two mornings earlier in the chancellor's office.
They had, in fact—once Raedenburg's request for a second interview
for his American friends had been made known—been invited to the
chancellor's new Berlin residence. They had arrived about thirty
minutes earlier, and were now chatting comfortably.

"Gentz tells me," Kolter said at length, "that you three
McCallums have a need that I might be able to help with."

"You did say, sir," replied Matthew with a laugh, "that you would
like to find a way to repay us—our son that is," he added, glancing
toward Tad, "for what he and the others uncovered."

"I meant every word. If I am able to help you, I certainly will.
What is the problem?"

"My wife," said Matthew, indicating Sabina with his hand, "was
raised northeast of here in what was then Germany but is now, thanks
to our Russian friends, in Poland."

Kolter nodded. He was well aware of the boundary problem.

"Her father was Heinrich von Dortmann—"

"Baron von Dortmann?" interrupted the chancellor. "The man
who hid Jews during the war . . . involved with Bonhoeffer?"

Sabina nodded with a smile.

"Then I am more honored to know you all than I realized," said
Kolter. "I knew of your father and admired him. So," he added as if

he was only piecing it all together for the first time, "my government was saved by none other than Baron von Dortmann's grandson?"

"Among others," laughed Tad.

"I see! Well—this is fascinating and unexpected." Kolter cast Matthew a sudden look of dawning recognition. "Say . . . haven't we met before?" he asked. "Talk of Dortmann jogs something in my memory regarding his son-in-law."

Matthew laughed lightly. "Yes, sir," he replied. "We've crossed paths briefly a time or two. I was with the U.S. State Department for some time."

"Of course! I do recall it now—forgive me for taking so long."

"It was many years ago," rejoined Matthew. "I was first in Berlin as John Kennedy's envoy, that's how far back I go."

Now it was Kolter's turn to laugh. "You predate my political career by several years! In any case, it is nice to see you again."

"Thank you."

"So . . . go on, go on—I am yet all the more intrigued."

"The baron, Sabina's father, owned a rather sizable estate," Matthew said, taking up the narrative again, "which of course was confiscated by the Russians once they took control of Poland and East Germany."

Kolter nodded as he took in the information, while Matthew went on to explain the difficulties he had encountered in attempting to regain the property on Sabina's behalf. When he was through he handed the chancellor the ancient deeds he had taken from the *Lebenshaus* dungeon years before.

Kolter looked them over with great interest. "Yes . . . yes," the chancellor said, "this small region of Poland has been a thorny spot for some others too, one of the unfortunate things even reunification has been unable satisfactorily to resolve."

"Is there anything that can be done for these people, Hans?" asked Raedenburg once Matthew was through. "Germany does owe them a great deal."

"Yes, you're right about that," mused the chancellor. Slowly he began pacing about the room, obviously deep in thought. The others waited silently.

"You know who else owes something," he said at length. "That's Poland. They're included in this aid package that it turns out is going to go through after all. We've not only saved democracy and freedom for their newly created government, they're going to get millions in economic assistance besides. I would say they owe us a great deal."

He turned around, face animated. "I think I might be able to pull it off!" he added.

"How?" asked two or three voices at once.

"I'll call Walesa!"

Glances of incredulity spread about the room.

"Lech already owes me more favors than I'm counting," said Kolter boisterously. "And now with these developments of the last two days . . . I'll simply ask him to give us the property back. I'll make it a personal condition, off the record of course, for Poland's receipt of its share of the aid."

"Is such a thing possible?" asked Matthew.

"Anything's possible! If Poland wants to be a democracy, they're going to have to get used to private ownership, even foreign ownership. What's to stop a German or an American from owning a home in Poland? It's the most reasonable thing in the world!" Kolter thought a moment more. "In fact," he said, striding now toward the phone on one of the tables in the spacious sitting room, "I'll call him right now!"

He picked up the receiver, waited a moment, and then Matthew, Sabina, and Tad heard him speak the authoritative words: "Get me Lech Walesa on the line."

128

Roses Will Bloom Again

• • •

Western Poland, near Niedersdorf

AS MANY YEARS AS SHE HAD DREAMED OF IT, THE SET-
ting was not one upon which Sabina Dortmann McCallum had
expected to set the gaze of her physical eyes again in this life.

She had imagined her beloved *Lebenshaus* ten thousand times in
those other eyes her father had helped nurture within her. But to
stand on the grounds of her daydreams again, with the great house of
her childhood behind, and the site of *Der Frühlingsgarten* sloping off
downward below her . . . it was a moment almost more full of
emotion than she could bear.

The hedged outline of her father's garden could clearly be made
out—if you knew what you were looking for. Both hedge and
everything within its borders was so overrun and wild that only one
who knew what had been there fifty years earlier could possibly
imagine its former shape and glory.

"We will make it all blossom and flourish again," said a voice
beside her, as if reading her thoughts. "Every tree shall bud, every
flower bloom."

Husband and wife had been standing motionless, hand in hand,
for three or four minutes in silence.

"Oh, Matthew," Sabina sighed, "do you really think it is possible?"

"What would your father say?"

Sabina smiled. "He would quote the Scotsman. I know the
passage by heart. It was always one of Papa's favorites."

"Then let's hear it. It seems more appropriate now than ever."

"*It is well enough known . . .*" Sabina began in a reflective tone, then paused. She could not separate the words from her father, as if he had loved them throughout his life because he apprehended their prophetic meaning and sensed that one day they would be uttered prayerfully over his *own* beloved garden as well. "*It is well enough known,*" Sabina began again after a moment, "*that if you dig deep in any old garden, such as this one, ancient—perhaps forgotten—flowers will appear. The fashion has changed, they have been neglected or uprooted, but all the time their life is hid below.*"

"I can hear the words as if your father were speaking them this very moment," said Matthew. "He would stand here only a few moments, and the excitement would begin to build for discovering all the hidden things waiting to explode from the earth out there."

Matthew pointed across the garden as he spoke.

"He would probably take as much joy in bringing the garden back to life as he had in giving it its beauty in the first place."

"He was always looking for life and meaning below the surface—whether in the character of God, one of the Scotsman's books, or in the dirt of his garden. It is one of his most enduring legacies."

"And he would be out there tomorrow morning on his hands and knees looking for that hidden life, with his gloves on and with pruning shears and a shovel beside him!" said Sabina, with a hint of the most loving laughter imaginable in her voice.

"And so will we," added Matthew. "What would he tackle first, do you suppose?" he asked.

Sabina thought a moment. "Hmm . . . probably the hedge, so as to establish a sense of order, then a few of the pathways, to enable him to move about . . . and, of course, the rose garden."

"Then I propose we adopt precisely the same plan—the moment all the paperwork is done and we can put our affairs back in order at home."

A week and a half had passed since their meeting with Chancellor Kolter. The day following the momentous interview they had made arrangements to delay their flight home, as had Joseph and Ursula their return to Israel.

Though red tape and delays could hardly keep from being part of the process, things had progressed far more rapidly than either Matthew or Sabina thought possible. They had expected months, even years . . . whereas the German chancellor, armed with copies of the deeds, had put the matter on such a fast track that huge progress was being made in mere days. There had been no resistance whatever from the Polish authorities once Kolter had explained the circumstances.

It would be a good opportunity, they said, to downscale a portion of the former Communist bureaucracy, and the site in question was not well laid out as a home for aging military officers anyway. They would be happy to part with it. The men would need to be relocated, however, and that might take some time, and the idea of Poland *giving* the property to the former owner might be troublesome.

Kolter reminded them of the aid.

Yes, that was true, replied Walesa, but then of course the aid would be forthcoming anyway.

In the end it was decided that the former Dortmann estate would be sold for three hundred thousand German marks, an arrangement that would have no ties to the aid package. Kolter's government would advance the funds, the chancellor had informed Matthew and Sabina yesterday, on behalf of the Historical Trust Foundation. The new deed would be drawn in the name of Sabina Dortmann McCallum and her heirs, with the proviso that, if the family should ever part with it, the estate would become the property of the trust as a historical site by which to commemorate the resistance of German people to the Nazis.

In exchange, some informal listings of *Lebenshaus* with other such sites, an attempt to recreate the house and grounds as nearly as possible according to its prewar design—for which funding assistance would be available—and a public opening once or twice a year were all that would be required of them.

With tears in their eyes, Matthew and Sabina heartily and gratefully agreed to Kolter's terms.

"Oh, and one more thing, Mrs. McCallum," the chancellor added. "Arrangements have been made for you to visit your former home—tomorrow afternoon."

Sabina's exclamation of joy was accompanied by a new onrush of happy weeping. "Thank you . . . thank you so much, Herr Kolter. You cannot imagine what this means to me!"

That had been yesterday, and now here they were.

A few moments more they stood quietly contemplating the garden and what they would do as soon as they had opportunity.

A noise from another direction interrupted their thoughts. They turned to see Lisel and Tad walking up the hill toward them, hand in hand, followed by Hermann and his wife.

"It would seem our son has been smitten by the German infection just as I was," said Matthew with a smile.

"It was I who was smitten," rejoined Sabina, "by the *American* infection."

Matthew laughed. "Do you suppose we ought to send them on a horseback ride into the woods over there?"

"If only we could!" sighed Sabina. "If only there were still horses and stables and riding paths and bridges."

"There *will* be—I promise!" said Matthew. "We will restore *Lebenshaus* to the full flower of its former glory in every way imaginable!"

"You were right, Mom," exclaimed Tad exuberantly as the four approached. "Now I know why you and Dad have been talking about this estate all my life!"

"And I know where my mysterious colleague *Karin Duftblatt* received her name!" added Hermann with a smile and wink toward Matthew.

"Oh, Hermann!" laughed Sabina. "It takes me all the way back to those days when I hear you say my old name."

"It is more wonderful here than I imagined!" added Frau Lamprecht.

"I'm anxious to see inside the house!" said Lisel.

"May we have a tour?" added Tad.

"A terrific idea!" said Matthew. "Sabina, lead the way!" Matthew turned toward the house. The others followed.

"Not me," said Sabina as they went. "You're the baron of the estate now. That duty falls to *you.*"

Matthew laughed. "I strenuously object to the title. There was, and always will remain, but one *Baron* of *Lebenshaus.* But I will consent to the honor you bestow upon me in his physical absence."

"Exactly what I would have expected my husband to say. So now I say to you . . . lead on!"

"I don't know if I will be able to prevent us from getting lost!"

"It won't be the first time! I'll assist you," laughed Sabina.

129

The Disclosing of Many Secrets

• • •

MEANWHILE, ON THE OTHER SIDE OF THE HOUSE, URSULA was showing Joseph around and telling him everything about the night her family had arrived through the tunnel into the *Lebenshaus* cellar.

They had just made their way around the corner of the great stone building, talking quietly with smiles on their faces, when they met the other six in the middle of what had once been the rear courtyard.

"We were just about to embark on a tour of the house!" said Matthew, hailing them with a wave. "I must caution you, however, that these brave souls have entrusted themselves into my care as their guide . . . so be warned before you join us!"

"Your counsel is duly heeded, my good man," rejoined Joseph. "But I think we shall fall in with these intrepid pilgrims notwithstanding the potential dangers. What say you, wife?"

"Whither thou goest . . . ," replied Ursula.

They all laughed.

"Actually, even if you didn't *goest thither,* I want to!" Ursula added. "I spent two years here—I want to see every corner where Sabina and Gisela and I played and talked and worked and hid other Jews like our family. I'm dying to see what it's like inside. Aren't you, Sabina?"

"Yes, but a little afraid too. I know it will be so changed."

"But only temporarily," reiterated Matthew. "Come, let us begin!"

He turned and marched off, leading the way back around to the front door, where the Polish official in charge of the institution was expecting them.

Over the next hour, there could not help but be many tears shed by those who had known the great house in its former condition, for indeed much was altered. Yet there were equal exclamations of delight at discoveries indicating that the basic structure had been preserved intact, with here and there rooms and corridors and walls that seemed they had not had so much as a hand laid on them in fifty years.

One such moment came halfway down the main staircase between the ground and first floors. Suddenly Sabina stopped and her eyes filled with tears.

"What is it?" asked Ursula, placing a loving arm around her.

"My fingers unexpectedly slid over a little rough spot on the underside of the banister," replied Sabina. "I'd forgotten all about it, but then suddenly remembered how I used to always feel for it as a child when I ran along here."

She showed them the spot. The others felt it.

"Such a tiny thing, but it made the years vanish away," said Sabina, wiping at her eyes. "I suppose it made me realize that in many ways I have changed more *myself* than has *Lebenshaus*. It's remarkably well preserved, even down to a little rough piece of wood like this."

"I was amazed how much the east wing of the top floor is exactly how I remember it," commented Ursula as they continued on.

"It always was the most 'secretive' part of the house," explained Sabina to the others. "That's where we hid most of our newcomers."

"Like our family when we arrived," said Ursula.

"That's also where you managed to lose me during the first tour of this house I ever took!" added Matthew with a laugh. "You were a mischievous young lady!"

"I was not!" laughed Sabina.

"You were too, but then that's why I fell in love with you."

"Oh, Matthew, will you forever be a romantic?"

"Forever! But now," he added, turning toward the others. "I have another region of the house to show you."

A few *ahs* and anticipatory exclamations followed, for at least two or three knew where Matthew was leading.

"Follow me . . . *downward!*" he said, heading off down the stairway. "I have saved the best for last!"

• • •

Gaining access to the underground portions of the house proved a bureaucratic obstacle in itself, for all entryways were sealed off and the man in charge knew nothing about them and was very nervous. It took two or three phone calls, both to Berlin and Warsaw, before he could be persuaded to allow Matthew and Tad access to his tools and a free hand to put them to whatever uses they deemed necessary.

Once they set about to dislodge one of the doors, it proved a remarkably easy task, and within another few minutes the eight visitors were descending the staircase into the cellar, where another door had to be pried open. Moments later they were moving into the damp, earthy darkness of the underground corridor.

Once the small entourage was standing on the dirt floor and light from two strong flashlights shone against its rough bare walls, neither Matthew nor Sabina could believe their eyes. Nothing was changed in all the years. Not a day seemed to have passed.

Now truly did the stories begin in earnest—Matthew's broken leg, Sabina's mysterious tapping, the hiding of the china box and roses, Matthew's sneaking in with Gustav on his trail, the old woman occupying the room of his earlier convalescence. Yet even as they reminisced and laughed, the earthen walls dulled the sounds of their voices. The somber setting produced a tomblike atmosphere of stillness into which they could not help feel they were intruding.

Matthew and Sabina led the way first the entire length of the corridor, to the room under the old small library. Nothing was altered except that the china box was missing, as a result of Matthew's visit in 1962.

They turned again. Now Matthew led, retracing their steps, halfway back the way they had come. Sabina was by now beside herself with anticipation to see the hidden rooms once more. Matthew explained to the others how he had first discovered the secret apparatus. He knelt down and proceeded to pull back the necessary stones, showed them the compartment where the key was laid, took it out, and inserted it into the mechanism. Dull clanks sounded. Door-bolts and levers revealed themselves. To everyone's amazement, a moment later they were all passing through the great stone door into the hidden corridor.

Matthew stepped forward into the yawning black cavity and now led with his light along its length, with Tad bringing up the rear with another, until at last they found themselves entering the hidden dungeon the baron and Rabbi Wissen had utilized as a clandestine workroom during the war.

Here too, everything was unchanged since Matthew had last seen it. Now finally did the sense fully settle upon them all that they had gone back in time to that former era of danger.

In much the same way and with many of the same emotive responses that Matthew had felt upon first laying eyes upon the ghostly scene thirty years before, all eight slowly and silently spread out, examining with reverence what they beheld.

For Sabina there could scarcely have been a more poignant place to be reminded of her father. Everywhere were visible and tangible reminders of his earthly presence—a few items of clothing, papers with notes from his own hand, scratchings to himself, pens and pencils, mildewed clothing, a few stray photographs, passports, iden-tity cards, so many odds and ends that reminded her of their wartime business, as well as the chair and corner of the table where she knew her father had come to privately pen many of the thoughts she had later read in his journals. She could not prevent her eyes filling with tears at everything upon which they fell.

Matthew, meanwhile, was busily engaged elsewhere. "Well, we'll soon find out if the electricity is still connected down here," he announced as he finished fixing the new light bulb he had brought into the socket hanging from the ceiling, while Joseph aimed the beam of the flashlight up to help guide his fingers.

Matthew now walked back over to the door and flipped the switch on the wall. Suddenly the whole underground chamber lit brightly.

"That's more like it!" exclaimed Matthew.

"I wondered what you were doing with that bulb earlier," said Ursula.

"I knew the one that was here couldn't possibly be good after all this time. And now I would say we will be able to conduct our search more effectively!"

"Search—what are you looking for, Dad?"

"Anything, Tad, my boy—though old Bismarck's gold tops the list."

"What gold!" exclaimed two or three voices at once.

"Rumor is that Bismarck was here, right in this very house. And a secret cache of Prussian gold disappeared at nearly the same time as he was in this area."

"Don't forget the evil neighbor," added Sabina.

"And the murder."

"I want to hear the whole story!" exclaimed an enthusiastic Lisel.

"Sabina?" said Matthew. "You probably heard old Eppie tell it more times than I did. I would say now it's *your* turn to be the baron and carry on the family tradition."

Sabina laughed. "I'll try," she said. "But I don't know if I remember every detail."

They all gathered around, as if a ghost story were about to begin—which, in truth, it was.

"The gold," Sabina began, "was from the Hohenzollern treasure belonging to Albert of Brandenberg and the original duchy of Prussia in the sixteenth century. How much of what Eppie said is fact and how much is myth, my father never knew—but the story is that Bismarck came here—"

"To *Lebenshaus?*" interrupted Tad.

"Yes, where he was on friendly terms with some great-grandfather of mine, I assume. Bismarck was said to have been here during the Prussian wars in the 1860s or early 1870s and to have brought with him a cache of Prussian gold for safekeeping with our relative who was a Prussian loyalist."

"But who was murdered?" put in Lisel excitedly.

"There was supposedly a neighbor, a certain Count von Schmundt, a spy for the Austrians, who contrived a way to sneak into the house here, somehow in these underportions, from the surrounding fields. My father always wondered if there was a secret passageway that was later closed off, but nothing was ever found—"

"Except the tunnel to the garden," said Matthew.

"Could they be the same?" Joseph asked.

"We never knew," answered Sabina. "In any event, Bismarck was said to have discovered the count down here, right in the dungeon here. A sword fight ensued, the count was killed, Bismarck eventually went on to unite Germany, and neither the gold nor Count von Schmundt were ever heard from again."

The dungeon fell silent. Notwithstanding the bright light, everyone became aware of the underground chill. Shudders followed.

"How much of it is true?" Hermann asked at length.

Sabina shrugged.

"I've wanted to explore the small room adjacent to that recess over here," said Matthew at length, "ever since I was here before. I didn't have time then, and I didn't have a strong flashlight. But if there is anything to the legend, it strikes me we might find clues there."

"My father never allowed us to go in there," said Sabina. "He kept that shelf in front of the entryway."

"I noticed that," said Matthew. "But now that I have a *young* man to help us three *old* men, we ought to be able to get it out of the way in short order."

By now Tad needed no further encouragement, and within sixty seconds they had the shelf moved back sufficiently to allow entrance.

Once again the two strong flashlights bathed the earthy darkness with light.

An even greater sense of ghostliness came over them as they slowly entered the small room. Its low ceiling gave a distinctly tomblike impression, as did the very shape of the cavity. It was eerily like standing inside a bigger-than-life, closed-in grave.

A quick look around revealed little of interest. Certainly no skeleton of a dead count lay stretched out on the dirt floor. A small low table stood to one side with a few rotted rags lying on it. A small spade, mostly rusted through, was leaning against one of the corners, and here and there about the room small holes and piles of dirt gave evidence that some kind of exploratory digging had once occurred.

"Someone was looking for *something,*" commented Joseph.

"The gold, do you suppose?" asked Ursula.

"If Bismarck's gold *is* here, there's plenty of time to find it later," said Matthew.

"I thought we actually might find the bones from a corpse!" laughed Sabina.

"You didn't really believe that legend about the murder of Gustav's ancestor?"

"Part of me couldn't help but wonder if he was buried somewhere beneath the house."

"But what about the gold, Dad? I want to find the gold!"

"We'll continue the search once the house is ours, Tad," said Matthew. "I'll let you loose down here, and you can turn over the place from top to bottom—and try to find either the gold . . . *or* the body."

"Maybe both!"

"You never know . . . and this shovel certainly is intriguing. But no one can get in and steal it in the meantime."

"Why not?"

"Because this time I'm taking the key to the hidden door with me!"

They turned and slowly filed out and back into the larger room known as the dungeon, which now seemed as bright as a sunlit day after the smaller coffin-chamber.

"I'm really looking for something else besides gold," said Matthew, glancing around now in earnest.

"I want to leave everything just as it is," said Sabina, "all the things on the table, the wartime activities Papa and Ursula's papa, the Rabbi, were involved in."

"That's an excellent idea," added Matthew, "especially if this house is to become a historic monument of wartime resistance to the Nazis."

"The only exception might be if we find any more of Papa's journals. Where were the others you took before, Matthew?"

Matthew showed her where he had found them and the other boxes of papers and records where he had located the old deeds to the property, which until two weeks ago had done no good. Suddenly they seemed to have been well worth retrieving after all.

"Speaking of Rabbi Wissen, I have my suspicions about *his* activity here as well," said Matthew.

"Suspicions—about my papa?" asked an incredulous Ursula.

Matthew laughed. "Suspicions, only in the sense that I think he might have left something here for safekeeping too, just as the baron did his journals—something of far more value, both temporal and spiritual, than Bismarck's gold."

Briefly Matthew explained to the others what they were looking for, and they spread throughout the room, being attentive to Sabina's request not to disturb anything more than was absolutely necessary.

There were shelves along two of the walls, two or three cabinets placed about, and several stacks and piles of boxes—some wooden, some stiff cardboard—all around the room in relative disarray, as well as an old oak filing cabinet. Nearly all these had been protected against dampness by elevating them off the floor atop wood slabs. Despite the wetness of the main underground corridor, here the dirt was dry and powdery. Thus, though mildew and rot and other signs of age were apparent, most of the room's contents were more well preserved than might have been expected.

Sabina walked to the table, slowly gazing one at a time over its contents, many of them evoking strange sensations of feelings she had had long ago. Matthew, meanwhile, was poring through the papers and folders in the filing cabinet, one drawer at a time. The others slowly looked up and down shelves and opened boxes, though there was no particular pattern or design to the search.

"Is this what you are looking for?" came a voice after ten or fifteen minutes.

They all turned to see Lisel, bent down on her knees, pulling at a small wooden crate below a stack of three or four cardboard boxes she had lifted aside onto the floor.

"I noticed that most of the boxes had labels showing," she said. "So this one struck my curiosity because it didn't. When I got the ones on top out of the way and pulled it out, I saw the label on the side toward the wall. Papa, could you lift this?" she said to Hermann.

By now Matthew had approached. "Please, allow me," he said to Lisel. He lifted the box up and out into the middle of the floor, turning it around as he did. On the side previously hidden from view were the clearly readable handwritten letters W-I-S-S-E-N.

"You may have found it, my girl," said Matthew in a soft and reverent voice. "Ursula, Joseph," he said turning toward his friends of so many years, "it appears my hunch was correct and that your father, Ursula, like Sabina's, made use of this hidden location to stow away what he felt might be in danger of falling into Nazi hands. It seems only fitting that you do the honors." He took a step back.

Ursula and Joseph approached slowly but eagerly, as if to them had been granted the privilege of peering into the very heart and soul of Ursula's departed father, the revered Rabbi Heziah Wissen, which indeed they were about to do. They knelt down and together lifted the lid and gazed inside, while six other heads slowly approached in a circle around them.

Ursula's were the first hands to probe the contents, her eyes filling with tears as she pulled out the top item, a bound journal not unlike those of the baron's Matthew had retrieved.

"I have wondered for years what became of this," she said softly. "I knew he kept a detailed diary when we were here at *Lebenshaus.* It was a time of great growth and spiritual insight for him. But after we left I never saw it again. It wasn't until after he was gone that I even remembered it."

"I'm sure it will be a treasure for you," said Sabina, placing a gentle hand on her friend's shoulder.

Joseph, meanwhile, had lifted out several packets and files and was thumbing through them. "Names and information concerning many of the Jewish families around Warsaw," he said after a minute. "He must have been trying to get this out of the country."

"Why wouldn't he just have destroyed it if there was danger of it falling into the hands of the Gestapo?" asked Tad.

"I doubt that was his concern," replied Joseph. "From the look of it, most of these individuals and families had already been killed or taken to concentration camps. But a great deal of the rabbi's work, both before and after the war, concerned verification of war crimes. I imagine he was trying to preserve these records until after the war for just that purpose."

Ursula, quietly weeping, was now drawing out several items she knew well—a candlestick their family had used longer than she could remember, the plate they had used for Passover Seder their last night at *Lebenshaus,* as well as a container with a few dried pieces of Passover matzoh. The last item she retrieved was her father's own bound copy of the Torah.

But it was Matthew who now, with eyes aglow, stretched out his hands to worshipfully remove the last item that had been stored safely away, wrapped in two soft towels, in the bottom of the crate. He knew what it was even as he began unwrapping the surrounding cloth. The baron had made Matthew well familiar with the sacred charge that rested in the rabbi's care, even though Rabbi Wissen had never, for the baron's own safety, told him what he had done with it when the baron had returned it into his hands when the Nazi danger intensified. Nor had he told a soul what he had hidden in the depths of the *Lebenshaus* dungeon. Better rest here for eternity, the rabbi reasoned later once the property was in the hands of the Communists, than fall into enemy hands. But if the baron or his descendants, or his own, should ever by God's grace return, and should they somehow be led to this discovery, the rabbi prayed they would know what to do with it.

Now both the baron's daughter and his own, along with their stalwart husbands of virtue, stood watching as the holy box that had been in the rabbi's safekeeping so long saw the light of other eyes for the first time in fifty years.

The small ancient receptacle of fired Russian clay was studded with brass braces and inlaid with jewels. Its four sides and top were colorfully painted with now-fading scenes, designs, and symbols of Russian Jewry.

Whatever the box itself was worth, and it must have been a great deal, it could not have compared by a fraction to the value—both historic and actual—of the ancient contents. Though Matthew had never seen the legendary stones, his hands trembled at the thought that in his hands he held the very diamonds from the breastplate of Moses' brother Aaron, dating all the way back to the time of the Exodus.

He drew in a deep breath, then handed the box to Joseph.

"Joseph, my friend and brother," he said softly, "knowing as I do of the rabbi's lifelong desire to restore these sacred stones and relics to the archives of the nation of Israel and his dream that they would one day rest again in a new temple in Jerusalem, I think you should take charge of them, as his son-in-law, to see his wishes fulfilled."

"Thank you, Matthew," said Joseph. "Ursula and I are deeply honored. Thank God for protecting them safely here for his people all this time."

"Amen!" said several of the onlookers.

"The prayers of those two mighty men who called themselves spiritual *cousins*," said Sabina, "my father the baron, and yours the rabbi, Ursula—were uttered by righteous men whom the Lord heeded."

The silence that followed as Joseph slowly opened the lid was the quiet of reverence and awe. God's presence was with them in the mystery chamber, and each of the eight of his four sons and four daughters felt it.

The stones were wrapped separately, as were the few other items, in folds of soft linen. Tenderly Joseph unwrapped each, then held them in one of his palms for the others to behold in their radiant splendor.

The silence lasted some time. There were many prayers of thanks and worship to be prayed. Many circles had been woven together among them, and this latest contained much symbolism for them all.

"It was always my father's belief that the Urim and Thummim had been taken out of the temple at Jerusalem in A.D. 70, just prior to the destruction of the city," said Ursula at length. "He never knew all the hands that had prayerfully kept them from that day until they were placed into his, but *God's* hand was certainly on them, whoever else's they may have been in along the way. That was why he always felt so strongly that it was incumbent upon him to see them safely restored."

"And we shall fulfill his dream," added Joseph.

"I am certain all Israel will rejoice," said Sabina.

130

Return Flight

• • •

ONCE AGAIN MATTHEW, SABINA, AND THADDEUS HEIN-
rich McCallum settled into their seats aboard the Lufthansa 747,
this time preparing to return to Washington. This time, however,
no thoughts of pending international intrigue, espionage, or mystery occupied the latter's mind.

One of the chief reasons was that beside him, instead of father or
mother, sat Lisel Lamprecht, who was joining them on their return
flight at the invitation of Tad's mother. She would spend a month's
visit, help Sabina pack, then return to Berlin, they hoped, with
Matthew and Sabina. If the final documentation regarding the transfer
of *Lebenshaus* had not been completed by that time, they had been
assured that all the old Polish veterans would have been relocated and
that the house would be available for their occupancy as they awaited
final closing paperwork.

Tad would remain behind at the Washington house at least
through the winter and spring, though he, like his parents, was busily
reevaluating his own future. He had followed in his father's footsteps
more than he would have anticipated possible when their trip began,
and he was now well on his way to falling in love with the certain
young German lady beside him. That fact, in addition to Matthew
and Sabina's decision to return to Europe to take up residence at the
estate they both loved so dearly, had sent strong gusty winds of change
suddenly blowing through their son's life.

Neither was Tad on this day daydreaming about spy adventures for
the simple reason that he had experienced enough of the real thing
firsthand. Now his problem was trying to figure out how to write

about it—and the conference as well—without divulging politically sensitive information about which Chancellor Kolter had sworn them all to secrecy.

"How can I possibly tell the story?" Tad asked, leaning across the aisle to his father in continuation of a conversation in which they had been engaged at the gate while awaiting boarding, *"without* actually telling it? There's such a huge part that *can't* be told."

"You'll come up with some creative way," replied Matthew. "Write about the conference. After all, that's why you were sent."

"Too boring . . . after all we went through *away* from the conference!"

"Write about the people you met. Andrassy, Udo and his wife, the fellowship there . . . others we met . . . Palacki, the Bialystok brotherhood . . . how about the Jewish/Christian links at *Lebenshaus* . . . what the baron did during the war . . . the sacred stones—or . . . write about Lisel!"

"There's not much of a story in that, Mr. McCallum," added Lisel with a laugh from the seat on the other side of Tad.

"I thought we were through with that *Mister* business."

"I'm sorry. It takes some getting used to."

"We Americans are uncomfortable with your European formality, aren't we, Tad, my boy?"

"Yep—don't like it a bit."

"How about contrasting what used to be East and West Germany," suggested Sabina in a new vein, "and the spiritual climate of each?" She was trying to be interested in Tad's dilemma, but in truth her thoughts were still at *Lebenshaus.*

"Everything you both say is good," said Tad. "Every idea could be an article in itself. But I was supposed to cover the conference, not all these other things."

"The *conference,*" repeated Matthew. "You know, it suddenly strikes me how much there were two separate stories going on, weren't there—the conference and the whole political thing you got drawn into. Yet how could you possibly write about the conference *without* mentioning the rest?"

"That's exactly it," said Tad. "They are so intrinsically intertwined."

"Parallel stories, going along right beside each other."

"There's an angle," put in Sabina, still visualizing Tad's article through the perspective of her thoughts regarding her former home. "It's just like something my father would say—parallel but separate stories, like two train tracks. The deeper meaning, you know— *wouldn't* my father say that, Matthew?"

"Exactly. Intrinsically linked, *both* part of the whole picture, impossible to separate . . . and yet never intersecting!"

"It is the perfect analogy of what happened to us," said Tad.

"There's the newsman coming to life!" laughed Matthew.

"It's just like Christianity," Tad went on, "the church, going along right beside the world . . . *in* the world, but not impacting it. Two separate tracks that *should* be completely intertwined but go along side-by-side never meeting."

"What does that have to do with the conference?"

"Everything! Here we were involved in a political plot of global magnitude, and none of our fellow conferees, other than Raedenburg, will probably ever hear a thing about it. Galanov and Bietmann's story, too, is just on a separate track than what most of them ever will give much attention to."

"Sounds like an editorial, not a news article."

Tad smiled. "Yeah, I guess you're right. I suppose enlightening everybody isn't my job, just reporting what happened. But still, it's such a sad statement on Christendom's impact when the world remains so untouched. Coexistent but nonintersecting stories. Double oblivion, each side toward the other. Parallel tracks of unknowing. But speaking of the conference," Tad asked, "did you and Palacki ever talk again?"

"No—Joseph saw him, but he didn't stick around long after his speech. From what I understand, Montgomery and MacPatrick spent the whole next day—while we were involved with Kolter and Galanov and the rest of it—trying to patch it up with him by phone and trying to get him back to accept the money and make amends."

"They no doubt wanted a good end-of-conference photo op of them all together."

"Right—so the outburst could be downplayed and written off to Palacki's temperamental nature."

"What do you think, Dad? Do you think conferences like that do any good? I have the feeling that nothing much will change as a result."

"I suppose that's how it strikes me too. Most of those people will go back home and continue doing exactly what they were doing before they came."

"The liberals will still be trying to feed the world's hungry without offering them eternal life; the conservatives still talking about saving three billion souls by the year 2000 with all their money and high-tech evangelistic techniques."

Matthew sighed. "Yeah, something like that, Tad, my boy. And the *balance* that a humble man in Galilee lived out during the brief years of his simple life on this earth will remain as invisible as it has been for most of the last two thousand years."

The four settled back into their seats for takeoff.

• • •

"Speaking of the part of our adventure that *can't* be told, did you see the papers this morning?" Matthew asked, turning one at a time to all three of his companions sometime after they were in the air.

"No, why?" asked Tad.

They had breakfasted with Raedenburg, Bietmann, and Galanov, and said their good-byes to their three friends earlier in the morning. Raedenburg had told them briefly of the continuing political fallout from the explosive session in the Bundestag.

The last they had seen them, the three brothers in Christ—a West German, an East German, and a Russian—were walking off together. Raedenburg had plans for their day together, he said, before they would all drive out to Bietmann's home for supper and an evening with the people of his fellowship.

"There was a long editorial speculating about what was behind Drexler's resignation," he explained. "The country's still in an uproar over it. Kolter's riding high again."

"Has there yet been any word about the Russian side of the thing?" asked Tad.

"I haven't seen anything. It was all downplayed. The summit between the presidents was canceled, of course, and Yeltsin's back in Moscow. I don't even think I've seen Desyatovsky's name mentioned in the two weeks since. I doubt anyone will ever know how close the Commonwealth came to blowing apart."

"What about your other friend . . . what was his name . . . the guy in the helicopter?" asked Matthew

"Bolotnikov. Nope, no mention of him either. Andrassy says we'll hear from him again, though."

"How so?"

"I don't know. He just says the guy has an uncanny knack for landing on his feet, no matter how many are falling around him."

"Well I hope I never see him."

They all fell silent.

Tad and Lisel were soon conversing amongst themselves. Matthew, however, found himself thinking again about Tad's potential article.

"There's too much," he said at length, as if thinking out loud.

"Too much what?" asked Sabina.

"Too many ideas, too many people, too many parallel stories and tracks. Too much happened for Tad to fit into just one article." He leaned across and smiled at his son. "You'll have to tell your editor it can't be done," he added with a tone of finality.

"What, Dad?" asked Tad.

"All that happened . . . it *can't* be put into an article."

"What's the solution then?"

"Simple," replied Matthew. "You'll have to write a book."

For Those Who Love Roses, the Story Never Ends

• • •

THE WEEKS WENT BY QUICKLY. SABINA HAD TO PINCH herself daily to reassure herself that it wasn't all a dream. Yet . . . here they were again—at *Lebenshaus!* And in a matter of just a few days, a week or two at most, it would belong to her again!

Autumn had come to the Polish countryside. Days were gradually shrinking. A nip could occasionally be felt in the air.

Her father had always said that no one would call this Pomeranian plain south of the Baltic the world's most beautiful land. It was flat and uninteresting, without snowcapped peaks of fairy tales or dense forests of legends. But this was a land that had caught her life up in *Das Märchen,* and she would always love it. And there were certainly legends and mysteries to be told about this house under her feet!

Sabina and Matthew had been standing on the outer balcony of the second floor of *Lebenshaus* gazing out over the fields and woodland about them for several minutes.

It was the first place they had come after their arrival only a short time ago. Their hearts had much to absorb, and this seemed the only location on the estate suitable for the task.

Some of the furnishings Matthew had arranged for had already arrived. More would be delivered this week. Realizing they had come this time to *live,* not merely to visit, changed the aspect of everything upon which their eyes fell.

The very thought was more than they could take in. The silences, sighs, and tears accompanying today's arrival and slow walk through the now-vacated house were heavy, deep, and filled with the most reverential and worshipful awareness of how *much* their Father loved them. What a *big* God indeed reigned in the universe.

"It's all pretty unbelievable, isn't it?" said Matthew softly, the first to break the silence.

Sabina drew in a long breath and then let it out in a contented sigh. "There's no other word for it," she said.

"God has been *so* good to us."

"I just want everyone in the world to know what a loving Father he is, and how much he longs to give them good gifts from out of his heart . . . if only they'll let him have his complete way with them."

They had both carried packages in their hands since leaving the car. They had been together so long there were no secrets between them, and they each knew what was coming. Yet they enjoyed playing out the game and knowing the ending nowise diminished the enjoyment of the process. Though there were no *new* secrets, there was a continual unfolding revelation of ways to tell one another the secret they had shared for fifty years.

Sabina was the first to break the silence that had followed. "I wanted to bring you every color," she said. "This day is so special, how could ten thousand roses possibly commemorate it?"

Matthew nodded. "I still can't believe we're actually here," he said.

"At first," Sabina went on, "I thought of giving you a yellow rose, in memory of that stormy night and the first roses we ever exchanged. In the end, though, I decided that it had to be red. With what other color could I say how much it means to me to be your wife . . . and how much I love you?

"I decided, however, to buy a growing, living rose." She now unwrapped the paper from around a single long-stemmed red rose. "This is a blossom from a plant that is down in the car," she added.

"I didn't see it," said Matthew.

"I had to sneak it into the trunk," laughed Sabina. "It will be the first one we will plant in the *new* rose garden of *Lebenshaus*. It will always remind us of *our* love and of this day . . . and our Father's bountiful goodness about which my father was so faithful to teach us."

"Amen! Thank you," said Matthew. "As many times as we do

this, you always manage to find new depths to explore in the secret of the rose."

"Your turn!" said Sabina.

Matthew took a breath. "Like you," he said, "I wanted to give you one of *every* color. In the end I had to make a decision too . . . and here it is." He pulled the paper off his thin, awkward parcel to reveal three beautifully shaped buds. "So here is a *yellow* for the first rose we exchanged, a *red* as symbol of the depths of our love, and a *white* to remember our wedding day and the two roses we hid down in the room three floors below us. All three will remind us of all our happy years together."

"Thank you, Matthew! You *are* a romantic!"

"As all three contain their secrets for us, they likewise contain the mysteries of God's love, which are the most treasured secrets of all and are impossible to exhaust."

She took them from his hand. "I will dry them and place them in a vase at the entryway of the house," said Sabina as she brought each of the three softly to her nose. "The story of the secret of the rose, and the Father's love out of which all other loves grow, will continue on forever."

"What a great idea!" said Matthew. "It's the perfect way for us to remind those who may see them of the discoveries of love we have made in our life together."

"I want everyone who ever visits this house," added Sabina, "to recognize the eternal fragrance of the Father's love, which he gave roses to help us know."

Matthew drew Sabina to his side, while Sabina placed her arm about his waist. They continued to gaze out across the countryside, their hearts full.

"We have had a good life together, Matthew," sighed Sabina at length. "You've made me so happy. I know I have told you before, but you have made my life a fairy tale!"

"Nothing more than any self-respecting knight on his white steed ought to do for his lady!" said Matthew, turning toward her and offering a slight bow.

"Oh, Matthew, my prince," laughed Sabina, "I do love you!"

"And I you, my princess Sabina!"

Afterword . . . from the Author

• • •

THE CHARACTERS THAT APPEAR IN MY STORIES ARE REAL to me. To whatever extent a man is capable of feeling such things, they are like children to whom I have given birth. Aspects of the person I am live through them. Though the realities of corporate publishing may from time to time bring about a premature death of certain of these literary children, they yet remain alive for me as their creator. That is why Andrassy Galanov, a character originally in another of my books, has reappeared here in this story of the rose. What his character prompted me to pour onto the page back then was deeply a part of me, part of the message I felt I had been given to tell. Though sales and marketing strategies at the time forced his tale to fade, this did nothing to diminish how vivid he remained in my heart and mind.

His story first appeared several years ago in the book entitled *Depths of Destiny.* It was intended as part of an ongoing series that did not materialize. Because much of the material and several of the threads in that story were intrinsic to longer-range plans, and because, as I said above, the characters were by then *real,* I have taken the unusual liberty (with consent of both publishers) of making use of a good deal from that former title—where it was able to fit smoothly into the ongoing flow of the Secret of the Rose series—in the writing of *Dawn of Liberty,* including certain elements of the plot line, several spiritual themes, as well as Galanov, whom you already know, and a few of the other characters.

At the same time, *Dawn of Liberty* is a newly written book in its entirety and represents the logical and creative culmination to the Secret of the Rose as planned and envisioned from the beginning. I sincerely hope those of you who did chance to encounter *Depths of Destiny* will enjoy *Dawn of Liberty* nonetheless that aspects of it may be familiar to you.

Writing for me is a very personal exercise. I write to *individuals*, not to a piece of paper or a computer screen. I like to know you are out there, and to know who you are and what you are thinking as I write to and for you.

It is always a pleasure, therefore, as well as an encouragement and an inspiration for my family and me to hear from you about what a certain book or character or insight out of one of the stories has meant in your life. As I have said on other occasions and in other books, you may not always get a reply, but I will read and appreciate whatever personal word you may want to say in response to any of my books.

Therefore, I invite you to write. I invite your comments, your sharing. I take your letters very personally, as one friend to another, even though, as I say, it may of necessity be a one-way correspondence.

Those of you who have enjoyed the books in the Secret of the Rose series may be interested to know that my most recent nonfiction title, *A God to Call Father,* grew out of the writing of *The Eleventh Hour.* You will no doubt see what I mean when you read it. I hope you will try to buy or borrow a copy, or check it out of your church library. In it I have amplified upon what to me is one of the most important truths we are privileged to learn in life—that God our Father is good . . . and that he loves us more than we can imagine!

Please read it, and let me know what God reveals to you about himself as a result.

Many of you who have read other of my works will know that the old Scottish writer of whom the baron was so fond was the Scotsman George MacDonald, my own literary and spiritual mentor. I do hope you will become familiar with his books. Many are available through

Bethany House Publishers. A complete list of both MacDonald's available titles and my own can be obtained by writing to me at the address below.

You may contact me either in care of Tyndale House Publishers, P.O. Box 80, Wheaton, IL 60189, or write me directly at 1707 E. Street, Eureka, CA 95501.

About the Author

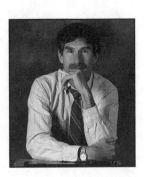

MICHAEL PHILLIPS is one of the premier fiction authors publishing in the Christian marketplace. He has authored more than fifty books, with total sales exceeding 4 million copies. He is also well known as the editor of the popular George MacDonald Classics series.

Phillips owns and operates a Christian bookstore on the West Coast. He and his wife, Judy, live with their three sons, Patrick, Gregory, and Robin, in Eureka, California.

Books by Michael Phillips

A God to Call Father

The Secret of the Rose
  The Eleventh Hour
  A Rose Remembered
  Escape to Freedom
  Dawn of Liberty
    TYNDALE HOUSE

**The Journals of
Corrie Belle Hollister**
  My Father's World★
  Daughter of Grace★
  On the Trail of the Truth
  A Place in the Sun
  Sea to Shining Sea
  Into the Long Dark Night
  Land of the Brave and the Free
  A Home for the Heart
  Grayfox (Zack Hollister's
    Journal)
    BETHANY HOUSE

The Stonewycke Trilogy★
  The Heather Hills of Stonewycke
  Flight from Stonewycke
  Lady of Stonewycke
    BETHANY HOUSE

The Stonewycke Legacy★
  Stranger at Stonewycke
  Shadows over Stonewycke
  Treasure of Stonewycke
    BETHANY HOUSE

The Highland Collection★
  Jamie MacLeod: Highland Lass
  Robbie Taggart: Highland Sailor
    BETHANY HOUSE

The Russians★
  The Crown and the Crucible
  A House Divided
  Travail and Triumph
    BETHANY HOUSE

**The Works of
George MacDonald**
    (Selected, compiled, and
    edited by Michael Phillips)
    BETHANY HOUSE

★with Judith Pella

If you enjoyed the Secret of the Rose series . . .

. . . this additional title by Michael Phillips will lead you to the kind of intimate relationship with God that is reflected in his characters.

A GOD TO CALL FATHER   0-8423-1392-5